PAMELA ATHERSTONE

We must never forget the "Generation Lost"

With Best Wishes,

Pam A

...Like Footprints in the Wind

A Generation Lost

outskirtspress

DENVER, COLORADO

...Like Footprints in the Wind
A Generation Lost
All Rights Reserved.
Copyright © 2013 Pamela Atherstone
v2.0

Cover Photo © 2013 JupiterImages Corporation. All rights reserved - used with permission.

Outskirts Press, Inc.
http://www.outskirtspress.com

ISBN: 978-1-4327-9773-7

Outskirts Press and the "OP" logo are trademarks belonging to Outskirts Press, Inc.

PRINTED IN THE UNITED STATES OF AMERICA

DEDICATION

Past: *This book is dedicated to the memory of those who lived through this horrific period of time. May we never forget.*

Present: *To those who seek to remember and document our forbearers, preserving the chronicles and telling the stories that will keep our pasts in the present.*

Future: *To my granddaughter, Natalie Rose, and all of those who descend from the Germans from Russia. My hope is that you will maintain the histories, be proud of who you are and where you came from, and never let such atrocities happen again.*

Why were the Germans in Russia in the first place?
A brief history has been included at the back of this book.

Thank You

This book would not have been written without the constant encouragement of the great people of the Writer's Workshop at the Modesto Institute of Continued Learning. But I wish to offer special gratitude to Shirley Irving and Martha Loeffler; these ladies had extraordinary input for which I will be forever grateful.

Additionally, the Thursday Evening Critique Group has been invaluable. The comments, suggestions and support of Mary Van Loon, Jan Sharp, and Teresa Dempewolf kept me on my toes and at my computer, writing and rewriting.

Furthermore, I am extremely grateful to all those who lived through these times, and had the courage to record their memories. This novel would not have been completed without the firm belief that by telling these stories the past would not ever be repeated.

And last, but most certainly not least, my husband, Jim. He may not understand why I am always at the computer, but he has allowed me the independence to pursue my dream.

Introduction

Growing up just three blocks from my grandparents gave me opportunities many of my childhood friends did not have. I spent almost as much time at their house as I did at home, and one would think I would have known nearly everything about them, especially my grandmother. It wasn't until I was well into my adult years, and my grandparents were long gone, that I discovered how little I actually knew.

My mother was an only child. I had known for many years that the man I called "Grandpa" was actually her step-father, and she had not seen her biological father since she was three. I also knew Grandma was one of six children who had been orphaned on the Canadian prairie at an early age, and she had grown up in a foundling home that sent the able children out to farms to work for their room and board. Grandma had somehow managed, throughout her life, to keep in touch with all of her siblings, even though the youngest had been adopted and both his Christian and surnames were changed. Family was very important to her.

When I would ask questions about her family heritage, she would tell me her people were French, Dutch and English. After all, her older sister had written this information down in a note book, and "if anybody knew, she would" was Grandma's response to me.

It was not until I was watching a PBS program in the late 1990s that I began to question this information seriously; it led me on a journey of discovery unlike any I had imagined. The program was called "Children of the Steppe; Children of the Prairie," and chronicled an ethnic group of Germans who immigrated to the United States from Russia in the late 1800's. All through this program I kept saying to myself, "Grandma used to do that," or "Grandma would say those things."

I had this strange feeling I was a part of these people, but couldn't understand how this could be.

Subsequently, the "genealogy bug" bit me hard. I began by talking to my mother and picking her brain for more information about Grandma. In the back of a closet at my mother's house, we found a large box of file folders full of paperwork from my grandparents' home. Mom had packed it away while cleaning out their house following Grandpa's passing in 1992. They lived at the same address in Bakersfield, California, for 54 years; the last eight of which Grandpa lived alone.

Grandma died in 1984 at the age of 78. She departed this life unexpectedly and peacefully in her sleep, surrounded by a houseful of visiting relatives. The previous evening was spent in the company of her younger sister and a cousin from Canada, and her younger brother and his extended family who lived near her in Bakersfield. The house rang with happy voices and laughter and the wafting aroma of freshly baked (and very German) apple-cinnamon strudel; a dish that always welcomed guests to her home. This was the way Grandma loved to live.

Perusing through that pile of papers proved more than interesting. Among the bits and pieces of my grandparents' lives was a marriage license issued in 1901 to Grandma's parents. There for all to see was the statement that her parents had been born in *Russia,* however, they were not of Slavic origins, but were actually ethnic Germans living in Russia. What a revelation that was! Now I was excited and eager to learn more.

But I soon discovered a gaping hole within the branches of my family tree. Information from Russia on family members, who remained behind when my great-grandparents emigrated, seems to be non-existent. The stories I unearthed regarding the history of the Germans in Russia, following the Revolution of 1917, explained these gaping holes and the lack of recorded information about the people. Knowledge of those inhabitants, and what they experienced, is relatively unknown among the general populations today, and the more I learn, the more

I wish to share the information with others. This has resulted in the story that follows. My version could be called creative non-fiction; it is based on many true accounts and chronicles, some personally recounted to me, from those who lived through those times. The names used are those of my own ancestors, as a tribute and remembrance. They are not forgotten.

The ten years of research has been more than an education, it has been a lesson in history, geography, humanity, relationships and life. It has caused me anguish, elation and frustration; initiating a deep look within myself for answers to questions I never thought I'd consider asking. It has grounded me in a way that I cannot explain, except to say that my roots run deep, and my tree is healthy, alive and growing.

MAP OF RUSSIA

Arctic Ocean

Siberian Sea

Barents Sea

Bering Sea

White Sea

St. Petersburg

Onega

Moscow

Odessa

Black Sea

Novosibirsk

Lake Baikal

Chita

Belogorsk

Khazakstan

Caspian Sea

China

Vladivostok

CHAPTER ONE

The Farmer's Fear

Darkness now covers the earth, and the people are in darkness. But the Lord will shine on you, and his Glory will appear over you. -Isaiah 60:2

LATE SUMMER, 1929

Johannes straightened from bending over his hoe. He stretched his back, removed the black wide-brimmed hat from his fair head and wiped perspiration from his brow with the back of his hand. He stopped to take in the panorama before him—acres and acres of good dark-loam soil that yielded excellent crops of potatoes, wheat, grapes, sunflowers and watermelons. Farming was hard work, but he had grown up tilling this soil, as had his father and grandfather, here in this fertile valley nestled between the Dniester and Bug rivers in the shadow of the Carpathian Mountains, just north of the great Black Sea. How he loved the smell of the rich musty dirt as he followed his horses behind the plow every spring, its aroma more enhanced with each summer rain.

It was now August and harvest would soon be upon him. It had been a good year. There was an abundance of produce to sustain his family through the heavy snows of winter, and if prices were good, he might even have a bit left over to put toward sending his eldest son to America. Jakob was quickly approaching his eighteenth year and conscription into the Russian military. If he could be spared those six years of agony, whatever money it took was well worth the expense. Johannes had done his time, he knew what was in store for Jakob, and he feared it could be even worse now, as there was talk of yet another impending war. Rumors in the village suggested that an up-and-coming leader in Germany was set on conquering all the lands in his grasp, and Russia was a prime target.

Johannes did not understand the politics involved. After all, he was German, as were his wife, their families, and all their friends. Everyone he knew spoke German as their first language, learning Russian only because they were forced to do so in school. Nevertheless, knowing the language had at times served him well, as he was better able to sell his crops in the Russian villages on the outskirts of the German settlements. Politically, the general thinking of local villagers was that if Germany conquered Russia, so be it, his people would easily assimilate; if Russia conquered Germany, then their lives would not change much from what they were presently. They had been through this before with the Russian revolution nearly twelve years earlier. But the people of his village had persevered, and managed to maintain their identity, and most importantly, their farms. They fought the ideas of "Papa Stalin's" new way of farming, or collectivization, and survived the famine that had engulfed much of Russia in the past few years. Johannes and his people were aware they were leading somewhat fortunate lives, and in spite of the ban on openly celebrating their love of God, they knew they were blessed.

The farmer took one more scan of the horizon prior to resuming his hoeing, his eyes settling on his son laboring a few rows over. *This land grows good strong sons as well as good crops*, he thought proudly to himself.

A cloud of dust rising from the south caught his attention. A chill traveled down his sweat-drenched back as he realized it was too early in the season for the bands of Romany to be arriving. The gypsy folk who assisted with the harvest did not usually arrive until early in September, and their horse drawn caravans seldom made so much dust, even in drought-stricken years. No, the oncoming dust cloud had to be …

"SOLDIERS!" He shouted to Jakob. "They will be coming to claim the boys! Hurry! Take one of the horses, ride to the village and alert the Byrgermeister. Then come straight home!"

Johannes began unhitching one of the horses from the wagon waiting to return them home after the day's work. The horses had been standing tied, dozing in the shade of a large tree, and were startled at the suddenness of Johannes' approach. Jakob took hold of Hans' harness and flung himself up on the big dapple gray's back, as Johannes tied off and shortened the lines; providing Jakob with reins to control the animal as he galloped hard into the village.

The second horse, Georg, began dancing in place eager to catch up to its teammate, not understanding why they had been separated, and causing Johannes great difficulty in unhitching the normally docile animal. There was no time to shorten the lines, so Johannes looped them into great coils and prayed he did not fall off; he feared becoming entangled and being dragged to death by the running animal. Johannes dug his heels into the sorrel's side, and urged the alarmed and confused creature up the road.

"Katerina, Katerina!" He shouted, as he rode up to their small home on the edge of the village. "Katerina, gather the children quickly, get them in the house, the soldiers are coming. I have sent Jakob to tell the Byrgermeister."

"Whose soldiers? Why the alarm? What's going on?" Katerina appeared in the doorway of their summer kitchen, wiping flour from her hands onto the full length white apron covering her simple faded-blue cotton dress. This morning her golden-blonde hair had been neatly braided across the top of her head and tucked under her ever-present white kerchief, but unruly strands had been making their escape as the day wore on. With the combination of the heat of the wood cook stove on the August afternoon, her thin build and the perspiration-generated dark circles around her sky-blue eyes, she appeared more exhausted than she really felt.

"I do not know whose soldiers," Johannes responded. "It does not really matter. I do not want the children exposed to whatever those men might do. This late in the afternoon they will be looking for a place to stay and food to eat. I do not want them here, but I cannot stop them. I can only try to protect you and the children from their actions. Mostly I have to keep Jakob from being taken by them."

"But he is not old enough," her voice faded in fear as she realized what Johannes was saying.

"If there is a war, do you think they will care about his age? He is big enough to handle a rifle. He, and all the other boys his size, is in danger if not hidden."

Tears welled up in Katerina's eyes as she yanked her apron off over her head. "Karolina, Magdalena, Heinreich and Anya are all at school. Konrad is playing behind the stable and Rosina is in her cradle." She was as much counting her children as stating their whereabouts. "I will head to the school." Katerina was nearly in a run as she flung open the small gate in the picket fence separating the barnyard from the plot that contained her household garden.

Johannes knew he should cool the overheated horse before he put him in the barn, but he felt there was no time. "Sorry boy," he tried to soothe the confused and sweating animal as he placed Georg in his stall. "I will brush you down later."

Hearing the commotion, Konrad appeared from around the edge of the stable, just as Johannes exited the building. The child's normally whitish-blond locks were caked in grime, as was the rest of him, from playing whatever games four-year-olds play in the soft dirt of a farm. A smile exploded across his face at the sight of his father. "Papi!" he yelled as his outstretched arms reached to be picked up.

"Konrad, what a mess you are, you need to come into the house now and get cleaned up for supper." Johannes smiled back in an effort to disguise his fear as much as possible, hoping his smallest son did not pick up on the anxiety he was feeling.

"But Papi, too early for supper. No one home from school." Konrad stood facing his father; an air of defiance enveloping him as he put his hands on his hips. "I do not want to go in."

"Please Konrad, not now. Mama has gone to get the others, Jakob will be home soon, and we have a lot to do to get ready."

"Ready for what?"

"I am not sure, son, we just have to be ready."

"No good, Papi. Want to know why."

"Konrad, I do not have time right now! Just get into the house and wait for Mama while I feed the animals."

"Okay, Papi. But Konrad no want to." Konrad knew when his father meant business and this was one of those times when he knew he had better obey.

Johannes quickly fed and milked the cow. Ilse was upset at being milked early and hurriedly. She was accustomed to Katerina's or Karolina's touch, and protested loudly at the change in her routine. As a result, she did not give her normal amount. Johannes took the partially-filled pail with him as he hurriedly threw feed to the chickens and geese in their pens, checked their water, and removed the few eggs from the nests of the setting hens. Just as he completed these chores, Jakob rode into the yard. The horse, not used to being run for any distance, was lathered with foamy sweat that dripped from his body. In the heat of the summer afternoon, steam could be seen rising from Han's flanks as his sides heaved with each gasping breath.

"Father, the Byrgermeister says to allow the soldiers into our house, if they so desire, and follow whatever instructions they might give. It is the best way for all of us to survive." Jakob jumped down off the horse and picked up a handful of straw to begin rubbing the exhausted animal down. He knew Hans should be cooled out prior to being given any water, and a good rubdown helped with the cooling process.

"The man is an idiot! He does not even know what army the soldiers are from, or what their intentions are. He can let them into his house if he so chooses, but they are not welcome in mine." Johannes slipped the harness off the over-heated horse and put a halter on its head as Jakob continued to rub the animal down.

"We do not have time to cool him properly, son, put him in his stall, but do not water him. He will cool off as he eats." Johannes felt a pang of guilt as he said these words. His horses always received the best of care; they were a major part of his livelihood, as well as nearly members of the family.

"But Father…," Jakob began.

Johannes looked at his oldest boy and slowly shook his head, "There just is no time. I do not like it either, but we must ready ourselves to deal with these soldiers. Here, take the milk bucket into the house and check on Konrad and Rosina; I will put the horse up."

As Jakob headed for the house, Johannes spotted Katerina arriving with their other children. He felt a sense of relief knowing no matter what happened they would all be together. He turned and led Hans into his stall, slipped the halter off and reached up and stroked the big horse's face. "Sorry old boy, I know this is not what you deserve, I hope to make it up to you somehow."

As he pitched hay to the tired horses, his mind raced with thoughts of what might be about to transpire. He realized that as much as he wanted to keep his family together, he was going to have to insist that Jakob leave— *keeping him out of the military is the only chance the boy has to stay alive long enough to get to the "promised land" of America.*

By the time Johannes arrived at the house Katerina had organized the children into various tasks preparing for an early supper. She knew not what was in store for her family, but they would enter the un-known with full stomachs. The one room serving as living, dining, winter kitchen, bath, and sleeping loft for the boys, was alive with ac-tivity. The summer kitchen, across the yard, kept the excessive heat of cooking and baking out of the main house, and it was here she dropped dumplings into the caldron of stew boiling on the wood stove, while the older girls set the table in the house. Despite Konrad's loud pro-tests, ten-year-old Anya scrubbed the filth off her little brother in the tub near the winter stove. Eleven-year-old Heinreich sat on the bare wood floor and played with baby Rosina. The closeness of the family, coupled with the diminutive size of the room they occupied, hindered any ability to maintain secrecy. Johannes took his place at the head of the table and asked the children to join him. Katerina arrived with her stew pot, the worry and fear evident on her ashen face, as she placed the vessel on the table.

"Children," Johannes began somberly, "Jakob must leave us for a time. Soldiers are coming and if they find him, Jakob will be taken to fight in their army. This decision is not easy for any of us, but especially for your mother and me. I need his help here on the farm and we all need his love and companionship, but he will be safer if he goes to Uncle Leopold's. Now we must pray for his safe journey."

A curtain of shock and dismay drew across Katerina's face, but she understood her husband's decision. She quietly moved over and stood behind Johannes, placing her hands upon his sagging shoulders and bowing her head. Tears silently slid down her cheeks and melted into the front of her apron. Johannes reached up and took her hand in his as he began to pray. The children sat in stunned silence; even baby Rosina seemed to be aware of the importance of this moment, possibly the last moment they might ever be together again as an entire family.

Loud knocking at the door interrupted Johannes' prayer. He threw a quick glance at Jakob, and then nodded his head toward the curtain hanging on the wall next to the stove. The drape covered a doorway leading into a hall that separated the girls' bedroom from Johannes and Katerina's; another door at the far end led to the stable area attached to the house.

"Take Konrad," Johannes whispered almost inaudibly. He knew if *anybody* said something about Jakob and his whereabouts, it would be his bluntly honest youngest son.

Jakob jumped to his feet and took Konrad by the arm. "Come, let us play hide and seek from the visitors." This was a game often played by Konrad, and Jakob knew it was the surest way to prevent a protest from his little brother. As the boys disappeared behind the curtain, Johannes rose from his chair to answer the persistent knocking.

Opening the door revealed not the expected uniformed soldier, but a man much like himself—about forty years old, of medium height, thin of build, dressed in the plain clothes of a fellow farmer.

"My name is Albert Lenz, I am from Freidenthal." He spoke in the same German dialect as Johannes and his family. "I have been sent by the commandant of the Russian army battalion setting up camp outside your village."

"Please come in, we were just sitting down for supper. You say there are soldiers outside the village, but you do not seem to be one of them." Johannes was somewhat surprised by this man's presence.

" No, I am not one of them," the man removed his hat and nodded politely toward Katerina, " but they are sending men like me to all the houses in the village to inform you that you will need to be packed up and ready to leave tomorrow. You will be joining those of us from the communities south of here, and others may be joining us as we move north."

"I fail to understand," Johannes replied with apprehension.

"The Russian soldiers are telling us that the German army will soon be raiding our villages, they are coming up from the south, and we are being moved north for our protection. It seems the German army considers those of us who are German, here in Russia, particularly dangerous. They call us spies and dissidents. We are being told we should only be gone about a month, or so, until the threat passes. You need to pack up anything you do not want stolen. Also you will need food and clothing for the journey."

"Where are they taking us?" Johannes questioned.

"We have not been told. The Russians say it is for our own safety that we do not know ahead of time, but that we will be provided for when we get to our final destination."

"I cannot leave now!" Johannes exclaimed. "Harvest time will be here soon. I need to harvest my crops so my family can survive the winter!"

"There will be nothing left to harvest." Herr Lenz responded sadly. "It will all become clear tomorrow." He looked around the room as he talked, sizing up the children sitting around the table.

"Are *these* all of your children?"

"There is a three-year-old who is playing at hiding from strangers," Johannes noticed Anya had quickly removed one plate from the table and hidden it under her skirt as part of the normal game Konrad played, but it still left one extra on the table.

The man nodded, "I see you have no older son, which is good, as the army is taking all boys over the age of thirteen. If they cannot shoot a rifle, they are being used to serve the soldiers food and water or to care for the horses." The man turned to leave, paused and continued, "Be ready to leave by noon tomorrow."

Herr Lenz had no sooner gone than all the children began talking at once. The cacophony only added to the tension pulling at Katerina as she tried to process what she had just heard. "QUIET!" she snapped. "Eat your supper and just be quiet!"

Johannes moved toward her, took her by the hand and led her past the drape into the narrow hallway. There he pulled her close, wrapping his muscular arms around her shaking body in a tight embrace. "We will get through this. I do not yet know how, but we will. God is with us. He will guide us. You heard Herr Lenz; we are not in this alone. I need you to be strong. I need you…I just *need* you."

She pulled free of his embrace, wiped the tears from her eyes and softly whispered, "What about Jakob?"

"Jakob must make his way to Leopold; I will give him instructions to help him. You need to prepare a bag of food and clothing light enough for him to carry. I will send my rifle and ammunition with him, and a letter for Leopold. I will ask my brother to find work for Jakob on a Turkish ship; he will be safe there."

Katerina inhaled deeply in an effort to control all the turmoil boiling within her. She nodded mechanically as she reentered the living space. Johannes retreated through the door into the stable where he found Jakob eagerly brushing one of the horses. Jakob gave a momentary look toward the hay loft over the cow's stall.

"I wonder where Konrad might be hiding?" Johannes said loudly. "I suppose I had better find him quickly, or he will miss his supper."

"Is the man gone?" A small voice chirped from overhead.

"Yes, he is gone," Johannes replied as he pretended to rummage through the horses' manger.

Konrad emerged from the pile of hay in which he had been hiding. "Jakob would not hide with me," the child pouted. "He said he would play only if the man came in here. He just brush Georg."

"Well, that was not a very good way to play with you, was it?"

Johannes motioned for Konrad to jump down from the loft into his waiting arms. "He might have been too easily found. You go and eat your supper; I will speak to Jakob about this."

"Yes, Papi, you tell him." Konrad was off like a flash back into the house.

"Konrad was right, Jakob, you should have hidden as well. You were lucky the visitor was from a neighboring village, if he had been a soldier he would have more than likely searched the house looking for older boys. I thought you understood that."

"Sorry, Father. I listened at the door and heard that the man was not a soldier, so I thought it safe not to hide. I thought cooling out the horses was a better use of my time than crouching in the hay."

"What if the man had not been alone? What if soldiers were checking around the house and yard looking for you while the man distracted us in the house?" Johannes was becoming agitated at the thought his son could have so easily been discovered.

"But it did not happen, I was safe here, and as I told Konrad, I would hide if I heard any noise that sounded like someone looking into things." Jakob was becoming a bit defensive in response to his father's agitation.

"What is done is done, Jakob, I am just trying to help you understand how serious this is. You must have heard also that the whole family has to leave tomorrow, so it is imperative you leave tonight. You will go to your Uncle Leopold; he will know what to do with you. I will write a letter for you to give to him. I will also write instructions for you to follow so you can get to his house safely."

"Yes, Father. Which horse can I take?"

"You must go on foot. It will be easier for you to disappear into the forest if you are not on horseback; you will make less noise and be less likely to draw the attention of the wolves. Besides, the family will need both horses to draw the wagon. THE WAGON! It is still out in the fields! I must retrieve it or we will have no way to take our things with us! Hurry, Jakob, help me harness the horses!"

Jakob removed the horses' collars from the hook on which they had been placed to dry, wiped them off with the sleeves of his shirt as best he could, and then placed them on the still sweating horses. Johannes threw a harness over each horse's back and began buckling the leather in place as Jakob bridled them. Johannes tucked the long straps of the traces up under the back band of the harness to keep them from being stepped on by either the horses or himself as he made his way back to his fields. He needed these straps intact in order to hitch the horses to the wagon. Jakob ran the lines from the bridles through the rings on the collars and back to his father's experienced hands. Johannes backed the horses around and lined them up with the big door that opened into the yard. As he left the barn he turned to Jakob, "Tell your mother where I have gone. Assist her with whatever needs to be done to get you ready to leave. I will be back soon. Above all, keep out of sight!"

Johannes clucked gently to the team and began the long walk. He began to pray. He was grateful for the opportunity to finally cool his horses properly, as he could not afford to have them stricken with colic in the morning. He was thankful for the time to reflect and think upon the events that had already taken place and those that were to be; but above all, he was appreciative of the time to make plans. By the time he returned he would know what to tell his oldest son about the journey ahead of him, what things he needed to watch for, how to find food, how to survive the unknown.

Approaching the main road out of the village, he was startled from of his thoughts by the snorting of his horses. It took him a moment to focus on what had upset them. Then he just stood and stared at the seemingly endless swarm of wagons and people spread out into the fields before him. The wagons were heavily loaded with household goods, and children roamed everywhere. He quickly understood the comment made by Herr Lenz that there would be nothing left to harvest. What was not trampled was being quickly eaten by the accompanying animals, the horses and milk cows, some with calves at their sides, were devouring all within their reach. How would he locate his own wagon in this amalgamation? He turned his team south along the road and the horses headed to his fields as if they were in their normal daily routine. Soon he spotted the tree in whose shade he and Jakob had eaten their noon meal; his wagon was still as he had left it a couple of hours earlier. He began maneuvering the horses toward the tree, but was soon stopped by a patrolling soldier.

"Where are you going?" The soldier stood with his rifle resting across his folded arms and spoke in Russian.

"This is my field." Johannes stated assertively. "That is my wagon under that tree," he pointed. "I am going to take it back to my home so I may pack it for tomorrow's journey." He feared his Russian was a little rusty, but he boldly stood his ground.

"Why did you leave it? Is it a common practice of yours? Do you not care what happens to your property?"

"One of my horses ran off." Johannes did not condone lying, but he could not think of any other explanation that would not reveal the presence of Jakob. "I needed the other to catch him, so the wagon was left."

The soldier nodded with some suspicion as he eyed the now cool but sweat-encrusted horses, and allowed Johannes to continue on his way. Johannes quickly hitched the horses to the wagon, stepped up to the seat and took a good long look out over his fields. He felt as if his entire life had just been ripped from his hands. All the hard work the whole family had put into growing those crops meant to provide for them through the coming winter was now destroyed. *What will we do now? What will we eat? How can we afford to start over again next year? What is to become of us?* While these thoughts raced through his mind, the idea that he might never see this land again did not even occur to him.

It was nearly dark by the time he drove back into the yard. To facilitate loading, he halted the horses so that the wagon was stopped near the door of the house. He then set the brake and dismounted, still holding the lines to the horses. The horses knew to stand quietly until told to move forward, so Johannes was able to unhitch them and take them back to their stalls and full mangers within a few minutes. Jakob met him in the barn. He lit the lantern and hung it from a rafter. He then took the lines from his father, guided the horses into their stalls and unharnessed them with the skill of a much older man. The collars were wiped off and hung to dry on their hooks, as caked sweat on a collar caused large sores on the horses' necks. The harness was laid out along the top of the manger wall to dry, in order to ensure the suppleness of the leather and to keep the harness from cracking and falling apart. A supple harness would also prevent the horses from being galled by cracked and worn leather. All of this was accomplished in a workmanlike way and in silence. When Jakob was finished, Johannes signaled for him to join in a final brushing of the horses for the night.

"Have you eaten supper?" Johannes asked.

"Yes." Jakob answered quietly.

"Good, it may be your last decent meal for awhile. Has your mother prepared your pack?"

"She was finishing as I came out here to help you. She had me select some clothes, wrapped up some bread and sausages into a towel, and tied it all up in my blanket."

"It will be adequate to get you on your way." Johannes moved around behind the horse he was brushing and joined Jakob. "I am giving you my rifle and ammunition."

Jakob was stunned by this statement. "Why? What will you do without your rifle? How will you hunt?"

"Do not worry about us. We will be traveling with many others. The soldiers have rifles. You are the one who will need to hunt for your food. You will need protection from the wolves and bears. You must take it with you."

"Yes, Father."

"When we are done here, I will write the letter to Uncle Leopold. He will know what to do for you. I will also write instructions on how to find his house once you get to his village. You must follow the river as it flows into the Black Sea—it will take you to Odessa. You will be able to hide in the forest along the shoreline during the day. If possible, that is when you should sleep, as well. Travel at night; you will be less likely to be seen by patrolling soldiers and will be better able to protect yourself from marauding wolves. Do not light a fire at night, it can be seen for great distances. A small fire during the day should be alright for cooking anything you might catch to eat. Do not shoot the rifle if you think people might be close. You will find villages along the river, but they may be empty now, or possibly full of soldiers. Stay away from them. Trust no one until you find your uncle. If you cannot find him, or it gets too dangerous for you to get to him, head to the sea. Odessa is a port where large ships come; they are continuously looking for workers. Try to find a ship headed for Turkey. Keep your head down and do what you are told. If you are spoken to in Russian, answer in Russian, if spoken to in German, answer in German; if you are approached in any other language keep silent until you are sure how you should respond. Do you have any questions?"

"If I go to Turkey, how will I find you? How will I know when I can come back?"

Johannes placed his hands on his son's strong shoulders. "If it is meant for us to be together again, we will be. You will know when the time is right; it may be in a few months, or years, or never. You must trust your heart. Now go and tell your brothers and sisters, and especially your mother, good bye."

Jakob withdrew to the house. In reflective silence, Johannes ran his hands over each horse's body one last time checking for anything he may have missed that might be cause of concern in the morning; he threw a bit more hay to the cow and put out the lantern, his mind occupied with thoughts for the day ahead.

By the time Johannes reentered the kitchen, Katerina had completed Jakob's pack and was fussing over what to load into the wagon. Johannes found some paper in the chest of drawers that was on the far wall of the room, sat down at the table and wrote the letters. Then he rose and retrieved his rifle from its supports on the wall, and lifted the leather pouch of ammunition from the nail behind the door. The other children stared wide-eyed at their father as he handed these precious items to Jakob. Finally Karolina broke the leaden silence.

"Is it really true? Is Jakob actually leaving us tonight? Why, Mama, why?" Her eyes were filled with tears at this inconceivable idea that she was losing her brother so suddenly. Being just a year younger than he, she had always known his presence in her life. Her connection to him ran deeper and stronger than it had with any of her other siblings.

"Dry your tears little sister, I will be fine." Jakob gave her a quick hug. "We will see each other again soon, I am sure. I am off on a great adventure to see Uncle Leopold. I am finally being treated like a man in this family, and there is nothing to be afraid of."

The other children closed in around him and he gave each an embrace. He lifted Rosina from her cradle, held her up and then pulled her close. "You will probably be walking, maybe even running, by the time I get back. Do not give Konrad too much trouble." He kissed her on the cheek and handed her to his mother.

Konrad wrapped his arms around his big brother's leg in an effort to keep him from leaving, but Jakob pulled him off and picked him up. "You look after Heinreich and your sisters for me, and be a big help to Mama."

"Why?" Konrad's question had many answers.

"That is something you will have to figure out for yourself, Konrad." Jakob answered as he put him down. He ruffled his little brother's silky hair and smiled, knowing Konrad would stew over the response for quite a while.

Katerina stepped forward and handed her son the bundle she had prepared for his trip. She knew she could not say much without bursting into tears again, so she simply said "I love you. God speed."

Jakob could only imagine how hard this must be for her. He kissed her cheek. "Do not be upset about me leaving. You have enough to worry about with your trip ahead, Mama. I will be fine. I love you." Jakob had become elated about the idea of being treated as a grown person, being allowed to leave on his own and fend for himself, even if it was only long enough to get to Uncle Leopold's.

Johannes removed the small Bible he carried in his shirt pocket and handed it to Jakob. "A few minutes each day will give you strength. But keep it hidden, as the godless Russians will kill you for believing in something they cannot control." With that he reached out and shook his son's hand. All that needed to be said had been said. Jakob opened the door and disappeared into the darkness.

CHAPTER TWO

The Journey

Johannes was up before the sun. There was much to be done before they could leave at midday. He dressed, lit the fire in the stove, making it ready for breakfast, and quietly went out the door. He enjoyed the last few minutes of dawn, listening to the day waking up, one small bird at a time. There was something especially reverent about this time of day, those few extraordinary minutes of silence as the night creatures settled into sleep and the day creatures awoke. He asked God to bless his family and thanked Him for the good life they shared together.

Eyeing his wagon near the door, he gave it a good going over. He normally took great care of his equipment, but he especially needed to know all was in proper order before entrusting his family in this wagon for any length of time. When he was satisfied, he proceeded to feed the animals, normally Jakob's chore. By the time he returned to the house, the rest of the family was up, dressed and doing their assigned morning tasks.

As the girls milked the cow and gathered the eggs, Johannes pulled up the picket fence that divided the garden from the barnyard and attached it to the sides of the wagon, extending the height of the sides. He then retrieved arched bows from the barn and fastened them to the fencing, forming a frame on which to secure a cloth cover over the wagon bed. He threw the oiled-linen cloth, which was used to protect the stacked hay during the winter months, over the bows and tied it firmly at each corner. Satisfied that his children would be protected from the heat of the summer sun, he entered his house.

Katerina was nursing Rosina. Magdalena and Anya were setting the table for breakfast, and Karolina was busy at the stove. Heinreich and Konrad were putting clothing into a wooden box. "Do we need to pack our coats and boots, Mama?" Heinreich asked.

"It is August, son, and we should be back by the end of next month, so I think not. Those items are large and heavy. We will need the space in the wagon for food."

"Yes, Mama."

"Mama, may I take my sewing box?" Anya asked. "I can work on my project while we are traveling." Anya had begun sewing her first apron and was anxious to finish it.

"That is a good idea, Anchen," her father responded, calling her by the nickname he had given her, "as we may need needles and thread to make repairs." Katerina frowned slightly at her husband's remark. "If the child's pleasure also means practicality, so be it," he said.

After breakfast, Johannes and the boys began loading the wagon with the household items necessary for the trip. The clothing chest was packed in behind the food storage box. Johannes put in a chair for Katerina to ride in while she nursed Rosina, and left a small space on the floor for the other children to sit. After that another trunk was put in containing dishes and household goods, the few things Katerina could not part with or allow the be stolen while they were gone. A washtub and a basket, containing the dishes and pots and pans they planned to use on the trip, were stowed in a corner. Next Johannes loaded four large sacks of flour and one of rye meal, then bags of potatoes, dried apples and peaches. Another box was filled with jars of preserved meat, pickled cabbage, beets and watermelon rind. Lastly, he added the loaves of bread Katerina prepared each week, and sugar and coffee to the load.

Katerina packed clothing and diaper cloths she needed for Rosina into a separate bag, while the girls stuffed bedding between the boxes and put their parents' feather-filled mattress in the open space of the wagon bed. The large family Bible was carefully hidden among the blankets.

It was finally time to hitch the horses and prepare to meet the rest of the village residents in the town square. Johannes tied their reluctant cow to the rear of the wagon. This was her time to be out in the pasture and she resented being deprived of her leisurely grazing. Opening all the gates to the poultry pens, Johannes allowed the chickens and geese to fend for themselves while the family was gone.

Katerina appeared in the doorway with two more items. She held Rosina's cradle with both hands; a small wooden box had been placed within it. "We will need the cradle. We can put it on the floorboard between us, and I will not leave our family photos, it is all I have left of Jakob."

Johannes nodded as he took them from her. He knew her attachment to the cradle went beyond Rosina's need to have a place to sleep. This was the cradle her father had made for her when Jakob was born, this was the cradle all of their children had been raised in, this was the cradle that had held little Johannes, the son lost to fever only weeks before Konrad was born.

All was now ready. As the children found their places among the many things in the wagon, Johannes returned to the house. He made sure the fire burnt out safely in the stove, placed the chairs upside-down on the table, and gave one last look around the room. All was in order and he hoped this was the way they would find it on their return.

Johannes assisted Katerina onto the wagon where she settled herself and accepted Rosina from Magdalena. He then placed the small box of photos in an opening under the seat that also contained various items used for harness repair. Finally, perching himself on the driver's seat and unwrapping the lines from the brake handle, he clucked to the horses and they headed out to the road.

In just a few minutes they met up with their neighbors, the Meirs, and fell in behind them as they proceeded to the center of the village. Katerina noticed right away that they were missing their oldest son. Somehow she felt better thinking the boys would meet up somewhere and Jakob was not alone.

By the time they reached the village center, most of the other residents were gathered and ready to take their place at the end of the line of wagons preceding them. Several Russian soldiers were milling around amongst the new arrivals, checking out the items in the wagons and inspecting the children. One soldier stood on the edge of the stone wall forming the town's communal horse trough and waved his rifle in the air in order to gain attention and silence; when he was satisfied that all could hear him, he spoke out in Russian-interspersed German.

"Welcome to our little journey! You have been made aware this is for your own protection. The German army believes you are enemies of their country and are set on killing *all of you!* While on this trip you will stay with your own village—do not join with the others! We will be watching to make sure you stay with your own! We will try to travel at least twenty-five kilometers each day, but I doubt we will make ten as slow as *you* people travel. Now get going!"

The Byrgermeister's wagon was the first to pull out, the rest followed and shortly thereafter, the entire village trailed behind the last of the other wagons. Almost as one, the villagers gasped as they first viewed their fields and the destruction of their crops from one night's stay of the caravan. The devastation was virtually unbelievable, as if a black cloud of locusts had invaded their countryside and eaten everything in sight.

When Katerina caught her breath she uttered softly, "Is this what we will do to others?"

"Yes." Johannes nodded his head slowly. "I am afraid so. We have no choice."

They traveled in silence for quite some time. The children were sadly watching their world disappear into the dust as the distance back home slowly stretched out behind them.

Konrad was the first to speak. "Papi, soldier coming."

"*Danke*, Konrad, I see him." Johannes responded.

The Russian soldier was mounted on a thin, dusty, bay horse that showed weariness from its forced march. As the soldier neared the wagon he smiled directly at Karolina, making her feel uneasy and the hair stand up on her neck.

"We do not stop until we reach tonight's rest point," he ordered.

Johannes asked, "How will I give my horses respite? How do we eat our afternoon meal? How do my children get relief from this constant movement? How does my wife tend to our infant?"

"You move too slowly for the horses to need a rest. If you choose to eat, it will be while you are driving. Your children can walk like the others if they tire from riding, and your wife will figure out how to tend the infant." The soldier was mocking Johannes and a bit of laughter rippled through his words. "If you stop for any reason, *you will be shot!*" That was his final declaration as he rode on to the next wagon.

Konrad started to whimper. Fear and anxiety were finally starting to grip his young intellect. Anya moved over next to him and put her arm around his shoulders, pulling him toward her. She rocked him from side to side in time with the horses' footsteps. She reached into the pocket of her skirt and removed a small hand-carved wooden doll. She was never without this token of love her father had made for her, and now she shared it with her frightened little brother. He fingered the doll's intricately carved features and after a brief few moments, laid his head upon Anya's lap, curled himself into a comma, and went to sleep.

Katerina turned slightly and looked back into the wagon; she gave Anya a knowing and comforting smile. *How quickly you are growing up, and what a good mother you will make,* Katerina mused. Anya took to looking after Konrad shortly after his birth, even though she was only five. He had come so soon after the death of little Johannes that Katerina just was not able to be a mother to any of her children for awhile, especially Konrad. The older girls had taken over the duties of the household, but Anya, almost immediately and without question, accepted the responsibility of caring for Konrad. She insured that he was clean and dry, and brought him to his mother when it was time to nurse. She spent hours rocking him in the cradle and quickly responded to his cries. She was constantly at his side when he needed comforting, as she was now, and hopefully as she would be forever. Katerina was proud of all her children, but Anya, with her nurturing instincts, was the kind of daughter she most wanted to raise.

The older girls were so very different. Karolina was headstrong and preferred to work in the fields alongside her father and brothers. While she was obedient and easily learned her household duties, she just did not seem domestic in her ways. Magdalena, on the other hand, was quiet and respectful, but continually seemed to be somewhere else in her thoughts. She did as she was told and performed her tasks well, but she seemed to drift into and out of her chores as if she were hovering on the edge of reality.

Katerina was jolted out of her thoughts by Heinreich.

"Mama, can we eat?"

"Yes, Heiner, have one of your sisters get bread out, and maybe some sausage. That will be easiest to handle. Prepare something for your father as well."

"Yes, Mama." Heinreich scrambled across the load in the wagon. Karolina had already begun to pull out from under the bedding the wooden box containing the bread. She took a loaf and tore it into eight pieces, one for each of them.

"Do you expect Rosina to eat bread?" Magdalena asked sarcastically. "Will she have sausage, too?"

"No." Karolina responded gloomily. "I was including Jakob."

"SHHHHHH!" Anya scolded in a hushed voice. "Do not say his name, especially in front of...." She pointed to Konrad asleep in her lap.

"I know!" Karolina snapped. "It was a mistake. I am sorry!" She put the last bit of bread back into the box as she got out a dried sausage. Separating it as best she could into seven pieces, she handed it out to each family member. Anya placed Konrad's share on the blanket next to her, so he could eat when he awoke.

CHAPTER THREE

Life on the Road

As the caravan continued on its northerly trek, Johannes became aware that they were out of the area of the German villages. Road signs were all in Russian, with no German translations. The Russian villages they passed through were somewhat different in their makeup, even though they were also agricultural in nature. *Unlikely there will be there any more additions to the group,* he thought, *probably a favorable circumstance, since we are nearly four hundred wagons strong.*

The travelers saw no local towns-people around the fields or in the villages. The unnaturalness of this produced an uneasy pall over the group, as they were sure the soldiers had commanded the people to hide from the eyes of the caravan, but they did not understand why this would be necessary.

Just before sunset the wagons were ordered off the road, into the wheat fields of a *kolkhoz,* a collective farm. Johannes knew of these farms because he and the other German farmers had resisted the Stalinist takeover of their own places. He thought of the condition in which his fields had been left the previous night, and he despaired knowing his family was preparing to camp on the wheat harvest that was to have sustained this village through the upcoming winter. He knew these farms were required to meet inflated government quotas, and how poorly the farmers were treated when the quotas were not realized. He did not understand why the Russian government was so callous to its own people. The great famine of the previous few years caused the loss of many people's lives. *Why does the government let them starve to death on good farmland? What is so wrong with letting farmers do what they have always done, the growing of crops that are right for the kind of soil they have, and selling their crops in a self-regulating market?* This was politics Johannes just could not fathom.

He maneuvered the horses into a clear area, dismounted from the wagon and began unhitching. Katerina and the girls began to unpack items to prepare supper, while Heinreich and Konrad struggled to dislodge a bedding roll from the wagon bed. As the dust from the day's travel settled, it mingled with the wheat chaff being stirred up as the other families engaged in their own activities to prepare for the night ahead.

Johannes tied the horses to the wagon on a long tether, allowing them to graze the wheat stalks. He did the same for the cow, but she was not used to so much walking and was totally exhausted, so she just collapsed onto the ground. Johannes scanned the area for an indication of water and noticed others hauling all manner of buckets toward the east. He removed the horses' water buckets from the side of the wagon and called to Karolina.

"Bring the cooking pot and follow me. Heinreich, you come, too. We will need your help."

"Yes, Papi." They answered in unison as Karolina grabbed the large iron caldron by its handle and rushed to meet her father. Heinreich had already taken one of the horses' buckets from his father and was making his way through the wheat toward the river bank. As he approached the top of the ledge overlooking the river, he stopped and stared at the water below him.

"Papi, we cannot use this water, it is full of mud."

"Yes, Heiner, we are at the end of a long line. With so many people upstream stirring up the waters, we are left with mud. Let us see what we can do." Johannes made his way down the bank to the water's edge, then looked both directions and across the river. About twenty feet out, the water was moving quickly enough that the mud was minimal.

"Karolina, go back to the wagon and get the longest rope you can find."

"Yes, Papi. Should I bring one of the horses, also?" she asked.

"Good girl; that is a grand idea! Bring Hans back with you." Johannes quickly figured out what she had in mind. Heiner stood on the riverbank somewhat bewildered as he watched his sister take off for the campsite.

"What are you going to do, Papi?" he asked. "Why do you need one of the horses?"

"If we fill the buckets by tossing them out there, way out in the middle of the river where it is cleaner, they will be too heavy to drag to shore. They will sink, and we will have to pull them out through the muddy part. We will end up with the same mud if we just fill them here at the shore's edge. But, if Karolina rides Hans into the middle, she can fill the bucket and pull it up onto him and bring it back to the shore out of the mud. Then we can have reasonably clean water to take back to camp."

Heinreich thought about this for a few moments. Finally a big smile came across his face as realization set in. "Also, if we let Hans drink while he is out there, that will be less water we will have to carry back to camp!"

"Heiner, be careful how you think. Finding ways to make your chores easier could be a sign of a future politician," Johannes playfully admonished.

Karolina quickly returned with Hans. The big grey horse cautiously stepped into the river, wary of the opaque, brown water hiding the river bottom he could not see. Johannes tied the rope to the handle of one of the buckets and handed it to Karolina. She urged the horse out into the swiftly running water and dropped the bucket into the cleanest area she could find. The big horse put his head down and drank in long gulping mouthfuls. When he was sated, he allowed himself to be turned around and ridden back up onto the shore as Karolina balanced the overflowing bucket in front of her. She handed the full bucket to her father and took the next empty bucket back out into the river, repeating the process, until all were filled, including the cooking pot. Johannes carried each full bucket up to the top of the riverbank and tied the handles together with the rope, allowing them to be slung across Han's back for the return trip to the campsite. Karolina and Heinreich carried the cooking pot between them as they followed their father and Hans back up the trail they had made through the wheat.

Hans' teammate, Georg, whinnied loudly as he saw his partner returning; causing Hans to toss his head and begin to trot. Water splashed out of the buckets and down the sides of the big horse. But Hans, being Hans, did not panic; instead, he felt the coolness of the water on his back and came to a complete stop, planting his feet wide apart, and giving himself a good shake. More water splashed out of the buckets as Johannes took a tighter hold on the halter. He and the children were laughing heartily as they returned with only about half of the water they started with.

Johannes removed the buckets from Hans's back, poured the remaining contents into one bucket and handed the empty bucket back to Karolina. "Better take Georg this time, let him drink, and fill the bucket for Ilse. That old cow will not mind a little mud, as long as she does not have to walk down to the river to get water for herself."

Katerina and Magdalena had already gouged a pit in the ground to form a hearth for the fire. They encircled it with stones they found along the edge of the roadway and tied stalks of dry wheat together to build a fire to cook the evening meal. The big pot was placed in the flames, but it would not be used for cooking tonight. The water was to be boiled and stored in a milk can for drinking the next day. A large iron pan was heated in the flames and sausage was added to it. Katerina removed a jar of beets from the food box, along with a jar of sauerkraut. She believed she should be frugal with what food they had; she was not sure how long it would have to last.

Soldiers patrolled past them several times through the evening, giving threatening motions with their rifles as they went by, but by midnight the entire area had quieted into only the sounds of periodic shuffling of horses and cattle as the camp drifted into an exhausted but wary sleep.

The sun had barely risen when trouble started in the far-off distance at the front of the caravan. Shouting was heard, followed by screaming and finally the echo of a gunshot. The encampment rapidly came alive with activity as everyone tried to find out what was happening. Soldiers quickly rode through the throng, bellowing orders to remain in place and stay with their villages. Johannes put the children to work preparing to break camp; if they were kept busy they would not be thinking about what might be happening.

It was not long before several more soldiers rode through, driving a number of skinny red cows before them. They stopped near the wagon and examined Ilse as she grazed at the end of her tether.

"We will take your cow," announced one of the soldiers. "She will be payment to the kolkhoz for your destroying the harvest." The young man was shouting as if he feared the muscular farmer standing before him. "Untie her and let her follow these other worn out excuses for meat as we drive them to the village."

Johannes calmly stepped toward Ilse and began to remove her tether, he did not want to lose her, but he had no choice in the matter. Unexpectedly, Karolina rushed forward and snatched the tether from his hands.

"You will not take my cow!" she screamed. "I raised her from a calf, she is mine and you cannot have her!"

Johannes reached out, grabbed his daughter by the arm, and removed the tether from Ilse all in one motion.

"PAPI, WHAT ARE YOU DOING? You cannot give them Ilse!" she cried out. "We need her milk, Konrad needs milk, please do not give her to them ...." her voice trailed away into sobs as she pulled herself free from her father's grip and fell to the ground.

"*Papi*, tell your spoiled daughter she will be next if she does not watch her insolence!" The soldier hissed through his teeth as he gave Ilse a pop on her hindquarters with a long stick to get her moving. "We will be watching you *kulaks* for any further trouble."

As Ilse joined the herd and the soldiers rode off, Johannes reached to help Karolina up from the ground. She jerked her arm away and flashed a look of tearful defiance toward him.

"Karolina, you must know I did not want to give Ilse to them. I know you children need her milk, but I also know that going against these soldiers will only result in harassment or death. Did you not hear the shot earlier? Do you think it was just a warning? I do not. I think we will see a fresh grave when we leave here today. Ilse will be better off with the people of the village. She gave no milk last night and less than half her normal amount this morning. She is not used to this kind of traveling, and we do not know what feed will be available for her on the rest of the trip. Would you rather see her butchered to feed the soldiers or just shot and left to die in the road?"

Karolina's tears were not easily stopped. Johannes helped her to her feet; she leaned on him, dampening the shoulder of his shirt.

"I have a feeling this will not be the last of our losses," Johannes sadly commented. "We must all be prepared for that possibility."

While the family continued to load the wagon and prepare for the day's travel ahead, the Byrgermeister went from camp to camp, talking with the head of each household. Soon he arrived and took Johannes aside to speak privately with him.

"I see you have lost your cow," Herr Becker said. "I assume the soldiers took her. Were there any problems?"

"Yes, they demanded we give her to the village for payment of our stay here. My daughter did not want to give her up—she was especially attached to that cow." Johannes was very matter of fact in his statement. He was not sure he trusted Herr Becker even though he had known him for many years. There was something about the way the man presented himself as someone much more powerful than the mayor of their village.

"I hope you did not anger the soldiers in any way. They came to me this morning and told me anyone who gave them trouble was to be dealt with severely. I suppose you heard the gunshot. That was a poor man from one of the villages who joined the trip near its start. They have been on the road for several weeks and are running out of food. The loss of their cow was far more harmful to them than you losing your cow. Now the family has no milk and one less to feed." Herr Becker turned to leave, but Johannes stopped him.

"The man, Herr Lenz from Freidenthal, who came to our house to tell us of this journey, declared we would only be gone from our farm for about a month, and now you are telling me some of these people have already been traveling for weeks? What more do you know? Where are we going, and when will we actually be able to return?"

Herr Becker shrugged his shoulders. "The soldiers are telling us little. Each evening they gather the village mayors into a group. As I am sure you are aware, last night was my first of these gatherings. We were informed there would be no more added to our company; we would be required to make payment to the kolkhoz that housed us the previous night, and we should reach our destination shortly. I was taken aside by the commandant of the soldiers and reminded that we were not to speak or mix with the people of the other villages in any way—on penalty of death."

Johannes had one more question. "The soldiers called us '*kulaks*,' what does it mean?"

Herr Becker was noticeably shaken by this inquiry. "*Kulak*, in Soviet terms, means 'wealthy farmer'; they are insisting those who farm their own land and are not a part of the collective are overly rich and their property needs to be taken for 'New Russia.' I had not heard the soldiers use the term, but if that is their assignment, we have all lost what ever we left behind."

Johannes felt the weight of uncertainty heavily upon his shoulders. "I must not say anything to my wife just yet. She will not understand and will want to return home."

"Nothing should be said to anyone. Any disruption in the journey will be cause for execution at the soldiers' hands. We must just do as we are told, and God willing, we will all come out of this alive. They are possibly just moving us to a kolkhoz a bit north of here, and maybe we will be settled soon." Herr Becker now seemed to be in a rush to leave, so Johannes let him go without another word.

There was something about Herr Becker's response that gave Johannes the feeling he knew more than he was saying and the question about their destination was one that should not have been asked as yet. "Time will tell," Johannes said to himself, "Time will tell."

One hot day after another ran together with a long, slow, dusty persistence. The ongoing trek through the collective farms blended one wheat field into another. After the first week, the children began walking beside the wagon in an effort to ease the strain on the horses.

During the early part of the journey, the travelers would stop briefly to squat along the trail to relieve themselves. But now, the heat of the sun, combined with the constant movement, dehydrated their bodies to the point that these stops, for the most part, became unnecessary.

"Katerina," Johannes sighed one afternoon, "I am going to have to ask you to walk with the children. I am guessing we have traveled about 400 kilometers, and the horses are exhausted. I do not know how much farther they will have to pull our wagon. I must do what I can to lighten the load."

"All right," she replied as Johannes pulled the horses to a halt. "But may I ride when Rosina needs to nurse?" she asked.

"Of course, I will walk and drive the horses from the ground. That will give them some relief. We should be stopping for the night soon, anyway." Johannes commented as he helped his wife down from the wagon.

Katerina shook her head, "I do not know how much longer our food will hold out either. I have tried to be frugal, but you and the children are becoming so thin. Each day we see more new graves by the road, graves of those who have no food, graves of those who can no longer tolerate this endless travel."

Johannes settled Rosina into her cradle on the floorboard by his feet. "You must remember, many of these families include old people, young mothers with tiny babies, and those who have given birth on the road. Those who began before us surely have not had substantial food for many days. This journey's toll is being paid with the lives of those who have been forced into taking it."

As the day wore on, Johannes noticed a definite change in the terrain around him. The road was more packed and solid. A village appeared on the horizon, a much larger village than any they had seen before, and most importantly, he saw railroad tracks coming in from the east.

The soldiers waved their rifles and shouted orders to pull off the road and set up camp for the night. A long sleek black car ominously drove past the extensive line of wagons, going slowly, as if the occupants were looking for someone in particular.

Heinrich grabbed his father's sleeve and pointed toward the car. "What is THAT?" he asked with some trepidation in his voice.

"That, my son, is an automobile. It is like a wagon without horses. You should be very cautious of it, as I would guess it is full of secret police or members of the local soviet."

"Papi, how do you know such things?"

"I saw many of these cars when I served my time in the army, and there was never anything good arriving in them. Here, help me unharness Hans."

After locating and hauling water to the horses, and while Katerina and the children prepared their meager supper of biscuits and sauerkraut, Johannes left camp and sought out the Byrgermeister.

"Herr Becker, do you know what is next for us? How much longer will my family have to travel under these conditions? My children suffer from too much walking and lack of proper fresh food. Each day, my wife makes less milk for our infant, and the child grows weak and refuses solid food. When will we be able to end this *evacuation?* Have we not traveled far enough from our village to avoid the oncoming armies?"

"Do not ask me those questions! I do not know!" Herr Becker was too easily agitated by Johannes' inquiry.

"I see there is a train in this village, will we be placed on it?" Johannes insisted on knowing something.

Herr Becker's face became purple-red with his rage as he lashed out, swinging his fists wildly toward Johannes' face. Johannes was caught by surprise and did not react quickly enough to miss being grazed across his left cheek.

"I told you, NO QUESTIONS! Too many questions and we will all die!" screamed Herr Becker as he tried to hit Johannes again.

Johannes quickly brought his hands up, catching Herr Becker's hands in mid air and pinning them to his sides.

"What is wrong with you, why are you acting this way?" Johannes was somewhat bewildered by these proceedings.

Frau Becker having heard the commotion ran to the two men. She saw the blood beginning to flow from Johannes' cheek and her husband's fortitude crumble before her.

"I am sorry for his hitting you," she apologized as she knelt beside her husband. "This has been a very trying time for him. The soldiers harass him every night asking about the people of our village. Who are Christians, who are Jews, who are against Stalin, who fought during the revolution and for which side....? Each night it is a new question, with new threats, and new penalties. Each night he returns to me with less strength and resolve. They tell him nothing of their plans for us. Do you not see that our family suffers also? Six days ago, I lost the child I was carrying. Our youngest son has become ill. I, too, wonder how much longer we can hold out before we all are left to die by the road." She seemed too drained to cry. She helped her husband to his feet and they began to return to their wagon.

Johannes removed his hat and wiped his cheek with his shirt sleeve. "I am sorry. I was not thinking beyond my own family. I know everyone is suffering. I realize those who began this trip before us are in even more distress. Everyday I see many new graves, and it frightens me. Tonight I saw the cars of the Soviets prowling the road past our camps, and I do not like it. Over and over again I pray we will soon see the end of this and we will be allowed to return home."

Frau Becker gave Johannes a momentary look of understanding. "Pray for us all," she whispered. "Pray for us all."

Johannes had no sooner returned to his family when a couple of soldiers rode in, their rifles aimed directly at his chest.

"Where have you been?" one of them demanded. "Why were you not in your camp? How did you come by that cut on your cheek?"

"I went to see the Byrgermeister of our village." Johannes simply responded.

"Why?" the soldier asked.

"I had questions for him that I wanted answered." Johannes would not give more information than he was specifically asked for, a trait he had learned in the army.

"What kind of questions?" the soldier asked.

"They were personal, and do not involve you."

"So personal that he hit you?" the soldier inquired, hoping to get more information.

Johannes simply nodded without saying another word.

The soldier lowered his rifle and turned his horse. "You kulak dogs fight like children; if he hit me, his wife would be digging his grave now! Stay in camp, no more butt sniffing and asking questions."

"Johannes, what happened?" Katerina asked as she placed a damp rag against the torn skin of his cheek.

"Herr Becker is a much tormented man. I did not realize what he has been put through as the mayor of our village. The soldiers have taken his pride and a bit of his soul. He needed to lash out at someone, and I foolishly demanded things from him he just could not give. I would rather have this scar on my cheek than the scar that will reside in his heart."

CHAPTER FOUR

The Interrogation

This night seemed cooler than previous ones. The waning moon shed little light upon those who slept beneath it. Sometime after midnight, Johannes was awakened by the sound of the car's tires as they slowly rolled by. He lay still as he heard the car stop and someone get out. The crunching of boot soles on gravel gave him a chill as he knew they were approaching him. He felt the cold hard steel of a rifle barrel being pushed into his shoulder. A hushed voice growled "Shhh," in his ear. Johannes rolled out from under his blanket without disturbing Katerina. He pulled his boots on and followed the beckoning uniform to the car. The rifle was now jabbing into his back, pushing him into the automobile.

"I do not know what you want, but I will not resist you," Johannes spoke softly as he entered the dark interior of the vehicle. "I only ask that you do not hurt my family."

Johannes was pushed into the back seat of the big black sedan. He nearly choked as he drew his first breath; the air was filled with the acrid smoke of a cheap Russian cigarette. Half of the seat was already occupied by a rotund, uniformed officer, his face briefly illuminated by the orange glow of the cigarette as he inhaled deeply. Johannes kept his eyes averted from the man's face; he did not want to see who might be responsible for whatever might be coming. Though, he did notice the insignia on his companion's sleeve—the sword-entwined hammer and sickle of the NKVD. This was not a regular soldier of the Russian army, but a member of the secret police. He again felt the cold steel of a gun barrel in his side, a silent reminder he was not in control and that he should do as he was told.

The car unhurriedly rolled through the village. Johannes wondered if this was an attempt to antagonize him in some way, or if his arrest was being kept silent for some special reason. He knew he would soon find out. He wanted to look out the windows, to get a better idea of the size of the village and the location of the railroad tracks, but each time he started to lift his eyes, the gun barrel sank further into his ribs.

Finally, the car pulled up in front of a long, narrow building. Johannes instantly recognized this building as a holding barn for the wheat of the kolkhoz. He also knew it would be empty at this point in time, just before harvest, and he began to worry about what else might be waiting for him there.

He closed his eyes and prayed silently. "God, please hold my family in your hands. I beg of you, do not let them suffer because of whatever I have done. Spare their lives, even if you do not spare mine."

The car came to a stop; the door was wrenched open and Johannes' arm was gripped tightly by a soldier from outside. "Get out, Fascist!" were the only words spoken. Johannes was jerked out of the car with such force that he fell to his knees. "Stand up! You Fascists have rubber for legs?"

Johannes stood and quickly found his balance; again he felt a rifle muzzle in his back, pushing him toward a small door in the barn being held open by his seatmate. As Johannes entered the barn, a large black rat scurried across the floor, and the soldier tossed the remainder of his cigarette toward it.

A lantern, sitting on a small table placed in the middle of the barn, shed a pallid light across the floor. What appeared to be a large map-book rested on the table next to the lantern, and a diminutive bespectacled man sat leafing through its pages. Plain wooden chairs had been placed across from each other a few feet from the table, just far enough away that the lantern's light did not fully shine upon them. Johannes was pushed down into a chair. The second soldier stood behind Johannes, assuming the stance of a guard.

"What is your name?" the NKVD officer asked in Russian, as he leaned into Johannes' face.

"Johannes Jahnle"

"What is your village?"

"Sofienthal."

"Give me your travel papers."

"I have no travel papers; we have not been given any papers."

"GIVE ME YOUR TRAVEL PAPERS!"

"I can not give you something I do not have! As I said, we have not been given any papers!"

The soldier turned to the small man with the big book. "Why does this man have no papers? All of these travelers were to be issued papers!"

"I will look into it, sir. He is from the last village that joined the trek; it is possible papers were not issued." He seemed to cower and draw away from the light as he responded.

"Well, you *are* the clerk! Find out and get them their papers!" the officer boomed back at him.

"Yes, sir," was the weak reply.

"Can you *at least* verify the information he has given me so far?"

The little man quickly turned pages, and finally settled on one. He ran his finger down through the information listed, stopping near the bottom of the page.

"Yes, here it is Comrade Commissar. House Number 29. Jahnle; Johannes and Katerina (Lutz). Farmer, soldier, 8 children; 4 boys, 4 girls."

The Commissar pulled a notebook from his shirt pocket and thumbed through a couple of pages. "Eight children? According to my sources you only have six with you. Four girls, but only two boys, where are your other sons?"

Johannes lifted his eyes and met the Commissar's gaze straight on, hoping to adequately disguise the lie he was about to tell. "One is dead; the other ran off to join the army," he calmly acknowledged.

"Really? Who's army? The army of the brave Russian workers and peasants, or the fascist pigs of Germany?" The commissar's voice rose with each word, emphasizing his hatred of the Germans.

"Why would he join the Germans?" Johannes asked as if bewildered by the implication. "I was a Russian soldier; it must be there in your book, and back in my wagon, I have those papers to prove it. Why would he not be a Russian soldier, too?"

"Because he is German, just like his father."

"But, I am a loyal Russian citizen…" Johannes began, but was quickly cut off.

"You were in a fight with…" the commissar consulted his notebook again, "Herr Becker, your village magistrate. WHY? What information were you trying to get from him that was so important? What information were you trying to pass along to the German fascists?"

"I was not trying to get information for any German army; I just wanted to know how much longer my family, all our families, are going to have to endure this trip we have been on. We were told it would only be a short time…" Johannes was again cut off by the commissar.

"So, you were trying to get information about your future location, so you could keep in contact with your spies! Who are your contacts? What is your affiliation with the German authorities?" The questions were being rapidly fired at Johannes in an attempt to trip him up, an attempt to get him to reveal his true nature.

"I TOLD YOU, I have no contacts with German authorities. I am a simple farmer. I have paid my taxes and obeyed Russian laws. I served the Russian army for six years and kept my paperwork up to date for future recruitment. I am sure you can verify this information." Johannes looked toward the clerk, who seemed to be taking notes at his table.

"How do I know you served the Russian army as a true soldier and not just to get training to be a kulak spy? How do I know you are not an enemy of the state? For all I know, you exchange messages with your son, and he reports back to the German wolves so they can plan their attack upon us." The words seethed through the commissar's teeth like a snake hissing at its prey.

"WE ARE RUSSIAN CITIZENS!" Johannes jumped to his feet in protest. The butt of the rifle held by the guard quickly found its way to the side of his head. Stunned, he reeled around to face his assailant, only to be struck again. Johannes fell to his knees and the rifle slammed into his back. He collapsed to the floor.

"Maybe, I should just shoot you now and save someone else the trouble later," the Commissar hissed.

The guard and the clerk pulled Johannes up and threw him back into the chair. Johannes could not focus his eyes or get a grip on the throbbing in his skull. He sat with his head between his legs and his hands over his ears trying to put together what had just happened. The commissar continued talking, but Johannes was not listening. The Russian words were falling into a jumble between the ebb and flow of the pain emanating from his head. Blood began to stream from his left ear, filling his hand, running down his arm onto his pant leg, and pooling on the floor at his feet.

The anger in the commissar's voice finally found its way through to Johannes, but Johannes was not sure to whom the anger was directed. "IDIOT!" was all he could make out. Someone slapped him across the face; it was as if a brick had been used. A bucket of water was poured over him, which only intensified the agony in his head. He felt safest not moving; he might tolerate more blows to his back, but not to his head. He heard more yelling, but could not make out the words. The rifle slammed into the side of his leg, just below the blood-soaked area.

"I SAID, ON YOUR FEET!" He finally heard the words, but did not know who spoke them. He tried to stand upright, but his knees would not support him and he fell to the floor, catching his chin on the back of the chair as he went down.

Soldiers on each side of him picked him up by his arms and dragged him out of the barn. He was thrown into the back of a waiting truck and driven back out to the caravan encampment. The truck stopped along the road, the soldiers rolled Johannes off the truck into the dirt, and drove off, just as the sun began to crest the Eastern horizon.

CHAPTER FIVE

Wounds

Katerina had been fully awake when the soldiers took Johannes, but out of fear that she, too, might be taken by the soldiers, she pretended to sleep. She did not want to take the chance that her children might be left alone. She had slept little during the past week, constantly listening for Rosina's quiet breathing as the nights slowly dragged out, hour by hour. The long days of walking, combined with the limited amount of food she had consumed, had nearly dried up the milk her little one needed. Katerina tried squeezing the milk from her breasts, in an effort to get every possible drop, until they were so tender that Rosina's feeble sucking had become painful. She encouraged Rosina to eat a bit of wheat gruel, but the baby would not—could not swallow the soft mush. Now, Rosina was too weak to even cry. *My child is dying*, she fretted, *how do I stop it?*

After the car left with Johannes, Katerina rose, wrapped the blanket around her shoulders and lifted Rosina to her breast. "Please, little one, please try," she whispered in desperation. "I do not know where they have taken your Papi; I do not know when we will see him again. I can only pray he will be returned to us soon. You must try to eat; you must be here for him." A tear slowly made its way down Katerina's cheek and fell lightly on the baby's face. Katerina watched as the drop rolled across her child's nearly transparent skin and disappeared into her white-blonde hair.

Rosina stirred slightly, opened her eyes momentarily, and then returned to her silent slumber. Katerina placed Rosina back into her cradle, knelt on the ground next to it, and placed one hand on the edge. She intended to rock her baby, but instead she began to cry. The cradle seemed to take hold of her and wrench the memories right out of her heart. Her mind was flooded with the recollections of losing little Johannes to fever; of not knowing where Jakob, the first child she had raised in this cradle, might be or if he were even still alive; remembering when her father had gifted this cradle to her, just a short time before he died of infection from the injuries he received in the Revolution.

"Dear God, PLEASE do not take Johannes away from me now! I cannot live without him; I can not face this journey alone! Please do not forsake us. Whatever you have in store for us, please allow Johannes to be here, please let him be by my side. I beg this of you!" The words rolled out through her tears with a desperation that she was not aware resided within her. As she allowed herself the release of the anguish gripping her, an arm wrapped itself around her waist.

"Mama, it is all right. We are all here to help you." Magdalena stroked the figure slumped beneath the blanket. She could feel the long braid of her mother's hair, and the ribs that did not show beneath her loose-fitting dress.

Katerina looked up briefly and saw her children gathered in a group behind her. She reached out and pulled them into a tight circle around her, and they all held each other until the sky began to turn a hazy grey and the stars no longer flickered in the night sky.

"We must start the chores," Katerina's words were muffled by emotion. Her tears had dried amid the love of her family. She stood up straight and smiled softly at Magdalena, "Thank you, 'Lena, I needed to know you were here."

"Yes, Mama. Papi will be here soon, you will see."

The horses had been watered and much of the camp broken up for the day when Herr Becker appeared.

"You had better come, Frau Jahnle. Johannes needs your help." He spoke in a hurried manner as he turned and started to leave her behind.

"Wait, Herr Becker, where is he? Is he all right? Can you not stop long enough to tell me what is happening?"

"I am sorry, Frau Jahnle, but he is in a bad way. He was left near my wagon a short time ago, and I feel it is your hand he needs now."

"Karolina, you and Magdalena finish packing the wagon, and keep an eye on Konrad. Anya, look after Rosina. I will be back as soon as possible. Heiner, get the horses harnessed!"

"Yes, Mama," the answer came as one from her children, as they began to undertake their assigned duties.

Katerina broke into a trot in order to keep up with Herr Becker's long stride. She wanted badly to run, but instead, tried hard to quell the fear growing inside her. The reality that she might lose Johannes was nipping at her heels, and she needed to get to him for assurance that he was still alive. As they approached the Byrgermeister's camp, she could see Johannes, slumped by the wheel of the wagon. Frau Becker was trying to wrap his head in cloth, but blood was soaking the cloth almost faster than she could swathe it.

"JOHANNES!" Katerina screamed as she ran to his side. "What have they done to you?"

He could not answer. His pain was almost more than he could endure, and Frau Becker's attempts at treating his wounds had only intensified his agony. He tried to push her away, but any movement fueled the fire within his muscles.

Why did they not just kill me and get it over with? was the thought that found its way through the recesses of his mind.

"Johannes, I am here. It is me, Katerina. Oh, what have they *done* to you?"

"Do not try to move him yet, he has lost a lot of blood. I am not sure how much damage has been done to his head, but his ear looks very bad." Frau Becker grasped Katerina by the arm. "Get your wagon up here and we will get him into it."

"Wait." Herr Becker spotted a soldier riding through the camps. The soldier appeared to be making some kind of announcement. Herr Becker began walking toward the soldier.

"STOP!" the soldier shouted at him. "You know you are not to mix with these other German dogs!"

"I was only trying to hear what you were saying." Herr Becker sounded apologetic.

"Stay where you are! I am coming to you next." The soldier spurred his horse, causing the beast to jump forward in a startled leap. "Mangy piece of dog meat!" the soldier responded with a hard jerk upon the reins. The horse's head flew up in pain, and then settled down into resolved obedience. "At least my horse knows his place, unlike you wretched kulaks."

The soldier came closer and saw Johannes lying in the dirt. "So, this is the Fascist who met his match with the Comrade Commissar last night. Too bad he is still among the living. Maybe he will now understand what we do to enemies of the state." The soldier growled his words like a wolf ready to snatch his prey. Then his voice changed into a sardonic utterance: "He is lucky though, as we will not be leaving this place today. Our orders are to hold you all here until we get further instructions. It seems this village was not issued travel documents, so *everyone* must stay here until you are all in possession of your papers." Without further comment he jerked his horse's head around and spurred him into a gallop back toward the village.

Frau Becker turned to Katerina, "I do not think it would be good to move your husband. You should bring your wagon here next to ours and set your camp here, then we will be able to care for him more easily."

Katerina nodded in stunned silence. She was still trying to get her mind around all that was happening. She was not accustomed to making decisions on her own; Johannes had always been there to guide her.

Frau Becker was going through things in her wagon and pulled a large ornate silver pot out from under some boxes. "My grandmother's samovar," she smiled sadly, "I have hidden tea inside it. We can make a poultice from the tea to help stop the blood and reduce some of the swelling around Herr Jahnle's ear. I can work on this while you get your family moved up here."

"Johannes," Katerina said distantly. "Please call him Johannes, and I am Katerina. If we are going to be living together we might as well use our given names."

"Yes, you are right. I am Sofia and my husband is Josef. You would think that after all these years living in the same village, we would have been using our given names before now."

"That is not who we are, nor how we were raised. It does not honor God to be so informal."

"*Honoring God* seems to be at the root of our problems. *Honoring God* is no longer allowed by our government and has led to your husband's situation. *Honoring God* has caused me to lose a child!" Frau Becker proclaimed. Her husband took the samovar out of her hands and set it on the back of the wagon. Then he came back, took hold of his wife's hand and glared at her.

"Watch what you say, woman, or you will have us all in worse shape than he is," he silenced her as he nodded his head toward Johannes. She said no more; instead she retreated to the samovar and began removing a large packet of tea leaves from its silvery insides.

By the time Katerina returned to the campsite, the children had packed their blankets and the cooking pot and loaded the wagon. The horses were hitched and the camp fire was out. Rosina was still in her cradle, which had not been moved.

"Mama, where is Papi?" Heinrich asked. "Why is he not with you?"

Katerina's attention was on Rosina as she rushed to the cradle to touch her baby. Rosina opened her eyes, squinted and closed them again. She was still breathing.

"Why was Rosina not put in the wagon?" she asked Anya.

"I thought you would want to put her in yourself, to make sure she was comfortable," Anya responded. "I thought if Papi was with you, you would want to hold her while he drove the horses."

"Yes, you are right. I do want her close to me. However, it seems we are not going to move far. The caravan has been given orders to stay here for a few days. Your father is not well and is at the Byrgermeister's camp. We will be joining him there. He may not be able to travel with us, anyway. It will depend on how quickly he can recover."

"Not well? Papi was fine yesterday! Where did he go? How did he become so sick in such a short amount of time?" Karolina knew in her heart something more was wrong than her mother was saying.

"You will find out soon enough, I guess; I should tell you now," Katerina sighed, as much from physical exhaustion as from emotional fatigue. "Papi was taken by the NKVD agents last night. They injured him badly. I do not know why. He will need us to look after him and take care of his wounds. Come on now, we must get moved quickly."

Katerina climbed up onto the wagon; Anya handed Rosina to her, and then placed the cradle into the back. "I cannot hold Rosina and the horses' lines, too. Heinrich needs to be up here as well, to drive the horses. We are not going far and he is light," Katerina commented.

"Yes, Mama." Heinreich did not try to conceal the delight he now felt. Driving the horses, even for a few meters, was an acknowledgement that he was quickly becoming a man.

In the half hour or so it took Katerina to return to the Becker's camp, Sofia had made several poultices from her tea packets and placed them on the worst of Johannes' wounds. She had also tried to clean up some of the lesser ones.

Katerina and the children found room to set up their camp. She left the children to organize the new site and care for the horses and, with Rosina in her arms, made her way to Johannes.

"Rosina, here is Papi," she crooned to her baby, hoping to get some kind of response from either of them. When she held Rosina out to Johannes, he tried to smile at her, but the swelling refused to let the muscles in his face move. He was too weak to hold her. He could not lift his head without pain coursing through every cell of his brain. He still did not fully understand the words being said to him.

Karolina arrived with a blanket and gasped at her first glance of her father. "Oh, PAPI!" she cried. "What has happened to you?"

With her free hand, Katerina took the blanket from Karolina's arms. "Please, go help Frau Becker. She is making some more tea poultices to soothe your father's wounds. We will talk more about this later. Wait, first go see that the children are occupied, I am not ready for them to see your father as yet."

"Yes, Mama," Karolina responded as she slowly backed away. She could not believe her eyes—this could not be *her* father lying on the ground; this person was grotesque and disfigured. How could *he* be her father?

Frau Becker returned to Johannes' side with a small basin of water and rags, and more tea bags. She also carried a bottle of schnapps. "This might relieve some of the pain, inside as well as out." She placed the bottle to his swollen lips, and he tried to swallow. The alcohol burned every place it touched, but finally found its way down his throat. She poured a small amount into the water and dipped the rags in.

"Hopefully, this will keep some of the infection out of your wounds. I know it will hurt, but it is all I have available."

"I cannot thank you enough for all you are doing," Katerina began, as she placed Rosina next to Johannes, and tried to tuck the blanket between him and the dirt he lay on.

"Please do not thank me. I think it is my husband's fault that Johannes is in this place. Had Josef not hit him yesterday, the NKVD would probably not have noticed Johannes. It takes little to arouse their suspicions and even less to stir their violence."

"But I thought Josef had been sent for questioning, as well."

"Yes," Sofia continued, "but because he is the Byrgermeister, the questions were intimidating but simple for him to answer. They asked about the number of people in the village and what their religion was, who was loyal to the Soviets and who might not be. He was only threatened with a beating and harm to me, and he did not receive any physical punishment except for a few humiliating slaps across the face. No, Josef's 'punishment' has been nothing compared to this. I only hope these injuries are not permanent. He has lost a lot of blood, and I fear he may not be strong enough to travel for more than a few days."

Katerina picked Rosina up and cuddled her. She wanted to try to get Rosina to nurse again, but there was no sucking response when she touched the baby's lips.

"I do not believe she will be traveling with us any further, either. She is too frail to nurse now …" Katerina's voice trailed off.

"I am sad for you. I lost the child I was carrying, and my youngest is ill. I do not think I can take much more of this insanely absurd trip."

Katerina was abruptly aware she had not seen any children around the Becker's camp. "Where are your children?"

"They are with Josef's brother and his family, a bit further up the line. After I saw Josef's reaction to your husband's questions yesterday, I thought it best to lessen the stress on him. With Friedreich being ill, I could not handle both of them."

"How did you get them there? We are not allowed to mix with the other villages."

"I waited for the soldiers to make their rounds just after dark last night, and moved from camp to camp until I found them, keeping low and out of sight as much as possible. It was one of those times that having only two children was a blessing."

Johannes reached for his wife's hand. His awareness of some of the women's words was apparent as he tried to speak. His puffed lips tried to form words, but all that would come out was a whispered "Rosina."

Sofia pulled back from working on Johannes' wounds and looked toward Katerina. She could see how frail the baby was and guessed she was not going to last much longer. Understanding her place was not between the parents and their child, she excused herself.

"I need to find some thread so I can try to stitch up the gash behind his ear. The tea seems to be working and the bleeding has finally stopped," she said as she rose to her feet and left.

Katerina sat on the ground, moving in close to Johannes, she placed her head upon his hip, and settled the small bundle that held their baby between them. Johannes reached out and pulled the blanket back far enough to see Rosina's face. A tear dropped imperceptibly from the corner of his eye, running through the split skin of his face, its salt stinging. Amidst the pain, the fatigue, the drained emotions, the numbness of hunger, the three of them shut their eyes and fell into the twilight of sleep.

The sun had reached its full height when Katerina was jolted awake by some unknown force. Was it a dream? Was it a mother's intuition? She sat upright and looked around her. She could see Frau Becker near the cooking fire; Anya and Magdalena were with her, possibly helping to prepare soup. Johannes was still asleep at her side. The small bundle in his lap was not moving; the shallow breathing had stopped. She picked up her baby and cradled her close to her breast, rocking back and forth from her waist, as if soothing the torment and agony from her child's tiny body. She bent her head to Rosina's face and kissed her amid the tears that flowed unceasingly from her heart.

"You are safe now, my little one." Katerina spoke in a barely audible whisper. "The angels will take care of you now."

Johannes stirred and opened his eyes. He saw Katerina's tears and knew Rosina was gone; he reached out to his grieving wife.

He desperately wanted to tell Katerina "I am here for you; I will help you through this. She is my daughter, too, and I love you both." But the words would not pass through the knot in his throat or his swollen lips. He placed his hand on his baby's body, looked into his wife's sorrowful eyes, and cried.

Frau Becker observed the couple's grief, gave them time to themselves, and then summoned the rest of the children.

"I am sorry," she said matter-of-factly, "but I believe your little sister has passed on. Your parents need all of you to be with them. We will finish preparing the meal later. I need to find Herr Becker …" her words drifted away as she removed herself from the children's presence.

"I no understand, Anchen." Konrad tugged on Anya's skirt as he watched his parents grieve.

"Rosina has died," she whispered.

"You mean the angels have come for her? Like the others Mama has told me about?"

"Yes, Konrad. Like the others."

"Why?" The predictable response of a four-year-old was touched with concern and trepidation, as well as an inability to understand what was happening around him.

Anya knelt on one knee so she could be meet her brother eye to eye. "She was too small to make this trip. She was not strong enough."

Konrad shook his head sadly, "No, she is not strong like me, she is too small."

Anya stood up, and pulled her little brother closer to her, "Now, you must be a big boy. Mama is very sad, and Papi is hurt. If you need anything, come to me or Karolina. Do you understand?"

"Yes, Anchen, I will come to you."

Katerina wiped the tears from Johannes' face, "We can not leave her here. I will not leave her in an unmarked hole by the road."

Johannes seemed pensive at first and she did not understand his hesitation. How could she know he was still unable to make sense of all of her words and was trying hard to organize everything that was going through his head? He finally nodded, more as a way to consol his wife than by agreement with her wishes. She continued to hold Rosina close to her, as if afraid to let her go.

Karolina was disturbed by her mother's actions. She had not seen her mother this way, not even when little Johannes died. She had cried, yes, but did not pick him up and hold him so longingly.

"Mama, I might be able to make my way through the soldiers to the village. I am sure there is a cemetery there," Karolina offered.

Katerina looked up at her daughter, "No, Karolina, thank you, but no. Even if you got past the soldiers and found a place in the village for her, we would not be allowed to bury her there. We would not be allowed to say prayers for her. No, we must find some place for her here, among our people."

"Mama, Frau Becker has returned to camp, maybe she can help us find a place to bury Rosina." Anya was still standing close and gently offered her idea, afraid of upsetting her mother further.

"Yes, ask Frau Becker...," Katerina seemed to be far away, distracted by the bundle in her arms.

"Papi, is that all right? May I ask Frau Becker?" Anya did not want to dismiss her father's rights to make decisions, no matter how badly he had been injured; he was still her father and the patriarch of the family.

Again Johannes nodded in agreement to a question he did not hear well enough to understand. He knew in his heart his children could make the decisions that were in the family's best interests at the moment. The unceasing pain in his head, accompanied with the new pain in his heart, consumed him. Frustrated with his inability to conquer the throbbing ache and weakness of his body and angered with the circumstances his family had been placed in, he thrust his fist into the ground.

Konrad jumped, startled by the violence of his father's action. He was frightened and confused, so he started to whimper.

Anya took Konrad by the hand and led him away. "Come with me, you can help find what we need," she told him quietly. "Mama and Papi do not need us here right now." They approached Frau Becker just as she was adding what looked like weeds to the caldron boiling on the fire. A few small potatoes occupied the pot as well.

"Sorrel and nettles will help strengthen your father," she said simply as the children approached her.

"Can you help dig us a place for Rosina?" Konrad blurted.

Anya was embarrassed by his bluntness. "Our little sister will not be traveling any further with us and we need a place to bury her. Mother was wondering if you might know of someplace safe for her."

Frau Becker smiled sadly at them. "I am not sure what we can do, but we will look and see if we can find someplace special for your sister." She put out her hand and beckoned for the children to follow.

Karolina and Magdalena busied themselves cleaning up the camp and setting out a few bowls for the soup. It did not seem like Frau Becker and the children had been gone long when Konrad came bounding back.

"We got a place for Rosina," he announced proudly.

Anya and Frau Becker were less enthusiastic, but did seem somewhat pleased with what they had located. "It is a very beautiful place," Anya told her sisters. "I believe Mama and Papi will like it."

"Where could you have possibly found a 'beautiful place' here? Where, among all these people, is a place that has not been turned to dust?" Magdalena was unconvinced any place suitable for Rosina could have been found, especially in such a short amount of time.

"Oh, Magdalena, come see! I show you! Karolina, come too!" Konrad was bursting with excitement; his four-year-old psyche not comprehending the gravity of the situation.

"Konrad, slow down! We will all go together, when Mama says it is the right time." Anya tried to quell the exuberance of her little brother as best she could. She was not sure why he did not comprehend the loss of their little sister or the sorrow she was feeling. She put her hand on his shoulder and lowered her voice. "Do you know what it means when someone dies? Do you know that you will never see Rosina again?"

"Yes," he pouted, "Mama says that when babies die, they are taken by the angels, and they can see us and talk to us and keep us safe. We will not see them, but they are always with us. So why are all of you so sad?"

Anya had no answer. "Let us help Frau Becker with the soup, maybe Mama will feel like going to see 'our special place' later," was all she could think of to say.

After seeing that the children were all fed, Frau Becker placed a ladle-full of soup into a bowl and carried it over to Johannes. She knelt down, filled a spoon with the warm broth and placed it against his lips. He tried to turn away, causing the broth to spill and run down his chin and onto his shirt.

"You must try to get some of this down," she said. "It will bring your strength back."

He was not ready to accept help from this woman, but he realized that he had no other choice. His wife remained next to him, rocking their baby, their dead child, in her arms as if Rosina was suffering from colic. He thought he could hear Katerina humming a lullaby, but he still was not sure what things he could actually hear and what were just noises within his head. He gave in and finally took a sip from the spoon. The broth was earthy and bitter, but somehow soothing at the same time. He was able to get it past his smashed and swollen lips as it did not have the fiery sting of the schnapps. He had not been conscious of his hunger until now. The soup was thin, but welcome.

Frau Becker gazed at Katerina with empathy; she understood the inescapable sorrow of the loss of a child. "There is a meadow in a small cove by the river not far from here. It is where I came across the sorrel for the soup. It has not been trampled, as it is somewhat hidden. I think that will be a good place to bury your daughter." Her voice was gentle as she reached out and placed her hand on Katerina's arm. Katerina looked at her, smiled faintly and continued rocking.

"I still must find some thread to stitch up this gash behind your ear," Frau Becker continued, trying to fill in the uncomfortable silence between Johannes' sips from the spoon.

"I have a sewing box in our wagon," Anya was standing behind Frau Becker, watching with interest as the woman fed her father. "I can go get it if you need it."

"Yes, child, that is just what is needed here."

Anya ran off toward the wagon and soon returned with her wooden box of thread and needles. She placed the box on the ground next to her father, pulled the split leather strip over the small attached wooden button and lifted the lid. The first thing she saw was her long-forgotten apron that she was so sure she was going to finish on this trip, but here it lay, just as she had placed it the evening before they left. She carefully lifted the white cloth from the box and looked for a fairly clean place to put it.

"What have you got there?" asked Frau Becker.

"My apron. It is nearly finished; I just need to complete the hem." Anya showed Frau Becker her prize.

Frau Becker examined the stitching, "You have done very nice work here. You would make a good nurse."

"A nurse?" Anya asked, somewhat perplexed by the comment.

"A nurse needs to be able to make tight, even stitches when sewing wounds. Your stitches are nearly perfect, which is very unusual for a girl your age. You have a talent that will serve you well."

"Are you a nurse?"

"I was, during the revolution. I was barely seventeen when I was placed in the army hospital. I was noticed because of my ability to make nice, small, even stitches. I learned many useful things as a nurse." She handed the apron back to Anya. "This is such a pretty piece, may I make a suggestion?"

Anya nodded, wondering what Frau Becker had in mind.

"I think your apron would make a very lovely gown to wrap your sister in for her burial. It would be a bit of you with her always."

Anya's face lit up. "Oh, Yes! I would like that very much! Do you agree, Mama? Rosina will be so pretty wrapped in my apron."

Katerina lifted her eyes from the bundle in her arms and looked directly at Anya. As she fixed her gaze on Anya's face, reality seemed to finally take hold. She placed Rosina's tiny body onto the blanket. "Yes, I agree, she will look pretty. We must wash her up first, though."

"If your older daughters will help you get the baby ready, I will take care of your husband. I have sent Josef to prepare the location for her." Frau Becker had already gathered a bucket of clean water and some cloth for cleaning.

Katerina struggled to her feet, her legs numb from sitting on the ground for so long. Magdalena gently picked Rosina up and took her to the back of their wagon, where she could be properly washed. Karolina followed with the water and cloths. Anya carefully folded the unfinished apron to keep it clean and joined her sisters. As with all things, this was a family of togetherness.

When all was ready, Anya and Konrad led their mother and siblings to the cove by the river. Frau Becker had been true to her word. The meadow was a green oasis in a desert of wheat. Herr Becker was standing near the center with a small shovel in his hands. He had completed the digging of the gravesite for Rosina. Heinreich stood next to him with a pair of twigs that he tied into a small cross.

Katerina placed Rosina into the hollowed out earth, pulled the edges of the white apron up over her face, and stepped back. Each of the children placed a small piece of cloth, torn from the ragged clothing they wore, into the grave.

It was too late in the fall to find flowers, so Anya laid her cherished wooden doll in Rosina's tiny hands. As Herr Becker began placing soil over the petite body, Katerina lead the children in prayer. When Herr Becker replaced the last of the soil, he stepped back.

"May I recite the twenty-third psalm?" he asked.

Katerina nodded her approval.

He began, "The Lord is my shepherd; ..." but quickly stopped. Katerina looked up to see two soldiers riding toward them. *Why now?* she agonized silently. *Why can we not have just one moment's peace?*

"What are you doing here?" demanded one of the riders. These were not the soldiers from the caravan.

"Burying my baby," Katerina's eyes pleaded for benevolence.

"Which village are you from?" the soldier asked, almost sounding sympathetic.

"Sofienthal," Herr Becker answered.

"I thought so," the soldier responded. "We are summoning all the people of your village to the Commissar's office so that your travel papers can be issued. Be there before sunset."

"What is this?" the other soldier had seen Heinreich's twig cross and removed it from the ground.

"Only a marker for the grave," Herr Becker quickly spoke.

"No Christian symbols! You may use one stick only to mark the grave!"

"I am sorry, it will not happen again." Herr Becker began untying the twigs.

"If you are truly Russian and not a German spy, you will say Russian burial rites." The soldier leaned over his horse and grabbed one of the twigs from Herr Becker's hands.

"Yes, we will do that, but we would like to be left alone in our grief, if that is possible," Katerina may have spoken out-of-turn, but she wanted only a little more time with her baby.

The soldiers rode off in silence as Herr Becker spoke the Russian proverb, "May the ground be soft, and your soul calm." However, once the riders were far enough away to be out of hearing, he continued the Psalm he had started. Then he ended with Psalm 46:1, "God is our refuge and strength, a very present help in trouble."

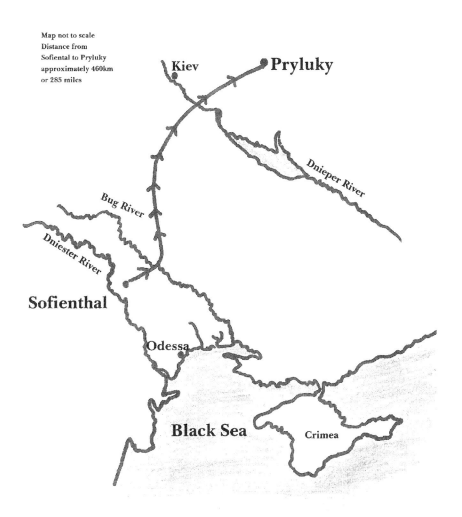

Map not to scale
Distance from
Sofiental to Pryluky
approximately 460km
or 285 miles

Kiev **Pryluky**

Dnieper River

Bug River

Dniester River

Sofienthal

Odessa

Black Sea Crimea

First Leg of the Jahnle Family Journey

CHAPTER SIX

The Train to Nowhere

Days passed without any further movement of the caravan, and the people were becoming restless. There was little wheat left for the animals to graze, and few of the human occupants had food either. Johannes' wounds were slowly healing and he was becoming stronger, due in large part to Sofia's uncanny ability to make soup from weeds and other local plants.

Katerina was called to the Commandant's office to receive travel papers for the family. There had been minimal questioning and no additional harassment from the soldiers, for which she was very thankful. As she was being escorted back to their campsite, she managed to catch sight of the town's name on a small sign. *Pryluky! We are in Pryluky? Johannes was right, we are more than four-hundred kilometers from home!*

Daylight was becoming noticeably shorter and the weather was beginning to change; the hot dusty afternoons were now preceded with dew-laden mornings and a distinct chill. Katerina wondered if her decision to leave the coats and boots behind was one that she was going to regret.

"It appears that Johannes is getting up and around a bit," Sofia Becker stood with her hands on her hips, watching Johannes with interest as he tried feebly to brush one of the horses. Anya was at his side, hovering like a little hen.

"Yes, he is stronger, thanks to you. We are very grateful." Katerina said. "Without your soup and medical training, he may not have survived. I do not believe that prayers alone would have pulled him through."

"Do not underestimate your husband's will power or his faith. My hands were put here for a reason. If not to give care where it is needed, then to train those who can," Sofia nodded toward Anya.

Katerina was surprised by this comment. "But, Anya is barely ten. She is too young; she just has simple household skills. She is actually behind, because I have not had the time or energy to work with her, as I would have at home."

"But what she has learned from you, she has learned well." Sofia gave a knowing look toward Anya. "I have not seen a child of her age with such a fine hand at stitching. She has watched every move I have made in dressing Johannes' wounds. I needed to explain only once how to clean and bandage them, and she has done an excellent job of keeping the infection out. Give her a chance; she will make a great nurse."

"Yes, she has done well with her father. But, you expect too much of her. She is still too small to be of any great service." Katerina had tired of this conversation; she picked up her cooking pot and headed for the river. "Anya! Come with me!" she called over her shoulder. "I need help getting water."

Sofia watched the two of them as they made their way down the trail through the trampled and unharvestable wheat stalks. She slowly shook her head and muttered to herself, "Katerina, you do not realize how wrong you are."

On the twelfth day of the encampment, Konrad and Heinreich were busy playing with the Becker's two boys. Nine-year-old Freidreich had recovered from his fever, and his eleven-year-old brother Helmut, was eager to return to his parents' camp. The older boys all knew each other from school and were excited to be able to romp in the dirt together; even allowing Konrad to join in their play.

A long low whistle echoed across the fields, causing the boys to stop their jostling in the dirt and look toward the village. A long assemblage of brown boxes formed a vast creature snaking its way toward the far side of the row of buildings that identified the town center, slowly stopping as it reached its objective.

"Heiner...?" Konrad's mouth gaped at the wondrous size of the thing.

"I do not know what it is, Konrad, I have never seen anything like it before." Heinreich gasped.

"It is a TRAIN!" Helmut exclaimed. "We rode on one last year when we went to Grandfather's house. The boxes are called 'cars', only the ones we rode in were rounder and had windows in the sides. We sat in rows of seats and looked out the windows, and the land went by so fast we could not even count the cows in the fields."

"And you know what else?" Freidreich added, "There was *food* in a special car. Mama told us. But we did not eat there. She brought our food; she said it was better to eat what we were used to."

"I would eat any kind of food right now," Heinreich sighed.

"Come on, Heiner, we got to tell Papi about the train!" Konrad pulled at Heinreich's sleeve, ripping what was left from the elbow down.

"KONRAD! Why did you do that?"

Tears welled up in Konrad's eyes, "Sorry, Heiner, I did not mean to, it just came apart when I touched you."

"All right, do not cry about it. Maybe Mama can fix it. I will race you back to the wagon!" With Heinreich in the lead, all the boys ran back to camp.

"MAMA, PAPI! Come see!" Konrad yelled breathlessly, as soon as he was near enough to catch sight of the wagon.

"What is it, Konrad? Are you all right?" Katerina rushed out to meet the boys.

"Mama, train!"

"Konrad, slow down. Heiner, what is he yelling about?"

"We were across the road, playing in the field and we heard a noise, and saw this big long thing going to the village, and Helmut said it was a train, but not like the one he rode on last year."

Johannes heard all the commotion; most of his hearing had returned, even though the pain continued. He worked his way around the wagon to where Katerina and the boys were standing. The Becker boys continued on to find their own parents. "What does the train look like?" Johannes asked.

"Like a great big snake." Konrad stretched his arms out to indicate how long the train was.

"Not exactly what I meant," Johannes managed a quick smile and rumpled Konrad's dirty blond locks. "Heiner, can you tell me a little more?"

"Yes, Papi, the cars—that is what Helmut called them—were like big brown boxes. Helmut said the train he rode on had rounder cars, with windows, but I could not see any windows, it just looked like boards. But, the front two cars were different. They were black and had chimneys with smoke coming out of them."

Johannes frowned and thought for a minute. "Sounds like cattle cars. Two engines usually mean they are pulling a heavy load. They may be bringing in troops or horses for the soldiers. Did you see any soldiers getting out of the cars?"

"No, Papi, we just saw the train stop in the village, then we came back here." Heinreich explained.

"I see. Well, if it involves us, I am sure the guards will tell us soon enough." Johannes was still feeling a bit light-headed and queasy. He moved closer to their wagon and leaned against it. Hans, the horse he had been brushing, was tied near enough to reach over and push his muzzle against Johannes' back, nearly knocking him off his feet. Johannes grabbed hold of the big horse's halter to steady himself, and then leaned into the muscular gray neck, bringing his hand up to brush the thick silvery forelock away from the horse's eyes. The horse's eye locked onto Johannes'. Hans took a deep breath and sighed contentedly.

The following morning, soldiers rode into camp. "Get ready to leave!" they shouted. "You must be ready in one hour!"

Katerina put the children to work breaking camp while she assisted Johannes in harnessing the horses. "I wonder how far we will be going this time," she commented to no one in particular.

Johannes completed hooking the horses to the wagon, and stood facing her. Even though the swelling had eased, his face was still pale and battered. He shook his head slowly and said, "I think as long as we are on the road, no matter what hardships we have to face, we are doing well. We have not been imprisoned, or separated from the children, or shot and left to die."

Katerina was not only shocked by his comment, but it was the melancholy in his voice that truly scared her. She had not realized, until now, the emotional toll her husband had paid. She took his hands in hers and faced him squarely. "Yes, you are right, but whatever you do, do not give up. With the grace of God we will survive whatever comes our way." She became pensive for a moment. "I must say goodbye to Rosina. Will you come?"

Johannes slowly shook his head. "I am not ready."

Katerina made her way alone to the gravesite. When she arrived, she felt her heart sink and her eyes filled with tears; the area had been thoroughly trampled by people looking for weeds to eat. The small stick that Heinreich placed as a marker was uprooted and broken. She made her way to the center of the cove and knelt where she remembered Rosina's grave to be. Carefully and deliberately she smoothed the upturned soil, softly humming her favorite hymn, lost in the moment of doing one last deed for her child. She found another small twig, not as straight or sturdy as the first, but deciding it would suffice, pulled the piece of Heinreich's shirt sleeve from the pocket of her apron and tied it to the twig, making a small flag-like marker. "Here my little one," she whispered, "is a small token of my love. Oh, how I wish I had a bit of pencil or a pen to write "Rosina" on this bit of fabric. You deserve so much more." With a final effort Katerina rose from the cold, damp ground and returned to camp, never looking back.

When all was ready, the mounted soldiers gave the order to begin pulling the wagons into line. But instead of continuing in the northerly direction they had been traveling for so many weeks, the wagons were directed west, toward the village. In less than half an hour, the lead wagons pulled into the train depot and lined up along the tracks. People were ordered off their wagons and, removing whatever they could carry, were placing their possessions into the box cars. Scores of armed soldiers emerged from the adjacent buildings and surrounded the remainder of the wagons, preventing any possible escape.

Heiner was riding alongside his father on the wagon's seat and keenly watched the activity before him. "Are we going to get to ride on the train?" There was excitement in his question.

"It appears so." Johannes did not like what he was seeing. The soldiers directed family after family into the boxcars. As soon as a number of families were in the cars, the big doors were rolled shut, and soldiers drove the wagons off to the far side of the tracks, unhitched the horses and led them to the rear-most cars. After what seemed like hours, Johannes was directed to stop his wagon near the middle of the train.

"Take only what you can carry!" a soldier shouted. "Clothes, food, and cooking pots! Water if you have any! Hurry! We have not got all day!"

"What will happen to our wagon and the horses?" Herr Becker asked from his wagon parked just in front of Johannes'. He was unwilling to make this sacrifice without at least some knowledge.

"The wagons are going to the villagers; what they cannot use, they will burn this winter for heat. The horses will go to the Army. The strong ones will be put to good use pulling cannon, the rest will be eaten." The soldier was looking at Hans and Georg as he made this statement. He reached out and placed his hand on Hans' shoulder. "This pair will likely pull cannon."

Johannes felt sick at the thought that his horses would be sent to the battlefield. He had seen what happened to cannon horses, and he almost wished his pair would die the quick death of a meat horse. He dismounted from the wagon and helped Katerina and the children unload the meager belongings they were allowed to place into the boxcar. As the soldier came to take the lines and drive the wagon away, Johannes made his way to the horses' heads. Reaching up and stroking the wide foreheads, he closed his eyes and prayed *Keep them safe, Oh Lord, they have been honest and faithful in their service.* All the while, the words of Proverbs 12:10 pierced his soul, *"A righteous man regardeth the life of his beast; But the heart of the wicked is cruel."* Aloud, he simply said, "Goodbye old friends, God Speed," and quickly turned away before anyone could see his tears.

Ten families were crammed in the boxcar, sixty or more people of all ages and sizes. A bit of straw scattered on the floor would serve as bedding. Katerina quickly located a bare spot along the back wall and placed her cooking pot and a blanket on the floor. She could see the ground beneath the boxcar through the openings between the slats, and feel the coldness of the air coming through. Johannes and the children joined her in getting settled as best they were able, placing their few belongings in the tiny space available to them, while trying to balance amid the jostling of the others as they were being packed in.

Karolina and Magdalena carried the milk can full of water between them and placed it with the cooking pot. Konrad and Heinreich squeezed their way to the outside wall of the boxcar and peered through the wall planks, watching as their wagon was driven away into the distance. Anya placed her armful of what was left of their clothing onto the blanket and sat heavily upon them. "I wish I could have brought my sewing box," she pouted.

"You can see there is no room for your box." Karolina answered testily. "Mama could not even find room for the family Bible, and you are worried about your silly sewing box."

Something about the word box sunk into Katerina's memory. "The BOX! The photo box in the wagon! Jakob!" She screamed as she tried desperately to get to the big doors of the boxcar. "I must have it, I cannot lose another child!" she sobbed as she tried to push her way through the people. She was too late. The big doors rolled shut. Screaming "JAKOB!" over and over, she thrust her arm through the horizontal slats, reaching out into the air, reaching for what she knew was lost and gone forever, reaching for the remnants of the life she would never know again.

Hers were neither the only tears, nor the only screams coming from that train. When it finally began to move from the station, sixty cattle cars swayed under the load of terrified humanity contained within its bowels, and twenty-five were filled with good farm horses.

As Katerina fell to the floor sobbing, others in the car were beginning to panic. There was a group realization that they had been caged; imprisoned; sealed in captivity; they pushed their way to the sides of the car trying desperately to escape, flailing themselves against the walls and floor. Katerina soon found herself being trampled in the terror of the moment.

"JOHANNES!" She screamed, "JOHANNES!" She covered her head with her hands, and curled into the smallest form she could manage. Feeling as though she could not breathe, she inched her way along the floor beneath the crush of feet and plunging bodies. She somehow knew to stay away from the corner, where she would be trapped. As she slowly progressed toward where she thought she had left her family, she felt a sharp pain as a boot struck her thigh, a second boot into her back made her want to jump up and run, but she could not get to her feet amongst the press of people.

A hand...she thought someone grabbed her hand. How could she be sure? She thought she heard her name, she tried hard to listen, tried hard to hear anything more than the screaming mob engulfing her. A firm two-handed grasp took hold of her right wrist and began pulling her along the floor. She instantly recognized that grip, knew the feel of those strong farmer's hands, and willed herself to move with them, toward them, toward Johannes.

"KATERINA!"

She could finally hear Johannes' voice above the din. She fought her way to him, half crawling—half pulling herself across the splintered planks of the floor. With one last effort she was finally in his arms. He pulled her to her feet and gripped her tightly, trying to steady both of them against the movement of the train and the force of people. He directed her to the wall where the children crouched; wide-eyed with terror, scared into alarmed silence, tears flowing from their faces. With the last of her energy, she joined her family and pulled everyone close about her. They all collapsed into a huddle, embraced together against the deluge of humanity besieging them.

The train rolled on. Evening approached and darkness settled on the landscape. As the shadowy fingers of night wrapped around the train, emotions began to calm, surrendering to the exhaustion and despair of the unwilling passengers. An uneasy quiet cloaked the over-loaded cattle cars as they rocked rhythmically along the rails.

Hours passed, or were they minutes, it was impossible to tell in the darkness. Konrad finally broke the silence with a hoarse whisper, "Mama, I am hungry."

In the dimness of the half-moon's light, Katerina reached out and felt for the small box that contained what was left of their food. Removing the lid revealed a dozen small dry biscuits and a single jar of pickled watermelon rind. Katerina removed half of the biscuits, giving one to each child and one to Johannes, and closed the box. She rose to her knees, removed the lid from the water can and dipped the attached cup into the top. When she handed the cup to Johannes, he pushed it away, so she handed it to Karolina. The children quickly ate their biscuits and washed them down with the water. Johannes noticed that Katerina had not taken a biscuit for herself and broke his in half, pushing it toward her. She shook her head.

"You need it more than I do," she said, "You are still not fully recovered."

"Will I ever be?" he asked. "Will we ever have a full meal again; will our children's stomachs ever not rumble from lack of food?"

She saw no point in responding, no point in providing fodder for the misery they all were feeling at that moment.

The night dragged on, the rumbling of the train blending into the constant noise of people talking in low voices, mothers trying to comfort hungry children, old women bemoaning their plight, babies crying. Few rested. The cold air coming up through the floorboards and in through the open slatted walls chilled everyone. Those with blankets tried to keep children and the elderly warm. Cooking pots were utilized as chamber pots, but there was no privacy.

Johannes positioned himself so that he could see out the side of the car. He thought he might be able recognize landscape from his days in the army, he hoped he could tell where they might be headed. Eventually the sky began to turn a pale gray. Johannes realized that the train was heading into the rising sun. "East! We are heading east. But why? There is nothing in the east. There is no arable land that I know about, only vast forests and tundra desert." The only person listening to his words was a grayed and long bearded old man lying in the sparse straw beside him.

The man pulled at his beard with work-gnarled hands, contemplating the words he had just heard. "Umm, yes, I agree with you. I do not know why we would head east." Then he rolled over, turning his back to Johannes, and seemed to return to sleep.

On the third day of incessant movement, the train pulled through a moderately-sized village, slowed and finally stopped on the far side. The horse cars were lined up with what appeared to be hastily built loading ramps and corrals. The wood of the fence rails reflected the green tint of newly sawn, un-dried lumber, and the posts were not well set into the hard ground. Rocks littered the open areas of the corrals between the short sparse grasses that grow in areas of permafrost.

Soldiers appeared at each of the passenger-laden cattle cars; they removed the locks and rolled the heavy doors back. "Everyone out, but stay close to your car! We are not staying long!" They shouted as they walked the length of each car, beating the sides with a large stick. However, no one rushed to the doors—cold, cramped muscles were not willing to stretch and move. Children well enough to be eager to be outside in the sunshine, remained to help their parents. Days without food had taken a toll on them all, and as the cars slowly emptied, this toll became more and more evident.

Johannes helped Katerina and the children off of the train. The air had a sharp chill, but there was no wind, for which they were thankful. Johannes returned for the old man he had spoken to that first morning, as he had not seen him leave the train. The old man was still asleep in the straw; in the same position Johannes last encountered him.

"Sir, can you get up?" Johannes asked quietly. Not receiving a response, he repeated his inquiry louder. "SIR, CAN YOU GET UP?" Johannes drew closer and leaned over the old man, then reached out and touched the shoulder of the ragged coat that enshrouded him. There was no response, just a stiff coldness. Johannes stood, whispered a short prayer, and then headed outside to look for his family. As he made his way to the doorway, a quick survey of the interior of the car revealed that the old man was not the only one who would not leave this village on this day.

A soldier met Johannes at the door. "How many are left?" he asked.

Johannes shrugged and shook his head, "Only the dead."

As Johannes headed for Katerina and the children, he looked down the length of the train and saw bodies laid out near each car; some had relatives mourning over them. *There will be more room in the cars tonight,* was a thought that passed through his mind, but he tried not to dwell on any of it.

Konrad came running and shouting, "Papi, come see the horses!" He bounced excitedly along his father's side, trying to get Johannes to follow. They walked toward the freshly-built corrals and Johannes quickly saw what Konrad was excited about. The horse-laden cars at the rear of the train had been emptied and the horses turned out into the corrals. The horses were milling about restlessly, looking for something to graze, establishing pecking orders, just enjoying being off the train and out onto open ground. Johannes noted that only the horses destined for the battle front to pull cannon had been transported on the train. He wondered where the rest had been taken. He quickly spotted Hans and Georg among the herd and mentally assessed their condition; they looked thin, but well.

Soldiers came through the groups of people recruiting as many of the older boys as were able. Heinreich was sized up by an older soldier Johannes had not seen before.

"You look strong enough. Can you handle a fork?" the man asked, as he placed his hand on Heinreich's shoulder.

"A fork for eating?" Heinreich's face lit up at this idea.

"Not quite," the soldier chuckled, "and at the same time, yes. The fork I meant is to feed the horses. But it might be worth some bread, if you do a good job."

"Then yes," Heinreich responded. "I can handle a fork." With that he joined the group of boys heading to the rear of the train, where a long flatbed wagon had arrived and pulled up beside the last car. Several soldiers had already opened the doors of the hay-stuffed car. The boys were distributed into two groups, those to unload the bundles of hay onto the wagon, and the others piling the hay for the optimum load and picking up any hay that fell to the ground. This took some time, as there were a nearly two- hundred horses to be fed, and many trips would be necessary to reload the wagon.

Shortly after Heinreich left the family, a rough-looking, large-bodied soldier came through recruiting able men. Approaching Johannes, he stated, "If you want bread, you will come with me." His tone did not indicate that there was any other choice to be made.

Johannes fell into the small crowd that gathered behind the soldier and they continued up the line of train cars, adding what few men existed among the families. When they reached the foremost cattle car, the soldier stopped and turned to his group of followers.

"You are to search each car and remove all remaining bodies. They will be placed in orderly rows on the far side of the tracks, out of the way. Do not worry about clothing, blankets or possessions, their families will take care of all remaining matters."

"Will they be given burial rites?" someone in the crowd asked.

"Later," was the response. "Just get those cars cleared quickly. There will be guards watching you at all times, so I suggest you leave well enough alone if you value your lives. Now hurry up and get moving!"

The men split up into groups of five or six and headed for the cars. Johannes was not surprised to see that the cars were nearly all the same on the inside, a few bodies lying among the piles of personal possessions on minimal strands of dirty straw. The men worked in silence as carefully, respectfully, each body was removed to the designated area.

Why will they not open the doors on the back side of the cars? It would make this job faster and easier, Johannes wondered to himself, but did not speak audibly. Instead he assisted another man with lifting the skin-covered skeleton of an elderly woman, carried her out of the car and over the coupling between the cars to the far side. There the bodies were placed in neat rows in the adjoining field; all ages, sizes and genders were represented, all were of German heritage.

It was nearly sundown by the time the chore was completed. The men dragged themselves, worn out mentally, emotionally and physically by the task they had just finalized. When they were ready to return to their families, a light wagon approached them, distributing half-loaves of coarse dry bread.

While the men were busy, the women returned to the cars and removed the pots that had been used as latrines, emptying them onto the tracks under the train. A few wagons from the village drove by, distributing "fresh bedding" for the cars, but once the loose bundles of straw were opened, they turned out to be soured and moldy. Much of this straw was thrown under the train into the sewage pools.

Heinreich returned, tightly gripping his pay, another half-loaf of the coarse dry bread. He was very tired and covered in hay chaff. "Mama, it itches," he complained.

Katerina brushed off his tattered clothing as best she could. "I do not know what to do for you," she said sadly. "At home I would have had you bathe, and washed your clothes, but here there is little I can do." She returned to their place on the train and opened the water can. Even though she and Johannes had been frugal with what they used, it was more than half empty, and there was no place to fill it. Carefully she reached into the can with the drinking cup and filled it half full, then dipped an edge of her apron hem into the cup. With that, she did her best to wash Heinreich's face, arms, hands and half-bare legs.

"Return to your quarters!" Soldiers ordered everyone back onto the train. "We will be leaving soon!"

There were protests. "What about our dead family members? Who will bury them? We need to have proper burial rites! Are we not getting any water? Food, we need food!" Anguish and confusion began to take control. The soldiers feared the situation would quickly get out of hand; shots were fired into the air.

"Get into the train, NOW! Or die here! German dogs are better off dead anyway," one of the soldiers shouted and waved his rifle toward those standing closest to him. Out of fear, frustration, and general exhaustion the crowd obeyed, cowed into obedience.

As the cars were loaded, the stench coming from the tracks beneath them was nearly overpowering, and they could only hope the train would begin moving soon. They questioned the wisdom of using the pots, wondering what other options they might have. The train slowly pulled away. The horses watched from their corrals, contentedly munching their hay. The bodies were left in the fields.

Once they were well underway, Katerina assessed the bread Johannes and Heinreich earned for their hard work. She quickly stashed one of the loaves into the food box, and then carefully broke the other into seven small pieces; they would all eat something tonight.

The train rumbled on for two more days. There was little conversation, and fewer noises coming from the children. Katerina carefully doled out the bread, making it last as long as possible. Daylight was disappearing earlier, and the air was becoming colder. For the most part, everyone sat in silence, trying to keep warm, trying to stay alive.

Just before daylight, the train pulled into a large station, with many tracks converging into one area. Slowly the big engines rolled over the track mechanism that allowed it to change tracks and its direction of travel. The train stopped, but no one came to open the doors on the cars. The boxcars that had held the horses and hay were uncoupled and left on the track. When the train pulled out of the station it was headed north. By mid-day, the terrain changed from sparse and rocky fields to heavy timber forests. Snow began to fall.

As dusk approached, the train again began to slow and stop. Johannes could see only heavy forest on both sides of the car. There was no village. His heart began to beat rapidly. He prayed.

"Dear Lord, please do not let them leave us here. We have no food or water, no protection from the weather. We are weak in body and soul. We need Your guidance and Your hand in our moment of need. We are but singular sheep in Your flock of many. But please do not forsake us; we need Your help now more than ever. Thank You for all the blessings You have bestowed upon us, we are grateful for all You have done. Amen."

Through the silence of the forest and the train's inhabitants, Johannes could hear soldiers coming. As they approached each car and opened the huge doors, one soldier held up a lantern, its light dimly illuminating the interior. The bark of the older soldier echoed through the car.

"One person from each family can come to the door and we will give you bread and water. Do not crowd! If there is no order we will not proceed."

Those in the car began to mill about, designating a family member to retrieve the food and water. Each family received a half-loaf of the hard bread and a small amount of water. As soon as all the families were handed their rations, the soldiers rolled the doors nearly shut, and then another command came.

"Give us your dead!"

There was a small group movement on the far side of the car as two families gave up their deceased members, both children. In tears and with much trepidation, the families handed the small bodies to the soldiers. The soldiers took the remains, quickly rolled the door closed and locked it. One by one, they turned and threw the corpses into the trees at the edge of the tracks. Screams and protests were ignored. The blackness that settled was more than just the disappearing of the lantern that the soldiers took with them.

The train resumed its northerly movement. Johannes reflected on how many people might have been left behind for wolf fodder, but he would never know the count…the shadows of the night would forever conceal the truth.

"Johannes, wake up. I think we are stopping again." Katerina was lying on her side between Johannes and the children. She rose up on one elbow and touched Johannes' shoulder. It was pre-dawn; she shivered as she rose from the warmth of Johannes's side. Snow had been falling for some time. Two days passed since their last stop, and no more bread or water had been distributed by the soldiers. The cattle car's occupants had been silent for a very long time, sleeping to the rhythms of the constant click-clacking of the wheels on the iron rails, rocked methodically by the swaying of the car. But now, that rhythm was changing, slowing, and gradually becoming louder.

Johannes sat up and peered out through the slats of the side wall. "There is less snow falling, I think I see lights in the distance, possibly houses," he whispered. "We must be coming into another village." He placed his face close to the slats, trying to get his nose out into the fresh air. "I think I smell the sea!" He was surprised at this as he had not realized they had traveled so far, nor that he had lost his sense of time and distance.

"How can we be near a sea?" Katerina responded. "Where in Russia is there a sea, other than the Black Sea at Odessa?"

"The only place I know of in the north that is connected to a sea is in Siberia. Why have we been brought here? What is there for us in Siberia?" There seemed to be no answers for Johannes' worried query.

"I doubt that the German army will look for us here, if that is really why we were brought this far." Katerina sighed and lay back down as she had no desire to stand. The collective warmth of the children was comforting to her and she did not wish to leave their presence just yet.

The train continued to slow and eventually stopped just outside of the village. The people in the cattle car began to stir, a low murmur of hushed voices hung in the cold air like smoke in a windless sky. It was just another stop on a long irrational journey.

Track of the Death Train

Pryluky to Onega
2,248 km or 1,396 miles

CHAPTER SEVEN
Onega, Arkhanglesk District

Thick forest bordered the west side of the tracks as the train approached the town. The aroma of freshly-sawn lumber mixed with the brininess of the wind blowing in off the sea. Snow fell lightly although it was not yet winter. The train sat silently as the sky lightened to a pale ash grey.

"Where are the soldiers? Why are they not opening the doors? Are we going to get food? Where are we? Why have we stopped?" The questions rose all around Johannes and Katerina. No one had come to open the doors; no soldiers could be seen along the tracks. Cries for help were heard coming from the other cars. People wanted off the train. While they were beyond experiencing the pangs of hunger, the cold leached into their bones. *Getting off this train, finding warmth somewhere, anywhere, is that too much to ask?* Johannes questioned.

It was nearly mid-day before the soldiers finally appeared. The doors were unlocked and rolled back. Armed guards stood lined up facing the cars. "Last stop! Get out and bring your belongings! Hurry up we have not got all day!" A gruff-looking man in a brown wool coat and an Army officer's hat stood at the door waving a rifle, indicating the direction the passengers were to exit. As those inside jumped out of the car into the snow, they were prodded to their feet with the aid of a rifle barrel and directed into a single-file line. They were then marched toward the front of the train.

Katerina quickly grabbed their blankets and stuffed the food box among them. The girls and Heinreich carried what clothing remained and the water can; they had opted to leave the excrement-filled cooking pot behind. Johannes lifted Konrad to his shoulders as they trudged after the many people from the other cars. As they neared a large clearing that opened onto the village, the soldiers stopped the procession, and then formed two lines leading away from the families.

"You will go where you are directed!" The officer's German speech was so smooth that the people thought he must surely be one of them. He must be there for their welfare and would look after them. "All men and boys over thirteen will go to the left! Women and girls over thirteen will go to the right! Children will remain where they are!"

Katerina grabbed Johannes' arm. "How can they separate us? What will happen to the children? Johannes, I do not like this!"

"Move out now!" A soldier stepped forward and yanked Katerina's grip from her husband. The muzzle of his rifle was pushed into her side. Karolina and Magdalena came up beside her and put their arms around their mother's waist, protecting her from the soldier and guiding her into the gauntlet of militia ahead.

Johannes handed Konrad to Heinreich. "Take care of him," was all he said.

"Yes, Papi."

Anya took Konrad's other hand. "Do not worry, Papi, we will take care of him together."

Johannes joined the group of men as they were marched toward the sea and a compound of wood-sided buildings that stood near a shipyard. The women were directed toward a series of small squat buildings near the lumber mill. The children, left next to the railroad tracks, whimpered and cried and shivered in the snow.

Soon a group of people in heavy coats and boots began to arrive. Some had come in wagons, others on foot. They walked down the line of children, examining the thin, frail, scantily clad figures. Some children were picked out of the group, measured, poked and prodded as if they were livestock in a sales' yard. Anya, Heinreich and Konrad clung to each other, watching the proceedings.

A bent black-cloaked figure slowly walked the line with the aid of a walking stick. Stopping in front of Anya, the figure reached out and touched her hair. Anya drew back in fear.

"It is alright, dear, I will not hurt you." A woman's voice came from under the hood of the cloak. She pulled her hood back revealing a kindly, but wrinkled face, framed with hair as white as the snow in the trees. The woman smiled, and her tiny black eyes disappeared into the folds of her cheeks. Anya did not understand the woman's Russian, but softened a bit when she saw her face. "Yes," the woman continued, "I think you will do just fine." She took Anya by the hand and tried to lead her back toward the village, but Anya resisted.

"I will not leave my brothers!" Anya shouted out of fear. "I will not go!"

The woman tapped her stick against Anya's leg. "Come child! You are coming with me!"

Anya backed away, looking for a place to run, and yet not wanting to leave her brothers. She turned to head back toward the train, but was stopped by a large hand gripping the upper part of her left arm. She looked up into the face of the German-speaking army officer.

"Where are you going?" His voice flowed easily, soothingly. "You cannot run away, there is no place to go except with this kind lady who wishes to give you a new home. Can you not see that she is crippled and needs your help? I am sure she will give you food and a warm place to sleep."

"I will not leave my brothers!" Anya tried to pull away from his grip. "I do not speak Russian, how will I understand what she wants? I do not want to go with her! I will NOT leave my brothers!"

"What is your name?" The officer asked.

"Anya," she huffed back, still trying to break his grip on her arm.

"Well, Anya, if I take charge of your brothers and make sure they are safe, will you go with this woman?"

Anya stopped fighting and relaxed a little. "You would do that? You would see that my brothers stay together and are taken care of?"

"Of course I will, as long as you go quietly with this poor old woman." The officer smiled showing tobacco-stained teeth as he released his grip.

"Then yes, I will go." Anya answered reluctantly, as she reached out for her brothers and hugged each of them tightly. "Do as this man says. Stay out of trouble. I will try to find you later. We will be together again, soon, I promise," she whispered.

"I told Papi that I would look after Konrad, Anchen, and I will." Heinreich spat out, a bit defensive. "I *am* older than you!"

The woman stepped forward and tapped Anya's shoulder, then pointed her stick toward the village. Anya nodded her head in reluctant obedience, and then followed the woman. She only looked back once and gave her brothers a slight wave. The army officer stood behind her brothers, a satisfied smile on his face, as Konrad waved back and shouted, "Bye, Anchen, bring me a treat when you come back!"

As Johannes and the other men and boys were marching toward the shipyard, Katerina and her teenaged daughters, Magdalena and Karolina, arrived at the barracks of the saw mill. They were ushered into a small dark room along with about forty other women and young girls.

"Mama, is this where we are to stay?" Magdalena asked.

"It appears so, child. But we are still together so we will make the best of it," Katerina answered as she stepped into the room and looked around her.

"But, Mama it is so… *dreadful!* I do not want to sleep on these dirt floors, it is too cold!"

"Hush, Magdalena! You will do what is necessary! Do you think Heinreich, Konrad or Anya will have a warm, dry place to sleep tonight? At least there is a roof over your head. There! You will sleep there!" Katerina pointed to rough-hewn wood planks that resembled wide shelves, nailed in three layers to the even rougher un-planed walls.

A single partition with a large table placed along it, partially divided the room into two sections of about thirty square meters each. Karolina explored the area behind the divider. "Mama, there is a stove here and a small stack of wood. We can cook!"

"Only if you have food," said Frau Becker as she walked up behind Katerina. Katerina was glad to have Sofia assigned to their group, since she did not know any of the other women who had been placed in this barracks. A familiar face, a familiar story was most welcome in strange circumstances.

"Surely they will provide food for us here. Mama, they *will* give us food, and water?" Magdalena asked anxiously.

"We will have to wait and see." Katerina reached out and put her hand on Magdalena's shoulder, "We are at the mercy of our captors, whoever they are. We can only do as we are told and pray for guidance. Now we must find a space to call our own, before they are all gone."

Karolina had already moved closer to the stove and placed her meager armload of clothes and bedding on the nearest plank. "Here, Mama, we can stay here."

"Is there room for one more? I would like to have Frau Becker with us." Katerina pushed Sofia ahead of her.

Several other women forced their way past Katerina and tried to claim the remaining bunks along the wall. It was soon apparent that there were not enough planks for everybody and shoving and scuffling began.

"Karolina, Magdalena, you will share a bed, Sofia and I will share another, that will make room for more to have them."

"But, Mama…" Magdalena whimpered in meager protest.

"Do as I say!" Katerina demanded.

There appeared to be no place to put their clothing, so Karolina lay what little they had on the planks and put the blankets over them. Katerina carefully placed the food box, which now contained only the jar of pickled watermelon rind, against the wall beneath the lowest bunk. She was not sure why she was still keeping this jar, but it had become very precious to her. She then went to see what could be done about lighting the fire in the stove to take some of the chill out of the room. Magdalena climbed onto the bunk and sat with her back to the wall, drawing her knees up to her chin. She intertwined her fingers around her legs and buried her head in silence.

Loud pounding on the door caused everyone to stop what they were doing. The door was thrown open. Occupying the majority of the doorway, a large figure clad in dark brown fur from head to foot, and with a fully-bearded face, appeared to be a Great Russian bear. He stood as if firmly planted to the ground; holding a lantern in front of him. Frightened, the women drew back against the far wall in stunned silence.

"I…am…IVAN!" He spoke slowly and loudly as if he thought the women were all deaf. "I …am…the…overseer. You…will…do… as…I…tell…you."

An indignant voice from the back of the room spoke up. "Many of us speak Russian, and those that do not will be told what you are telling us. You do not need to yell or treat us like children."

"All right then…. I will proceed. You will receive food twice a day, but you must earn it. You will be fed tonight and tomorrow morning. After your morning meal you will be taken to the forest to help harvest the trees. You will be issued *toloni* according to the amount of work you do. This can be redeemed for food at each meal."

"We can not work in the snow; we do not have proper clothing! We are weak from hunger. We need soap for baths. Where are our children? What has happened to our families?" The uproar from the women was allowed to continue for a few minutes until Ivan had had enough.

"SILENCE!" he boomed over the din. When the room quieted he again spoke. "You will work in the clothes you have. I have asked the army to provide more suitable working garments; they will come when they come. You will have to work if you want to eat. Water is available in the well across the compound, or you can heat snow on the stove for bathing, and there is a sanitation facility behind the third barracks to the east. When you are in camp you may visit the other barracks, but you are not to leave the compound unless directed to do so. Anyone found outside her assigned areas will be taken by the soldiers." He handed the lantern to the nearest woman. "I will bring another later," and he left, leaving the door wide open in his wake.

Katerina quickly found a small scrap of wood and headed for the lantern. "I need to get the stove lit; it will get colder after nightfall." She seemed to have to need to explain herself, the need to be busy doing something, anything to take her mind off the children she had been forced to leave behind.

It was not long before Katerina had the stove burning brightly, its heat emanating throughout the barracks. The warm glow seemed to have a calming effect on the women as they settled in to their new surroundings.

Just after sunset, Ivan returned. "I have brought your food," he announced as he flung the door open, without knocking this time. "Ah, I see you have been able to light your stove. Good. Some of the other barracks are not so clever and are still trying to get theirs lit. Some, I am afraid, may never get the job done." A wry smile exposed a few teeth under his thick mustache.

Another man had been standing behind Ivan, but was unseen through Ivan's bulk, until he stepped around the enormous figure blocking him. This man was carrying a large pot of a thin liquid substance. A loaf of dark bread was tucked under each arm. He placed the pot on the table and the bread beside it and then left the room. He returned shortly with a stack of small bowls and spoons. Ivan placed another lantern on the table; the two of them quickly left, again leaving the door wide open in their path.

The ravenous women grabbed for the bowls, some seized the bread. Arguing followed. It seemed few were willing to share. Sofia stepped forward, placing herself between the caldron and the women.

"STOP IT!" she shouted. "STOP IT!"

The women seemed to freeze in place, taken by surprise at the force in Sofia's voice. "We all need food. We are all in this together. Form a line! Karolina, come here and help me serve the soup. The bread is already gone. This will not happen again, not if we are going to survive!"

As children caught in some naughty deed, the women obeyed Sofia's orders. The soup, which was no more than a pot of hot water with potatoes and beets, was distributed as equally as possible. Sofia took the last bowl, which was less than half full and contained only a small bit of beet.

"Please take this," one of the women pulled a small piece of the bread from her skirt pocket. "You are right about needing to share. I am sorry."

Sofia accepted the bread, placing it in her bowl, letting it soak up the broth. "Thank you," was her only response.

After finishing their meal, the women retreated to their bunks. Hoping to make the light last longer, one of the lanterns was put out. A few ventured into the compound looking for the "sanitary facility," while many just sat and cried for their lost families. Some, like Magdalena, withdrew into themselves, shutting out the rest of the world and all that was happening around them.

CHAPTER EIGHT

Fish Stew

A massive Norwegian freighter dominated the shipyard. Numerous men and boys, similar to the group Johannes belonged to, were loading freshly cut lumber into its holds. The cold wind blowing off the surface of the White Sea chilled Johannes to the bone, causing him to shiver in his tattered clothes. Marching single-file through the light snow, he and the others hunched into the wind, trying to keep up with the soldiers leading them.

Tall fences of barbed-wire formed a barrier into and out of the shipyard, and as they approached the large entrance gate a soldier yelled, "HALT!" A door opened on the small shack near the gate, and a guard carrying a big rifle emerged and conversed inaudibly with the soldier leading the rag-tag group of men. The guard turned and pulled a metal chain from under his coat. The chain was attached to the shiny black belt girdling his waist, and a large key hung from the unfettered end. He used the key to unfasten the big lock on the gate and swung the gate open just wide enough to let the men pass. Once they were all inside, the gate was closed and relocked from the outside, and the guard returned to his shack.

"HALT!" The soldier at the head of the line again yelled as he stopped and turned to face the line of men. He brandished his rifle as if to bolster his own confidence. The weary men stood silently, waiting, wondering. A man dressed in an officer's heavy wool coat emerged from a nearby building and swaggered down the steps from the entrance; he approached the freezing cluster of men as if he were the supreme ruler of the world. Johannes recognized his uniform and the insignias of his epaulets.

"The Camp Commandant," he whispered to the man standing nearest him.

The chief officer strode down the line of men, shaking his head in disgust and revulsion as he sized up his new workers. When he finished his perusal, he placed himself midway up the line and faced the group.

"I am Comrade Commandant Solokov! You have been brought here to work for me; you will obey all of my orders. Your job will be to load the lumber from the mill onto the ships. You will be paid for your work. I am the right hand of Stalin! Remember that and you will do well." He spun on his heels and retreated back into the structure from whence he came.

The men were hustled back into a single-file line and their march continued through the compound. When they reached another small building much like the guard shack at the gate, they were again stopped. Another soldier exited from the building and spoke to their leader, then directed his attention to the line of men and boys.

"One at a time you will enter this room and provide your name, village, and any other information you may be asked. Then you will be issued sleeping quarters and something to eat. Tomorrow you will begin your new jobs." He returned to his station within the building.

Johannes observed as, one by one, the men disappeared into the little building, and then were escorted out where they vanished into a row of barracks nearby. He waited; his mind raced with thoughts of what he had endured the last time he had had to answer questions, and now more questions would be asked of him, and he wondered how he should answer. Finally it was his turn to go before the inquisitor.

"Name?"

"Johannes Jahnle."

"Age?"

"Thirty-nine…no, forty."

"You do not know your age? You have trouble answering this simple question?"

Johannes straightened himself up and stood nearly at attention. "I was thirty-nine when we left our home, but I believe I have had a birthday since, I have lost track of the days."

The soldier looked at him for a moment, and then returned his gaze to his books.

"Village?"

"Sofienthal."

"How many in your family?"

"My wife and ...five children." Johannes' head dropped with this statement.

"Why did you hesitate with *that* answer?"

"We have lost children on this journey, and one before we left."

"Yes, you and many others from what I have heard so far. Kulak Fascists seem to breed like rats. The fewer mouths I have to feed, the better off the rest of Russia is!"

Johannes bit his lip to prevent lashing out with words he would likely regret. *Without my German ancestors and brethren, thousands of acres of barren steppe land would not have been farmed, and you and your people would have starved long ago!* He wanted desperately to say these words, he wanted to make this soldier choke on the words he had just spoken, but he was sure that saying anything would be a death sentence, and it would not be an instant death. He had already tasted the blood of what could be done.

He again straightened up and stood tall facing the questioner with his chin slightly elevated.

"You stand like a soldier. Were you in the Revolution? For whose army did you fight?" the soldier asked.

"The Red Army, of course!" Johannes lied. How he wished the Czar were still in power instead of Stalin and his Communists. But he knew he could show no loyalty to what was or what might have been...and stay alive.

The soldier slammed the book shut, stood and proceeded to the corner of the room where a wide white cloth hung against the wall. A tripod held a large camera, the lens facing the cloth.

"Stand here!" he demanded. Johannes stood facing the camera; a bright flash lit his face, momentarily causing shadows to emphasize his deepening wrinkles. The soldier took hold of Johannes' right hand, placed it onto a large ink pad, and forced it onto the blank page of an open book, leaving the prints of his fingers upon the paper.

"Now, go. You will be directed to your quarters."

Johannes was led to a large barracks, much like the one he had stayed in during his military duty. The building was long and low, and appeared to be sided with white-washed slats of heavy thick wood. Inside, rows of metal two-tiered beds filled the single room; intertwined ropes formed the sleeping surface. Between every other row of beds, a metal wash-stand stood with a large grey pitcher and a small cloth on top. Beneath each bedframe a metal chamber pot sat upon the bare wood floor.

The men and boys who had gone before him had already claimed their beds, so Johannes selected the one next in line. He had taken one blanket and a few clothes from Katerina when they had been separated; he placed these on the bed and lay upon them. He shivered, but did not think it was from the cold. This room seemed warm, at least warmer than it had been outside, but his body would not cease its relentless shaking. He stood and pulled the clothes from the bed and put them all on, and wrapped the blanket about him, but the shaking continued. He was very tired. He returned to the bunk and tried to settle down enough to get some rest, but he could not get Katerina and the children off his mind. *If only they would bring food, maybe the shaking would stop.* He watched a louse crawl up over the edge of the blanket. He quickly flicked it away with a sigh. He had not experienced lice since his army days, but had seen them in the warm crevices of his body for several days now. *One is a thousand, a thousand a million.* His mind was wandering in many different directions at once. He wanted to sleep, but sleep seemed to be out of reach. The room continued to fill with additional men from the train. There was little conversation, just mumbling and groaning as they tried to settle in.

A loud noise at the far end of the room caused Johannes to sit up. Several soldiers trouped into the barracks, pushing a large cart containing an enormous vessel of steaming liquid.

"Stay on your bunks! Your stew will be brought to you!" The

Russian announcement was tempered with a Norwegian accent. The man accompanying the soldiers did not appear to be a soldier himself, but rather a full-sized rotund rendition of the troll *Moki,* the long-bearded little man of legend who lived under bridges and extracted tolls from those who tried to cross.

The clothes Moki was wearing were different than any Johannes had seen before. The white pants and shirt were loose fitting and the material was quilted. They appeared to have some warmth as the man was not wearing an overcoat. His head was topped with a slouched leather hat; the brim hung low over his eyes in front and covered his neck in back. The discoloration of the leather exposed the waxy coating that made the hat water-proof. He stepped up to the cart and began ladling the stew into small bowls. The full bowls were then handed to the soldiers, who in turn delivered them to the men on the beds.

Johannes received his bowl and gazed at its contents. What appeared to be the white flesh of some kind of fish floated among shards of cabbage. There was a distinct smell emanating from the rising steam. He cautiously sipped a spoonful of broth, avoiding the solids. The heat of the broth filled his mouth and slid down his throat, warming him from the inside. When he had consumed all of the liquid, he set the bowl aside on the metal edge of his bed.

"You are not eating all of your stew?" the man in the upper bunk asked.

"No," Johannes answered. "I have not eaten in many days, I am afraid solid food would not be accepted by my stomach. I prefer to take this nourishment a little at a time."

"You are a fool, sir. We do not know when we will get another chance to eat! It may be tomorrow, it may be never!"

"If you would like what remains of mine, here, please help yourself." Johannes handed the bowl up to him. The man took it and swallowed the contents all at once, without even using his spoon.

"*Danke,*" he commented as he wiped his mouth with the end of his ragged sleeve. "You do not know what you are missing."

Though very tired, Johannes could not sleep. His thoughts of

Katerina and the children dominated his presence. *We have not been separated like this since I was forced into service during the revolution,* he reflected, *and our separation was forced then, as now. Why? What have I done to deserve this? What have any of us done? Why are we prisoners in our own land?* His thoughts began to drift back to the farm and the night before they left. *Jakob, my oldest son, where has fate taken you? Are you still alive and well? Did you find your uncle in Odessa? Have you escaped this nightmare? How I wish I knew what has happened to you.* Then he turned his contemplation to God and began to pray. *Please look after my family, please watch over them and do not let them suffer. Jakob must be kept out of this dreadful situation, please protect him. And my youngest, left behind in the snow, shield them from unnecessary suffering; I beg of you, they are only babies....* Johannes was jolted out of his prayer by a loud groan from the man in the upper bunk.

"What is wrong?" Johannes whispered.

Agonized moaning was the only response. Soon others joined in the excruciating chorus of distress, doubled over in pain and anguish. Some left their beds and rushed for the doors, only to find them firmly locked. Banging against the thick wood, they screamed to be let out. The room filled with the stench of diarrhea as the men could no longer control their bodily functions. Many dropped to the floor in heaps of unbearable pain as their intestines protested in torment to the cabbage and fish stew they had consumed.

As much as he wanted to help, Johannes knew there was nothing he could do. He took his blanket and retreated to the far corner of the room, hoping he, too, would not be so banefully afflicted. A few others joined him, others like himself that had abstained from eating the solids in the stew.

While the hours of the night passed, the moaning and shrieks of pain fell into quiet whimpering, but the reek of human excrement became nearly unbearable. Johannes felt along the wall until he located a bit of cold air leaking into the room. Working until his fingers bled, he dug at the small hole until it enlarged enough that he could get his nose into it, breathing in the frigid, but fresh air. He shared his treasure with those around him until the early light of dawn brought the welcome sight of soldiers opening the great doors.

"WHAT GOES ON HERE?" the first soldier through the door shouted as he took in the condition of the room, and the men and boys strewn about the floor. He quickly drew back as the disgusting odor that filled the room rose to meet his nose. "Do not go in there," he said as he pushed his companion aside, running to the outside corner of the building to relieve himself of his morning meal. When he was able, the soldier returned to the doorway. The influx of the cold morning air had eased the smell somewhat, and he was able to take in the situation a little more thoroughly, though strictly from the threshold of the doorway.

Joining him at the entrance, his colleague took in the state of affairs before him, and drew back in horror. "Stalin save us! What disease have these people wrought upon us? Is this something we will all be afflicted with? I must inform the commandant!" The words flowed behind him as he turned and ran off into the direction of the camp commander's office.

Being of braver substance than his comrade, the first soldier took a deep breath and cautiously entered the barracks. Using his rifle barrel as a prod, he gently poked at a few of the heaps of flesh and bones crumpled on the floor before him. Some moved in response to his nudging, others did not. "Is anybody standing?" he queried the room.

"Over here…a few of us," Johannes responded weakly.

"Come here so I can see you," the soldier demanded.

Slowly, the dozen or so men who had huddled with Johannes through the night, stepped gingerly among those on the floor. As they approached the soldier he raised his rifle as a warning for them not to come too close. "Stop there— let me see who you are!"

The men stood in a ragged group as the soldier examined the tattered, emaciated, wanton figures before him.

"We are too weak, too tired, and too cold, to cause you trouble," Johannes said quietly as he stared down the rifle barrel before him.

The Camp Commandant appeared at the door, his face contorted as he took in the situation and the stench that offended his senses. "What plague have you brought into this shipyard?" he demanded.

"Only the plague of hunger," Johannes responded.

"HUNGER! How can you claim hunger? You were all fed well last night! And this is how you repay us? You have no gratitude for your benefactors! You are as the horses that refuse to work on Monday, give them good feed and a day of rest, and they repay their owners with colic and laziness!" The more the commandant spoke, the angrier he became.

One of the men standing behind Johannes unexpectedly stepped out of the crowd, "Typhus!" he stated. "We have Typhus."

The commandant stepped back away from the men and looked over his shoulder as if he were seeking a place to run. "I knew it! I knew you kulaks brought some plague with you. Hunger, hah! Typhus. Typhus is the reason for this…" His hand made a large sweeping motion as he turned and quickly made his way out of the building. He stopped, and then faced the soldier. "Get the doctor, see what he can do. I need men to work, not lay around sick while I feed them and provide shelter for them."

"Yes, Comrade Commandant!" The soldier snapped to attention and saluted smartly. He closed and locked the doors.

"Why did you tell them we had Typhus?" Johannes asked the man who had spoken up.

"I have seen his kind before, when I served in the army. He would not have accepted that he, or any of his staff, had done anything wrong. Thinking that they fed us in error would only give him cause to further our suffering. Typhus is common among prisoners of all kinds. Have you not seen lice on you or your bunkmates? While some may die, many are cured of the disease, so it was a believable reason for the illness. Also, you heard him request the doctor. Maybe we will receive some sympathy, or at least some assistance for our plight."

Johannes gave a slight smile. "You are a very smart man." He extended his hand, "I am Johannes."

The hand was accepted, and with a quick shake, the man said "I am Paul."

In a short time the doors were again unlocked, and a number of soldiers entered accompanied by an older man dressed in a quilted white suit similar to the one the Norwegian cook had worn. He carried a black leather bag in his left hand. He inspected the room with a slow gaze and shook his head in a deliberate manner.

"Get all of these men out of this sewage pit!" he demanded of the soldiers. "Take them to the empty barracks on the east side of the hospital."

"But, comrade doctor, we have no orders to do this. The commandant has not approved such a move." A lieutenant stepped forward to address the doctor.

"I cannot treat these men in this mess, and I need them closer to my medical supplies so they can be tended. Do you want me to tell the commandant that you were the one responsible for the spread of Typhus throughout the camp?"

"No, Sir!" the lieutenant stated. "Hurry, get these men out of here and to the barracks as the doctor has requested!" he commanded the soldiers in his platoon. "Just do not touch anything or anybody you do not have to."

Johannes, Paul and the others still able to stand and walk on their own were the first to be escorted out of the contaminated building. As they approached the alternate barracks, they were stopped next to a small structure. One by one, each man was instructed to enter. When Johannes went in, he discovered that this was a shower room. A soldier stood inside, wielding yet another rifle.

"Remove all of your clothes and step into the stall," he ordered.

Johannes did as he was told. The water flowed quickly across his body, and though not very hot, stung sharply as it contacted his thin skin. He was handed a lump of harsh-smelling lye soap, which he used to scrub himself under the close scrutiny of the guard. When he was done, he was handed a piece of cloth with which to dry. Finally, the guard gave him a white quilted suit and a pair of felt shoes. When he was dressed, he was escorted outside. The light snow, that had been falling off and on since they arrived, now turned to rain. The felt shoes soaked up the water rapidly and his feet became very cold, though the suit warmed the rest of his body comfortably. Several of the other men who had gone before him, were waiting in a close group, and when about ten of them were ready, they were marched to the barracks.

Upon entering the building, they saw that it was nearly the same as the first, except the beds were furnished with blankets, and a well-stoked wood stove glowed in the center of the room. Johannes chose his bed, removed his wet shoes, and placed them near the stove. Others did the same as they filtered into the room. By evening, only about half of the men he had roomed with the night before were relocated with him. Most had come under their own energy, some had been carried in on stretchers, and all had been washed and redressed in the white quilted suits.

The doctor appeared, accompanied by the Norwegian cook and his cart with the soup vessel on it. Johannes groaned at the thought of the misery last night's soup had caused.

"This is merely broth," the doctor announced. "It will not cause the distress of the fish stew. You may eat it freely."

Johannes cautiously took the bowl that was handed to him. The broth was hot and smelled of vegetables, but was nearly clear. Even the bowl seemed cleaner and more welcoming than that of the night before. He took a sip and let the broth sit in his mouth for a bit, feeling its warmth and wetness as it flowed down his throat.

The doctor approached Johannes and examined him with his eyes. "How did you not suffer like the others?"

Johannes lowered his bowl and met the doctor's gaze. "I only drank the liquid from the stew."

"Why did you not consume the solids? Were you not hungry? Have you not been without food for awhile?" The doctor's inquiries seemed endless.

"Yes, I was very hungry, and I did want to eat it all," Johannes began. "But, I have seen the ravage of starvation before; it was a common sight during the revolution. Therefore, I knew what I could not do."

"I see," said the doctor, as he nodded his head in thought. "Good. I have been taking the temperatures of those who were placed in the infirmary, and have found little evidence of fever. From what I have seen so far, I do not believe Typhus is currently a problem, but we must be ever diligent." With that he continued on his rounds among the other men, and Johannes finished his broth.

CHAPTER NINE
Kulak Pups

As Heinreich and Konrad stood watching Anya reluctantly being led away by the cloak-covered old lady, the soldier standing behind them prepared to be on his way.

"Where are we going?" Heinreich asked as he watched the soldier pick through a few of the belongings the prisoners left behind on the snow near the railroad cars.

"*We* are not going anywhere, *I* am returning to my company and my job." He quickly thumbed through the pages of a Bible he picked up from the ground, not finding anything of value within its pages, he tossed it behind him, and continued his rummaging of the remaining items.

"You told Anya that you would look after us."

"Yes, I did say that, but only to get her to go with that poor old woman." The soldier stopped his rooting and faced the boys.

"But you *promised* to take care of us!" Heinreich's statement was as much a plea as it was insistence.

"I did no such thing! I only told her I would take charge of you and see that you were safe, and I have done that. You are safe, are you not? And I have been in charge of you since she left." His wry smile and nonchalant attitude bewildered Heinreich.

"But she has only been gone a few minutes!"

"I do not remember saying exactly how long I would take charge of you, so I think I can call the job done whenever *I* want, and *I* say it is done now. You *kulak pups* get going now, and leave me to my work."

Konrad pulled on his brother's ragged shirt-tail, "Where is the puppy?" he whispered.

Heinreich pushed his brother away then returned his questions to the soldier. "Why do you call us kulak pups? What does that mean?"

As Konrad tried to hide behind his brother for protection, the soldier leaned into Heinreich's face, "Did you ever have a dog?"

"No, Papi said dogs were too much trouble."

"And did he say why?"

"He said that dogs would only work when they were told to, otherwise they were lazy and only wanted to be fed. He said they would get into trouble and raid the hen house, and dig holes in the yard, and chew up everything they could. He said dogs had to be kept on a chain unless they were working as they were told."

The soldier's easy smile shrouded his quickly working mind. "And did you have a cat?"

"Oh, yes, we always had cats. Papi said cats are good."

"And why was it good to have a cat and not a dog?"

"Cats keep the mice out of the grain. Papi said cats are working even when they seem to be asleep, 'cause they are always listening for the mice, and they can wake up and jump on one before the mouse knows it."

"Well now, I think you will be able to understand why I call you *kulak pups*. Your people are German, not Russian, am I right?"

"We do not speak Russian, is that what you mean?"

"You do not speak Russian, you do not worship the Russian god, you do not live in Russian villages, and you do not recognize the great Comrade Stalin as your superior leader. Do you?"

"I am only eleven; I do not understand what you are talking about."

"That is exactly what I am getting at! Eleven-year-old Russian children know what god they must worship, they know Comrade Stalin very well! That is why you are *kulaks*— German-bred problems for the good Russians to deal with. We Russians are like the cats. We are always working, even when we sleep. But you Germans, you are like the dogs who do not work unless they are told to do so, and must be kept on a chain to keep out of trouble. I have no place to put you, so I must turn you loose to raid hen houses and cause damage wherever you go, that is your ilk, that is your destiny, should you live so long." With his words, the soldier's face twisted into a mask of disgust and revulsion, and he pushed Heinreich away from him.

Heinreich, numb with confusion and fear, just stood staring at the soldier. Finally he mustered up what courage he had left and said, "But, you speak German like me, how can you be Russian?"

"I am *Russian*, because my father was Russian. I speak *German* because my mother was German and she taught me your language and your ways, but she did not teach me your deceitfulness. She did not teach me what to do when her own people fought the true Russians, when her own people shot her in the street for being a Russian spy because she was married to my father. The Revolution taught me many things about how *your* people lie and cheat and turn against their own kind when the situation suits them. My father, a true Russian, taught me the right way to live, the right way to love my country, the right way to treat those who suck the goodness out of our land for their own wealth and fortune."

During his tirade, the soldier raised his arm as if to slap down the German devil before him. Heinreich raised both hands in front of his face and cowered back away from the blow he expected to receive, but as he stepped back he tripped over Konrad, and they both fell into a heap, in the snow, crying. The soldier seemed to come to his senses, lowered his arm and stomped off toward the troops gathered at the front of the train.

Konrad recovered quickly when he realized he had not been hurt. "Where is the puppy?" he again asked Heinreich.

"There is no puppy!" Heinreich, still reeling from the words the soldier had hurled at him, pulled himself out of the tangle with his little brother and just sat there, sobbing. Konrad stood up and began exploring through the rubble the soldier had rejected.

"Look, Heiner, I found a coat!" He lifted the dark brown wool garment and put it on. What was left of the item hung on Konrad like a mufti's robe. His arms, lost in the hanging sleeves, flapped in the air resembling a fledgling eagle learning to fly. He twisted and turned trying to get a look at himself, finally falling back into the snowy mud puddle he had made with his feet. He giggled quietly, afraid of bothering his big brother. Heinreich looked up, wiped his tears away, rose to his feet and stood over Konrad. He reached down, helped his brother up and put his arm around the shoulders covered in the now-wet coat.

"Well, I guess we are on our own now, Konrad. We should go see what else we can find to keep us warm."

"And eat, too?"

"We will not find food on the train, Konrad. We will have to go to the village for that."

"And get a puppy?"

"We will see, Konrad, we will see."

"Heiner, look." Konrad pointed at several small children huddled together in the shadow of the train. The boys had been so wrapped up in their fear of being left by the soldier they had not seen the others, and only now realized they were not alone—there were many other children scattered along the string of boxcars that brought them. Tiny babies too ill to be taken in by the villagers lay swaddled in whatever coverings their desperate parents could find and those that were not already dead, soon would be. Girls and boys in small family groups wandered, or stood, or sat in the snow, confused and bewildered, wondering what to do next. Many cried. Some watched in wonderment as older children searched through the few items that had been left behind.

"HEINER, OVER HERE!" A familiar voice rang out a short distance down the tracks. Heinreich looked up to see Helmut Becker waving exuberantly.

"Come on Konrad, it is Helmut and Friedreich. Let us go see what they are doing."

The boys quickly made their way to Helmut. When they met, Heinreich and Helmut embraced, jumping around in an uncoordinated excited dance. Their families were separated when they were put on the train and now the boys exulted in the reunion. Konrad stood back far enough to keep from being knocked over and soon spotted Friedreich climbing over a coupling joint between two cars.

"Helmut! Come here, look at this!" Friedreich called to his brother. Helmut and Heinreich made their way through the mud to Friedreich.

"What have you got?" Helmut asked.

"Look, over there…" Friedreich pointed into the distance. A small dilapidated building sat at the edge of the woods, its roof partially collapsing under the expanse of thick green moss growing upon it. Tiny pines sprouting around the foundation, pushing their way through the layered rock base, caused the framework to sit askew.

"We must go see if there is any food in there," Helmut waved for the others to follow. As Heinreich and Helmut climbed over the coupling after Friedreich, Konrad found a way to crawl underneath. The boys seemed oblivious to the cold, eager at the thought of finding food, or at least a place to sleep. Approaching the structure they saw that it was not much larger than their mothers' summer kitchens. Heinreich cautiously pushed against the splintered wood door. Slowly, it creaked open.

"Stay here," Helmut ordered the smaller boys as he and Heinreich prepared to enter.

"Hey, I saw it first! And I am not a baby like he is!" Friedreich was indignant at the idea that he would be left behind on this great new adventure.

"Oh, alright, you can come. Konrad, you have to stay here until we know it is safe." Helmut demanded.

Konrad nodded in disappointment, but as the older boys entered the little building, he saw movement at the edge of the tree line. Ever-curious, he wandered off to find what was there.

As they entered through the doorway, the boys were aware that there was nothing adventurous before them. Just a single room with a dirt floor covered in pine needles. The dirty, soot-encrusted walls tilted and strained against the weight of the moss-covered roof. A rusted iron stove stood in the far corner.

"No food here," Helmut sighed.

"No, but we can sleep here, it smells better than the train."

"Yes, Heiner, good idea. This hut is ours and we can go hunting from here. We can have a fire to keep us warm and a roof to keep us dry."

Heinreich looked up at the moss creeping through the opening of the roof and down the wall. "Well, sort of…" he responded.

Friedreich kicked through the pine needles, disturbing a few small black beetles. He stomped at them as they tried to hurry back into their hidden existence. "I do not like it here," he said.

"Well, Freddy, you will have to like it for now. It is getting dark and we have no place else to go." Helmut cuffed his smaller brother on the shoulder to put him in his place. The boys decided they would need more pine needles to sleep on and some wood for the stove, so they headed back out onto the porch.

Heinreich stopped short as he came out of the door. He had temporarily forgotten about Konrad. He had expected his little brother to wait as he was told, but the porch was vacant. "Where is Konrad?"

The boys looked all around the exterior of the building, but Konrad was just not there.

"Not to worry," Helmut said. "He will come back when it gets dark. He will not want to be away from you, Heiner."

"Maybe…" Heiner was not sure if he should be worried about Konrad or glad that he might be free of having to worry about him. Guilt began to sneak its way into his thoughts; after all, Konrad was only four.

"We can not waste our time looking for him right now," Helmut cautioned, "we need to be getting our beds ready before it gets dark. And we need to be looking for something to eat, as well." Helmut had decided that he should be the leader of this group; he was, after all, a month older than Heinreich. "Maybe we will find Konrad while we are looking for food."

"Yes, that is when he will turn up!" Heinreich brightened at the idea that Konrad would just appear while they were busy doing something else, something more important than searching for a lost child.

The boys foraged around the edge of the forest, gathering pine boughs for sleeping and pinecones and small branches for burning in the stove. They returned to the shack and set up their beds. Helmut cleaned a mouse nest out of the stove and proceeded to place the pinecones and branches inside.

"What are you going to light it with?" Friedreich asked.

"Oh," Helmut responded. He stopped what he was doing and sat on a pile of needles. "I guess I forgot we needed fire to make fire."

"*Dumkopf,*" Friedreich scoffed.

"I am going out to look for Konrad." Heinreich said as he headed for the door. "You do not have to come." He wanted very much for the others to accompany him, but he felt that Helmut really did not want Konrad with them.

"Do not get lost," Friedreich's sarcasm surprised Heinreich.

"What is wrong with you?" Heinreich asked.

"Nothing." Friedreich could not explain what he was feeling; he just did not like the idea that his brother might like Heiner more than him.

Heinreich headed off to the forest to search among the trees. He found a number of small caves formed by brush-covered fallen trees; some were coated in light snow. He called "Konrad!" over and over, but got no response. He decided to circle back toward the shack when he heard quick, short footsteps rustling through the brush behind him. He stopped and turned in the direction of the noise. A small figure emerged through the trees.

"HEINER, LOOK, PUPPY!" Konrad held up a small grey ball of squirming fur for Heinreich to see.

"Konrad! Where have you been? I have been looking everywhere for you!"

Konrad drew the animal close to his chest and wrapped him arms over it. Heinreich's anger scared him and he was afraid it would scare his puppy, too.

"You made me alone, I saw *hund* by trees, so I went to go see it, but it kept going away, so I tried to come back, but then I found puppy. And then I hear you calling me."

"Let me see your puppy."

"NO"

"Please, Konrad. I just want to see what it looks like."

"Okay," Konrad responded warily as he handed the creature to Heinreich.

Heinreich took the warm bundle into his arms and perused the grey face. It whimpered and squirmed, trying to escape the strange hold on it. It was soft. The grey down-like fur, tipped with specks of black, wafted in the breeze floating through the branches of the larch trees that surrounded them. Its dark brown eyes stared up at him as if studying his face.

"You are right, Konrad, it is a puppy, a little boy puppy. He is pretty small; I wonder where his mother is and why she would have left him alone out here in the forest?"

"Give him back," Konrad reached out for the puppy.

"You know we can not keep him, we have nothing to feed it with. We do not even have food for us...wait, maybe if there is a dog close, there is an owner close. There must be a farm or something close by where we might get food. But we will have to come back tomorrow. It is too dark now to look. I just hope we can find our way back to the shack."

Konrad cuddled the puppy close to him and followed his brother through the trees. They soon found the shack and joined the boys inside.

"Did you bring food?" Helmut asked as soon as they entered the dark room. A sliver of moonlight, coming through the open area in the roof, formed a rivulet of pale light across the floor. Helmut and Friedreich sat against the far wall, huddled close for warmth.

"No, but I found Konrad."

"And, Konrad found puppy." Konrad happily declared.

"Oh great, maybe we can eat the puppy." Helmut was disgusted that his minions had not brought food.

"NO!" Konrad screamed.

"Oh, forget it! I was not serious. Really, you found a puppy? You are sure it is a puppy, and not a skunk or muskrat or something?"

"Yes, he really did find a puppy. And maybe tomorrow we can find who owns it and get some food from them." Heinreich wanted to please his friend with his grand idea.

"We will have to wait until tomorrow then."

The boys crowded together into a cluster, with the puppy in the middle. Before long, the puppy began to whimper with hunger.

Out in the forest, the pup's mother returned to her den. Not finding her lone pup where she left him, she sniffed and rooted through the dried leaves and pine needles, frantically searching for her lost offspring.

The young female had had her pups late in the season. Her inexperience already resulted in the loss of two of her litter, and now her last was missing, gone from the cozy den where she left it while she hunted for sustenance for herself. She paced anxiously, nose to the ground searching for any sign of her pup's scent. The only trace she picked up was one she feared and hated; the smell of a human. She lifted her head, and with her nose to the air tried to discern the direction the human had traveled.

A sound gathered in the deepest part of her, emanating forth as a long and wailing cry; a mother's forlorn call to her youngster, a pack subordinate calling for the comfort of family. Soon she was joined by other members of her group. An impressive silver male was the first to emerge from the shadows, his lips pulled back into a threatening snarl as he snapped at the female's throat in greeting. She quickly dropped to the ground whining and wagging her tail in short, quick jerks as a sign of submission. Almost as soon as he accepted her customary groveling, more grey figures appeared from the trees and joined in the time-honored tradition of the wolf pack. Six females and three males gathered in a yelping, animated group.

Once properly reunited, they quickly set out on their hunt for the missing pup. Moving like silent apparitions through the Siberian forest, they picked up the scent of the human. Coming upon a clearing and singling out the scent of human, more pungent than the first, the wolves determined that a larger creature had been present. Now more cautious, more alert to the danger that lay ahead, they softly padded through the undergrowth, arriving by the shack at the edge of the trees.

The wolves knew this shack. They often smelled the stench of death surrounding the ground around it. It was a hunter's cabin, and many of their kind had fallen at the hands of these humans. This cabin marked the border between the protective forest and the human presence that now occupied the wolves' centuries-old hunting grounds and migration route to the East.

The big male stopped short when he reached the edge of the tree line. The rest of the pack understood his unspoken command, and stopped behind him, all except the young female. Her teats were very full and the uncomfortable pressure made her yearn for her lone pup. The waning moon's dim light shone upon the little shack, casting a shadow across the clearing toward the trees, enabling the young female to remain hidden as she carefully approached the building. When she was very near, she halted, lifted her head and emitted a long low cry, calling her pup to her.

The pup squirmed and wriggled in Konrad's arms, as it started squealing out of hunger and excitement. Konrad held the pup tighter, nearly smothering it in the huge sleeves of his coat.

"Did you hear that?" Helmut whispered in the dark.

"What is it?" Heinreich was fully awake now and drew closer to the other boys.

"I think it might be a ghost…or maybe the Devil." Freidreich shivered, but it was not the cold that caused him to do so.

The puppy squealed again.

"Or maybe the mother of this puppy," Helmut groped in the dark for Konrad's bundle. "I think we should put it outside."

"NO!" Konrad hollered emphatically. "It is mine!"

"But, Konrad, what if that is its mother, she might come in to get him, then we will all be in trouble. He is hungry, he wants his mother." Heinreich pleaded with his little brother.

"NO!" Konrad insisted. "I am hungry; I want my Mama, too."

"Please, Konrad…." Heinreich's voice trailed off into silence as he heard a snuffling noise around the base of the door. The boys drew tighter into their little circle.

Outside, the young she-wolf whined softly as the silver male came in response to the pup's cries. The rest of the pack followed his lead and soon they were all circling the shack quietly, heads low, detecting the many smells that scented the ground. The big male stopped, backed off a bit and hesitated as if calculating his next step. The young mother returned to the door, inhaling the odors around the threshold, whining, agitated, excited. Unseen, the pack leader disappeared around the far edge of the building. The rest of the pack milled around the female, waiting for her next move.

Unable to contain herself any longer, she threw her body against the door, and it flew open. The boys screamed, the pup screamed, the female snarled and growled. Bolstered by the entrance of the rest of the pack, she charged the cluster of humans that kept her from her youngster. Suddenly, a loud crack emanated throughout the room as the big male broke through the mossy roof, collapsing it into the middle of the mêlée.

The pack began to fight amongst themselves, the pup temporarily forgotten. In the seconds that passed, Heinreich pulled at Konrad, as he tried to run to the door. Konrad gripped the puppy harder. The big male soon recovered from his unexpected fall and gave a quick bark of command to the others, reminding them why they were there. The pup gave a muffled squeak, trying to call to its mother through Konrad's over-protective grasp. The female lunged for her pup, grabbing Konrad by the throat. The other wolves followed her action, latching onto whatever tender flesh was within their reach.

A gun-shot rang out. All movement ceased. The closeness of the wolves' howls had aroused nearby patrolling soldiers. Hearing the commotion within the shack, they quickly assumed the wolves had cornered a small animal of some sort. It would be an easy hunt, and a pleasant distraction from guarding the empty train. A second shot through the open door caused one of the wolves to drop, landing motionless on the pine-needle strewn floor.

Some of the wolves used fissures in the collapsed roof as a means of escape. More shots rang out, followed by hearty laughter as the soldiers' bullets found their marks. Finally, all was silent once again.

Holding a lantern out before him, one of the soldiers entered the shack. He was surprised by what he found. The light from his lamp glowed softly upon two dead wolves, a magnificent silver male and a small but milk-heavy female. As he shined the light further around the room, his eyes took in a scene of blood and terror. Three boys lay dead, their bodies mangled by the wolves. A wolf pup lay crushed beneath the youngest child. He remembered this child, one of the German saplings left behind at the train. "Looks like he got his puppy, after all," he mumbled to himself.

Behind the soldier something stirred in the rubble. Fredreich had been caught under the collapsed roof. Obviously in pain, he whimpered as he tried to free himself. The soldier stepped closer, pulled his sidearm and fired one quick shot, then grabbed the tail of the silver male and dragged the wolf outside.

"This one will make a fine pelt for a new winter coat," he announced as he met his partner, who had already begun to skin one of the other members of the pack. "There is a small female inside, but her pelt is pretty ragged, not good for much. We need to burn this little cabin, or the stench from the dead wolves will soon draw others." He threw his lantern inside the door, and the pine-needles exploded into flame.

CHAPTER TEN

The Iniquitous Forest

Katerina woke with a jerk. Her dreams had taken her somewhere she did not want to go. She lay silently in the dark, barely breathing, trying to understand the feeling that was permeating her deepest soul. She realized that Sofia, lying next to her on the hard wooden plank, was crying softly. Katerina reached over and took Sofia's hand, "What is wrong?" she whispered.

Sofia shifted her body closer and gripped Katerina's hand harder. "I do not know for sure," she whispered back. "I have a feeling something has happened to my boys."

Katerina reached up and brushed Sofia's hair away from her face. "We must trust in God to take care of our children. The villagers will take them in. You will see, one day we will bear witness to how our children have grown under the care of these people. Your boys will do well, they are strong and obedient; they will make good workers for any family that accepts them. My Konrad, however, he is so small and so thin from having no food. But I must have faith that he is nurtured and loved by his new parents."

Sofia closed her eyes; a large tear drop rolled across her nose and onto the wooden plank. She sighed a deeply emotional and deeply tired sigh. "Yes," she whispered, "you are right, they will be fine, I must believe that, I must believe that...." Slowly she drifted back into a fitful sleep.

Katerina could not return to her slumber, she was wide awake and her mind was picturing her children, one by one. Her thoughts turned to her youngest daughter. *Anya, my Anya, you are the one I am most frightened about; my precious daughter, so young, so vulnerable. Will you be taken by a family? Will you find warmth and bread? Will you be loved and nurtured? Oh God, please, please protect her.* Katerina fell into silent prayer, one after another, for all of her children, for her husband, for Sofia's family, and finally for herself. Just as she began to drift off into sleep, the door flew open and crashed against the wall. It was still dark out, and the cold air flowed in like an ocean wave upon the shore.

"Get up, you lazy hags!" Ivan bellowed as he shone his lantern around the room. "You have work to do! I have brought food; you have one-half hour to be ready to work. I will be back for you then." He placed his lantern on the table, returned to the doorway and brought a large kettle of something steaming and placed it next to the lantern. "Hurry up!" he roared again as he left.

The women moaned and shivered in the dark and cold. Slowly the room came to life as someone lit the lanterns and stoked the fire in the stove. Another tasted the thick white liquid that filled the kettle. "Not intolerable," she said, "something like oatmeal soup, at least it warms the insides."

There was no need to dress, as they had all slept in whatever clothing they brought with them. Those who managed to bring hair brushes tried to return their long hair to their usual braided buns. Most took the opportunity to have a small bowl of the gruel.

Katerina took filled bowls to her girls. "Here, you must eat; we do not know what lies before us, or when we will be allowed to eat again," she said as she handed the bowls to her daughters as they sat on the edge of their sleeping-plank.

Karolina quickly downed hers, but Magdalena's spoon was dipped repeatedly, slowly, into the contents. "Magdalena, you must eat," Katerina implored.

Magdalena slipped the spoon into her mouth, pulled it back out and threw it on the floor, the bowl quickly following. She shifted her body, moving back against the wall, partially turning away from her mother. She drew her legs up to her chest and withdrew into herself, as she had done the previous evening. Katerina could not understand what was happening to her child. "You must be hungry," she pleaded with Magdalena. "You must eat something." Magdalena did not move.

"Mother, ignore her, she is just being Magdalena. You know how she can be." Karolina had little use for her sister's introverted dispo-sition. She had often been the one to complete Magdalena's chores when Magdalena was in one of her moods.

"Now is not the time to act like this Magdalena, please, please eat *something*," Katerina again insisted. But, Magdalena would not move.

Again the door flew open without warning, revealing Ivan, the man-bear, standing in its wake. "Line up outside, *now!*" he command-ed. The women quickly stopped what they were doing and obeyed the brusque demand. Katerina grabbed Magdalena by the arm and dragged her outside to line up with the others. The women stood shivering in the frigid early-morning darkness, murmuring amongst themselves, wondering what was coming next. "QUIET!" Ivan demand. The wom-en stood in silence.

Katerina was distracted by the movement of lanterns in the dis-tance. She looked past her group and saw many other women being escorted from similar barracks buildings by armed soldiers. *Where are they being taken,* she wondered, *will we follow? What are we being subjected to?* Her distracted thoughts were quickly brought back into focus with Ivan's next proclamation.

"You will be issued tools for work. You will be taken into the forest to cut down trees. Some of you will be taken to the sawmill to plank the trunks for transport."

Mumbling among the women ensued as Ivan's instructions were translated to those who did not speak Russian. Questioning responses caused Ivan to call again for quiet. "What is the problem here? Are you women so lazy that you do not know how to work?"

Sofia stepped forward. "It is not that we cannot work, but that we have never seen logging before. Where we come from, we have few trees, mostly birch and oak. Our men have always cut the wood for our use. Most of us have never even seen a tree fall."

Ivan's broad grin could only be seen by the exposure of his few remaining teeth from behind his thick beard. "You will learn then. You will learn…or you will *die*," he announced with assurance. A soldier approached and spoke in low tones to Ivan. Ivan nodded in agreement then returned his attention to the group of women. "I do not suppose that any of you can handle a horse?" The women remained silent for several seconds. "I thought not," he said as he shook his head in disgust.

Karolina raised her hand somewhat cautiously. "I can handle horses; I worked next to my father in the fields with our team."

"Karolina, NO!" Katerina grabbed her daughter's arm and pulled it down to her side. "Never offer to do anything for these people!" she warned in German.

"But, Mama, I love working with horses; you know that. I would rather do anything with a horse than cut trees down in the forest."

Ivan stepped forward and removed Karolina's arm from her mother's grasp. "Come with me then."

Several soldiers holding lanterns escorted the remainder of the women to a large tool shed, where they were made to accept a tool in exchange for signing their names and home villages on a roster. Further instructions informed them that all tools were to be accounted for at the end of each workday, and anything broken or missing was to be paid for out of the *toloni* they earned. Most had not seen such tools as they had been handed and had no idea how they were to be used. At length, they were all loaded with their tools into the backs of large freight wagons and transported to the edge of the great forest.

The sky had lightened enough for them to see the yellowing trees before them. Few spoke as they rode, saving their energies for the task ahead. Towering larches loomed out of the early morning shadows, frost lacing the edges of the boughs that hung low over the dirt track that led them to where the trees were to be harvested. Soon the wagons entered a large clearing; rime clung to the top edges of muddy wheel ruts.

"Get down. Bring the tools!" a soldier ordered. One by one the women dismounted the wagons, each gripping the tool that had been issued to her. Another wagon arrived full of men from the village.

"These men are here to teach you how to bring these trees down. You will only cut the trees with the white markings and only below those markings! You will be divided up into those who will actually cut the trees down and those who will clean the trees for transport," the soldier continued.

The village men each selected three or four women and led them into the forest; there they demonstrated the proper way to wedge the trunk and insert the two-man saws. The women soon learned how hard this job was going to be. With no gloves for protection, their frozen hands were soon covered with blisters, but they did not feel them. The handles of the saws were quickly coated in blood from their inexperienced, tender hands. Katerina and Sofia had been put on a saw and worked well together, each picking up the rhythm of the movement of the saw. Their backs and shoulders soon ached with their efforts.

Many of the younger girls, including Magdalena, had been given small axes with which to remove the branches from the trees after they fell. Most worked quickly as they had been instructed, out of fear and intimidation by the soldiers. Magdalena, however, put in only a half-hearted effort. Her movements were slow, mechanical, her thoughts somewhere else.

As the sun rose and the day progressed, Katerina observed Karolina walking behind a fully-harnessed sturdy-looking horse, maneuvering it into the clearing. Some of the men rolled a huge stripped log onto the dirt track and attached a chain around one end. Karolina easily backed the big horse up to the trailing ends of the chain and attached the trace straps from the harness to it. Standing next to the log, she spoke in soft tones and with a slight movement of the lines asked the horse to move forward. He obediently dropped his head and leaned forward into the collar. He dug his hind legs into the mucky snow and pushed his shoulders into the collar, tightening the traces until the chain became taut and the great log began to slide forward. The horse took another, slow deliberate step and again the log moved. Mud and snow piled up against the leading edge of the log, making the horse pull harder. Karolina stopped the horse and said "*rechts*," as she gave a gentle pull on the right line requesting that he pull to his right. The horse immediately obeyed and the log rolled over the rut it had been digging and up onto an area of packed snow. The horse eased up on his efforts as the log slid smoothly and they were soon on a steady pace headed for the mill.

Sofia noticed Katerina watching Karolina and stopped pulling on the saw. Straightening her back and wiping her brow she said, "Karolina handles the horse well, she will be a prized worker." Katerina nodded in agreement and thanks, and returned to the saw.

Magdalena also observed Karolina working with the horse. Jealously and anger permeated her thoughts. *Why does she have such an easy job? Why am I cutting branches off these trees—these dead, good-for-nothing trees, in this dead good-for-nothing place? I want to go home! I do not have to do this; I am not one of them!* She threw her axe in the snow, acting like she had hurt her hand, and briefly waited for a response. The others were working too hard to notice, and she realized that she had not seen a soldier in a while. So she cautiously, slowly, headed for the tree line. Once within the protection of the thick trunks, she began to run. Not knowing which direction she was headed and not really caring, she just kept moving. *I am free! I am free!* The thoughts raced through her mind as quickly as she ran. She pushed her way through some thicker undergrowth, and as she found her way to the other side, a small clearing opened up before her. Just as she entered the open space, Ivan appeared before her. He grabbed her wrists in his large hands. In Russian he demanded, "Where do you think you are going, child?"

"You are hurting me!" she cried as she tried to pull away from his grasp, not fully understanding his question.

"I said, where do you think you are going? ANSWER ME!"

"*LASSEN SIE MICH LOS!*" She screamed, "LET ME GO!"

"Why are you so far away from the work area? Why were you running? You think I have not noticed that you have not been working? Have you spent all morning planning your little get-away?" Magdalena still did not understand him and continued to struggle against his grip. "Maybe you think you are too young to work? Then I will teach you to be a woman!" he sneered. His agitation at her struggling and pulling away caused him to fling his arms and, momentarily, he lost his grip;

she slipped through his hands but her body was still retreating from his. She flew off balance, falling backwards against the base of a tree and hitting her head. She lost consciousness and lay limply in the snow.

Ivan's ire overcame him as he reached for her. He began tearing at her clothes. "I will teach you!" he bellowed. He grabbed her arm again and pulled her out into the clearing. He was standing over her when a soldier appeared.

"Is there a problem here?"

"No problem, just an attempted runaway. She seems to have fallen and hit her head," Ivan lied as he feigned concern for her well-being. "I will take her to the infirmary."

"Better I do that," the soldier responded. "You should return and supervise the new workers." Ivan was still boiling when he stomped off into the forest, but he said nothing more. He knew his presence here was tenuous at best; he had been released from prison under a decree allowing convicts supervisory status in the labor camps if they voluntarily served their terms under military administration. His previous indiscretions were to be kept concealed as long as he did his job.

Magdalena slowly lifted her hand and put it against her head. "Are you alright? Can you rise?" the soldier asked in German.

"I think so," she responded groggily.

"Good, then you can return to your position." He helped her to her feet. She clutched what was left of her torn clothing and tied them about herself. The guard took her by the hand and escorted her back to her axe.

CHAPTER ELEVEN

Anya's New Life

Anya managed to get a couple more glances of her brothers, before she and the old woman turned a corner into an alleyway at the edge of the village. Given that the soldier assured her that her brothers would be safe, Anya obediently followed the woman. It seemed to Anya that the path they were taking was skirting the main part of the village, as they walked behind a number of small houses and yards. The child was intrigued at how differently this village appeared from her home in Sofienthal. The town itself was somewhat larger, but the houses were closer together and she thought they looked smaller, and did not seem to include quarters for large animals.

Small lean-tos, placed against the backs of the houses, contained a few chickens, but she did not see any geese. Anya thought about how much she loved her mother's geese; they would often follow her around the yard waiting for a chance to get into the fenced garden. Sometimes Mama allowed her to let them in so they could eat the weeds. It was Anya's job to watch them and keep them out of the newly sprouting vegetables, but this was a task she very much enjoyed. In the evenings, Mama let her feed the chickens and geese and lock them into their pens to keep them safe. *Will I ever have geese again?*

Taking in as many sights and sounds and smells as she possibly could while following along, Anya observed the old woman limping as she traveled. She watched as the matron used the crooked old stick to brace herself when the footing was slick, or soggy, or uneven, and how the woman's cloak gathered mud, caking the hem as it dragged through the slushy mire.

After what seemed like an hour, Anya realized that they were no longer passing houses, and seemed to be entering the forest. Soon, they arrived at a small cottage in a large meadow. Anya was entranced with the ornate floral carvings that decorated the eaves beneath the fanciful crested roof of the otherwise plain little building. A well-worn path led them through browning grass and dying flowers still poking up through the snow, to the doorstep, where the woman finally stopped, turned and faced Anya.

"*Zdyes zhdat*," she said in Russian as she dropped her hand palm-down toward the step at the entrance of the cottage. Anya did not know the words, but understood the motion and stood still. The old woman disappeared into the little cottage. Returning with a grey wool blanket, she handed it to Anya and began jabbing a finger toward her.

Oh, I hope she is not going to make me sleep out here, Anya began to worry. *It will be so cold tonight. What kind of woman is this? Is she going to be a cruel old witch? Is she like the old woman in the* 'Hansel and Gretel' *story Mama often told? Will she put me in a cage and feed me 'til I am plump enough to eat? I wish I could have left a trail of bread crumbs…but I have no crumbs…I have no bread…I have nothing to leave a trail with.*

The woman shook her head and in a calming voice said, "I only want you to leave those filthy clothes outside; here wrap yourself in this blanket and we will get you cleaned up." But Anya did not understand. The woman saw the fear in Anya's eyes and again tried to soothe the child with her voice. "I am Sonia," the woman said pointing to her chest. "Soh-nee-ya," she repeated slowly. "I will not hurt you. I only want to help."

Anya looked into the woman's face and somehow seemed reassured. "Anya, Awn-yah," the child answered pointing to herself.

"Anya," the woman said with a slight smile, and again indicated for Anya to remove her clothing and wrap herself in the blanket. Still unsure of what the woman was going to do to her, Anya slowly removed what was left of her dress and socks and shoes. Sonia quickly wrapped the child in the blanket and escorted her into the cottage.

Anya's heart beat rapidly as she walked through the doorway at Sonia's urging. Cautiously stepping upon the curly-brown fur hide that served as a rug, Anya stood shivering, even though there was a fire burning warmly in the fireplace on the far side of the room. Pulling the blanket closer about her and looking around, she was amazed to see that the walls were made of large round tree trunks lying on their sides. The bark had been removed, but the wood was still coarse enough to trap small particles of ash from the fireplace, causing the walls to be dark and foreboding. This seemed to be the only room to the whole house. In the far corner a small bed, neatly covered in more brown fur, was pushed tightly against the wall, flanking one side of the fireplace. The opposite wall sported a long sideboard that appeared to serve as the food preparation area. Above and below the entire length of the sideboard, simple cloth curtains over framed cupboards hid whatever possessions Sonia owned. A large black kettle hung in the fireplace. The only other furniture in the room was a modest straight-backed wooden chair, a small square table with a lantern centered upon it, and a spinning wheel. The afternoon daylight softly illuminated the room from the one window cut into the wall to the right of the door. *At least there is no cage or large oven,* Anya thought with some relief as she took in all that was around her.

Sonia removed a metal tub from under the sideboard and placed it on the floor near Anya. Removing the kettle from the fireplace, she poured steaming hot water into the tub. Anya watched with interest as Sonia busied herself removing small cloth bags from the cupboard. One of the bags was placed into the hot water. Soon the room was filled with an amazing floral aroma, the likes of which Anya had not smelled before. Sonia placed her hand into the water to check the temperature, and then indicated for Anya to get in.

Warily, Anya dropped the blanket and slowly stepped into the tub. The water was hot, but not scalding. She gradually sat down and the warmth flowed over her like the sun on an early summer's day. Closing her eyes allowed the sweet fragrance to seep into her brain and her thoughts turned to the first flowers that emerged through the snow each spring. Sonia dipped a cup into the water, pouring it down Anya's back, then took another cloth bag and began scrubbing Anya's nearly translucent skin. Sonia constantly and tenderly spoke in Russian; her tones comforting, soothing to Anya's ears. Finally, Sonia poured water over Anya's head and sprinkled the contents of another bag into her hair. Using both hands she scrubbed thoroughly down to Anya's scalp. Anya flinched a bit at first, as her hair had not been washed in months and her scalp was very tender, but Sonia perceived the sensitivity and eased up a bit on her scouring. The water had cooled by the time Sonia finished and Anya was ready to leave the bath. She stood and reached for the blanket, but Sonia pulled it away, handing a clean blanket to Anya. Anya wrapped herself and stepped out onto the animal hide. She watched as Sonia struggled with the water-filled tub, dragging it outside and dumping it into the snow. Anya's hair dripped down her back, causing a wet streak down the blanket.

Sonia briskly rubbed the blanket that encircled Anya, drying and warming her little body at the same time. Anya's thoughts were of her mother; *this is just how Mama always dries us after a winter bath.* Sonia then wrapped Anya's head in a muslin cloth to defray any more water from dripping onto the floor. With some effort, Sonia pulled a large wooden box from beneath the bed. Carefully, she opened the box and removed several items. Anya saw several wool blankets woven with intricate designs, and what appeared to be an apron of fine white lace. Finally, Sonia pulled a tightly wrapped bundle from the box. The bundle was draped in white cloth and tied with a thin leather cord. She untied the cord, removed the cloth and held up a small pale-brown dress. With obvious effort, Sonia handed the dress to Anya.

Anya was intrigued by the dress. It did not seem to be made of any cloth that she was familiar with. It was soft and finely stitched. The neckline was embroidered with green thread in a tiny leaf pattern, and the hem was embellished with a zigzag pattern in variegated colors. Anya removed the muslin covering from her hair and pulled the dress on over her head, as there was no opening except for the neck. It was a tad too big and hung nearly to the floor, but she immediately felt its warmth and its smoothness against her bare skin. Anya ran her hands down her sides feeling the buttery softness of the material, still unsure as to what it might be made of. She saw that Sonia was watching her intently; tears formed in the old woman's eyes. Anya looked directly at Sonia and smiled. Sonia smiled back.

Using her walking stick, Sonia pulled herself up from her position in front of the box and went to the far side of the fireplace. There she removed a small pair of fur boots from their place on the floor. Sonia indicated that Anya should sit on the chair, and handed the boots to the child. Anya easily slipped into the too-big boots. The fur-crowned tops came well above her knees, but like the dress, they too were very warm. As Anya admired the clothing she had been given, Sonia began combing the long, wet, blonde locks that fell across Anya's shoulders. Soon they were plaited into a loose braid. Anya could not believe how wonderful she felt. She had not been this warm and comfortable in a very long time. She did not even feel the hunger that had been a constant companion for weeks. Sitting upon the hide on the floor, Anya closed her eyes and saw only her mother, in their home in Sofienthal. She was happy.

When she awoke, day had turned into night. She found herself curled up on the hide and covered with one of the wool blankets. The fireplace crackled and lit the room with an orange glow. Seeing the back of an old woman hunched over a kettle on the hearth, stirring its contents, Anya momentarily forgot where she was and cried out a startled "MAMA!"

The woman turned to face her. *This is not Mama!* Anya drew back against the wall in fear. The woman smiled and made soft shushing sounds. Gradually, Anya's memory of the morning and afternoon returned, and calmness swept over her. "Sonia," she said in recognition.

The woman smiled gently and softly spoke only one word, "Anya." Taking a cup from the sideboard and filling it with broth from the kettle, Sonia offered it to the child. Anya sat up, crossed her legs in the middle of the brown hide she had been sleeping on, and gladly took the cup and began to drink, but the dark brown broth was very hot. Pulling back for a second, Anya then blew across the surface of the broth cooling it slightly, as her mother had often shown her. Slowly and carefully sipping the contents, as it warmed her mouth and throat, she did not recognize the flavor or smell, but found it appealing. Anya looked up to see Sonia sitting in the chair next to the small table. She, too, had some of the broth, although hers was in a deep bowl and she sipped it from a carved wooden spoon.

Anya had barely finished the contents of her cup when she lay back upon the hide, pulled the blanket over her, and returned to a very deep sleep.

A shuffling noise, combined with the 'kerplunk' of a fresh log being put into the fireplace, awoke Anya from her dreams. Except for the renewed glow from the hearth, the room was still dark. Anya pulled the blanket tighter about her and lay watching, as Sonia lit the lantern and proceeded to start her day. Soon, however, Anya realized that she would have to get up and find a place to relieve herself. She quietly rose to her feet and neatly folded the blanket, placing it back upon the furry rug on which she had slept.

Sonia heard the rustling and turned to face the child. "*Dobry Utra*," she said quietly. Anya smiled and shrugged her shoulders to indicate that she did not understand the words. Sonia pointed out the window, "*Utra*" she repeated.

"*Utra?*" Anya questioned. *Did she mean outside, or darkness, or night? I wish I understood. I hope I can make her understand.*

"*Toilettenhäuschen?*" Anya asked. Sonia looked perplexed, so Anya stood with her knees together and placed her hand over her crotch. "*Toilettenhäuschen*" she repeated.

Sonia smiled, picked up a squat palm-sized candle from the sideboard and lit it with a small stick from the fireplace, then took Anya's hand and led her out the door to a tiny building behind the cottage. This little structure was weatherworn and in need of some repair, but Anya noted that it also sported the same ornate eave carvings and roof crest of the cottage. Sonia opened the narrow door and directed Anya to enter. "*Tualyet…tual…yet*," she pronounced slowly.

"*Tualyet!*" Anya repeated eagerly, "*tualyet*." Sonia nodded, handed Anya the brightly burning little candle and closed the door after Anya entered. Sonia waited for Anya to take care of herself then led the child back to the cottage.

As they approached the door Sonia stopped and faced the little log cabin, then lifted her arms over her head and spread them wide. "*Izby*," she declared.

"*Izby*," Anya again repeated the word Sonia used. "*Häuschen*," she returned in German.

Sonia nodded "*Häuschen*."

Once they returned to the warmth inside the cottage, Sonia prepared a light gruel for the two of them. Handing Anya a bowl of the gruel, Sonia said, "*Kasha*." Then pulling yet another small linen bag from her cupboard, Sonia placed it in a cup and dipped a ladle into the boiling caldron hanging over the fire. Steam rose from the ladle as she poured its contents into the cup. After a few seconds, the process was repeated with a second cup, but it was allowed to steep for a longer period of time. Sonia handed the first cup to Anya with the words "*gribnoy chay*." Anya accepted the cup of pale brown liquid and brought it up to her face. She inhaled deeply. She did not know what the substance was, but it smelled like the freshly-plowed dirt of their farm, mixed with the anise seed that her mother used when baking Christmas cookies. The child took a sip, and found the taste to be much like the mushrooms that her sisters often picked in the woods near their home. It felt good as it flowed into her empty stomach. She followed it with a spoonful of the pale-yellow gruel. Thinking, *this Kasha is alright, but it needs honey, Mama always gave us honey and fresh butter on our morning cereal;* Anya decided that she should eat whatever was offered, as there might not be another meal to follow if she did not.

By the time Anya finished her breakfast, the sky had faded into a pale gray, but the closeness of the large trees kept the cottage shrouded in their shadows, leaving her still unsure as to whether it was day or night. When Sonia completed her meal, she rose from her chair and filled a wash basin full of hot water. Washing her face and hands and arms, she then indicated for Anya to do the same. Anya followed Sonia's example, splashing the warm water across her face and rubbing her arms with her wet hands. Sonia smiled simply. Anya smiled back. Sonia gestured for Anya to sit in the chair. Once Anya was settled,

Sonia carefully undid what was left of the loose braid she had put in Anya's hair the night before and gently combed the long blonde locks. Anya enjoyed the attention. Sonia's gnarled hands had some difficulty hanging onto the hair, but she eventually got the braid tight enough to hold for the day. Once happy with the look of the braid, Sonia tied a bit of yarn at the end. She laid the comb on the table and began to wrap a scarf around her own hair.

Anya rose from the chair and touched Sonia's arm. When Sonia turned to inquire what the child wanted, she saw her standing behind the chair with the comb in her hand. Sonia placed the scarf on the table and sat upon the chair. Anya began to painstakingly unwind the hair that encircled Sonia's head, removing a few metal pins as she proceeded. The hair was thick and heavy, very unlike her own soft flighty tresses. She marveled at the way the snow-white frame around Sonia's face streaked into silver and finally black. When the bun was totally unwound, Anya discovered that Sonia's hair nearly reached the floor. She was amazed. *Mama's hair is the longest I have ever seen,* she mused, *but it only went to her waist. How can anybody's hair get so long? How old this woman must be to have hair like this.* Anya combed and combed and combed, until her arms were very tired. She did not think that she could braid this hair, so she began twisting it and wrapping it around Sonia's head, pinning it as she felt it was necessary. When she was done, the resulting bun hung slightly to the left, with some places loose and others quite tight. She stood in front of Sonia with a disheartened look upon her face as Sonia reached up and made a few adjustments. Then the wrinkles in Sonia's face deepened, nearly hiding her dark eyes, as she began to laugh. Anya thought Sonia must be laughing at her unsatisfactory efforts and began to cry.

"*Nyet, nyet*, little one, you must not cry. I laugh not at you, but at the joy of having you here." Sonia pulled Anya to her, hugging the child tightly. Again, Anya did not understand the words, but the warmth of this strange old woman conveyed all that needed to be said. Anya picked the headscarf up off the table and handed it to Sonia. This time they both laughed.

CHAPTER TWELVE

A Grave Discovery

"I need men strong enough to dig." The sergeant entered the doctor's office, pulled a cigarette from his jacket pocket and proceeded to light it with a match. He took a long draw, causing it to glow a bright orange. "How soon will these men be ready to work?"

"Some are ready now," the doctor said, as he removed his coat, and settled onto a tall stool in one corner of his office, which adjoined the infirmary where Johannes and the others had been taken. "How much digging do you expect them to do? Some are more able than others."

"That will depend on how many bodies we have to dispose of; to my knowledge there has been no official count, but most of the bodies will be small, so I do not foresee any huge amount of digging. But it must be done before the ground freezes for the winter, or we will be battling more than just the "German" wolves.

The doctor pulled a pipe from his pocket, and tapped it on the edge of the table placed along the wall next to him. He removed a small brown envelope from his breast pocket and scooped the pipe's bowl through the tobacco it held. Using his index finger he pushed the tobacco tightly into the pipe, then he took the sergeant's cigarette and touched it to the tobacco, puffing the pipe to life; a cloud of smoke partially obscured his face for a brief moment. "Yes, it must be done soon. I will make a list of the men who I think might be able to complete the task. I will have it ready by the forenoon."

The sergeant nodded, took another draw from the cigarette, and left the doctor to his responsibilities. Returning a few hours later, the sergeant picked up the list of names, gathered a few troops and headed for the infirmary.

Johannes watched from his bed as the doors opened and the soldiers filed in; the sergeant was the last to enter. The sergeant stood in the doorway perusing a piece of paper, then reached into his coat and pulled a pair of glasses from the inside pocket. Hooking the glasses' frames over his ears, he spoke loudly: "As I read your name, you will fall in line behind these soldiers. There will be no talking." The sergeant read name after name until he finally called out "Johannes Jahnle." Johannes quietly slipped from his bunk and walked across the room and stood behind the man that had been called before him. When the sergeant was satisfied that he had enough men to complete the job that was to be done, he signaled to the troops to lead the men out of the infirmary.

The men were marched in single file through the shipyard. Johannes realized that they were headed back the way they had come in a few days before. *Where are they taking us? Surely they are not taking us back to the train, and if so, for what purpose? Are they going to shoot us where we stand, or send us even farther from what is left of our families? Why will they not tell us what is going on?* Johannes' mind was full of questions, but he knew there would be answers only when his captors were ready to give them.

They approached the side of the train farthest from the village and were ordered to stop. They stood in silence for several minutes; the only sounds were some low-voiced mumblings among the guards. A large truck rumbled up behind them and came to a quick stop, nearly hitting the last man in the line; gravel-filled snow flew up around the wheels of the vehicle. Two more soldiers jumped out of the back of the truck and began throwing shovels out into the snow.

"Each of you will take a shovel and begin digging. I want a hole as wide and long as one of these boxcars, and as deep as a man is tall," the sergeant commanded.

One voice spoke out from the back of the line. "Are we digging our own graves? Are you going to shoot us and dump us into this hole?"

The sergeant smiled, then sneered, "If that is what you want, it can be arranged!"

One of the soldiers took a shovel and began to draw a line indicating the boundaries of the hole to be dug. Johannes stepped up and placed the tip of his shovel against the line; he braced his right foot against the top of the blade and pushed. There was a good deal of resistance before the blade broke through the surface into the top layer of the cold tundra. As the others joined him in his efforts, the hole began to take shape and slowly grew deeper. Johannes was feeling the effects of the lack of food, the lack of regular work, and residuals from the injuries that had been inflicted upon him at his inquisition. *I am not myself, if we were back on the farm, I would have no trouble digging this hole alone, yet now it is all I can do to lift this shovel full of soil,* he worried. *What will happen to me if I cannot complete this task? What other tasks are facing us? How soon will we be shot for not being able to do what is demanded of us? I should only be thinking of what is at hand presently. I know better than to let my mind drift into the unknown, it is not productive to let my mind wander. It is not within my military training to allow these thoughts. I must keep my mind centered...shovel in...shovel out...shovel in...shovel out...*

Johannes did not know how long he had been digging when one of the soldiers tapped him on the shoulder with the barrel of a rifle. "Leave the shovel and come with me," the soldier stated. Johannes dropped the shovel where he stood and followed the soldier to the front of the train. The engine stood like a silent iron giant, cold and severe in the afternoon's gray light. There, Johannes joined about a dozen others guarded by two additional soldiers.

"In groups of two, you will walk the length of this train and gather the bodies laying along-side the tracks," one of the soldiers commanded. "You will then take the bodies to the hole for burying. Use these sleds for transport." He pointed his rifle toward a small pile of boards and ropes.

Johannes stepped over and picked up one of the ropes attached to four wide flat boards roughly nailed together. Paul, the man he had befriended at the barracks, joined him, and they set off down the tracks past the engine and the coal car, dragging the sled behind them. They neared the first boxcar and it was soon apparent what bodies the soldiers had meant. Five small children, two of them tiny babies, lay in the mud and snow— still, cold, ashen. Neither man could prevent the tears that rolled down their cheeks and into their beards. Working in silence, Johannes and Paul carefully picked up the corpses and placed them on the sled. Other men moved past them and began picking up bodies further down the line. Johannes watched closely as each load heading back to the hole passed him; but he did not see any of his children on those sleds. *I can only hope they will not be among them, I must pray for their protection,* he thought. As he and Paul took each filled sled back to the hole, they watched in horror and sorrow as the children's bodies were thrown into it, like so much garbage. They knew their companions were under orders to work as quickly as possible, but they were not prepared for the seeming callousness of their fellow villagers.

As one frail boy's remains were tossed into the hole, Paul suddenly screamed "NO!" He followed the child's body into the hole and grabbed for it. "PAULY," he yelled as he reached for the body. "You can not have *my son!*"

"Get out of there now!" the soldier on the edge of the hole commanded. "GET OUT OF THERE, OR I WILL SHOOT YOU WHERE YOU STAND!"

Paul ignored the command as he cradled the child in his arms, sobbing uncontrollably. "No, no, not my Pauly. Oh, Pauly, what has happened to you? Why did you not go to the village? Where are your sisters? Oh, Pauly…" Paul's words came to an abrupt halt as a shot rang out. He stood like a statue; the child's body slowly fell from his grasp and back into the abyss. Paul started to turn, and looked up at the soldier standing on the rim of the massive grave. The soldier lowered his rifle as Paul collapsed and fell lifelessly into the same space where his child's body had just landed.

"Any more disobedience will be met with the same fate," the sergeant shouted to those who were waiting with their filled sleds at the edge of the hole. "NOW RETURN TO YOUR TASK!"

Johannes hung his head in despair, and pulling the sled, returned alone to the boxcars. He had to travel more than half the length of the train before coming to two more dead children. As he prepared to lift the first child onto the sled, something caught his eye. He had seen

many items in the snow today, bits and pieces of the people who had
been forced onto this train, but here was something he had not seen
before. A black leather-bound *Bible* lay spread open in the snow, its
pages ruffling in the breeze. Johannes picked it up and shoved it into
the waistband of his pants. *I feel like a common thief,* he thought, *but this
is something I cannot leave behind. I will put it to good use; I must put it to
good use.*

"What are you up to?" A patrolling soldier had seen Johannes leave
the sled and came to see why.

"I thought there was another body here," Johannes responded, "but
it was just this piece of cloth." He kicked at a bit of black fabric that
lay in the snow.

"Umm," the soldier muttered. "Just keep to your job."

"Yes sir," Johannes replied. He picked up the remaining child and
placed him on the sled. His heart pounded. He could feel his face flush
hotly with the adrenaline that rushed through his veins, feeling the
presence of the Bible in his waistband. Continuing down the length of
the train, glancing briefly between the cars as he went, Johannes' attention was momentarily drawn to a fire smoldering at the edge of the
woods. *Looks like it might have been a small cabin of some sort,* he thought
in passing, *it is no concern of mine.* Johannes worked alone, loading the
bodies of six more children onto his sled. He began his trek back to the
mass grave, he proceeded more slowly than before, as the ground had
become sodden under the repeated traversing of the loaded sleds, and
now his sled bogged down under the weight of the bodies. The wind
began to blow cold air off the sea, and Johannes dropped his head for
protection and leaned into it, pulling with his remaining strength even
though his feet were soaked and numb, his hands cramped around the
rope.

As the sun set on the village, Johannes finally reached the front of
the train; turning to cross the tracks, he slipped on the ice-coated rail.
The sled stopped fast, catching on the lip of the tie-plate holding the
rails together. Johannes strained against the rope, but the sled would
not budge. He gathered the rope into his frozen hands and tried to

lift the end of the sled over the rail, but he was unable to get a solid enough stance on the wet ground. Finally he reached down, planning on lifting the edge of the makeshift sled up onto the rail. As he bent over, the Bible slipped out of his waistband and fell down the inside of his pant leg, dropping into the snow at his feet. He quickly stole a look around him to ascertain the whereabouts of the soldiers, not realizing one had come up behind him.

"What have you got there?" the soldier demanded.

Johannes jumped with surprise at the man's voice. A lump wedged firmly in Johannes' throat; he thought he might vomit from the fear that welled up inside him. He could hide it no longer, so he picked the Bible up out of the snow and carefully, reluctantly, handed it to the soldier.

"Where did you get this?"

Johannes hung his head; he wanted to disguise his fear, but it was shame that overwhelmed his being. "I found it while loading bodies, sir," his voice hoarse and shaking.

"Why did you take it? Do you plan to sell it somehow? Are you a thief?"

"No, sir, I only intended to use it to comfort the souls of these children."

"Comfort! COMFORT? How can these rotting corpses be comforted? You kulaks all think that the world will be comforted if you pray and read your Bibles. If you wish to pray —pray to Stalin, he is your god now. He is your savior and salvation." The soldier sniggered as the words traversed his lips; he began ripping the pages from the book's bindings and scattering them about. When he was satisfied that he had destroyed this instrument of derision, he stepped over and kicked the corner of the sled with his heavy black boot. The body of a tiny girl, maybe around the age of three, rolled off the pile and into the mud.

The disrespect of the soldier set Johannes' inner being into a boiling rage, and he could contain himself no longer as the fear and exhaustion turned to anger. "Savior and salvation?" The words seethed through Johannes' teeth. "You dare call Stalin a god? He is no more than a criminal, excised from his church and exiled. Were it not for the gullibility of the communists who elected him to office and the death of Lenin, he would be nothing more than a third-class secretary. Can you not see what is happening around you? This land is becoming a nation of slaves to your 'god' Stalin. There will be no salvation under his hand—only death and destruction. Maybe the German army that you fear is the *real* salvation. I hope Stalin suffers his fate as he has made us suffer!"

"Shut your mouth you German dog! Shut it now or I will shut it forever!" The soldier raised his rifle to Johannes' chest. Johannes grabbed the barrel and jerked the rifle from the soldier's hands. Even though taken by surprise, the soldier quickly reacted, grabbing hold of the rifle's stock. The two men fought for control of the weapon. Johannes managed to get both hands on the barrel, his numb fingers gripping as tightly as they could. Mustering all the strength he had, Johannes wrenched the gun completely away from the soldier, but his weak, tired, frozen fingers could not maintain their grasp. While the rifle flew through the air, Johannes tried to regain his grip; he felt the sharp curve of the trigger momentarily hanging on the end of his index finger. An explosive crack reverberated through his chest and filled his ears. Pain swept through his head, splitting his brain, as if his skull was being crushed from every direction. His hands flew up over his ears and he dropped to the ground in agony, steel and earth and bone and tissue coming together and ripped apart—all at the same time. Blackness enveloped him, and with the blackness, peace.

Pale light filtered into his thoughts, but the ringing in his ears drowned out all external sound. Slowly, deliberately, he opened his eyes. *Where am I?* he wondered, *am I dead or alive?* He tried to raise his head, but the pain slammed into him, and he knew that any movement would only intensify his agony. He lay still, trying to get his bearings. He was on his stomach, the crusty stickiness of dried blood tightened his cheek, he was on something softly lumpy and yet hard. He was cold. He could not remember how he got here; he did not even know where "here" was. Time passed. Twilight emerged. Slowly, ever so slowly, Johannes finally raised his head enough to look about him. Snow fell from his face. Reality jolted his consciousness and his stomach churned in revulsion.

The truth of his situation made him want to get up and run, run as far away from this place as he possibly could, but he was unable to go anywhere. The intense agony that ripped through his head with each change in his position caused an overwhelming, nauseating spinning of the world about him. *I cannot stay here. I cannot lie upon the bodies of the children. I must get out of this grave. Why am I even here?*

He managed to bring his right arm up and brace it against the body under him. His arm tingled with numbness as the blood began to flow back through his veins. Slowly he drew his left arm into the same position and pushed, but there was no strength in his left arm. His hand slipped out from under him, and his body rolled over the dead children, lodging him against the edge of the dirt chasm. His head again exploded in pain; he closed his eyes until the world stopped spinning. With a great effort, he managed to sit up with his back against the dirt wall. As he fought the weakness that flowed over him, he considered his condition. *Why am I here?* He remembered the fight with the soldier and the gun going off. *Am I shot? Where? My head?* He reached up and felt around his skull, but found no open wound, just the blood running from his previously damaged ear. *Did the soldiers think they killed me? Was I left for dead? Is that why I am here?* He closed his eyes against the horror that lay before him, and eased his head back against the cold dirt. *Why did they leave this pit of bodies open? Was it because night came upon them, and they could no longer see to work? Can I get myself out of this? If I do, where will I go? How long will I have before I am caught? It will be daylight soon and the soldiers will return. If I am going to leave it must be now.*

He turned himself around and rose up on his knees to determine how far up he would have to climb. He was amazed that the top edge of the hole was barely above his head. He lifted himself up far enough that he could hook his elbows over the top edge of the soil berm and supported his weight while he positioned his feet under him. He again momentarily closed his eyes against the pain and whirling in his head. The pain masked the numbing coldness that enveloped the remainder of his body. He pulled himself over the edge and onto the muddy embankment. He lay on his stomach and looked around him. Snow began to fall. He spied the smoldering building in the distance. *If I can make it that far, at least I will have warmth.* The elusive feeling of comfort overrode any rationale of his thoughts.

He managed to get to his feet, but he could not stand erect without becoming sick. He slumped over and with his knees bent, began to move as quickly as he could toward the forest's edge and the pile of ashes. He had just reached the first of the large evergreen trees when the wet Siberian sky unleashed its fury on the landscape around him. The cold drenching rain soon turned to heavy wet snow, obliterating muddy trails and obscuring the bodies in the grave.

Johannes sought protection amongst the exposed roots of a large tree, pulling damp needles about him, and sat silently, waiting. He closed his eyes. *No! I do not want to sleep. I must watch for the troops that will surely be looking for me. Scriptures. Maybe if I recite scriptures.* But his mind seemed to play tricks on him. He could not think of any specific verse, only a jumble of bits and pieces of many, like the shredded pages of the Bible that the soldier destroyed. Before long, his damaged and exhausted body overpowered his vulnerable common sense and he drifted into oblivion.

CHAPTER THIRTEEN
Russian Salvation

A cherub in the forest gazed upon him…he was floating…a woman's hands touched his face…a child's voice…warmth. Johannes was aware of fleeting moments as he faded in and out of consciousness. When the cloudy murk cleared from his head, he opened his eyes upon a small but cozy room.

"Mama, I think the sailor is awake." The voice came from a little girl standing near him. The words were barely audible, though she appeared to be speaking loudly. Johannes closed his eyes briefly as his brain labored at trying to make sense of the words, muffled and foreign, and yet he understood their meaning.

A woman appeared. She reached out and placed a hand on his forehead, checking for fever. Johannes felt the cracked dryness of her skin, rough and work-worn, as she tenderly brought her hand under his chin and rolled his head, exposing his right ear.

"Can you hear me?" she asked.

He looked upon her face in silence, still processing what was going on around him. Her voice was more clearly heard than the child's had been. With effort, he slowly nodded in acknowledgement. She again turned his head, exposing his damaged ear this time, and repeated her inquiry. "Can you hear me?"

He saw her lips move, but no sound came from them. She shook her head sympathetically, and looked into his eyes. "I thought so. Your ear was bleeding heavily when we found you. Do you know what happened to you?"

Johannes turned his head so he could hear her words, but he was still not sure why they were not clear in his mind. He tried to remember where he was. He looked at the woman, but did not recognize her. She was small and dark, and slouched under the weight of her heavy black dress and apron, no resemblance at all to his Katerina. *Where is Katerina?* he wondered with uncertainty, *who is this woman? Why am I having such trouble understanding her words?* He closed his eyes again; he was tired and trying to think exhausted his frail body. He listened to the voices around him, *a girl-child, two young boys and the woman,* he decided. *I must be in their house, but why and where is this place? How did I get here? What happened to me? Remember, I must remember...* The voices lulled him into sleep.

Happy children were playing in the snow, laughing, running, energized with the coolness of the white flakes that filtered from the sky...floating in the air, then falling to the ground motionless, suddenly a great chasm opens, swallowing the children as they fight to climb out....

Johannes awoke with a start, sweating and his heart pounding. He tried to sit up, to escape the visions in his head, but he only managed to roll weakly onto his side. The room was quiet and dark, except for a small candle glowing faintly in the far corner. He could see a woman sitting in a chair next to a small iron stove; her hands resting on her lap held a bit of fabric that she had been sewing, and her head drooped onto her chest as she dozed. Johannes watched in silence, again trying to make sense of where he was. Slowly he began remembering: the soldiers coming to his farm, sending his eldest son Jakob off to Odessa, the journey north by wagon, the death of baby Rosina, the interrogation and beating, then the overcrowded train, their arrival near the White Sea and the separation from his family, and the sleds full of children's bodies as they were dumped into the mass grave, and lastly the struggle with the soldier and the rifle firing.

Russian, the woman is speaking Russian! Johannes realized. *She may not know I am German. Is that why she took me in? Will soldiers be coming for me? I wish I knew.* He rolled over onto his back again and stared into the darkness. *Silence is my best friend for now,* he rationalized. He was unable to return to sleep; his mind replayed the events of the past few months over and over again. He heard the woman stir and saw her getting up from her chair.

"You are awake," she said as she gently wiped tears from his face with her apron. "You must be remembering what happened to you."

He turned his head away from her and closed his eyes against the reality of his life, hoping, praying it would all go away.

"It is alright, sleep, regain your strength, then we will see what must be done with you," she whispered, but he did not hear her.

Before daylight emerged through the small window over his head, Johannes heard the children up and about. A lamp had been lit and was sitting on a large table in the center of the room. He watched as one of the boys—about ten, Johannes surmised—stoked the fire in the wood stove. The other boy, slightly older, came in the door with a large bucket of water and poured some of it into a kettle on the stove. The girl, maybe five or six, appeared at Johannes' bedside and peered closely into his face.

"Mama, he is awake again!" she shouted at him. He made an effort to smile at her and started to reach for her hand, but she pulled away frightened by his movement.

"Katya, leave him alone." The woman grabbed the child by the arm and pulled her back. "Eat your breakfast so you can help your brothers." The little girl joined the boys at the table and began eating from the steaming bowl that awaited her.

"If you are up to it, I think you should eat, too." The woman handed him a cup that contained a bit of boiled cereal. "I have tea, as well, if you would like." She placed another cup on the floor, next to the bed.

Johannes braced himself with his hands and lifted up into a semi-sitting position in the bed. He placed a spoonful of the hot cereal into his mouth and let it dissolve on his tongue. Though bland in flavor and thin in texture, the cereal was appreciated. He watched as the children quickly devoured their share along with the small biscuits that the woman gave each child. She placed several more of the biscuits into a small cloth sack, tied it with a piece of twine and handed it to the oldest boy.

"You will be on your own again today," she told her children. "I expect that the visitor should be up and about by tomorrow, and then I can come with you." The oldest boy nodded, put a heavy coat on his little sister, tying it at the waist with a piece of rope, and donned his own coat. The younger boy was already out of the door. When the children were gone, she came back to Johannes and took the empty cup from his hand.

"The children have gone to gather wood in the forest, which is how we make enough money to live on. I also take in sewing, repairing uniforms for some of the Norwegian sailors that come into the port with the big ships. My daughter thinks you are one of those sailors because of your white clothing. I am not sure. The material is much like the uniforms that I repair, but it is made differently. Are you Norwegian?"

Johannes looked into the woman's dark eyes as he decided how he should answer this question. He chose to remain silent, nodding as if he did not fully understand her words.

She shrugged and began to turn away, but suddenly her eyes narrowed and she blurted out, "Are you a kulak?"

Johannes could not let this question go unanswered. He looked into the woman's piercing dark eyes, "No, I am Russian like you." His voice was barely audible, hoarse and frail, as he had not spoken in several days, but she heard every word. She considered his whispering a feeble attempt to conceal the strange accent she thought she perceived.

"Where do you come from?" The curtness in her voice revealed her misgivings about bringing this man into her home.

"I am from an area near the Black Sea, in the southern part of Russia." His voice was getting stronger, but so was his accent, something he could not control no matter how hard he wished he could.

"You do not speak like any Russian I have known," she retorted.

"Nor do you," he responded.

"What do you mean? I was born and raised right here in *this* house! I can be nothing else but a Russian!"

"As am I," he managed a slight smile. "I, too, was born and raised in Russia, on the land of my father and his father. I am merely a farmer from another part of Russia, but I am very much Russian."

"I am not sure that I believe you. I have heard that kulaks have been brought from the South and put to work in the sawmill and shipyard. How do I know that you are not one of them? Will soldiers come and beat down my door looking for you?"

Johannes shrugged and asked. "What is a kulak?"

She looked at him in amazement, "You say you are Russian, but you do not know what a kulak is?"

"I have heard the term many times, but no one has ever explained it to me."

"They are the wealthy German land-owners that have invaded the south; they are rebellious and want to rule Russia, taking away all our rights as Russian citizens!" The tone of her voice raised in fear and dread at the thought that she might lose what she now had.

Johannes quickly realized the necessity of calming this woman's fears and doubts if he was to remain free of the soldiers' rifles. Should he speak the truth of his plight? How much should he tell this stranger if he was to remain out of the hands of the Soviets? He dropped his head in sadness, "The only wealth I have ever known has been my family. The love of my wife and children were everything to me, and now they are all gone and I have nothing."

"What has happened to your family?"

"I do not know for sure, but I believe they are all dead. Our village was raided by the NKVD, and my family was separated. I have had no contact with any of them. I can only assume they are all gone."

She seemed to understand his loss and let her guard down. She drew closer to him. "Why are you here?" she asked. "Why were you beaten and left for dead? Will the soldiers or the NKVD come for you?"

"I really do not know. I remember being taken to the infirmary at the shipyard, then crawling through the forest. I do not know anything else." He wanted to end this conversation before he said something he should not. "My head hurts. There is a constant whine in my ears." He placed a hand over his left ear, grimaced in pain, and lay back down on the bed.

She removed the tea cup from the floor and stood looking down on him. The taut lines in her face had softened with his story, but now worry began to take hold.

"I am a widow," she said. "My husband worked in the sawmill, it was good work, we lived well. Then one day a blade broke, cutting him deeply. He died of infection two weeks later. That was winter before last. I was left with the children to feed, so I began sewing for others and making a few rubles. But the soldiers arrived and brought the kulaks to work in the sawmill, taking the jobs from the villagers. Now no one can afford new clothes, so I sew for the Norwegian sailors, but it is not steady work. Gathering wood for the fires of those that cannot gather for themselves is our only other source of money to live on. I cannot afford to feed you for long, nor can I allow the soldiers to take me away for harboring a runaway."

"I am not a runaway. The soldiers may not be looking for me as I believe they think I am already dead. They have no time to hunt down an injured sailor, Norwegian or Russian. Besides, if I were a sailor, I could no longer sail, not with these ears, as I will have no balance and will only be sick all the time. I am useless to them. Please let me stay, at least for awhile, I will earn my keep, you will see."

"I am not sure I trust you. How do I know you speak the truth? How do I know the soldiers will not come? How will I protect my children?"

"Have faith and take a chance, or hand me over to the soldiers, the choice is yours. That is all I can offer right now."

"*Faith?* You use that word rather boldly. Do you have faith? Are you religious? Do you dare worship under the noses of the NKVD? Or are you a plant, here to undermine the beliefs of our village and those who still prefer to pray? Oh, God Almighty, what have I done? What terror have I wrought upon my children?" She began to sob as she dropped to her knees, clasping her hands in forgiveness.

"No, wait! I *am* a man of faith! I have not been sent here to cause you harm. Faith and belief in God have been the foundation upon which my family has always lived. I was a soldier in the White Army; I fought so that we could keep our faith...." Johannes stopped abruptly, hoping he had not said too much. She was possibly testing him; *she* could be an agent of the NKVD. His hands began to sweat. He nervously smoothed the blanket that lay over him in an attempt to dry his palms, but the tell-tale redness could not be hidden.

She quieted, but did not rise. He could see her lips moving in quiet prayer. She reached into a pocket in her apron and brought forth a strip of leather. A gilt-edged triangle at each end of the strip, and tiny tight knots formed the body of the leather rope. She thrust it towards Johannes, "Recite your prayers; I want to hear you pray!"

Johannes did not take the *lestovka* from her. "I am not Orthodox, I am Evangelical. I will pray with you, but we recount the prayers we know, or read from the Bible, we do not chant the Rosary."

"Then convince me that you know something of the Bible, convince me that you are a religious man. Make me believe that I have not erred in my judgment by bringing you here."

Johannes paused for a moment then began, "There hath no temptation taken you, but God is faithful, who will not suffer you to be tempted above that ye are able; but will the temptation to the end of profits, that ye may endure."

She was not totally convinced, "Book and chapter?' she asked.

"1 Corinthians 10:13."

She thought for a moment, "Now I will pick one. What does Mark 12:30 say?"

Johannes hesitated briefly, "And thou shalt love the LORD thy God with all your heart, and with all thy soul, and with all thy mind, and with all thy strength. That is the great commandment." ... As we are discussing strength, I have another that might give you reassurance, Psalm 27:1... 'The Lord is my light and my salvation; Whom shall I fear! The Lord is the strength of my life; of whom shall I be afraid!"

"Your words are similar to those I am familiar with, but they differ," she still doubted this man.

"I quote from the Bible of Martin Luther; it is the one from which I was taught. As I said previously, I am not Orthodox, my people are Evangelicals."

The straightforwardness in his words bolstered her confidence and eased her anxiety; maybe she had not made a bad choice after all. Maybe he would be as helpful as he promised.

"I am Elena," she introduced herself.

"Yanochan," he answered, using his best Russian translation.

CHAPTER FOURTEEN

...And Fear Ran Beside Her

As fall iced over into winter, the women of the lumber camp grew accustomed to their fate. Their hands became calloused and hard as they wielded their axes and drew their saws. Days started early. They were awakened at six every morning to the clanging of a railroad spike pounding against a piece of iron, and the incessant yelling of *"Davai! Davai!* Come on, Come on!" Their morning rations of gruel and bread were found at the door to their barracks by the time they were up. At seven, they were expected to be assembled for roll call, standing in the cold darkness in front of their buildings, ready to return to the forest.

"Karolina, eat your bread, you cannot live just on the gruel," Katerina said to her eldest daughter as she saw the bread disappear into a pocket.

"I will be fine, Mama. The bread is for Boris. He is much like old Hans, he loves when I bring him a treat, and I think he works harder because of it."

"Oh Karolina, I might have known it was for that horse. What is it with you and horses? You should not deny yourself, especially for a horse that does not belong to you."

Karolina had grown to love this horse. She devoted extra time to him each morning and evening brushing his thick brown coat. She spoke only kind words to him and slipped him a bit of bread when she could. He returned her kindness with a welcoming nicker each morning when she entered the barn. Karolina knew she could not make her mother understand. When she was with Boris, nothing else mattered. With him pulling in front of her, the endless hours of hard labor quickly passed

Karolina shrugged. "Mama, does it really matter? Boris and I bring in more logs than any of the other teams, and I think he puts more of his heart into the work because I treat him well. He helps me earn enough extra *Toloni* to feed us. Without him, Magdalena would not eat."

Katerina could not disagree. While Magdalena had recovered physically from her incident in the forest with Ivan, she had become more reticent. She worked only enough to satisfy the soldiers. Ivan hung around Magdalena on a frequent basis. Often standing with his hands buried deep into his pockets, he would laugh maliciously when she could not, or would not, complete her work of stripping the trees. He seemed to thoroughly enjoy her emotional breakdowns, taunting her when she wept openly out of frustration, helplessness or anger, driving her deeper into the depression that had engulfed her fragile psyche. His favorite taunt was threatening her with time in the "detention chamber."

All of the women had been shown this horrible little stone building on the outskirts of the compound. Barely big enough for a large dog, its cement floor retained a permanent pool of black slimy water that reeked of the rotted straw that had been placed within for bedding. As they were each shown the inside, Ivan announced "If you do not work to your quotas you will spend your time in here!" Quotas were not made known, and more than one woman spent a night in this place, and the stories they told were enough to keep the workers on task. Some women had not returned from the chamber, and their whereabouts were still unknown.

Katerina tried every way she could to protect her daughter. She feared Ivan's intentions toward her thirteen-year-old. "Magdalena is too young for you," she told him. "She is not ready to become a woman!"

"And what will you give me to leave her alone?" he asked.

"You know I have nothing to give you. No...wait...," Katerina retrieved her precious jar of pickled watermelon rind. "This is all I have; take it and leave us alone, *please!*" Katerina's bribe seemed to have worked. Ivan had not bothered Magdalena for about a week.

However, today, at the end of roll call, Ivan singled out Magdalena.

"Since you do not seem to like working in the forest, I have a special job for you." He reached out and took her arm, pulling her out of line.

"Leave her alone! You promised!" Katerina yelled.

"Do not worry, woman. I am only putting her to work in another part of the compound. She is going to be tending the sheep in the barns. She will be back tonight." Ivan growled as he carted Magdalena away.

Ivan led her through the compound and across a field to a large barn. The big double door was closed tight against the cold. He eased one side open enough for entry, and pushed the reluctant Magdalena inside. The interior of the barn was dimly lit with lanterns that hung from overhead beams. Her first sensation was of the warmth that was held in by the high wooden walls. Sheep bleated at their arrival, and Magdalena saw that beyond the row of empty horse stalls, low-fenced pens were filled with thickly-wooled ewes, many heavy with their unborn lambs. In one corner a large brown ox stood tied to a ring in the wall.

"Your new job is to take the sledge that sits outside and hook it to that ox. Then you will go out into the field, load hay on the sledge and bring it in to feed these sheep. The sheep belong to the Commandant, and he wants all his ewes to lamb easily before spring. They will only do that if they are properly fed. Do you understand?"

Magdalena nodded her head.

Ivan turned to leave, and then sneered, "I will be watching you."

When Ivan was gone, Magdalena cautiously made her way to the ox. She murmured unintelligible words to him, reaching towards him with her hand outstretched. She had never encountered an ox before. She had grown up with a family cow, but this ox was much larger than Ilse had been. He stood with his head down, his huge black eyes watching her. He did not move when she placed her hands on his shoulder. *This might be easy*, she thought. *I can do this.* She untied the beast from the wall and led him outside. He stood while she placed a hayfork into the back of the massive sledge. She fitted the yoke over his neck, and placed the leather britchen harness about his rump. Finally, she attached the reins and pulling chains to the rings at either end of the yoke arch, and attached the trailing ends of the chains to the sledge. She asked him to move forward, but he just stood. She tried slapping him with the lead rope, but he only shook his head. The temperature was dropping. "It will be snowing soon," she hollered at him. "We have to get going now!" But the animal refused to move. Out of desperation she hit him with a stick she found along the edge of the barn.

The ox gave a loud bellow. She hit him again, harder, irritated at his stubbornness and that he would keep her out in the cold unnecessarily. The ox bellowed again then took off at a run. The suddenness of his movement caught Magdalena off guard, and she fell into the tracks left by the sledge as it trailed behind the ox. She watched helplessly as the ox loped through the field, head and tail held skyward. The sledge overturned and began dragging in the snow-covered hay stubble, slowing the ox. Soon the sledge became so heavy with accumulated snow that the ox had to stop. Magdalena jumped to her feet and ran to the now exhausted bovine. She got down on her knees and used her hands to clear snow from the sledge; bracing her shoulder against its flat surface, she was able to upright the device. She untangled the reins from around the animal's legs and turned him toward the haystack at the edge of the field.

"Now, maybe you will work," was all she said to him.

When she got to the hay, the huge stack loomed over her head. It was covered in snow and she had to dig through the crust to get to the fodder beneath. Realizing that the hayfork was no longer on the sledge where she had placed it, she turned to look across the field. She threw her hands up into the air, then dropped them down to her sides in disgust, as she headed down the track back toward the barn. While she was gone, the ox grazed on the hay that had been cleared of the snow. Returning with the hayfork in hand, she began loading hay onto the sledge. The feed was very heavy, as it was wet from the moisture of the snow. This would have been difficult labor for a grown man, yet this small girl worked and struggled until the sledge was nearly full. The short northern day quickly turned to night before she made it back to the barn. The sheep were restless, milling about the stalls, waiting to be fed. She struggled to open the barn's door wide enough to allow the ox to pull the sledge inside. As she was closing the door, Ivan appeared in the opening.

"What took you so long?" he bellowed. "These sheep should have been fed hours ago. Now they are upset and restless. Do you want them to loose their lambs? The Commandant will have me whipped if these ewes loose their lambs! Is that what you want? You know you will get twice what I get, do you not? I think I will have to teach you how to work harder and faster!" he snarled.

Magdalena shrank from his presence and tried to get out of his way. She still did not fully understand his Russian, but she got most of the meaning. He grabbed her and threw her to the ground. She started to scream, but choked it back. "The sheep still need to be fed," she cried. "I must feed them or you will be blamed."

He stopped short and thought for a moment. He calmed himself. "Yes, you are right, little one," his voice had become eerily quiet and gentle. "See that they are fed as quickly as possible." He turned and left the barn with no further comment.

Magdalena was not sure what he wanted from her, but she could plainly see he was up to something. She unharnessed the ox and tied him in his stall, gave him a bucket of water and placed hay in his manger. Next, she fed the sheep as quickly as she could, intent on getting back to the barracks and her mother's protection. She left the barn and began racing down the lane to the compound as if fear was running beside her. Tears streaking her face turned to ice as they reached her chin. The frigid night air felt like splinters lodging in her lungs as she tried to breathe. She thought she heard the ground pounding behind her, but she did not stop to look.

"Stop! Stop now!" Ivan's voice penetrated the pounding of her heart in her ears. The pounding, the pounding, the rhythmical pounding, he is *on horseback*! She felt him grab her arm as he galloped past, dragging her off her feet. He reined his horse right and turned back toward the barn. She struggled, trying to grab him with her free arm. He lost his grip, dropping her into the snow. She managed to get to her feet and began running toward the nearest building. He yanked his horse, turned around and came up behind her, grabbing her long blond hair. She felt pain in the back of her head as she again lost her footing. He dragged her along the rutted roadway until her arms and legs were a bloody pulp; she tried to scream but the cold air froze in her throat. He rode back through the hay field and let go of her half way across. The bed of nails formed by the frozen stubble pierced through her skin, but she did not feel it. She lay covered in blood. Ivan began to ride off, but she managed an agonizing moan. He rode back and forced his horse to step across her mangled body. "I hope this time you have learned your lesson. You will not cause me further trouble, you little kulak monster!" He rode away, a tuft of blonde hair still in his fist.

Katerina paced the barracks. "Where is she? Where is Magdalena?"

"She will be back soon, you will see," Sofia tried to comfort her friend as best she could.

Katerina continued to fret, and by bedtime she was frantic. "I must go find her. I have to find her!" she cried.

"You know we cannot leave the barracks, you will be shot in your tracks. She will come," Sofia insisted.

"Mama, please. You must get some rest, or you will not be able to work tomorrow. Then what? Magdalena is likely sleeping with the sheep, she will be fine." Karolina did not believe her words, but she had to try to console her mother.

Just as they were about to turn out the lanterns, Ivan stormed into the room and sought out Katerina. "Your lazy child did not complete her task," he bellowed. "She has been sent to the detention chamber until further notice." He left as quickly as he came. No questions asked, no answers given.

Katerina cried uncontrollably all night. In her heart, she knew she would never see her daughter again; if she was not already dead, she soon would be. All the women in the barracks grieved the loss of another child. Inside the barracks they prayed loudly. Outside, the snow fell in silence.

CHAPTER FIFTEEN

What Is in a Name?

Ten-year-old girls need mothers, or at least mother-figures in their lives. As a result, Anya quickly formed a deep connection to Sonia. As the winter deepened, Sonia patiently taught Anya many things, things a child should know, as well as many things the average child would never know. Anya was a willing student and quick to learn. Through trial and error, she learned much Russian, so that conversation with Sonia had become commonplace. In addition, Sonia made an effort to learn German from Anya, which pleased the child and increased her admiration of this grandmotherly spirit in her life.

One early morning, Anya was helping prepare dough for the heavy black bread Sonia baked weekly. As Anya mixed the rye flour and dark syrup, she seemed deep in thought.

"Sonia?"

"Yes, child."

"Would it be alright if I called you Oma?"

"I do not know what Oma means, but it sounds nice. Why do you wish to call me something other than my name?"

"My Mama always called her mother Oma; I think it means mother's mother. When I think of my Oma, it is your face that I see."

Sonia smiled at the thought that Anya wanted her to become part of her family. "I think that is a very good idea, especially if Oma is easier for you to remember than Sonia. I like Oma. Please tell me about your Oma."

Anya's face clouded slightly, "Well," she began, "I really do not remember much about her. She lived many kilometers from our farm with my Uncle Heinreich. It is he who one of my brothers was named after. Mama mostly went to visit by herself, leaving us children with Papi to take care of the farm. One time that I remember though, Oma came to stay with us for a month. She baked with Mama every day. And she brought wonderful gifts, like *Halva* and olives."

"I know what olives are," Sonia interrupted, "but I am not familiar with…what did you call it again?"

"*Halva*. It is sweet and smooth, kind of like cheese and yet different. It would crumble in your hand. Some of it also had green nuts in it, so it was crunchy. Oma said it came from Turkey and was made with ground-up seeds. I do not know about that; I just know how good it tasted."

"Well, if it was made of seeds and nuts, it must have been wonderful!" Sonia smiled as she took a large handful of dough from the curing bowl and kneaded it into the mixture Anya had prepared. "There, we will have to wait for this dough to rise; we might as well have some tea, and you can tell me more about your Oma."

Anya went to the cupboard near the sink and pulled two brownish-grey cups from the shelf. They were made of heavy crockery clay, like the bowls in which they were using to make the bread dough. Sonia removed a packet of herbs from a small tin, placed a bit in each cup and poured boiling water from the kettle over the leaves. From a plate on the counter, Sonia selected a few spice cookies she had taught Anya how to bake earlier in the week and laid them on the table. Once settled in their chairs they waited for the tea to steep and cool sufficiently to drink.

"Oma was old, like you…" Anya began again, "And she had trouble walking, also like you. But when she came for a visit last spring, she used two walking sticks, and she had trouble saying her words. Mama said it was a problem in her head, but I do not know what it was. I just know she was different, she did not do all the things with us that she had done before. Mama was very sad when Oma and Uncle Heinreich went home."

"And do you wish to call me Oma because I am old and do not walk as you? Or do you think I have something wrong with my brain?" Sonia teased.

"Oh, no!" Anya exclaimed. "I want to call you Oma because you smell like I remember her."

Sonia's dark eyes widened at this remark. "Smell? What do you mean by that?"

Anya closed her eyes as she thought about her Oma. "You know, it is a lot of things, warm bread, spicy cookies, the smoke of the cook stove and fireplace. Mama had it too, but hers had *baby* smells mixed in it." Anya wrinkled her nose at that idea. Then her face again started to cloud as she thought more about her Mama. "Do you think I will ever see my Mama again? Or my Papi, or any of the rest of my family? I was supposed to take care of my brothers when we were left at the train, but I came here with you. Do you think they are alright?"

"You told me that the soldier said he would look after your brothers and see that they were safe. I do not think you should worry about them. I do not know what to tell you about the rest of your family. I expect my son to come visit in a few weeks, maybe he can find out some things for you."

"Son?" Anya seemed startled at the idea that Sonia might have children of her own. "You have not mentioned a son before. Where is he, what is he like?"

Sonia sipped her tea, not responding to Anya's questions right away. She set the cup down and broke a bit of cookie off and placed it in her mouth before she spoke again. "My son is probably closer in age to your father than he is to you. He is married and has a family of his own. I have three grandchildren, all boys. However, I do not see them but maybe once every other year or so."

"Why?" Anya asked, her interest peaked by this revelation.

"Anya, you have willingly commented on my age and difficulties walking. You have commented on my "smell" and even my hair. But you have never mentioned that I do not look like you, nor do I look like most Russians."

Anya shrugged. "The only Russians I have seen have been the soldiers, and many of them were German like us. How are you different from 'most Russians'? I do not think I understand what you mean."

"I am very short, my eyes are not round like yours, and my cheek bones stick out. That is because I am not Russian; I am Selkup. My people are native Siberians; we were here before the Russians."

"But you speak Russian, and you live in a Russian village."

"Only out of necessity. When the Russians invaded our territory a few hundred years ago, our people were forced to learn to speak Russian and learn Russian ways. But we also maintain our native language and way of life. Our people are nomads. Do you know what a nomad is?"

"I think so. During harvest season the Romany people come to help us out. Papi called them nomads; he said it was because they wander all over the country and do not have houses and such."

"Yes, that is exactly what a nomad is. My people herd the reindeer and hunt and fish in the vast areas beyond the Ob River. We have few permanent villages; we take our homes with us when we travel. It is a hard life, but a good one. However, sometimes we have to find a situation that is not so hard. Then we settle in a permanent place, like this one. But my son and his family still follow the old ways, so I see little of them. My son comes twice a year to bring meat and fish to me. In turn, I gather and dry mushrooms and berries and leaves, and make tea and herb potions for him. These items are needed to keep his family healthy through the long dark winters. I also go to the village markets and make arrangements for other supplies that the clan might need. When he arrives he will be with about a dozen other men, and they will gather the needed supplies while Rodin comes to visit me."

"I have not heard that name before, is it Selkup? "

"Yes, dear, the Selkup language is part of the Samoyed people's language. The Samoyeds are a large group of many nomadic tribes that live all over Siberia, and all of our languages are a bit different, but we can understand each other. We name our children after that which we see around us. Rodin means 'Bright Flame.' He was born just as the sun was setting; it was a very brilliant orange, the color of a bright flame in the evening fire."

"Oh, that is a wonderful way to name a child. Anya does not mean anything. I was just named after my father's aunt."

"When the time is right, we will give you a Selkup name. But you will have to make that decision. You will have to find a name that pleases you and still describes who you are. You have an advantage in this way; babies can not chose their own names, and parents do not always know what the child will turn out to be. My 'Bright Flame' has done well to match his name. He has always been ready to help when needed, providing warmth and comfort to those around him."

"Yes, I would like to have a Selkup name. I want to think on this, and you will have to help me, because I will not know the word."

Sonia stood and stretched her back. "Time to bake the bread. Maybe we can call you baker. That would be *Peka'r*."

"No, I think I will find another name. But thank you anyway, Oma."

CHAPTER SIXTEEN

Ivan's Reprimand

"Ivan, report to the Commandant's office." The young soldier stood just inside the door of Ivan's meager quarters. Shifting the weight of the heavy rifle that hung in a sling over his shoulder, he turned and left the way he came. Ivan felt a twinge in his gut as he put his vodka glass on the table next to his bed.

"Now what," he grumbled to himself. Ivan donned his coat and followed the soldier out of the door, stomping through the snowy sludge of the compound to a concrete building on the far side of the square lot, where the soldiers sometimes practiced their drills. The snow had stopped falling, but the wind was blowing fiercely off the sea. The yellow glow of an electric light shone from a central window telling Ivan that the commandant was there and waiting. Knocking politely, Ivan slowly opened the door, "Comrade Commandant, you wish to see me?"

"Ivan, come in!" The commandant stood behind a work-worn desk, the gouges and scratches that appeared between the piles of scattered papers told of its many years of use. An old light bulb hung from an exposed ceiling wire, casting a murky ray over the room. He pointed to a plain wooden chair located in front of his desk, inviting Ivan to sit. Ivan settled his dark, heavy bulk onto the chair. The senior officer picked a folder up from the desk-top and began thumbing through its pages while he remained standing. "Ivan, your file states that you were sent to work for me from the Rostov prison, and you were sent there as punishment for crimes against young women in your village. Is that correct?"

Ivan's eyes focused on a chiseled notch in the otherwise simple square legs of the desk, "Yes, Commandant."

"And you were suspected in the mysterious disappearances of your sister and her schoolmate. But, since there were no bodies ever found, your suggestion that they ran off to Moscow to find rich husbands was accepted by the authorities. Is that right?"

Ivan nodded in response.

"You were sentenced to five years hard labor, but you were given the option to serve out your sentence here, under my command, in order to ease the burden on the prison system and leave more space for dissidents."

"Yes, comrade, that is true, but what is your interest in these matters now? Why am I here?" Ivan's agitation was becoming evident, and he glowered at the commandant as if to challenge his power.

The commanding officer slammed the file onto his desk. A man of medium build and obviously physically fit, his authority out-weighed Ivan's bulk, and there was no fear in his manner. He planted his palms on the desktop and leaned across the piles of papers toward Ivan. "My ewes have lost two more lambs this week! Do you understand what that means to me? Do you not understand why it is important to keep my ewes healthy and happy? These sheep are not just a fanciful dream; they are a road to success. If I can prove to my superiors that sheep can be kept and produced in this area, to feed and clothe the masses, to off-set the poverty and starvation of our people, then I will achieve great recognition. I have entrusted their care to you, because I thought you could manage this simple project, but what is happening to my ewes? Why am I losing their progeny before they are carried to proper term? How hard is it to feed and water these creatures, to keep them warm and happy?"

The parts of Ivan's face that could be discerned around the heavy beard were turning a deep red as his blood began a slow boil. "I keep assigning the task of feeding the ewes to the kulak girls who are not doing their part in the forest. But the lazy whelps do not seem to be able to handle even the easiest tasks."

"Well, maybe *that* is the problem!" The commandant's anger was becoming evident as his voice rose. "I gave this job to *you*, not those frail waifs that Central Command sends me to clear the forest! It was *you* I put in charge of the ewes' care, not the kulak girls...or *anyone else*!"

"But Commandant, my hands are full trying to get the women to meet the quotas in the forest. I do not have time to feed sheep." Ivan clenched his hands around the arms of the chair as he tried to control his anger.

"Yes, ...my guards tell me that the girls you take to tend the sheep have a tendency to disappear after a day or two in the barn. While no one has reported seeing anything suspicious, it is strange they just seem to vanish. Do they run off to find rich husbands, too?"

"No sir. When they do not complete their tasks with the sheep, I put them in the detention chamber for punishment, but these kulak weaklings do not have the wits to make it through one simple night."

"That may be, but I find it interesting that none of my men have seen any of these women or girls leaving the chamber –dead or alive – why is that?"

"I go to release them in the early morning, while *your men* are still chatting over their morning tea. The bits of flesh and bones I find are not worth feeding to the curs that roam the village streets."

"So where *do* they go?"

"In the sewage ditch behind the tool shed, for the rats to have their fill." Ivan bit his lip after he made this statement; he worried that he said too much and wondered where this conversation was leading.

The commandant sat down slowly and was silent for a few moments, contemplating what he was going to do about this situation. When he spoke it was with the coolness expected of a seasoned military commander. "Ivan, I need these ewes to produce as many lambs as possible. It is very important to me that they are cared for in the best possible manner. I am taking you off the forest detail. My soldiers can handle the women. You will be solely in charge of the ewes. And, I warn you that if there is more than ten-percent loss of the flock come spring, you will be returned to prison to complete your sentence. Do you understand?"

"But, Commandant, I was not sent here to..." Ivan's protest was quickly subdued.

"Would you rather go back to prison now?

"No sir! I will tend to the sheep as you wish."

"You are a wise man, Ivan. Now return to your quarters before I remove your privilege to roam the compound at will."

"Yes, Commandant," was Ivan's quiet response as he opened the door and stepped back out into the cold, dark night.

As the women lined up for roll call the following morning, the lack of Ivan's presence was quickly noted and became the topic of furtive glances and occasional murmuring among them. Little could be said as they stood trying to hold their ground against the icy wind that buffeted them, chilling them to the bones. The soldiers keeping the women in line, said nothing.

It had been two weeks since Magdalena's disappearance, and Katerina wondered if Ivan's absence was somehow connected. She knew that several other girls had also disappeared under Ivan's "personal attention," and she was torn between hoping that he was being punished and horrified that she would never know what really happened to her daughter.

Riding in the open wagons to the forest was especially difficult on this day, as the wind blew harder and harder. The women wrapped their faces and hands in whatever they had available to help prevent the frost bite that would eat away at any exposed area. Several women already suffered black noses and cheeks from poorly protected faces. Katerina and Sofia huddled together, their heads down, sitting on their hands, trying to keep the chill at bay.

They arrived in the clearing where they would begin the day's cutting, got down off the wagon and began their trek to their first tree. Katerina and Sofia kept shoulder to shoulder feeding off each other's strength as they trudged through the forest. Finally, Katerina braved the cold long enough to remove the length of cloth that covered her nose and mouth.

"Do you think I will ever know the truth about Magdalena? Will I ever know what happened to her?" Katerina whispered hoarsely.

Sofia stopped and faced Katerina; tears welled up in her pale blue eyes as she, too, removed her facial covering. "Katerina you are as close to me as anybody has ever been. You are friend, companion, partner and confidant. If we were sisters we could not be closer. So I feel you already know the answer to your question. The Soviets do not care about any of us, we will never know what has happened to our children or husbands or any of our people. Future generations will never know we even existed..." she paused and turned Katerina to face the path they had just traversed. The wind was blowing loose snow over their tracks. Sofia's voice trailed away as she continued, "we will all just vanish...*like footprints in the wind.*"

CHAPTER SEVENTEEN

An Uneasy Acceptance

"I want you gone as soon as the weather permits," Elena said one morning as she served Johannes a cup of tea. "You cannot hide in my house forever." She began clearing the children's breakfast bowls off the table and placing them in the wash pan. The fierce Siberian wind had stopped blowing, so she sent the children to gather wood.

"Yes, I agree," Johannes nodded slowly as he sipped the hot liquid. He had gained a little weight on Elena's meager servings of gruel and stew and bread, and his strength was returning, even if the hearing in his left ear was not. His relationship with Elena was tenuous, and though they lived under the same roof, no firm trust had yet developed between them; they were still very much strangers to each other.

"My neighbors will be wondering and gossiping, no doubt, about who you are and why you are here. The children have been warned not to speak of you, but Katya is still small and her mouth flows like the Ob River. But so far I have only heard her refer to you as 'the sailor'. That might be a good story to keep. This town is full of sailors and there are a number of houses that allow them to stay for room and board while they await loading or repair of their ships."

"If you are satisfied with that story, then I will accept it, as well. I may, after all, be such a sailor. I still remember little of what actually happened in the forest." Johannes regretted lying to Elena, but he could not allow her or anyone, to know the truth.

As the days passed, Johannes became restless. He was bored with being alone in the house day after day with nothing to do. He felt pangs of guilt for having to depend on Elena for his keep. Something was needed to occupy his hands and his mind; after all, he had always subscribed to the belief that "idle hands are the devil's workshop." He began to find small repairs that needed doing, things a husband would normally take care of in a house. Still, Elena had somehow managed to keep abreast of most of the repairs, so there was little for Johannes to fix.

One morning after Elena and the children left for their daily trek to gather wood in the forest, Johannes located a small knife in the cooking area. After sharpening the knife on the rock edge of the hearth, he pulled a bit of wood off the stack by the stove. He placed a chair near the fire and sat down and started to carve bits off the piece of fir. By the time Elena and the children returned from the forest, Johannes had completed his project.

Katya was the first to spot the finely crafted doll sitting in the middle of the table. "Mama, look!" she exclaimed with glee, pointing to the object. "Can I have it?"

Elena picked the doll up and looked closely. She ran her fingers over the figure. The smoothness of the doll's surface belied the fact that Johannes had only a small knife to work with. "It is beautiful." She looked at Johannes with wondering eyes.

"I made her for you, Katya. She is all yours." Johannes smiled. He was pleased to see the excitement in the little girl's face.

Elena admonished Katya with, "What do you say, Katya?" as she handed the doll to her child.

"*Spasiba*, Thank you," was the somewhat bashful response as Katya took the doll and headed for her bed, where she sat and carefully caressed the object.

"You do beautiful work. Are you a toy-maker or a sculptor?" Elena asked.

"I am only a sailor," Johannes shrugged as he glanced toward the boys taking note of their mother's actions. "Sailors often have many idle hours sitting on a ship, and carving becomes a simple pastime."

Elena took note of Johannes' response and nodded in silent agreement. "Children, maybe Yanochan can make something for each of you."

Viktor rushed to Johannes' side. "Uncle Yanochan, will you make a wooden ship for me? I love ships. Papa used to take us to the shipyard to see the giant ships being loaded with the lumber from the mill, but Mama does not have time for that."

"He is not your uncle!" Pavel quickly reprimanded his little brother. "He is just a visitor that we are feeding." Pavel's resentment of Johannes' presence was apparent in the tone of his voice.

"Viktor, why do you call Yanochan 'uncle'?" Elena asked with curiosity, as her son had never known an uncle before.

"My friend Renata said that there is a man living in her house, and she calls him uncle." Viktor pouted at his brother. "Her mother told her that a man living in their house that is not her father, must be an uncle, so Yanochan must be an uncle."

Elena shot a guarded look at her eldest son, and then smiled at her youngest one. "Yanochan is just a sailor staying with us until he is well enough to return to his ship. But I see no reason why you cannot call him uncle."

"But, Mother…" Pavel started to whine.

"We will talk *later*, Pavel." Elena sternly retorted.

Johannes quickly picked up on Pavel's hostility; he had felt it developing for some time. "Pavel, I know I am just visiting. I appreciate that you are the man of the house, and that you are the one who needs to be strong for your family. I thank you for allowing me to stay here. I have already discussed with your mother that I will be leaving in the spring. But, until then, I would like to be your friend and a friend to your brother and sister. If it is easier for your brother to call me uncle, what is the harm in that? Why can I not be your uncle, too?"

Pavel stood deep in thought, a frown on his face. Finally he responded, "If Viktor wants to call you uncle, he can. But, I will call you Yanochan, as Mother does."

Johannes extended his hand, "We shall shake on it, man to man."

Pavel grinned and offered his hand in friendship.

'But what about my ship?" Viktor interjected.

"I would love to make a ship for you, if your mother approves. It will give me something to do as my strength returns. Can I make something for you, too, Pavel?"

"I do not need a toy, I am not a child." There was a hint of disappointment in Pavel's voice.

Viktor cupped his hand to Johannes' good ear and loudly whispered, "He likes dogs."

CHAPTER EIGHTEEN

Horse Sense

Boris stood quietly as Karolina groomed him one last time before returning to her quarters. The sweat he generated as he pulled the big logs to the mill turned to clumps of frozen mud that hung from his long shaggy coat.

"Have to get these tangles out of your hide," Karolina crooned to the big horse. "We can not take the chance of your getting sores from the harness, now can we?" She tied small bunches of his bedding-straw into brush-like bundles that she scrubbed against his hair helping to loosen the caked mud. She worked long after the other girls had bedded their horses down and left the barn for the night.

By the time she finished, Boris had emptied his manger and began stomping restlessly as he stood tied in his narrow stall. "Alright, old boy, I will see if I can find you some more hay, but do not think you will always get me to rummage for you," she laughed as she left his pen and headed outside into the adjoining hayfield.

She made her way through the muddy snow to the haystack on the far side of the field. She knew this stack was to feed the sheep housed in the back of the barn, but she had garnered a bit of hay from it before, and no one had seemed to notice. *A little bit here and there would do Boris a lot of good, and the sheep will not miss it*, she thought as she pulled an armload from the back side of the stack. She returned to Boris and filled his manger. She gave him one last pat on his big rump as she squeezed her way out of his stall. Just as she cleared Boris' backside, she looked up and her eyes met Ivan's.

"You little wench!" Ivan bellowed. "I saw you stealing hay for that horse!"

"I was not stealing," Karolina retorted. "This horse belongs to the Soviets the same as the sheep and the hay. So how can I be stealing?"

"You little bit of sass! You know these horses are on rations, the same as all the other 'animals' in this compound. If too much is fed now, there will be none left by spring."

"My horse works harder than any of the others; we bring in more logs each day than anybody else. He deserves extra hay!"

"*Your horse?* I thought you just said he was the property of the Soviets. Now he is *your* horse? Well, if he is your horse, then you *are* stealing!" Ivan reached out and grabbed at Karolina's arm, but she was too quick for him. She pulled out of his grip and dove back into the stall, under Boris' belly.

The horse's head flew up from his manger at the sudden movements around him, and he stomped his big hind foot as a warning. Ivan ignored the horse and rushed in to grab at Karolina again. Boris flattened his ears against the sides of his head. With the aim of a well-trained marksman, the big horse planted both hind feet directly in Ivan's abdomen. Ivan stumbled back, stunned by the force that hit him. Karolina crawled closer to Boris' front feet and huddled there; waiting to see what Ivan was going to do next.

Ivan fell into the aisle-way of the barn. He rolled over onto his hands and knees and slowly rose to his feet, gasping for air. He braced himself against the stall of another work horse. "I will kill you and that beast!" he hissed with what little breath he could gather.

Karolina crawled out from under Boris. As she made her way into the aisle, she saw that Ivan was blocking her escape out of the barn's entrance, so she turned and ran toward the sheep pens in the back. Opening the gates of the sheep's pens, she hoped for a way to divert Ivan's attention. The ewes were already milling about restlessly, as Ivan had not yet fed them; they immediately took advantage of the openings, crowding into the passageway and slowing Ivan's progress.

"GET BACK HERE!" Ivan shouted as the sheep leapt past him, heading for the open barn door. Karolina continued to open gates and chase the ewes toward Ivan. Unexpectedly, Ivan grabbed at his left side, and staggered. Just as blood-filled vomit spewed from his mouth, he fell against the wooden panel that separated two more of the horses. As he crumpled to the floor, Karolina swiftly followed the ewes past him and out of the barn. Without even stopping to look, she ran all the way back to the barracks.

She remained outside in the cold until she was able to breathe normally. She wondered whether she should tell somebody about Ivan, but she was terrified of being punished for stealing hay. The dreadful image of the detention chamber refused to leave her mind. Instead, she calmly entered the barracks and made her way to her bed.

"Karolina, you have missed supper again, but I saved a bit of stew for you." Katerina offered the bowl to Karolina, but Karolina set it aside. Katerina sensed something was not right with her daughter. "What is going on?"

"Nothing, Mother," Karolina responded quietly. "I was just tending to Boris."

"Karolina, it is not like you to lie to me. Please tell me what has happened."

"Mother, I am all right. I am just tired and do not want to eat."

"Child, if you do not eat, you will not be able to keep up your strength to do your work or tend to that horse."

"Mother, I am fine. Please just let me rest."

Katerina was not happy with her daughter's response, but said no more as Karolina curled onto her sleeping plank and pulled her one blanket over her head.

"Commandant! The sheep have escaped!" The soldier hollered as he pounded on the door to the Commandant's quarters.

The commanding officer threw the door open and stood half-dressed in the morning darkness. "What do you mean they have escaped?" he roared.

"The early guard saw two in the field a while ago. He went to the barn to check the others but found only empty pens."

"WHERE IS IVAN? I want him here immediately!"

"Ivan was found in the barn. He is dead. He has hoof marks on his clothes. I think one of the horses kicked him in the stomach."

"What was he doing with the horses? His assignment was to tend the sheep! WHERE ARE MY SHEEP?"

"I have sent men out to look for them, sir, but most seem to be near the hayfields."

"Well, get them in as soon as possible. There had better not be any more loss of my lambs! If Ivan were not already dead, I would see that he soon was." The commandant slammed the door in anger, and he returned to dress himself for breakfast.

Karolina rose slowly from her bunk. Though tired, she slept little through the night. She dreaded returning to the barn this morning and possibly facing the wrath of Ivan again. She worried that Ivan may have done something horrible to Boris in retaliation for her turning the sheep loose and running from his ire.

"Karolina, what is wrong with you?" Katerina was more concerned than ever about her daughter. Karolina was not keeping to her normal morning rush to see Boris.

"I told you last night, nothing is wrong. I am just tired."

Sofia approached Katerina, took her by the arm and led her away from Karolina. "There is rumor that Ivan is dead," she whispered quietly. "He was found in the barn this morning."

The blood rushed from Katerina's face. *Is that why Karolina is acting so strangely? Did she have something to do with this? What has Ivan done to her?* The questions came quickly and jumbled visions of her daughter and Ivan raced vicariously through her mind.

Katerina returned to Karolina's side, but said nothing to her daughter. *There are too many prying eyes and ears in this room; I must talk to my daughter in private, but where and how? There is no privacy here.* Katerina tried to feign normalcy through the morning, but she was desperate to speak to Karolina. She knew that if the rumor was true, something would probably be said during roll call; questions would be asked; the authorities would want to know details and possible suspects.

As they stood in the pre-dawn cold waiting for their names to be called, Katerina took Karolina's hand in hers, and pulled her daughter close.

"Did you seek vengeance for Magdalena's disappearance?" Katerina murmured in her daughter's ear.

"Mother, NO! Why would you think that?"

"There is rumor that Ivan was found dead in the barn."

Karolina's face turned white and she staggered back in shock and dismay. "Oh, Mother, Ivan was alive when I left the barn last night. Please believe me!"

"Hush, daughter. Yes, I do believe you. But, the other women in our unit saw you come in late last night. They will suspect something!" Katerina insisted under her breath.

Their whispering was interrupted by the officer calling out the roll. When he was satisfied that all were present he stepped aside and the Commandant moved in front of the huddled group of women. "Ivan is no longer here," he announced matter-of-factly. It seemed that Ivan's disappearance was to be as little noted as the disappearance of Magdalena and the other girls. "I need someone to feed my sheep, are any of you experienced with livestock?"

"Mother...the barn is warmer than the forest...and I will help with the feeding." Karolina pushed her mother toward the commander.

Katerina stood somewhat perplexed by Karolina's actions, but as several other women also stepped forward, she did not resist. The senior officer slowly walked past the women, sizing each one up as if they were livestock being presented for purchase. Finally he turned around and stopped in front of Katerina, "This one will do," he said to his aide. Katerina's brain raced into action.

"Excuse me, Commandant, but may I make a request?" Katerina shyly asked.

"What is it?" The Commandant was surprised that this woman would have the mettle to speak directly to him, much less make a request.

"The woman that shares my saw in the forest will not have a partner now; would it be possible for her to join me in the barn? With two of us working together, we will be able to attend the sheep more completely, and will give the ewes more attention during lambing."

The Commandant stopped to ponder this request briefly. He turned his gaze to his assistant, "When does the next train of kulak workers arrive?"

"Friday."

"Then, yes, I will allow it. By tonight, I want an inventory of my ewes and an estimate of the number of lambs that are expected. Is that understood?"

"Yes, Commandant, you will have that information by tonight," Katerina was pleased with herself for her confidence; and she was excited that Sofia would be joining her in the warm barn.

As soon as the women were released from their line-up, Karolina raced to the barn to check on Boris. She was elated when she heard his welcoming nicker as she entered. Her eyes filled with tears of relief as she placed his morning hay in his manger. She threw her arms around his thick neck in an ecstatic hug. "Thank you," she whispered in his shaggy ear. The big horse stopped chewing briefly and turned his head toward her, puffing softly from his rippling nostrils. His indifference to the previous night's events calmed Karolina's soul.

CHAPTER NINETEEN

Warmth

Anya awoke to a quiet swooshing in the snow outside the cottage. She lay in the coziness of her woolen blanket and listened intently, wondering what was causing the strange noises. Sonia's soft snoring disrupted Anya's ability to hear the muffled sounds, so she rose slowly and quietly tip-toed to the small window near the door. She eased the cloth curtain back from the lower corner and tried to look through the blurry isinglass. She could see little in the darkness, but made out the shadow of a man moving past the window. Noiselessly, she shrank back in fear. The silence of the moment was pierced by the shrill yipping of an animal and a hushed voice. The yipping ceased instantly. The slamming of her heart against her chest caused Anya to take a short deep breath. But her childish curiosity got the better of her and she eased up to take another look out of the window. She again pulled the curtain back, not thinking about the waning glow that emanated from the hearth behind her.

The movement in the window caught the attention of one of the creatures, and it looked directly at Anya. The light reflected in its eyes glowed a bright red, then disappeared into the blackness. Tears began to flow down Anya's cheeks and she ran to Sonia's bedside. "Oma!" she whispered frantically, "Oma!"

Sonia woke with a start and quickly sat up. "What is it? What is wrong, little one?"

Anya put her finger to her lips. "Wolves! There are wolves outside the door!" she whispered urgently.

Sonia pulled the child into her bed and wrapped her in a blanket and brushed the tears from Anya's face. "Stay here while I see. This is not the time of year for the wolves." Sonia threw a hide over her shoulders for warmth and placed a log on the flickering embers. The fire sprang to life, licking at the shards of bark clinging to the surface of the wood and illuminating the room. Anya moved closer to the wall and wrapped the blanket tighter around her.

"Wolves do not like fire," Sonia said as she reached for the latch on the door. Sonia opened the door slowly; the chill from outside rushed across the floor and lapped at Anya's bare toes. Anya drew her feet up under her and pulled the blanket over them. She did not want Sonia to reveal herself to whatever was out there, but she was too scared to speak. Sonia peeked out the door, and then threw it open in welcome. Clasping her hands together in delight she excitedly exclaimed "Rodin!"

Anya watched in silence as a rotund figure dressed in light-brown skins stepped into the cottage. His head was covered in a parka lined with long grey fur. He pushed the parka back off his head, revealing his dark skin and black hair. Reaching out to her son, Sonia's arms disappeared in the thick folds of his coat. When she released her embrace, Rodin removed his coat and hung it from a peg on the wall near the door. He was now half the girth of the man that stood there only moments before.

Anya watched with curiosity. She wondered why the coat was inside-out with the heavy long fur on the inside and the tanned hide on the outside. She had never seen anything like this before. She also noticed the smoothness of the outer surface and the bright-colored embroidery that zigzagged around the hem. The embroidery matched that of the dress Sonia had given her to wear the first day she came here. She remembered how tenderly Sonia had handled the dress when she replaced it in the box beneath her bed.

Rodin spoke to his mother, but Anya did not understand the words. Sonia hugged her son again then said in Russian, "You must meet Anya."

Rodin was led to Sonia's bedside. "Nothing here but a bundle of blanket," he said with a laugh, as he pretended to poke at the mound huddled against the wall. "And where did you find this un-melted snowflake— in one of your mushroom patches?"

"Anya, this is my son, Rodin. I told you about him. Please do not be afraid. He will not hurt you. Rodin, this is Anya. She has come to live with me, so you do not have to worry so much about me being alone here in the forest."

Anya slowly lowered the blanket and smiled shyly at this man standing before her. Then she eased herself off of the bed and stood in front of him. "Why do you wear your coat inside out?" she asked bashfully.

Rodin was perplexed by her question. He turned and looked at his coat hanging from the peg. Then his mouth widened into a huge smile revealing a gaping space between his two front teeth, and his eyes disappeared behind the almond-shaped lids. "It is warmer that way," he laughed.

"How can that be?" Anya could not fathom the reasoning. Animals wear their fur on the outside.

Rodin began explaining that the fur next to his body sealed in the air and his own warmth while the skin-side repelled water on rainy days. While he was talking, Sonia handed her son a cup of tea and indicated that he should sit at the table. She motioned to Anya in a silent instruction to get dressed, shifted the hide shawl on her own shoulders and joined her son at the table.

Anya pulled her dress on over her nightclothes. Sonia had sewn this dress for her; a simple tunic of light blue wool, called a *sarafan*. Sitting on the edge of Sonia's bed, Anya tugged the fur boots onto her cold feet. The boots soon warmed her freezing toes. Finally she donned the muslin apron she and Sonia had made to protect her clothes, and tied it in place. Without a word, she placed another log on the fire and poured hot water from the kettle into her waiting cup. There were no chairs left, so she settled herself cross-legged on the fur rug near the hearth.

Rodin watched with interest. "How old are you?" he finally asked.

"Ten," she answered between sips of the hot liquid.

"You are tall for ten," he observed.

"Not where I come from. I am the same as the others."

"Where do you come from? How did you get here?" Rodin was not oblivious to the trains that had arrived with the German prisoners; he just wanted to engage Anya in conversation.

"My village is Sofienthal. Soldiers made us leave our farm, and we went with our horses and wagons until we got to a place where we were put on a train. Then after a long time the train stopped at the village near here, and we had to get off in the snow, and our Mamas and Papis were taken away. Then Oma brought me here." The words flowed so quickly Rodin could barely understand.

"Who is Oma?" he asked his mother.

Sonia smiled. "Me," she responded. "Anya has chosen to call me by a family name, a name she called her grandmother."

He nodded, recognizing the need for this child to be connected to family.

Without warning, Anya jumped to her feet, nearly spilling what was left in her cup. She ran to Sonia and whispered in her ear, her eyes filled with trepidation.

Sonia took Anya's hands in hers and gazed into her face. "No dear, there are no wolves. What you saw are Rodin's sled dogs. They are resting for now."

"That reminds me," he spoke with concern in his voice. "Miko was not travelling well. I need to check his feet for soreness."

"Bring him in by the fire, Rodin. The light will be better here even after the sun comes up, if it comes up today." Sonia pulled a ragged blanket from under her mattress and spread it on the floor as Rodin put his coat on and went outside.

As soon as the door opened and the dogs saw Rodin they erupted into a chorus of howling and yipping. He shouted a command that silenced them. The dogs were tied individually to trees surrounding the pathway to the cottage, and Rodin made his way to a big male. He untied the dog and returned to the cottage with the dog following closely behind. Once inside the cottage, the dog quickly went to the blanket and lay upon it.

Anya was taken with the magnificence of this creature. He was twice the size of the farm dogs she had seen in her village. He looked much like the pictures of wolves she was shown in school, but his silver hair was long and thick. His pointed ears were enhanced with black tips and stood at attention as his deep-yellow eyes watched Rodin's every move. His face was white, as were his legs and underside, and his muzzle seemed to form a smile as his mouth opened to pant while he lay in the warm room.

"He would love to be petted," Rodin said to Anya.

Anya got down on the floor next to the dog and placed her hands onto the dog's back. He looked up at her, then rolled over onto his side with a satisfied groan. Anya ran her fingers through his thick fur; she could feel his tight well-formed muscles beneath the soft dense undercoat. Rodin knelt on the other side of the dog and reached across to examine the pads of his feet. Anya realized that Miko's feet were as big as Rodin's hands and long, soft hairs grew between the hard, black pads on his soles.

"Does it tickle?" Anya asked as she lightly brushed the toe hairs. The big dog twitched slightly and relaxed with a deep sigh of contentment.

"Here it is!" Rodin exclaimed as he spread the toes on Miko's back left foot. The dog raised his head and looked at his master. On one side of the center pad a small crack had opened up and was inflamed and obviously sore. Sonia handed her son a small jar of salve and a strip of cloth. The dog's foot was treated and the cloth was wrapped into a boot-like bandage around the injured foot. "He must have cut it on some ice. He will be fine now. By tomorrow, he will be ready to run again. Alright, old boy, back out with you."

"Does he have to go back out so soon? I have never been with a dog before, not this close," Anya pleaded.

"You did not have a dog on your farm?" Sonia asked in amazement. "I would think all farms had dogs to keep the wolves away."

"No, Papi would not allow us to have a dog. He did not like the ones on the farms around us, but maybe he never saw a dog like this one. I think if he had seen this dog he might have liked dogs."

"He can stay a few more minutes, but it might be too warm in here for him. He is built to be outside, and I do not want him sick from becoming too hot." Rodin stated.

"No, I do not want him to get sick. Maybe...you better take him out," Anya decided.

Rodin stood and the dog stood as well, waving his plume of a tail slowly over his back. Sonia gave the dog a bit of spice cookie and stroked his head.

"Mother, you will spoil him," Rodin admonished. "You know better."

"A little medicine for his soul will heal his foot faster," Sonia winked at Anya as Rodin led the dog back out into the grey morning.

CHAPTER TWENTY

Of Wood and Flesh

Being limited to the confines of Elena's small house during the winter gave Johannes many hours to perfect his already ample carving skills. While the children were at school, or out gathering wood with their mother, Johannes completed many beautiful items, each unique in its own way. The ship for Viktor was far beyond the child's expectations, as it was not just a simple wooden boat but an actual ship with portholes and smoke stacks.

The dog Johannes carved for Pavel was received with less excitement, however. Long floppy ears drooped on either side of a square-muzzled face resting on smallish paws. The dog itself was curled into a sleeping position with a somewhat bony hip protruding from its side and a long skinny tail curled around its rump.

"What kind of animal is this?" Pavel demanded when Johannes handed him the figure.

"It is a dog. I thought you liked dogs." Johannes answered, a bit perplexed by the question.

"This is not a dog!" Pavel's eyes filled with tears of disappointment as he threw the figure to the floor and ran for his bed.

"PAVEL! Get back here and apologize!" Elena reprimanded her son. "What is wrong with you?"

Pavel choked back his tears and returned to stand in front of Johannes. "You made a beautiful doll for Katya and a great ship for Viktor. But you must not like me, because you made this odd-looking thing and called it a dog. The one thing I have always wanted is a dog. Before his accident, Papa promised to let me have a dog." Pavel whimpered in disillusionment.

"I am sorry you do not like the dog I made for you," Johannes reached out and placed his hands on Pavel's shoulders. "I made it to look like the dogs I am familiar with, the dogs on the farms around my village."

"I do not understand. How can dogs be so different? A dog is a dog. They are just tame wolves," Pavel declared.

"Evidently not," Johannes shrugged, "dogs seem to be different in different parts of Russia. People can be different, why not dogs?"

Pavel picked the little carving up and fingered it, turning it over in his hands and looking at it from all angles. "If this is a dog, where is its hair?"

"This dog has short hair that lies close to its body."

"How does it stay warm, then? It will not survive a winter!"

"The winters are not so cold where this dog lives. And," Johannes continued, "this dog would spend the winter next to its owner's hearth."

"Do you mean the dog is allowed to live in the house?"

"Yes, sometimes. It depends on the person who has the dog. Some farmers like having their dogs close. I think it makes them feel important. Others make their dogs sleep in the barn with the livestock, where they should be."

"Where does your dog sleep?" Pavel asked.

"I do not have a dog."

"Well, not now, but when you live at your home, where does your dog sleep?"

"I do not like dogs," Johannes finally admitted. "I will not have a dog."

"Why not?" Pavel could not believe that anyone would not want a dog.

"I find that dogs cause more trouble than they are worth. When they are not chasing livestock or killing chickens, they dig holes. Good work horses are hurt by stepping in those holes. And if that is not enough, when they are not causing trouble, they are lazy and sleep underfoot."

"NO! Dogs are not like that!" Pavel exclaimed. "You do not know what a REAL dog is!"

Elena thought it might be time to step in and settle this. "I think you are both right. Pavel, maybe you need to show Yanochan what a Siberian dog is like, and then maybe he can carve a proper dog for you. I have heard that the *Sami's* are in the village. You may take Yanochan to meet them and their dogs tomorrow."

"Can we go? Can we go?" Viktor and Katya chimed in unison.

"Not this time," Elena softly replied, "Pavel and Yanochan must make this trip alone. Besides, I need you two to help me with the wood."

Though very disappointed, the children said nothing more. Pavel, however, was elated at the idea that he could show his knowledge about the dogs.

Later that night, after the children were asleep, Elena sat sewing by the fire. Johannes sat on the opposite side of the hearth working on a large flat curing bowl for Elena's bread-making. Elena noted his deep concentration as he sat and worked the wood, bit by bit, out of the center of the bowl. She was startled when he suddenly spoke.

"You told Pavel that the *Sami's* are in the village. Who are they?"

"Native tribesmen from the east, across the Taz River. They are no-mads that the Soviets hire as hunters." She shifted the garment in her lap and continued sewing.

"The Soviets? Then I should avoid these people, if they are em-ployed by the Soviets!"

Elena thought for a moment. "I have heard that they dislike the Soviets, but like being paid for what they do naturally. The Sami's have come to trade for many years, likely since the village was built. They bring in meat to barter for staples like flour and potatoes, when avail-able. Now, they are paid to bring in meat for the soldiers. Both sides get what they want, I guess."

"You said they had dogs. For hunting?"

"Not from what I have seen. The dogs are used to haul the sledges full of deer meat, and sometimes fish, into the village and supplies back out to their camps."

"I think Pavel and I will have an interesting day tomorrow." Johannes lifted the bowl from his lap and placed it on the table. He stretched his back and slowly rose to his feet. He carefully placed the knife behind a small porcelain dish on the mantelpiece, and headed for his cot. He nodded a polite good-night to Elena, "Time for my prayers."

Soon after breakfast Pavel put on his heavy overcoat and boots. "Hurry Yanochan, we must see the dogs. The light will not last long!"

Elena handed Johannes a thick wool coat, its dark grey hem nearly touched the floor and the cuffs of the sleeves ended just below his knuckles. "My husband was a rather large man," she said.

Johannes picked up the pair of boots that were warming by the fire. He pulled them on and felt his feet shifting from side to side in the wide toe bed. He removed the boots, placed some bits of material Elena handed him into the toes, and returned the boots to his feet. Katya giggled as Johannes stomped around the room trying to work the material into place. Finally, Elena handed him a finely knitted balaclava. He pulled the hood down over his ears and nearly to his shoulders; it was roomy but would still keep him warm. When they were ready, Pavel slipped several of Johannes' carved dolls into his coat pocket, and rushed to the door, nearly shoving Johannes through it in his haste.

The cold blast of air in Johannes' face nearly caused him to lose his breath. It had been awhile since he had been out of the house, and the winter was even colder than he imagined. He put his head down and followed Pavel through the narrow streets, slipping occasionally on the slick stones that lined the way. Not realizing how little his muscles had been used, his legs now ached from the cold and the lack of exercise. Dragging the too-big boots through the hardened snow was a laborious task, and was causing him to sweat under the heavy coat.

At length, the street opened up into a broad square in the center of the village. A large conical tent dominated the square, and was surrounded by dogs—lots of dogs. Interspersed among the dogs were small-statured men dressed in thick, hooded coats, busily involved in various tasks: tending to the dogs, keeping a cooking-fire near the tent going, visiting with villagers and their children.

Johannes recognized the tent. "That is a Yurt! These people are Mongols!" he exclaimed. "But where are their ponies?"

Pavel looked at Johannes as if he were crazy. "These are *Sami's* and they do *not* have ponies!" Pavel was about to continue his protest when he heard his name called.

"PAVEL! How good to see you!"

Pavel ran with his arms widespread to the Sami calling to him. "YERIK!" Pavel shouted excitedly as he ran toward the man.

Johannes approached the happy assembly slowly, allowing Pavel to enjoy his obviously ecstatic moment with this stranger. The Sami noticed the reticent approach, and releasing his grip on Pavel, asked, "Who is this Pavel? Your new father?"

Pavel drew back and shot a shocked look at Johannes. "NO! This is just someone who is staying with us. This is Yanochan. He is a sailor that was injured, and is staying only long enough to get well and go back to his ship." Pavel's smile turned to a scowl, as if to remind Johannes who was head of the house.

"I am Yerik," the Sami responded in accented Russian and an outstretched mittened hand. "Young Pavel, here, visits me every time my men and I come to this village."

"Where is Suka?" Pavel asked.

"She is on the far side of the tent, tied near Sos."

Pavel was off like a flash, running as best he could across the slippery tromped snow in the square. Johannes and Yerik stood watching as the boy disappeared around the curve of the yurt. Yerik was the first to speak, "Pavel is a good boy. He has a special affection for my white female, Suka. I am not sure why that is, other than he was to get one of Suka's pups a few years ago, before his father died."

"Pavel was supposed to tell me about dogs today, but I am not sure he will have the time, maybe later."

Yerik laughed, "I think Pavel's attention is distracted for now. What would you like to know?"

"I am curious about your people. I met many Mongols years ago, when I was in the army. They lived in yurts like yours, and looked much like you, but they were horsemen, very skilled horsemen. It is legend that they taught the Cossacks many of their riding and fighting skills."

"Yes, tribal stories tell of the Mongol people of the south. But our languages and culture are very different. We are Selkup people, but the locals call us Sami's, as most of the natives in this area are of the Samoyed tribe. Our homes are called sampas, not yurts. The Mongol horses would not tolerate our cold, so our people have turned to the native animals for survival. Once, wolves were tamed and used for hunting. Over many years the wolves were bred into the dogs you see here." Yerik led Johannes over to one of the dogs nearest where they were standing. He untied the dog from its stake and made him stand quietly.

"You see his legs?" Yerik removed a mitten and ran his hand down the dog's foreleg, then continued, "these dogs have thicker bones than a wolf. The muscles over the shoulders and back are larger, too. That is for pulling our heavy loads of meat and supplies. These dogs can also haul a man for many kilometers without tiring. Their ability to run for hours comes from the wolf. They still look much like their wolven brethren, but they are larger and their hair is thicker. They are also good with our families… that is a necessity, as our children often play with them when we are not traveling."

Johannes' listened intently to Yerik's words. He filled his eyes and mind with the being that stood before him. He had not seen any dog like this or known a dog that would work so hard for its master. When Yerik finished his assessment of the dog, Johannes ventured a simple question, "What do you feed them to keep them in such good shape?"

Yerik shrugged. "What ever is available. They eat meat or fish. We feed them the remains of what we hunt or catch. When we are on a supply run, like this, we bring meat for them."

Now I know why Pavel was so disappointed in the dog I carved for him. I will have to make him a new one, Johannes thought to himself as he stroked the big dog's back.

Just before the pale light of the afternoon disappeared, Pavel returned to Johannes with a large piece of meat tucked inside his coat. Johannes' questioning look brought an immediate response. "I traded two of your dolls for the meat," Pavel revealed. "I did not think you would mind."

"No, Pavel, I do not mind. In fact, I think you made a very good trade. Had I known what you had in mind, I would have offered to bring more. I think this is a good thing for me to do, a small contribution to your mother's kindness to me. But, if I carve you a new dog—a Sami dog—then I hope you will keep it."

"Oh, yes! A Sami dog! I will keep it forever!" Pavel handed the meat to Johannes and ran ahead toward home.

CHAPTER TWENTY-ONE

Sheltered Moments

Grief-ridden sobbing of new arrivals, accompanied by those who suffered from the additional loss of a close companion or loved one, often kept the women awake through the long cold nights. The barracks was an odd combination of the stark realities of their new lives, the reassuring routine of work, and minimalist meals. It was becoming apparent that only those of strong faith, will, and determination would live long enough to see where this ordeal would lead them.

Katerina and Sofia fed off each other's spirits, and bolstered by Karolina's youthful energy, thrived where others did not. Their assignment to care for the sheep was anticipated with guarded expectations. The cognizance that they would not be laboring in the forest, wading through the deep snow and battling the icy winds, renewed their morale.

Katerina and Sofia entered the large barn to conduct their inventory of the sheep, as they had promised the commandant they would do. Their first encounter upon opening the great barn doors was the stench that overwhelmed their senses. Shocked to see the filth Ivan left in his wake, the women picked their way through the aisle to the pens.

"It is no wonder the ewes have lost lambs," Katerina exclaimed. "I think we have more work here than expected."

Without comment, Sofia took the rake down from its peg on the wall and started pulling soiled straw and hay from one of the sheep pens. Meanwhile, Katerina waded through the muck in the ox's stall and untied him from his stanchion. She found his yoke and harness and led him outside to his sledge. When she had him hitched, Katerina led the ox back into the barn pulling the empty flatbed, and placed him just outside the sheep pens.

"Poor old bag of bones, I wonder if you have a name." Katerina mused as she patted the beast on his broad forehead.

Sofia briefly stopped her raking and gave the ox an appraising look. "I doubt it. I am sure Ivan would not have bothered with a name. He is a pitiful looking beast, though; looks even worse off than we do. I think I might be inclined to call him *Kozha*."

"This poor creature needs to be given a real name, not something like 'leather', he will meet that fate soon enough. No, I think I will call him…*Sacha*."

"I do suppose that 'helper' is appropriate, because we are going to need all the help we can get to please 'Comrade Commandant' *and* his sheep," Sofia asserted.

Once satisfied that the ox had an appropriate name, Katerina dug into the growing mound of soiled straw and began piling it onto the sledge. When it was sufficiently loaded, she asked the ox to pull the heavy mass outside. They traveled a distance from the barn into the stubble field, and Katerina raked the manure-filled bedding off into the snow. This was the first of many loads that would be taken out through the day.

It was late afternoon before the women were pleased with the cleanliness of the pens. They turned the ewes out into the barn's aisle while they laid fresh straw into the pens and fresh fodder in the mangers. As each ewe was allowed back into her pen, she was counted and felt for the presence of a lamb in the womb.

As Sofia prepared the report for the commandant, Katerina tended to Sacha. Since Katerina cleaned his stall when she was cleaning the sheep's pens, all was now fresh for him. While the ox had quickly learned the day's routine, and eagerly obeyed the kind words that were spoken to him through the day, he now balked at returning to his spotless stall.

Instead of battling with the beast, Katerina left him standing in the aisle. She searched around the horses' area and found one of the straw bundles the girls used as brushes, and gave the ox a complete rubdown. He stood with his head outstretched and lapped his long tongue over his nose-ring in contentment. When Katerina was finished, the ox finally followed her into the stall and instinctively stood next to the chain that hung from his tie-ring; but Katerina did not connect him to the chain. Instead, she found a loose board and slid it across the opening, allowing the ox to have his freedom to move about. He stood with his nose to the wall and rolled his eye around to watch Katerina as she filled his manger with hay. When she brought a fresh pail of water to him, she stood outside the improvised gate and softly called his name. Sacha swung his rear end around so that he stood parallel to the wall, and bawled a plea for her to bring the water closer.

"Oh, you poor confused thing," Katerina crooned, "you can come here for your water, you are no longer tied short."

The ox still did not move. Katerina again called his name and enticed him with a slosh of the bucket. Finally, cautiously, Sacha took a step away from the wall. Realizing he was not going to have his nose jerked back by the ring and chain, he completed his journey to the bucket and drank deeply from its contents. When sated, he plopped his body down in the straw and contentedly gazed at Katerina as he began to slowly chew his cud.

Sofia came up beside Katerina and stood watching the ox. "If I did not know better, I would swear that animal is smiling. Tell me, did you actually milk your cow, or did she just hand you a full bucket twice a day?" Sofia gently teased.

"As a matter of fact, she made her own butter, too," Katerina tried to laugh, but was too exhausted. With that, she pulled her clothing tight around her, covered her head, slipped her arm under Sofia's and headed for the barn door and the cold reality that waited outside.

CHAPTER TWENTY-TWO

Small Gifts

As the winter winds died down and the longer presence of the spring sun began turning the snow to mush, the Selkups returned to Onega for one last supply run before heading into the eastern tundra for the summer.

Elena quietly slipped out of her house before sunrise and made her way to the town square. Through the winter, she spent many hours considering how she would approach this situation, and now she was sure the time had come to set things in motion.

It did not take long for her to single out Yerik in the town square. She moved him away from the main camp, and they spoke in hushed voices and subtle hand movements. Before leaving, she handed Yerik a fabric sack, as if to seal a deal.

Upon her return to the house, she found Johannes and the children preparing the morning meal. Johannes' strength had fully returned, and now he tried to help Elena with the children and the chores.

"Mama, where have you been? Why did you leave without us?" Katya was always full of questions. Johannes wanted to know what Elena was up to, as well, but he said nothing.

"I had business to take care of," Elena responded. "Now hurry, you need to be off to school."

When the children finished their pasty gruel, and Elena saw that they were clean and ready, she accompanied them out of the door. Once satisfied that they were gone for the day, she went back inside to find Johannes clearing the table of the dirty dishes. She approached him and took the bowls out of his hands, setting them down on the side-board. "I need to talk to you." Her words were spoken with a solemness that alarmed Johannes. She indicated that he was to sit at the table, then she sat across from him.

"You are getting stronger by the day," she began, "and I have seen how restless you are becoming. With the upcoming warmer weather, you will desire to be outside. Being trapped in my house is not how you should live. I am afraid to allow you to be where the neighbors might question who you are and why you are here. Prying eyes and rattling tongues abound. I do not want soldiers invading my house in the middle of the night and taking me from my children. I told you some time ago that I wanted you gone by spring, and now that time has come."

"But...where will I go?" Johannes asked.

"The Sami's are in the square. I spoke with Yerik this morning. He said you may travel with them for the summer. If you can hunt and fish, you can earn your meals and a place to stay. They will take you far away from here."

"What will you tell the children? Pavel has become quite attached to me, you know that. He needs a man in his life for guidance. He needs a father."

Elena could not let Johannes know how she really felt about him, as she too was quite attached. Instead she took on a demeanor colder than the ice that hung from the eaves. She narrowed her eyes and swallowed the lump in her throat. "Suka has a litter of pups. I traded some of your carvings for one of them. Pavel will be distracted with his new charge." With those words, Elena rose to her feet turning away from Johannes. She grabbed her coat and headed for the door. "I have additional arrangements to make," she sputtered as she practically ran out. Once far enough away that Johannes would not see her, she stopped, sank into the muddy slush and sobbed.

Johannes just sat at the table in silence, stunned and confused by Elena's words and manner. He knew she wanted him to leave, but so quickly and without warning? *I love the children. How can I just leave them without some explanation?* he pondered. *They have needed me as much as I have needed them. I did not have an option to say goodbye to my own children. I have got to be able to tell them why I must go. How can Elena be so callous?*

Oh, Katerina, how I miss you. I have not sinned against you, but I do have feelings for Elena. Is that wrong? I feel I am only half a man without my family, without you, without someone to care for and care about. Oh Lord, if ever I have needed guidance, it is now.

Elena was gone nearly an hour, and when she returned found Johannes sitting on the edge of his cot, her Bible in his hands. Deep in prayer, he did not acknowledge her return, so she quietly sat in her chair and busied herself with some sewing.

Several minutes passed in silence before Johannes raised his head and looked at her. When their eyes met, she could see the grief in his face and even though she felt she had nothing more to cry with, she found she had to fight back her own tears, so she quickly looked away. Rising from her chair, and taking the kettle from the hearth, she fixed them both a cup of tea. Placing Johannes' cup on the table, she returned to her chair. She sat with both hands around the cup, absorbing its warmth and contemplating the wisps of steam that ascended from the hot brown liquid. Finally, she was ready to speak.

"The Sami's will be here for two more days. They will leave early on the third day. Yerik said he will come for you just before they leave, while it is still dark. He will knock two times on the window and you are to meet them in the square as quickly as you can be there. That will give us time to prepare the children for your departure. Yerik is bringing the pup tomorrow. I will take Pavel to see the puppies and allow him to choose the pup this afternoon. He will know your carvings paid for the pup."

"Thank you." Johannes was unable to say much, but he appreciated the opportunity to say good-bye to the children.

"I think it is best to tell the children that you will be returning to a ship. They will accept that explanation."

"Yes, I am sure you are right. I will do my best to make it easy for them." Johannes left his cot and went to the fireplace. He selected a piece of wood, knocked some of the loose bark from its surface, and laid it in his chair. He reached up and took the knife from behind the plate on the mantel and sharpened it on a piece of flint the children found for him in the forest. "I will make a few more carvings for you to use for trading. Maybe you can obtain fresh vegetables for the children later this summer." Nothing further was said about Johannes' leaving.

Once the news was revealed to the children about the impending acquisition of a puppy, the house came alive with excitement. Pavel picked a black and silver female from Suka's litter. The pup had one amber and one dazzling blue eye. With Yerik's help, Pavel selected the name Fayina, meaning free one. Johannes assisted Pavel with building a suitable pen and shelter at the back of the house. The next afternoon, Yerik delivered the squirming bundle to six eager hands all wanting to touch the pup at once. As soon as the children were calmed and the pup was settled into her new surroundings, Elena called everybody into the house to warm up with a cup of strong tea.

Yerik excused himself, "I must return to my dogs and prepare my sled; my people will be leaving early." He gave a quick glance and an almost imperceptible nod to Johannes. Johannes returned the signal.

Soon after Yerik's departure, Johannes sat down in the chair he occupied while carving, and called the children to him. "I, too, am leaving early in the morning. Your mother has done a good job tending to my injuries, and now I am strong enough to return to my ship." The boys backed away as if Johannes had just announced that he had some contagious disease. Their eyes clouded over, but their stares never left Johannes' face.

Katya, however, stood with her feet apart and defiantly placed her hands on her hips. "Well, you just cannot leave. Who will make my dolls for me?" Her stern voice and matter-of-fact demeanor caused Johannes to smile broadly.

"Well, little one, I guess I will just have to send some dolls to you. I am sure I will have time to carve a few dolls while I am sailing on the ship."

With a wide wave of her arm, Katya said, "All right, you may go."

"Thank you for your permission, Katya. I would not be able to leave without it." As Johannes hugged the very self-assured Katya, Viktor pulled at Johannes' sleeve.

"Can I go with you? Can I go on the ship? I am small, I do not eat much. I could share your bed. Please, Uncle Yanochan, please?" Viktor's pleas came in rapid succession, and Johannes needed a moment before he could answer. Katya squirmed away as he pulled Viktor close.

"No, Viktor, I am sorry, but I cannot take you with me. There really is no room on a cargo ship for a child of any size. It is just too dangerous, and the crew's quarters are very small. Crew members work around the clock, so beds are often shared as it is. We must eat quickly, and if the seas are rough, we seldom eat at all. In a few years you will be old enough to become a sailor. When that time comes, you will be able to go on a ship whenever you want." Johannes cupped Viktor's chin with his large hand and wiped a single tear from the boy's cheek with his thumb, as Viktor faintly nodded his head in understanding.

Pavel could not contain his feelings any longer and began to cry. "No, you cannot go now! Who will help me train Fayina? How will I know what to do? Who will help Mama care for us?"

Johannes had anticipated Pavel's reaction. Once he had broken through Pavel's crust, they spent their winter developing a close father-son relationship. Johannes regretted having to be the one to cause Pavel to lose a second 'father' in his young life.

Johannes took a deep breath to steady his voice. "Pavel, you were the man of this house before I came. You have always asserted your leadership, and I have respected that. Now, you will return to your true place. Your mother needs your help, and you know that this family lived just fine before I came. Indeed, I put a burden on you and your mother." Johannes stopped for a breath and glanced at Elena. She looked back, but said nothing. Johannes continued, "Fayina will grow quickly, and with Yerik's instructions you will go far in her training. Fayina will trust your instincts; you must as well. She will teach you as much as you teach her. If you find yourself in a situation where you are not sure what you should do—listen to your heart and follow what you feel. You will be alright; you will do well." Johannes stood up, walked over to his cot and pulled a small cloth-wrapped bundle from under the blanket. As he handed the bundle to Pavel he continued, "I have made something for you. I hope it will keep me in your memory and maybe help you make important decisions regarding Fayina."

As Pavel carefully unwrapped the bundle, a stunning figure of a sled-dog emerged in his hands. "It's Suka!" he gasped as he ran his fingers over the form, feeling the texture of the carved hair draping down the sides of the dog. The sharpness of the erect triangular ears contrasted with the smoothness of the wood as it shaped the pointed muzzle, straight legs and large feet. The striking curve of the tail as it arched into a plume over the dog's back completed the near-perfect representation of Suka. "Oh Yanochan, she's beautiful!"

"I hope I have met your expectations. Because of you, I have learned what a *real* dog is and how one should look. You have taught me to appreciate how important dogs are, and how helpful they can be. I will always remember you for that."

"That means you will never come back here?" Pavel did not take his eyes off the figure; he could not bear to look at Johannes.

Johannes fixed his eyes on Elena as he answered. "One never knows where life will take him, only God knows that. I did not set out to live in your house, but I was brought here. I did not intend to love you, all of you, but I do, just as I love my own family, wherever they may be. Now it is time for me to leave, and I do not know if I will ever be back; if God so wishes, then I may return someday. All I can ask is that you remember me as fondly as I will remember you."

Johannes knelt on one knee and drew the children to him. Wrapping his arms about the three of them, he kissed each child on the cheek. As if knowing a distraction was in need, Fayina broke into a refrain of yips and whines and cries, and as one, the children ran out the door to console the pup.

Afraid to fall asleep and of not hearing Yerik's signal, Johannes dozed fitfully through the night. Finally, he heard the two light taps on the window. Johannes quietly and quickly left his bed, the moon shown through the window just enough that he could get around the room without crashing into furniture and making noise. Before retiring for the night, Elena put a number of her husband's clothing items into a burlap sack and placed it by the door for Johannes. Now, Johannes added the small carving knife and flint to the sack and tied the piece of rope tight about the opening. He pulled on the fur boots and donned the heavy wool coat and fur hat Elena had given him. Then he went to each child's bed and kissed the occupant lightly on the cheek. Fayina squirmed happily in Pavel's arms. Finally, Johannes made his way to Elena's bedside. Her deep and rhythmic breathing assured Johannes that she was in a deep sleep. He brushed a strand of hair from her cheek, bent over and kissed her softly and placed an object on her pillow. "Thank you, Elena. I will never forget you, please do not forget me," he whispered nearly inaudibly.

As Johannes turned to leave, Elena opened her eyes and watched. She did not want him to know that she, too, had been awake through the night. She clutched the edge of her blanket, to keep herself from calling out to him. She shivered when the cold draft whisked into the house as Johannes disappeared into the darkness. Finding the object on her pillow, she closed her hand around the carving of a single perfect rosebud. A tear fell, lodging itself between the petals. *I will never forget, Yanochan, I will never forget.*

CHAPTER TWENTY-THREE

Promises

As Anya made her way to the privy behind Sonia's cottage, she squinted against the brightness of the sun beaming through the tall firs. The icy breeze that penetrated her clothing told her that spring had not arrived quite yet, but the lengthening daylight was an indication that it was not far off. When she returned to the cottage, she found Sonia at the table busily making bread. "Oma, why are you baking bread now? Today is not baking day."

Sonia brushed a stray bit of hair from her forehead with the back of one of her flour-coated hands, leaving a dusty off-white streak in its place. The unconscious gesture brought a flood of memories and feelings as Anya pictured her mother making the same quick movement.

"Rodin will be coming soon. I must make extra bread for him and his men. Here, help me get this dough ready," Sonia offered, as she continued her kneading on the tough brown dough.

Anya washed her hands in the basin on the sideboard and pulled her apron on over her clothing. She stood next to Sonia and pulled a bit of dough from the large mixing bowl in the center of the table. Silently, she worked the dough as her thoughts clung to the image of her mother making bread in their kitchen on the farm. These pictures lead to new pictures, scenes of her father and brothers and sisters, memories of happy moments together. Tears began flowing as Anya turned from her work. She left the dough on the table and ran for her sleeping mat. She began sobbing loudly as she dropped to her knees, hunched over, her hands covering her face.

Sonia was taken by surprise. She, too, left her dough on the table, and wiping her hands on her apron, went to Anya's side. Even though she had great difficulty with her crooked aching legs, Sonia got down on the floor next to Anya and placed her arms around the child. "What is wrong, little one? Why do you cry this way?" Anya did not respond, except to release a flow of more intensity. Her body shook with every sob; she gulped for air then began sobbing again. Sonia did not know what to make of this. She gripped the child tighter. Anya gave in to the comfort of Sonia's body and collapsed into her lap. Sonia began rocking slowly from side to side, hoping to soothe Anya's troubled soul. "Oh, my little one, what has gotten into you?" Sonia softly crooned; her voice gently easing its way into Anya's mind. "Do you realize that in the nearly six months we have been together, this is the first time I have actually seen you cry? Oh, there have been little accidents, like the needle prick while you were sewing, and when you cut hand while chopping wood, or your bruised ego when your fingers could not keep up with the spinning wheel, but Anya, you only whimpered a bit and drew on your courage and spirit to get you through it. What makes you cry so hard, now?"

Sonia felt Anya's body begin to relax; the crying eased a bit. She continued to soothe the child, stroking Anya's forehead with her gnarled work-worn hands. Anya finally began taking deep breaths; the sobbing ceased and only quiet tears continued to dampen her reddened cheeks. As Sonia's rhythmic swaying continued to calm her, Anya finally spoke. "I miss Mama," she whispered.

"I am sure you do, little one," Sonia murmured back, "I am sure you do. Daughters should not be torn away from their mothers at such a young age. Girls need their mothers to teach them the many things they need to know about life. The connection between a mother and her daughter is unlike any other. I am sure your Mama misses you as much as you miss her." Sonia continued to stroke Anya's forehead. Anya did not want to move; Sonia's warmth enveloped her and held her in a near trance of peace and comfort. She closed her eyes as Sonia spoke again. "You have told me of the horrid trek that led you to me. I often wonder now why I chose you, why I was the one that separated you from your brothers that awful day. Had I known what you had been through, would I have taken you? I cannot honestly say. But I do know that you have been a blessing to me. Not only have you done what was expected of you, but you have nested yourself into my heart. You are my daughter now, but I cannot expect you to forget your own family or from where you came. I can only hope you can accept this old worn-out woman as your teacher."

Anya looked up at Sonia. "Oma, you are my Oma, but I miss Mama...I miss home." Anya picked up the hem of Sonia's apron and began working it with her fingers, rubbing in a slow circle, as she did to her mother's hem when she was hurt or upset. There was something soothing about this motion. "Will I ever see them again? Will I ever go back to the farm?"

"I do not know, little one, I do not know." Sonia sat silently for a few more minutes, keeping Anya close to her, rocking slowly, lost in her own thoughts. It was Anya's words that startled her out of her day dreams.

"We must finish the bread, or Rodin will not have any to give the others." Anya hopped to her feet and offered a hand to Sonia. Sonia struggled to rise, but her legs would not support her. Anya pushed the chair closer to Sonia. Sonia pulled herself up onto the chair and turned her body to enable her to sit on it.

"Anya, I have a favor to ask."

"Yes, Oma, what is it?"

"The next time you need a good cry, please do it on my bed, it will be much easier for me."

A smile brightened Anya's face, "I will try to remember, Oma, at least until I am big enough to get you off the floor myself. Now we must finish the bread." Sonia stiffly rose from the chair and joined Anya at the table to knead the heavy dough.

Early the next morning, Anya woke to the shooshing of the sled on the mushy snow as Rodin arrived at the cottage. The dogs yipped and whined as they came to a stop near the door. Excitedly, Anya hurriedly pulled her clothes and boots on and quickly straightened her sleeping mat. Sonia was already up and making tea over the freshly stoked fire.

"Take the lantern out to Rodin and see if he needs your help,"

Sonia instructed the eager child. Anya grabbed the softly glowing lantern off the table and headed toward the door.

"Put your coat on! Do you want to freeze to death?" Sonia admonished.

Anya set the lantern down and jumped into her coat, and then with the speed of Mercury she was out of the door. "Rodin!" she hollered. "Rodin! I am so glad to see you. Here is the lantern; can I help unharness the dogs? Do they need to be fed and watered? Can I take them into the trees?"

"Whoa, Snowflake, slow down! How can I answer your questions if you ask them so rapidly?" Rodin laughed as he put his mittened hands on Anya's shoulders. When he had her attention, he took the lantern from her hand. "I had better take this," he said. "I am not staying long; the dogs have only been in harness for a short time, so they do not need food nor water or a trip to the trees. But I am sure Miko would like a good hug." Rodin tied his lead dog to a tree, removed a large sack from the bed of the sled and went into the cottage. As Anya made her way to the big dog at the back of the pack, the remainder of the team took advantage of the time for a quick nap. When she reached Miko, she knelt in the snow and threw her arms around the dog's furry neck.

"I am glad to see you are doing well, Miko. I have been worried about you."

The dog wagged his tail and licked Anya's face; he sat on his haunches, then eased his front legs forward until he was fully prone in the snow, panting from the morning run. Anya laid her head against his side, absorbing the vibration of the rapid breaths, listening to the thumping of his heart. In a few minutes the panting ceased, and Miko lowered his head onto his front paws and closed his eyes for a quick nap. Anya realized she was getting wet as the snow melted beneath her, so she stood up. Miko was on his feet instantly, as well. "Sorry, boy, I did not mean to disturb your nap. I need to get into the cottage before I get too wet and cold." She gave the dog one last hug. "Have a safe trip, be a good boy and mind Rodin." As swift as a lizard, his tongue shot across her nose. She giggled as she wiped her face with her sleeve.

"You have fish breath!" she declared as she headed back for the cottage.

Rodin was warming himself over a cup of hot tea, and Sonia was busy wrapping the loaves of bread in cloth when Anya re-entered the cottage. She removed her coat and hung it on its peg and began assisting Sonia with the bread.

"Why are you not staying, Rodin? I thought the spring run was when you spent the most time here," Anya asked.

He set his cup on the table. "I did not stop on our way to the village because we had a very heavy load of meat for the soldiers. It was a good winter for hunting and fishing. The soldiers will eat meat for quite awhile this year. The commandant paid us well; we have enough supplies to take back to our people to last us through the summer and fall. So my time was spent delivering our meat and loading supplies for the trip back."

"Oh," Anya replied, disappointment in her voice. "I was hoping to spend more time with you; I wanted to ride on the sled with you."

"I am sorry, little snowflake, maybe when I come back in the fall we can do those things."

"Why do you call me Snowflake?"

"Because you are so white."

"I am?"

"Compared to our people, you are," Rodin stated as he pulled back his sleeve and put his forearm next to Anya's, his olive skin contrasting against her porcelain exterior.

"Oh." She smiled at Rodin's contrast.

Rodin reached into the bag of meat and fish he brought for his mother and pulled out an object wrapped in soft deer skin and handed it to Anya. "Maybe this will keep you busy until I return."

Anya carefully opened the skin revealing an elegantly carved wooden doll. She gasped with recognition.

"Do you like it?" Rodin asked.

"Where did it come from? Who made it? It is exactly like the one my Papi made for me when I was little! Have you seen my Papi? Do you know where he is?" Anya pleaded.

"No, I do not know your Papi. Yerik traded one of Suka's pups for a bag full of carvings. They came from a woman in the village. That is all I know about it." Rodin turned to his mother and continued, "Yerik also picked up a passenger. It seems there is an injured sailor who needs a new job. He claims he can hunt and fish. If he can not earn his keep, he will end up on the train to Vladivostok."

Sonia raised an eyebrow at this last comment. "You had better be careful. Do not anger the government by hiding fugitives."

"Yerik says the man is Norwegian, not one of the kulaks from the camp. I have not seen him yet, as we loaded up before sunrise. Everyone else has gone on ahead, so I will meet him tonight when we camp. I had better get going now, or I will be left to the wolves and bears."

Sonia smiled. "Too early in the season for either, but I suppose the clan will want my bread with their fish tonight, so yes, you must get going."

Rodin started to rise from the chair when Anya wrapped her arms around his neck, hugging him tightly. "Thank you," she whispered. "The doll is very beautiful."

"I will talk to Yerik for you and see if he knows anything about its maker."

Anya's face lit up, her bright blue eyes sparkled. "Oh, please, please do, Rodin. I must know who made this doll."

Rodin smiled and nodded as he placed his hand against her rosy cheek, "Yes, little Snowflake. But in the meanwhile, do not melt before I return."

Sonia also gave her son a warm embrace, "Have a safe journey, return soon."

"As soon as I can, mother, as soon as I can." With that, Rodin was out of the door, untied his excited dogs, gave a quick command, and was gone.

Anya examined the doll closely, rewrapped it carefully in the deer skin, and put it under the corner of her sleeping mat. "My Papi is close, I know this now. I will not cry for my family anymore, Oma."

CHAPTER TWENTY-FOUR
Illness and Indignity

As the women stood in the chill of the early morning, waiting for their daily roll-call to be completed, they heard the distant whistle of the train as it pulled into Onega.

"We will have to make room for the new inmates," Sofia whispered to Katerina.

Katerina nodded and sighed sadly at the thought of more families being wrenched apart, more children left to die by the edge of the railroad tracks, more women crying their hearts out for many nights to come, and more bodies to carry out of the barracks as the new additions withered under the onslaught of work and lack of adequate food.

By evening, fourteen women had been moved into Barracks Four, but these were not new arrivals. As they settled their few belongings into their new quarters, the other women began questioning what was going on.

"The soldiers are no longer taking the girls from their mothers," was the response. "They are being allowed to stay in the camp, as long as their mothers work hard enough to feed them all. In order to keep them together, we are being moved here."

"But, what of the boys? Are they going with their fathers?"

"We have been told that the boys are being sent to school, all but the babies. No one is told what happens to the babies."

Within the week that followed, several of the new arrivals became ill. Suggesting that the illness was caused by homesickness or avoidance of hard work, the camp commander refused to look into the situation. Soon the camp seemed to be seized by an epidemic of some sort, and it even affected the women who had been there the longest.

Karolina awoke one morning to a throbbing headache. She

cautiously sat up on her bunk, only to be ravaged by a flowing tide of chills that emanated from her toes and travelled straight up through her body to her skull. She groaned in agony and lay back upon the bunk.

Katerina placed her hand on her daughter's reddened forehead, feeling the heat of the fever that consumed her body. A tiny brown louse emerged from Karolina's hairline and crawled across the back of Katerina's hand. Even though all of the women had been accustomed for quite some time to picking lice from their bodies, the movement of this tiny creature, shadowed by the sallow light of the morning lantern, made her jump. Her reaction was swift and deadly as she flung the insect to the floor and stomped on it. Just as quickly, the recognition of the cause of her daughter's illness hit her. "TYPHUS!" she screamed as she pushed Sofia away and ran outside.

Katerina ran as fast as she could manage to the Commandant's office. His guard tried to block her as she rushed him, knocking him off balance and into the wall. She hit the door full force, flinging it back, and burst into the office. The camp commander was standing with his back to the door, drawing a cup of strong tea from a large silver samovar on a side table. Startled at the sudden intrusion, he lost his grip on the cup and it fell to the floor; the fine china shattering into a plethora of many small pieces.

"WHAT IS GOING ON?" he yelled, upset over the mess at his feet. Looking up and expecting to see one of his men, he was shocked to see Katerina standing before him. "Why are you here? What is so urgent that you have caused this mess? Well, speak up woman!"

Breathlessly Katerina tried to get the words out. "Typhus," she whispered between gulps of air, "Typhus."

"What *are* you talking about? What about typhus?" he demanded.

The guard regained his balance and came up behind Katerina, grabbing her elbow and pulling it back. She yanked out of his grip and managed enough breath to speak again. "The illness in the camp, the illness that my daughter has, is typhus. You need to do something! You need to get a doctor!"

"And why do I care that the women have, what did you call it, typhus?"

"Commandant, sir, I have heard of typhus," the guard interrupted.

The officer in charge looked with surprise at his underling, and when he saw the fear in the man's face he knew something was truly wrong. "Well? What is it that you have heard?"

The guard stood straight and faced his superior, "I have heard that this disease spreads quickly and can obliterate an entire camp in a very short time, but that there is prevention. A doctor would be a wise acquisition, sir."

"Fascist German kulaks bringing death and disease into my camp!" the commandant sputtered angrily at Katerina. He looked at the guard, regained his composure and calmly replied, "Then I must do what I must do. Here take this woman back to her barracks, I will decide on her punishment later." He dismissed them with a short wave of his hand.

As the guard escorted Katerina back across the compound, he kept his distance by carrying his rifle so that the muzzle pointed at her back. When they were close enough that she could enter the barracks, he returned the rifle to its place on his shoulder, and sprinted away, back across the compound to his post.

Katerina had only a quick chance to check on her daughter before roll-call. Karolina tried to rise and join the others headed out into the cold morning air. "Do not get up," Katerina admonished, "stay in bed, a doctor will be here later."

"But mother, if I do not work, I will not eat, *we* will not eat. Who will feed and care for Boris?"

"Karolina, if you go to the forest and die there, who will ever feed Boris? I will look after him, but you must stay here and get better. I have already let the guards know that you will be here in bed today."

Karolina finally gave in to her pounding head and aching body, and she lay back down on her plank. Katerina found a small piece of cloth, went outside and wrapped a bit of snow in it, returned and placed it on her daughter's head. Karolina closed her eyes, accepting her mother's attempt at comforting her.

By the time the women returned from their daily toil, changes had been made to their compound. One of the barracks, worst hit by the disease, had been turned into a rudimentary infirmary. Those who were so sick that they had remained behind that morning were moved into the central location for the doctor's inspection. Katerina tried to get in to see her daughter, but was turned back at the door by two guards. She stood with several other women holding vigil in a huddled group outside of the sick-room, quietly in prayer for their loved ones. Soon a long, black sedan pulled into the compound scattering the women as it stopped just outside the door of the barracks.

The driver's door opened and a woman stepped out. She stood straight and stiff in her perfect Russian uniform, her black hair severely pulled back into a bun under her flat brown cap. Her tight-fitting fuscous jacket was cinched in the middle with a shiny brown belt, while her shoulders squared off under bright-red epaulets. She stepped forward and began a slow methodical pace around the car, outstretching her long legs in their knee-high black boots; khaki riding britches billowed prominently at her thighs, defiantly advertising her feigned authority to the pitiful group before her.

She arrived at the rear passenger door of the car and snapped it open, standing at attention as she waited for the occupant to exit. The women, remaining in their huddled group, expected to see a high ranking official depart from the car.

A portly, grey-haired gentleman in a heavy fur coat unfolded himself from the back seat. From his mouth, he removed the pipe he had been smoking, tapped the glowing tobacco out of its bowl into the snow, and with his free hand, reached back into the sedan to pull out a black leather bag. When he was satisfied that the pipe was cool enough, he placed it in a side pocket of his coat, adjusted his wire-rimmed glasses and took a good look at the group watching him. He seemed disgusted at the sight of the emaciated, dirty creatures clustered in the congelation of mud and snow. Turning to the Russian uniform beside him, he uttered a heavy sigh and said, "Take me to the sick ones."

After the doctor and his aide disappeared into the building, a camp guard arrived and ordered the women back to their quarters. "My daughter is in there!" Katerina pleaded with the guard, "I need to know how she is."

The guard leveled his ever-present rifle parallel to his waist and pushed it toward the group. "Return to your barracks now, or suffer the consequences!" he demanded. The women reluctantly disbursed, slowly trudging through the icy mush back to their quarters.

Sofia greeted Katerina at the door, "Any news?"

Katerina quietly said, "The doctor has arrived."

Not caring what would happen to them if discovered, the worried but hopeful assemblage spent the night in a prayer vigil.

At morning roll-call the women were informed that they would not be going to their respective jobs. Instead they were to line up for inspection by the doctor.

The doctor arrived on foot, accompanied by one of the familiar camp troops. His impeccably uniformed aide from the night before did not seem to be present anywhere in the compound. The doctor carefully looked at each woman in the line, but touched none of them. When he arrived and stood in front of Katerina, a glimmer of recognition softened his weary face. "Do you have someone in the infirmary?" he asked her.

"My daughter." The words masked a thousand questions.

"Can you describe her for me?"

"Karolina is about eighteen, I think, blonde, less frail than most of us."

"Ah," the doctor nodded. "That one is strong, not only of body, but mind. She kept insisting that she needed to get to Boris. Her young man? A soldier, maybe?"

Katerina smiled a weary, concerned, motherly smile. "No, Boris is her logging horse. A man should be so lucky as to have her care as much for him as she does for that animal. Please, can you tell me how she is?"

The doctor placed his hand on Katerina's shoulder, "I wish they were all as strong as your Karolina. It will be rough for a few more days, but I think she will do fine. However, once the fever is broken it may take some time for her to regain her strength."

"Thank you, doctor, thank you."

The doctor started to walk away, and then asked another question. "When was the last time you women bathed?"

"We have little to wash with. Some of us collect snow or rainwater in our cooking pots and heat it on the stove. Mostly, we just wash our faces, hands and arms as best we can. We have no soap or clean towels to dry with."

"And your hair, how do you wash your hair?"

"We have not had that ability since we left our homes." Katerina reached up and brushed the loose strands around her braid with the back of her hand.

"Thank you for your honesty," the doctor replied as he moved on down the line.

When the doctor was satisfied with his inspection, he appeared in the commandant's office. "I have not been properly introduced, I am Anton Sorokov. As you might know, I am the shipyard's physician."

The camp commander shook the doctor's hand in earnest. "I am Commandant Alexei Volkvoi. Thank you, comrade, for coming so quickly. What is the status of my compound? Will this disease kill my troops?"

"Not if handled correctly and quickly. However, I wonder, how have you been able to avoid rampant illness in this camp before now?"

Taking some offence at the question, the commander stood up straight and puffed his chest in a manly display. "I treat these women fairly! They are fed as well as I am allowed to feed them, they have warm sleeping quarters, what more do you think they need?"

The doctor quickly saw he would get nowhere with this man and decided to change his approach. Lowering his voice into a calming tone he began, "Do your troops have bathing facilities?"

"Of course!" the commandant responded. "My troops have all that they need, and sometimes more!"

"And the women, how do they bathe?"

"They have no reason to bathe; they only need to work!"

"But Comrade Volkvoi, a woman's structure is such that she needs to bathe to remain healthy. How many women have you lost in this camp?"

"Only the ones that are too weak to do what is required of them, or the ones who are imprudent enough to get hurt in the forest."

"If you wish to maintain the health and well-being of your work-force and your troops, then you will have to accept that some changes must be made, and soon. You have an outbreak of typhus in this camp…"

"Yes, I know. The last trainload of those kulak fascists brought it with them. They will do what they can to destroy the Soviet benevo-lence we offer them."

"That may be, Comrade Volkvoi, but the disease is easily prevent-ed. You see, it is carried by body lice, and your women are covered in them. The first thing that must be done is to have them bathe and burn their clothing."

"If I burn their clothing, what will they wear? I have not been pro-vided with any apparel for these women!"

"I will arrange for the attire. I will have shipyard uniforms sent over. Now, please make plans for them to use the soldiers' facilities for bathing, and give them soap and clean towels or blankets for drying. Then we will address the additional measures that must be taken to stop the spread of this epidemic before it affects your men."

The women were waiting in their barracks when the soldiers came for them several hours later. One building at a time was emptied as the women were marched to the soldiers' latrine. Outside of the box-like chamber, they were ordered to disrobe leaving their clothing in the snow. Protests brought only laughter and leering from their unsympa-thetic sentries. Katerina and Sofia remained close to each other as they were ordered inside the building, still not knowing what was going to happen to them. The sight of the skeletal forms ahead of them nearly made them ill, until they realized that they, too, appeared like the others.

Once inside, a row of bare chairs were lined up across the cement floor. Half of the women were instructed to sit in the chairs, the other half were handed scissors. Each one was ordered to cut the hair off the woman seated before her. Tears flowed openly as thick locks and braids hit the floor. When the first group was done, places were switched and the process was repeated.

As Sofia removed Katerina's braid, Katerina asked "My hair has never been cut before; how will this change me?"

When the task was completed, the women were given hard bars of lye soap and sent to the open shower stalls. "Scrub thoroughly, even your heads," the men ordered.

The water was lukewarm, but the ladies reveled in the feeling of cleanliness. Even the leering eyes did not phase their meager pleasure at finally being able to wash themselves. As they finished, the soldiers handed out woolen blankets to dry their bodies and they were led into another room.

"You have been provided with new clothes," a young man announced. "But first you will have to be powdered to prevent the return of the lice."

"What kind of powder prevents lice?" one of the inmates inquired.

"They call it Chlordane. It is a good insecticide. It is used in America all the time, so it must be good," the man with the dusting bottle laughed.

Still naked, the joy of the shower wearing off, the women endured a cloud of chemicals. Lastly, they were handed tunics and trousers made of white quilted cloth. The clothing came in one size only, extra large. As the material tented over their boney bodies, cold air rushed in under the intended protection of the material. Each was given a woolen scarf, and a pair of rubber-like boots, but no stockings.

Upon returning to their quarters, the women witnessed piles of burning matter outside each barracks building. Inside, they found their few belongings ransacked. The handmade quilts and coverlets they had brought from home were all gone, replaced by hard scratchy woolen blankets on their sleeping planks. The pungent aroma of the chemicals

they had been sprayed with permeated the air. Bibles and family photos, carefully hidden under loose boards or within the quilts' layers
had been discovered and burned. There was little left to remind them
of their previous lives.

Katerina sat stiffly on the edge of her bunk. Sofia sat next to her.
"If this is what we have to endure for not being sick, what are they
putting Karolina through? What treatments is she receiving?" Unable
to control her emotions any longer, Katerina broke down into body-
wrenching sobs. Sofia placed her arms around her friend and held her
close for several minutes. As Katerina's tears eased and she began to
calm herself, Sofia reached up and stroked Katerina's forehead, letting
her fingers wander through the scant inch of hair that was left. "I am
sorry I had to do that to you."

Katerina sighed, "It feels like boar's bristles."

Sofia smiled softly. "Mine, too. Josef always said I was pig-headed, I
guess this proves it." Too distressed by all that was going on around her
to laugh at Sofia's meager attempt at humor, Katerina dried her eyes
with the heels of her palms and looked at Sofia with an improvised
smile of acceptance.

It was three days before Katerina was let into the infirmary to see
her daughter. Her eyes widened in shock and dismay at the sight of
Karolina, lying between the folds of a clean woolen blanket, her thin
bluish skin, which had been thoroughly scrubbed, pulled taut over her
hardened muscles, and topping it all was her bare head, completely
shaved. Karolina was awake, and reached for her mother; a wan smile
feebly traversed her lips. The doctor approached them— an air of gentle compassion on his face. "She is doing well, this one. Such power of
will she has."

"How soon will she be able to come back to me? How much
strength has she lost? Is there something I can do for her?"

"Oh, it will be at least another week, I should think. I want to be
sure she is truly able to return to work."

"Yes, doctor. "

"My name is Sorokov, Anton Sorokov; I was told you were the one who recognized the fever in the first place. May I ask how you knew it was typhus? Few people know the symptoms. The camp commandant was not even familiar with the name. Are you a nurse by chance?"

"No, sir, I am not a nurse. However, my bunkmate was, at one time, and even she did not know the problem at first. My husband dealt with the disease during the revolution. He saw many good soldiers lost in the trenches to the malady and often questioned how such a tiny insect could cause so much grief. When my daughter became ill, and I saw the louse emerge from her hair, typhus instantly came to my mind. I really did not know for sure, it was just a response."

"You did well, Madam, you did well. Tell me, if your husband made it through the revolution, do you know where he is now?"

"Last I saw him he was being led to the shipyard with the other men from our train. We have been told nothing more," Katerina answered cautiously.

"And how long have you been here, in this camp?"

"We arrived in late fall of 1929. But I have no idea how long we have been here, we have no clocks or calendars, only the passing of the seasons."

"You must have been on one of the early trains. Today is the twelfth of March, 1931. If you will tell me your husband's name, I might be able to discover where he is at present. There are big changes coming to the shipyard. Many of the detainees are being transferred to the new project in the west."

"A new project?"

"Yes, our great leader, Stalin, has devised a way to connect the White Sea to Lake Onega through a massive canal. It is to be a bit over 200 kilometers long and will allow ships to reach the northern ports during the winter... supply ships that are currently unable to traverse the frozen waters of the White Sea. The plan is to employ detainees from the various camps in the area to build this great and wonderful canal. Your husband, if he is still alive, will likely be sent to this project."

Katerina thought for a moment. *Will I put Johannes in jeopardy by giving his name to this man? He seems caring enough, but is he really a spy? What should I do? I really want to know about Johannes.* Finally, an idea came to her. "Doctor Sorokov, sir, I would very much like to know about my husband, but so would all of the other women. Would it be possible to be provided with a list of all those who will be going to the project? Then I can see, like the others, my husband's name in print, and I will be happy."

"That will be quite an undertaking; the list will be quite long."

"But, the morale of the women here would benefit greatly. Just knowing that our husbands are being sent to work on this magnificent project would strengthen the wills of those who feel all is lost for us. It would make them happy. Happy people work harder and Papa Stalin would profit from increased productivity in this camp."

"You make a good argument, Frau....I do not remember your name."

Without thinking, Katerina instantly responded, "Jahnle, Katerina Jahnle." As soon as the words slipped past her lips, a chill of realization slithered down her spine. Would this man be able to determine Johannes' name from hers? How could she protect her husband and yet, know where he was?

The doctor paused for a moment. "Jahnle," he repeated, "Jahnle. Why do I know that name? It is a different name, not common like Wagner or Lutz. You said you came in the fall of twenty-nine...why do I know that name?"

The blood rushed from Katerina's face, she felt weak and sick. *What have I done?* she repeated to herself over and over. She knew she could not let the doctor see the confusion that twisted her soul. She clenched Karolina's hand more and more tightly as she felt she was losing her grip on her senses. Her knees felt as if they could bear her weight no longer, so she slowly sat on the edge of Karolina's bunk, masking her desire to collapse onto the floor. Fighting with every bit of her being, she kept the tears at bay. Even though she tried very hard not to look at the doctor, his eyes finally met hers.

"Frau Jahnle…are you ill?" He placed his hand against her fore-head, "You are very warm, but I do not think you have the fever. Can you come with me?" He helped her up and supported her as she walked on wobbly legs to a chair that had been placed next to an im-provised desk of wooden boxes and planks. When she was seated, he took a thermometer out of the breast pocket of his coat and placed it in her mouth. She sat, her elbows on the desk's top, supporting her head with her hands. He removed the thermometer from her mouth and squinted at the small instrument. "No fever," he commented. "You might be having a reaction to the louse treatment. Wait here a minute."

She stayed seated, her head still supported by her hands, staring down at the desktop, and waited for the doctor to return. Her mind was so distorted under the weight of her indiscretion, she could not put thoughts together. She could only envision Johannes being hauled before a firing squad, or bound and beaten by soldiers, not knowing that it was she who betrayed him. *But, he has done nothing wrong, why should he be killed? Maybe there is no reason for my imagination to run so wild*, she admonished herself.

When the doctor returned, he handed her a small white pill, and a tin cup filled with water. "Here, take this; it should make you feel better." As Katerina swallowed the pill, the doctor lowered his ample body gingerly onto the desk. "Katerina…you did say your name was Katerina? Katerina, I have been thinking and trying to remember why I recognize your name and I believe I now know." She put the cup onto the desk and looked at the doctor; his voice was somehow soothing to her raw nerves. "The train you arrived on was one of the first, and we, meaning those running the shipyard and myself at the hospital, were not prepared to deal with the number of people that the government sent us. The first night there were many sick men, because they were fed stew that their starving bodies could not handle. I remember one man in particular who had the wisdom not to eat the stew. He told me he had experienced the 'ravage of starvation' during the revolution. This man I speak of had suffered some sort of injury to his left ear, there were scars and deafness."

Katerina caught her breath and her eyes quickly met the doctor's. Her swift reaction affirmed the doctor's suspicion that he was remembering the correct individual.

"A few days later," the doctor continued, "I was asked to make a list of names of the strongest individuals left in my infirmary. Jahnle... I believe the first name was Johannes, was on that list. Those men were returned to the train to bury the bodies of the children who were left behind to die in the snow. I am not sure what happened next, I have only heard rumors and stories." The doctor took Katerina's hand, and enveloped it between both of his. "I am sorry to tell you this, but it seems there was some sort of altercation with a guard. In the scuffle the guard's rifle fired, and your husband was shot and killed. I heard he died quickly and was buried with the children."

Katerina slowly pulled her hand away from the doctor. "Thank you for the information, doctor," she said calmly. "I am feeling better now, I must return to my daughter." She stood to leave, and Dr. Sorokov wondered if she had heard anything he had just told her. She offered her hand in friendship and goodbye, "my husband would not have fought with a soldier without a reason. That makes me believe he found the bodies of our children. If so, I have only Karolina now and she must be my only concern." The doctor watched in stunned silence as Katerina made her way back to her daughter.

Katerina reached Karolina's bedside, but her daughter was asleep. Taking Karolina's hand in hers, Katerina sat quietly on the edge of the bed. She revisited the doctor's words and was surprised at her own lack of feeling about what she had just heard. *I feel so numb, so insensitive, so distant. Why? Has my heart become so hard that I cannot cry for the loss of my husband and children? Are there no tears left in me?* Then without another thought, she began reciting a verse from 1 Corinthians. She repeated it over and over, remembering the last time she had spoken these words, remembering the day she and Johannes recited them together as part of their wedding vows.

Beareth all things, believeth all things, hopeth all things, endureth all things.

CHAPTER TWENTY-FIVE

Anya's Shield

It was very early when Anya awoke with a special excitement; Sonia was taking her to the village market today. Sonia only made this trip once or twice each summer, and until today, always alone.

"Oma, you have never allowed me to go into Onega before; you have always said that the village is a dangerous place for me. Why are you taking me now?" Anya asked as she dressed for the trek.

"Anya, you have asked many times to go with me to the village, and I have always said no. I have felt it was just too dangerous. But, you are about thirteen years old now, and I think you are old enough to know how to find your way to the village. There will come a time when you must be able to go there on your own. You must learn how to talk to the people, and you must do so without revealing who you really are."

"But why, Oma?"

Sonia sat on the edge of her bed, struggling to pull on her deer-hide boots. "This past winter has not been good to me, child. My bones ache, my joints no longer move without pain. I fear I can no longer make this trip alone, but we need things that the forest cannot provide. Flour for our bread is not a gift from our trees, but from the grasses of the south." She groaned softly as she gave one last hard tug at the boot. Finally standing up and taking hold of her walking stick, she straightened as she leaned on the staff for support. Anya noticed that, even around the house, Sonia was becoming more and more reliant on this knobby length of wood, and made sure it was always within Sonia's reach.

Sonia picked up her leather knapsack from the table and gave it to Anya. "Carry this for me, please; it is full of mushrooms and herbs for trading. When we arrive, keep your head covered, dear, and say as little as possible to the villagers. That will help avoid too many questions."

"But, Oma, why should I avoid questions? What questions will be asked of me?"

"People will see that you are different from me. They will want to know where you came from, how you came to live with me."

Anya was puzzled. "You needed to bring me here. You needed my help. When you took me from the train, it was a good thing. The soldier said it was. Surely many of the other children were taken in by the people of the village; there should be a lot of children like me living there, even my brothers. Why would it matter now?" Anya followed Sonia, picking her way through the woods to the main path.

"On my past trips into the village, I have not seen many children as fair as you. I think that few, if any of the others, were given homes. I do not know what may have happened to the other children that came with you, but I am sure they are not here."

"Is that why you keep me in the forest, away from the others, away from school?"

Sonia paused in the middle of the well-worn foot path. Anya knew that Sonia needed to stop frequently and rest, but she was anxious to get to Onega; wanting to keep moving, she began to step around the old woman. The walking stick quickly came up off the ground and blocked Anya's path. In her haste, the girl's lack of attention nearly caused her to step on a small, dark-green grass snake gliding across the trail, hunting toads for its supper.

Sonia scowled, but said nothing of Anya's near indiscretion. Instead, she returned the stick to its place and just stood, deep in thought. She looked at Anya and noted that this girl would soon turn into a stunningly beautiful young woman. The delicate features enhanced by pale golden locks and sea-blue eyes contrasted starkly to Sonia's furrowed dark shell. Sonia had been very protective of her young charge. Yes, she had kept Anya away from the school in the village, at first fearing that taunts and threats by the other children would too deeply injure Anya's spirit, then as time progressed, it was to keep her from physical harm. But Anya was not without an education. Sonia made her read aloud from the Bible every night, and they would discuss the comparisons and contrasts with the Selkup native beliefs. The child was taught to gather fresh plants from the forest and dry them for winter consumption, and Anya became adept at brewing the teas and potions for which Sonia was known. Mastering the skills to create cut-lace and fine embroidery, kneading the black rye-bread dough and tending the heavy loaves as they baked by the fire, and learning to sew deer hides together to make the warm, protective clothing the Selkups depended on through the arctic winters, was Anya's testament to Sonia's teaching principles.

The old woman took Anya's delicate hand into her arthritic aged one and spoke softly, "Many things have changed since I brought you here. There is much in the world that you do not yet understand. Your people are said to be enemies of the government and are no longer welcome in Russia. They are considered spies and criminals, and I believe your parents were taken to the labor camps because of who they are and not anything they have done. You and your brothers and all of the other children that arrived with you—and on the later trains—are not supposed to be alive. That is why I protect you. I have heard the stories in the village on past visits, but I did not think you were old enough to learn of these things. Now, I see that you are reaching womanhood, and there are things you must gain knowledge of, beyond the skills I have taught you."

Anya listened silently, watching the snake slip into the grass on the far side of the path. Sonia returned to hobbling up the trail; Anya shifted the knapsack on her shoulder, and as she began to follow, asked, "Will I ever be able to visit the village on my own?"

Sonia expected questions, lots of questions, but was a bit surprised by one so simple and direct. "I have to see how today goes. But, yes, there will come a time when you must be able to do this on your own, and I believe you will do just fine."

They walked on in silence for some time before Anya finally spoke once more. "Oma, I know that I will never see my real family again, and I am alright with that because you and Rodin are my family now.

The villagers will just have to get used to me being different. I think they are the ones who are different, so every time I am asked a question about who I am, I will ask them the same question." Sonia smiled in response.

It was mid-morning when they finally reached the edge of town. As they left the protection of the forest, the air became significantly warmer, and the ground was wet from a late night downpour. Anya covered her head with her scarf in an attempt to silence the buzz of the mosquitoes that swarmed around her. She and Sonia slogged through the long grass along the unpaved road that led to the town, avoiding the water-filled ruts of the sticky red-brown muck of the lane. As they got closer, Sonia turned and proceeded through a narrow alleyway behind rows of houses.

Anya scrutinized each building as they passed. She observed that most of them were made of some type of wood, either slats or squares or a mis-match of each, unpainted and rotting from the damp air. The roofs were formed from large sheets of rippled tin, some shining in the summer sunlight, others a mottled dirty red from rust eating away at the surface. For the most part, the houses seemed to be many times the size of Sonia's cottage, and she wondered how many rooms each had within. Some houses were connected with solid wooden fences between them, and where Anya could see into the yards that were formed by these fences, she caught sight of small vegetable gardens or chicken houses.

A few of the residences sported small pens along the alley itself, most constructed of short pickets wired together around a large box-like structure. These pens were occupied by dogs, all resembling the sled dogs of Rodin's tribesmen— some more than others. The dogs all seemed to know Sonia and wagged their tails happily at her presence. She spoke to them in Selkup as she passed each pen, and the dogs seemed content with her attention. As Anya approached, however, the dogs eagerly strained against their barriers, anxious to examine this newcomer. Following Sonia's lead, she spoke to each of the dogs in a soft voice; just saying "Hello" was often satisfactory. One dog caught

Anya's attention, and she stopped for a better look. A sleek black and silver female with one amber and one blue eye stood on the ramp to her doghouse. Behind the dog and above the entry, a small wooden plaque had the word "Fayina" painted in a child's Cyrillic scrawl. The dog stared at Anya with an aloofness that resembled supremacy.

"You act like you are something really special; are you the empress?" Anya asked.

Sonia turned and looked to see who Anya was talking to. "Yes, she is royalty. She is one of Miko's pups, by Yerik's Suka. The family must be at the market, because this animal is usually in the house." Sonia shook her head at the thought of a house dog.

When they finally reached the town square, it was filled with people. Anya was not prepared for the crowds and shyly drew herself behind Sonia, who ignored the child and went about her business. It was not long, though, before a group of children gathered in Sonia's wake.

A boy about Anya's age began shouting "Witch, Witch" and throwing small pebbles at Sonia. Others waved sticks in the air, as if warding off demons. Another hollered, "She is why we cannot go into the forest alone; she eats children for supper! All but this one, it seems." The group laughed as they pointed their sticks at Anya.

Anya was astonished and angered at the same time. A deep burning sensation arose within her, and she turned to face the gang. She stood up straight with her arms outstretched like eagle's wings, and curled her fingers into talons. Her scarf fell back over her shoulders, uncovering her platinum locks. Her ice-blue eyes glared. She said nothing as she stood her ground. She did not have to.

"It is a ghost! The witch has brought a ghost to steal our souls!" The children screamed as they ran off in all directions. Tears formed in Anya's eyes. The feeling that her heart had been wrenched out of her chest and thrown upon the ground caused a coldness to flow through her and she began to shiver. Sonia replaced the errant scarf, and put her arm around Anya's shoulders. She knew Anya would need time for the anger and surprise and the resulting adrenalin-rush to subside.

"I am accustomed to the taunts of the children," Sonia sighed, "but, I did not expect this."

A woman selling vegetables stepped forward, "Are you alright? Those children are horrid; I will speak to their parents."

Sonia waved the woman off, "Thank you for your concern, but that is not necessary. We are not hurt. Children only know what they learn from their parents, and it seems tolerance is not a readily learned behavior here."

The woman handed Sonia a small bunch of carrots, "I do not know where this child came from, but she is not a ghost. Instead, I think you have found an angel," the woman looked up toward the running children, "and I think you should keep her close."

"Thank you, and yes, I intend to do just that." Sonia smiled, placed the carrots into the knapsack, and put her arm around Anya's waist, guiding her back to the main road and out of the village.

The women traveled in silence as they proceeded back to the protection of the forest. At length, Sonia said, "When the time comes, I feel you would be better off joining Rodin's family, and not returning to the village."

"Oma, I will just stay with you. I have no reason to leave, ever."

If only that were true, little one, if only that were true, Sonia reflected.

CHAPTER TWENTY-SIX

What Gain Hath the Worker From His Toil?

The years slipped into oblivion for the women of the labor camps. Changes appeared in the compound—changes reflecting the transformation of the civilized world; changes echoing the politics and policies of the Soviet government toward the *Russlanddeutschen*, the ethnic German-Russians; changes hinting at the malevolence yet to come.

The lumber camp was at first encircled by a barbed wire fence, but as more trains arrived, swelling the population of the compound, the fences were replaced with high walls of reinforced concrete crowned with coils of the "Devil's Rope." The barracks buildings, suffering through the ravages of winter and the humidity of summer, decayed around the women attempting to live within. There seemed to be no Soviet policy of repairing or replacing such structures.

The national famine was felt within the work camps, as much as, or possibly more so, than in the rest of the country. The issuance of ration cards, *toloni*, and meals in the form of stew, or gruel and bread, had been replaced with handouts of 800 grams (28 ounces) of bread each day, but only to those who actually worked. And to those whose work was exemplary, an additional offering of 500 grams of sugar (about one pound) per month was presented. Those who were too ill, too crippled, too exhausted to work received nothing.

Each morning, the women were ordered to carry the bodies of those who had not survived the night to a large storehouse where food reserves had previously been kept. Where the corpses were taken from there, no one seemed to know.

The doctor had been good on his word of procuring a list of all the men taken from the shipyard to work on Stalin's White Sea-Baltic Canal. It had been posted on the infirmary wall for all to see. Katerina did not find Johannes' name listed, confirming the doctor's words of Johannes' death. Sofia found Josef's name there. However, his name was also listed on a subsequent register of those who died during the construction. Sofia grieved for months, but through faith and Katerina's constant strength, she finally accepted her loss.

The winter of 1933 was a particularly harsh one. In January, temperatures dropped below minus 36 degrees Fahrenheit. The few hours of murky daylight were quickly replaced by the unforgiving shadows of the night. The women continued to labor in the forest.

It had been nearly two years since Karolina's bout with typhus; as soon as she was able, she returned to her job of hauling logs to the mill. Now, she was tramping through the snow behind Boris as he pulled the heavy loads. The horse's thick, long hair-coat caked in clumps of salty ice as sweat from his effort rose to the surface and froze. Moist air expelled from his nostrils crystallized almost instantly, then burst with a barely audible tinkle, something the older women called "the whisper of the stars." Working in the pallid glow of gas lanterns, barely able to see the road ahead of them, Karolina no longer wasted energy trying to talk to the horse over the howl of the wind; her face was blackened with frostbite, her lips frozen to the scarf that covered them.

Boris had already lost the tips of his ears to the frozen air. His eyes, watering from the force of the unrelenting flurries, were nearly frozen shut. He plodded along blindly, relying solely on Karolina's guidance. Together, they had made a multitude of trips to the sawmill and this load was their last before the shift ended. The load consisted of two large trunks chained together behind the big horse.

Karolina guided Boris carefully along the skid road toward the slope that led to the landing where the logs would be held prior to being processed at the mill. Her hands, wrapped in strips of cloth, were nearly petrified from the cold. She had not felt her feet for hours, but she really had not noticed. It was just another day in the forest for the two of them. Cold, bored and inattentive, Karolina's mind wandered.

She had every confidence that Boris knew the track he was to follow, especially since the downhill grade made the final leg of their journey easier on him. Besides, her hands were too numb to pull on the lines.

Boris, eyes closed, dropped his head and put his shoulder into the collar, waiting for the inevitable signal from Karolina that he could ease up as they turned into the roadway. He felt no tug on the line, so he continued on straight. He had gone about twenty feet when Karolina realized he was not turning as expected. She picked up the left line and pulled, but with her frozen hands she could not feel the tension on the rein, so she gave a hard tug. The surprising jerk on his mouth caused Boris' head to fly up in surprise. He began to step left, but caught his large hoof on a small stump that stood as a marker at the edge of the road. As he fell to his knees, he jammed the stump into his chest, knocking the wind out of him. Karolina dropped the lines and started to run to the horse as he floundered in the snow. She stumbled, arose, and stumbled again, unable to make her feet move as she intended. Boris struggled to get to his feet, but snow balled up in the soles of his hooves, and he was unable to get a grip on the slick ground. His struggling caused his heavy body to begin a slow slide down the slope. He continued his fight to stand, but his harness tangled in the chain traces attached to the logs, and the more he fought, the faster he slid down the hill. Karolina finally reached the horse's head and grabbed hold of his bridle, trying to steady him, trying to give him something to brace against.

Boris' struggle caused one log to flip over the other, twisting in the chains that secured them. They, also, began a slow precarious slide down the hill. The logs outweighed Boris and dragged him along their path. Karolina's frozen fingers could not let go of the bridle, and she, too, was pulled into the slipping load. Logs, horse and human tumbled as one down the soggy knoll. The seconds that it took for this to happen seemed like an eternity to Karolina. She felt her fingers, then her arm, snap like dry twigs. Her trailing scarf caught on the hames cap of Boris' collar, tightened around her face and throat, and pulled her under him as he rolled.

Two guards, warming themselves by a barrel full of wood scraps burning in the holding yard, heard the clamor up the road. Grabbing their rifles and lanterns, they ran toward the noise. Arriving at the scene, they saw the logs, entwined in their chains, blocking the road. A deep groan emanated in the darkness. Lifting their lanterns skyward, they spotted the great horse on his side, tangled and torn. He was bleeding from his chest and a foreleg lay awkwardly under him.

"He will have to be put out of his misery," one of the men uttered as he put the rifle to the horse's head and pulled the trigger. He stooped to take a closer look at the animal, "This is Boris, so where is his girl? She is never far from him."

His colleague moved around the horse, "Here!" he declared. "She is under him!"

Several additional soldiers, hearing the unexpected gunshot, arrived on the scene; a couple of them rolled Boris' body over, revealing Karolina. She was laying face down in the sludge. One man reached down and turned her over. A voice from the group asked "Well…infirmary or storehouse?"

"Storehouse. Her neck is broken."

"She was a good worker, we will lose production output."

"And we lost a good horse, too."

When Karolina had not shown up at the barracks by bedtime, Katerina knew she lost another child. She lay upon Karolina's empty sleeping plank and waited in the dark. She said no prayers; she shed no tears. She let the emptiness consume her.

It was Sofia who shed the tears that night. She cried for the loss of her best friend's child, a young woman she knew well; she cried for her own losses, home and family; but mostly she cried for the inevitable loss of Katerina.

Arriving in the barn the next morning, Katerina found Boris' stall empty. She slowly entered it and sank upon the straw in the corner. Sofia silently went to work feeding the sheep and ox, and cleaning the pens; she willingly expected she would do double duty today. Katerina sat and stared into the abyss of her lost soul. Despite her emptiness, she soon joined Sofia in the sheep pens, throwing herself into her work without a word. Sofia respected her friend's grief and did not try to initiate conversation.

Upon returning to their quarters at the end of the day, Sofia and Katerina discovered that another woman had moved into Karolina's sleeping area. Katerina said nothing. She crawled onto the plank that she shared with Sofia, and curled herself tightly against the cold wall. Sofia wrapped Katerina in her blanket and whispered, "Be strong and take heart, you must put your trust in the Lord."

Katerina pulled the blanket closer about her and closed her eyes. Softly, distantly, she spoke the words that came to her, words she knew well from her Bible, "'My grief is beyond healing; my heart is broken.' 'My soul is exceeding sorrowful, even unto death: abide ye here and watch with me.' *Wir werden uns wieder im Himmel treffen.*, we will meet again in Heaven."

The words cut through Sofia. *Katerina is willing herself to die! We only have each other now, and I am not about to lose the person I depend on for physical, mental, and spiritual strength!*

"'No man hath power over the spirit to retain the spirit, neither hath he power in the day of death…!' these are the words of the Bible you should quote!" she angrily exclaimed. Guilt instantly seized her heart for saying these words to someone so deep in grief. Biting back her sorrow, she lay upon the bunk and wrapped her arms about Katerina's shoulders. Taking a deep breath to calm her words, she quietly exhaled a simple prayer, "'Find rest, O my soul, in God alone; my hope comes from Him.'"

Arkhangelsk Oblast

White Sea

River Mazen

River Taz

● Arkhangelsk

●Onega

Karelia

Komi Republic

River Northern Dvina

Vologda Oblast

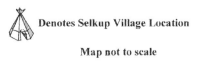

Denotes Selkup Village Location

Map not to scale

CHAPTER TWENTY-SEVEN

Anya's Journey

EARLY APRIL 1934

Anya looked forward to the early spring and late fall visits of Rodin and his dogs. Their arrival meant she and Sonia would have a fresh supply of meat and fish, a welcome change to the berries, mushrooms, onions and wild cabbages of the woods. Rodin's arrival also meant days of cooking and preparation of the meat for sausages and the smoking and salting of the fish. When they were not busy with food preparation, Anya reveled in Rodin's stories of his adventures hunting the taiga and tundra, herding the reindeer that his tribe managed for the Soviets, and laughing as he described the errors and missteps of the foreign stranger who had come to live with the tribe.

"Where did this man come from?" she asked.

"I was told he is a sailor from Norway, but I do not think so. While his hunting skills are quite adequate, his fishing abilities have been lacking. I think he must have been a farmer of some sort. He is good with the herds, and can milk a cow faster than most of the women," Rodin laughed heartily.

"Why do you laugh?" Anya asked

"Only women milk our cows!" He explained through his chuckles.

"My Papi used to milk our cow when Mama was too busy with my brothers and sisters. He never thought it was funny," Anya shrugged.

"I guess that is another difference in our people from yours, Snowflake, especially since our cows are semi-tamed reindeer with large antlers."

"Tell me more, Rodin. I want to know more about this stranger in your clan."

"He stays with Yerik's family; he was quick to learn how to take a *sampa* apart and pack it on the *pulk* for transport. He seems to have no problem keeping up with the herds as we travel to the feeding grounds. He spends time with the children of the camp, and teaches them to carve antler and bits of wood." Rodin looked at Anya, "He is very pale like you, but he seems tough enough to keep up with us."

There was one question Anya was nearly afraid to ask, but the answer was very important to her. She took a deep breath and braced herself. "What is his name?'

"They call him Yanochan." Rodin answered casually, not understanding Anya's hesitation.

"Yanochan," she repeated quietly, as her heart sunk in disappointment.

"Why did you ask, little one?" Sonia was listening to the conversation and noted Anya's discontent.

"When Rodin talks about this man…I feel…he sounds very much like my Papi. I was hoping he really was Papi. But, I guess I was just being silly." Anya fought her tears of embarrassment and disillusionment.

"Well, maybe someday, you will find your Papi. But, do not plan your days on such a quest, as I fear it may be a distant one," Sonia embraced the child warmly.

The winter of Anya's fifteenth birthday had been an especially hard one on Sonia. Even though Anya kept the little cottage unbearably warm by over loading the fireplace with large logs, Sonia complained of the cold. She kept to her bed most days, and Anya found it necessary to improvise a chamber pot from one of the cooking caldrons, as Sonia could no longer make the journey to the '*Toilettenhäuschen*'.

As spring crept into the forest, and the first blooms of crocus emerged through the snow, Sonia became more unresponsive to Anya's efforts to assist her daily needs. Sonia spoke little, and when she did she only repeated "Malvina," over and over.

Anya prayed that Rodin would arrive soon. She feared that Sonia was going to die and leave her alone— in the cottage, in the forest, isolated from the world. It was a glorious day for Anya when she heard the tantara of the dogs' yips and barks as Rodin pulled up outside the cottage door. She was sitting on the edge of Sonia's bed, knotting colored threads together into a belt for her simple shapeless sarafan and chatting idly to keep Sonia calm, when she heard Rodin arrive. She dropped her work as she ran to the door to greet the man she had come to know as a brother.

"RODIN!" she shouted as she flew out of the door and embraced the somewhat surprised man tying his dogs to the trees. "Oh, Rodin, I am so glad to see you."

As Rodin embraced Anya, he looked over her shoulder toward the open door, expecting to see his mother standing there. The doorway remained empty. As he peeled himself free from this young woman, who was now as tall as he, Rodin noted Anya's uncharacteristically disheveled appearance and her tired eyes. "Where is Mother?" he asked calmly.

"Oh Rodin, it has been a hard winter on her. She is too frail to leave her bed. I am doing my best to care for her."

"Can you finish tying the dogs while I go to her?" Rodin asked.

"Yes, yes…of course."

When she was done with the dogs, Anya quietly entered the cottage. Rodin was standing over Sonia, talking to her in their Selkup language. Sonia reached for him and mumbled something unintelligible to Anya's ears. Rodin turned to Anya.

"She is asking for the '*teetypy*', our village shaman. She wishes to speak to the spirit of my sister, Malvina. She knows she is going to die soon, and wants to let my sister know that she will be joining her in the higher world."

Anya was familiar with the Selkup belief of the division of life into three spheres: the middle world, or one's physical life; the under world, where you did not want to be, ever; the higher world, where you went when you died. She and Sonia often discussed the similarities between the Selkup 'spheres' and the Christian beliefs of Heaven and Hell. What Anya was surprised to hear was the reference to Malvina as Rodin's sister. In all the time Anya had been with Sonia, a sister to Rodin was never mentioned.

The image of the doeskin dress that Sonia let Anya wear that first day flashed in her memory. The care that Sonia took in handling the dress, and the loving way she put the dress back into its box under her bed, should have alerted Anya to the possibility that a young girl had preceded her in this cottage, but she had not given it any more thought than if it had been any other garment.

Rodin moved to the chair by the table. He sat and watched his mother. Still wearing his heavy parka and boots, he began to sweat in the overheated room, but paid no attention to his own discomfort as he contemplated what to do.

Anya pulled at the edge of his coat, "You had better give this to me, or you will suffocate in here. Oma seems to be unable to keep warm, so I have been keeping the fire fed."

Rodin stood and removed his coat and handed it to Anya. He returned to the chair, and turned his gaze to his mother. Sonia drifted off into a tranquil sleep, reassured by the presence of her son. "Our village is three days travel from here. The shaman was in the village when we left, he had not yet departed for his summer dwelling in the forest. I will stay here tonight, to give the dogs time to rest. Tomorrow I will go into Onega and find Yerik and a couple of the other men for the trip back to our village."

"That means you will be gone at least six days?" Anya asked with trepidation in her voice; she did not want to be left alone again.

"Six days? Why would…Oh, no, I mean that I will gather the men to help me take Mother and you to our village. I will be back tomorrow afternoon, and we can leave early the following day."

"Why do you need the others?" Anya was still a bit confused.

"The dogs cannot pull the sled with three people in it. Or were you planning on staying here?"

"No, please do not leave me here alone in the forest! I very much want to go with you and Oma!"

"Then, after I leave tomorrow, you will need to pack up the things we will take with us, but nothing too heavy. Keep the dogs in your thoughts as you prepare the load. We will need food for the trip, and basic supplies, but cooking pots and baking pans can stay here."

"I understand," Anya responded, "but now, what if I use them tonight and prepare something for all of us to eat?"

"Good thinking, Snowflake. I will get some meat from the sled, and then settle the dogs for the night while you are making supper."

As Anya cooked, she thought about what things she should pack and what to leave behind. She already understood about the pots and pans, but she would have to ask Rodin about other items, like the spinning wheel and her sleeping mat. Anya made a quick fish soup with the fresh sturgeon Rodin gave her, and some of the dried mushrooms and wild onions she and Sonia had gathered last fall. Slices of freshly baked rye bread were added to the fare, along with a sweet hot tea of huckleberry blossoms and bilberries.

Rodin ate in silence as Anya tried to get Sonia to accept a morsel of bread soaked in the soup. When he had his fill, he pushed himself away from the table and wiped his mouth on his sleeve. "Mother has taught you well. You will have to teach my wife how to make this soup; she always overcooks the fish."

Anya smiled at the compliment. "I am surprised that she cooks the fish at all. Oma says you prefer your fish raw."

"Yes, there is nothing better than good raw fresh fish; we all eat it that way. But, there are times when my wife insists on making soup, and she cooks the fish until it disappears."

Anya quickly cleaned up the dishes, attended to Sonia's needs, then sat on the floor at Rodin's feet. This was her way of telling him she wanted one of his tales of adventure while hunting or fishing. Tonight, however, she had a special request. "Tell me about Malvina," she requested in a soft voice.

"If that is what you want. There is really not much to tell. Malvina was born three years after I was. The following summer we lost our father. He was fishing on the River Taz, and had caught a large pike in his stake net. As he was struggling to pull the fish into his boat, the net lodged on a snag under the water. Somehow the tangle of fish and net pulled him into the water, and he was swept away in the strong current. Our people always made sure we had food and a house; our village works that way. The shaman took Mother under his wing and taught her the ways of the forest— the secrets of the teas and potions for healing.

"Traditionally, when our girls reach the age of thirteen they are honored with a special ceremony to guide them into womanhood. Malvina asked for a special dress for the ceremony, so she and Mother worked all that winter preparing the dress and a pair of boots for the spring rites. She looked so pretty in that dress..." Rodin stopped talking as he stared off into the distance, the vision of his sister twirling gracefully in the dress filled his memory.

"That is the dress in the box under Oma's bed," Anya said.

"You have seen it then? Did you think it was beautiful?"

"Oh, yes, it is so soft and the pattern around the edge is wonderful." Anya was not sure she should mention that she had actually worn the dress once, or that she had worn the boots until her feet outgrew them. "So what happened to Malvina?"

"Malvina was out with the reindeer herd during the spring thaw. She was with several girls moving the herd to fresh ground, when a fissure in the ice opened up. Malvina, along with several cows, fell through the opening. One of the other girls saw what happened, but could do nothing to help. The tundra can be a very dangerous place, especially during the thaw."

"Why has Oma not told me any of this? Until she became ill, I had never heard Malvina's name."

"Mother suffered much from Malvina's loss. She was sure she had angered the spirits by learning the shaman's secrets. She felt shamed and disgraced. The shaman and our people tried to show her that it was not her fault, but she would have none of it. She left me with an uncle, took the dress and boots and disappeared into the forest for many years. After a long time our people thought she must be dead, then one day she just appeared. Her leg had been injured in a fall from a tree while escaping a bear's attack. She rejoined the clan for a short time, but remained detached, in her own world up here…" Rodin pointed to his head.

"I was happy that she returned, but our closeness suffered from her absence. I never really got to know her, in the same way, again. After a few months, she told me she was leaving once more. That is when she came to this place. She has never spoken completely of her life during her absence, nor have I asked. When she came here, she offered to keep the village stocked with the herbs and teas and healing potions that we need, and the tribe was pleased. Over the years we have become closer, but she never returned to our village; she has not met my wife. She has seen my children, because I have brought them here on occasion, but she does not know them, not like a grandmother should." Rodin rose from the chair, indicating that he was finished talking for the night. He shook out his fur bedroll and placed it on the floor on the far side of the room, away from the heat of the fire.

Anya checked on Sonia one more time, banked the fire for the night, blew out the lantern and settled onto her own mat.

The morning dawned gray, and a light rain drizzled through the trees, as Rodin removed a sufficient amount of meat from his sled for the trip home and handed it to Anya to include in her packed items. After feeding and harnessing the dogs, and saying a quick goodbye to his mother and Anya, he was gone. Anya began emptying the cupboards of the collection of forest herbage and preserved meats. She put them into a variety of small leather and cloth sacks that she and Sonia used on their trips into the woods when they gathered fresh plants. She folded and piled her and Sonia's few items of clothing onto the table, along with dishes and other kitchen items.

Rodin returned late that afternoon, accompanied by three of his clansmen and their sleds and dogs. The other men settled their dogs, built a fire and set up a sleeping tent in a clearing near the cottage. Rodin had sold the remaining meat and fish and now returned with an empty sled to transport his mother.

Anya was busy preparing the evening meal when Rodin entered the cottage. Sonia was sleeping.

"I see you have been busy," Rodin commented when he saw the piles of possessions around the room.

"I am still not sure what all we should take, there was more in these cupboards than I thought," Anya sighed. "I realize that we must leave the table and chairs and Oma's bed, but I was wondering about the spinning wheel, and the bear rug I sleep on."

Rodin picked through the items on the table and set a few easily breakable things aside. "Your rug is needed; you will be covered with it in the sled and sleep on it at night. I think there will be room for the wheel if we dismantle it and bundle it securely. I would suggest that you wear as much of your clothing as possible; you will appreciate the warmth, and it will take less room. Mother's clothes and some of the other cloth items can be used to wrap the dishes. Where is the box with Malvina's dress? We must find room for that."

Anya knelt by Sonia's bed and reached underneath. She gently pulled the box toward her so she would not disturb the restful sleep of the old woman. Once clear of the bed, she stood and lifted the box and placed it on the table. Rodin pushed the toggle, made from a bit of antler, through the slit in the leather latch and opened the box. He removed the dress and held it up to the light, a smile of remembrance unfurled across his face.

"MALVINA!" Sonia cried from her bed as she reached toward the dress silhouetted in the lantern light, "Malvina...." Her voice drifted softly as she returned to her slumber.

Rodin quickly returned the dress to its box and latched it shut. As he placed the box on the floor by the door, Anya asked, "What will happen to it?"

"We will take it with us to the shaman. This dress will serve as the passage between Mother and Malvina's spirit. When the time comes, it will be hung in a tree near her coffin-boat as an offering to the spirit-ancestors as Mother travels the 'sea of the dead.'"

"Rodin," Anya hesitated before continuing, "is it a bad thing if someone else wore the dress?"

Rodin took a long look at Anya, seeing her uneasiness and anticipating her concern. "Not necessarily, why?" He wondered if she had worn the dress without his mother knowing.

"When I first arrived—when Oma first brought me here—I had only the clothing I was wearing, and it was tattered and filthy. Oma bathed me and put the dress on me that night. I wore it until the next afternoon, when she found something more suitable for me. I did not know about Malvina, I just thought it was a very pretty dress." Anya choked back her tears of guilt and despair at the thought of having ruined the dress.

"Under those circumstances, I believe there will not be a problem, unless you defiled it by killing an animal or conjuring up evil spirits while wearing it." Rodin grinned as he teased her.

"Oh, No!" she declared, "I never would have done anything like that!"

"Then there is nothing to worry about," Rodin reassured her.

The following morning the sleds were loaded and the dogs were hitched and ready to run. Rodin carefully carried his mother out and tucked her into his sled, making sure she was warm and comfortable. Sonia reached up, feebly took hold of Rodin's sleeve, and smiled. She was wide awake and ready to make this journey.

Heavily garbed in layers of clothes, Anya carefully stepped into Yerik's sled and cautiously sat on the mound of clothing and blankets already placed in the basket. Yerik threw her bear hide sleeping mat over her and pushed the edges in tightly around her. She could feel the knots in the leather bindings that formed the sides of the basket and the tethers that held it to the sled, but she knew she would have to get used to the discomfort. She slipped her hand into the pocket of her coat and wrapped her fingers around the wooden doll that resided there. The doll was nearly worn smooth in many places; it had been her constant comfort in the five years since Rodin presented it to her, and at the moment it soothed some of her anxiety and apprehension about the trip she was now taking. Until now, she had not realized how afraid she was to leave the cottage behind. The last time she had been wrenched from her home resulted in a terrible journey, but she settled down here with Sonia and she eventually found happiness. Where was this trip taking her?

Rodin gave a quick shout-out to his dogs, and they were off at an easy trot down the forest trail. Yerik followed close behind and the others soon shadowed after them. Anya had taken short trips with Rodin before, so, expecting the excitement of the ride, she relaxed back into her seat and peered over the furry hide. Once the dogs reached their stride and realized they were headed for home, they traveled quietly, saving their strength for the trek ahead. Except for the occasional command to the dogs from the mushers, the silence of the forest was broken only by the swoosh of sled runners as they glided over the snow. Their travels took them through clear-cut areas left behind by the logging operations of the lumber camp. Anya thought of her family, and wondered if her mother or sisters had traversed these places, and if she might catch a glimpse of them along the way. However, she soon realized that the Selkups were not going where any people might be encountered, only through deserted, empty regions of barren woodlands.

By early afternoon they left all vestiges of the forest and started out across the open tundra. The dog teams transformed from columns into compact triangles behind their leading females. The sleds moved parallel to each other across the naked plain. Anya looked upon the vast openness at the endless expanse of snow, broken only by rolling hills and frozen lakes. As she soaked in the sight before her she thought, *the snow and hills are beautiful, but merciless in their starkness. They make me feel small and unimportant.* She glanced over at Rodin and the bundled, sleeping, Sonia. He was concentrating on his dogs, but seemed to have a reverent look to him. *I see similar feelings in Rodin's face. This is his land, and yet, somehow, he seems humbled by it.*

In the distance, a howl pierced the stillness, the singular cry of a wolf. It did not go unnoticed by the men or the dogs, as all heads turned to the east. Anya searched the terrain, seeing nothing except gray sky. Tears formed in her eyes, but they were not from dread or fear of the wolf. They were not even from the cold wind that stung her face. *I understand the wolf's song,* she realized, *he cries out to be recognized in this vast and lonely land. His howl grabs at my heart and chills my spine, and yet I feel as one with him. He is me, and I, him, as he cries out for his family, cries out for all that is lost forever.* She again took comfort in the doll in her pocket, running her fingers over its features, caressing it in her palm.

The dogs altered their direction a bit to the west, but continued north toward the village. Anya closed her eyes against the wind and her thoughts, erasing her tears with the edge of the hide. She breathed in the familiar scent of the tanned bear, intermingled with the aromatic essence of the cottage. She remembered the day she had wandered too far, and Sonia's resultant admonition to stay close to the cottage and not meander off into the forest alone. "*A call for help might well go unheard, or, if heard, unfound,*" Sonia had cautioned, "*but if you do get lost, you must find the strength within yourself to survive. It is that strength and that strength alone that will see you through the very worst of times. It is the strength the wolves rely on, it is the strength the bears depend on, it is the strength of the land and the sea and the sky combined within you that will allow you to carry on.*"

Anya finally conquered the fear that had been sitting heavily on her shoulders since they left the cottage. She looked across the arctic plain and let her eyes sweep the open expanse of sky. *I do have that strength; I can feel it building within me. I am excited about what lies ahead, no matter the outcome. The wolf's cry says I must do this, I can do this, I will do this!*

CHAPTER TWENTY-EIGHT

The Night Revealed

Anya woke with a start. Her head was in a fog, and she could not remember what, or if, she was dreaming. Opening her eyes, she found herself staring at the top of a small tent. Still unsure of her whereabouts, she raised herself up on one elbow. Sonia slept quietly beside her. Anya reached out and rested her hand on the old woman's chest. Reassured that Sonia was breathing and alive, Anya eased herself back onto her mat. Now she was quite awake and aware of the circumstances that brought her here. She lay gazing at the tent's crown and took in the dance of light and shadow that played across the doe-hide covering. She had often watched the shadows of the tall trees that surrounded the cottage dance in the wind and the moonlight. Sometimes she saw the bright reflections of the pale greens and bright reds of the *aurora borealis*, as they shone into the small meadows near the cottage, but the shadows on the tent somehow seemed different. She was drawn to rise from the warmth of her bed and peer through the flap that formed a door.

The kaleidoscope of undulating colors rippling across the clear black sky and reflecting on the open snow-laden tundra caused Anya to suck in her breath. Having slept in her clothing, she quickly donned her boots and threw a blanket about her shoulders. Cautiously, she stood in the snow at the entrance of the tent, staring; her mouth agape. She closed her eyes against the forming tears, and opened her arms wide, absorbing the beauty into her soul. She felt the current of the lights flow in and out of her, and she followed the pull of their splendor. She felt as if God had grasped her heart and was pulling her toward Him as she stumbled awe-struck through the snow.

Something grabbed her arm and startled her out of her euphoria. Blinking through her enchantment, Anya turned toward the interloper.

Yerik removed his hand from her arm, a look of knowing concern on his face. "The wolves would relish your tender flesh, but I am afraid you would be hardly more than a midnight snack for them." His admonishment came with a slightly amused smile. "You have not seen the lights before? I am surprised."

Regaining her senses and still a bit annoyed at having been wrenched from her reverie, Anya retorted, "Yes, I have seen the lights before." Realizing she did not comprehend what had happened, she lowered her voice and whispered, "Just not like this."

"Ah," Yerik nodded, "This is why Rodin asked me to keep an eye out for you as I watched for wolves tonight. He knew you would be drawn by the fever of the spirits."

"I... I do not understand."

"It seems that Rodin did not warn you of this, so I will explain," Yerik huffed a sigh of annoyance and led Anya to the campfire that glowed nearby. He tossed a fresh log on the fire; as it settled into the coals, the flare jumped and licked the edges of the wood. Orange and red sparks exploded into the air. Anya put her hands out over the flame and accepted its heat. Yerik stood next to her and also reached for the flame, clapping his gloved hands together, as if he were trying to get the blood to flow through frozen fingers again. He was finally ready to continue his discourse.

"Our people believe the lights are the spirits of our ancestors. Through their radiance the ancestors reach out to us in many ways. They light the way and guide us across the tundra to our homes. They help us to see the shadows of the wolves that follow our path and stalk us in the night. If death is near, they beckon for us to join them in the higher world. When a foreigner, such as yourself, comes into their vision, the ancestors test the newcomer, drawing them into the path of the wolf or the crevice of the ice, just to see if there is strength enough to resist the deception. But, if the ancestors deem the stranger to be worthy, they will also provide for the hungry, leading them to the herds of wild deer, or the rivers filled with fish."

"...*und ich werde bleiben im Hause des HERRN immerdar*," the words flowed from Anya's lips so naturally, she hardly even knew she had spoken.

"What did you say?" Yerik asked.

"Just the last words to a prayer I was taught as a child. Something about what you were saying made me think of them. Your people are Russian Orthodox, which is what Sonia told me, so I would think you should know the Twenty-third Psalm."

"*Some* of our people do follow the Orthodox customs, but many do not, and I am one of them. I prefer the old ways of the ancestors. So tell me of this prayer, I am curious." He shifted his feet in the snow and moved closer to the fire. One of the dogs stood up and stretched, circled his sleeping spot three times, then lay back down to sleep.

"It has been a long time since I have even thought of it. The last time I heard it was when my baby sister died and we buried her along the river on our way to Siberia." Anya stood silently for a moment, thinking, then slowly started reciting, remembering the cherished words as she spoke. *"Der HERR ist mein Hirte, mir wird nichts mangeln..."* She stopped in mid-sentence, realizing she was reciting the passage as she had learned it—in German. Taking a deep breath she began again, slowly at first, translating the words into Russian for Yerik. "The LORD is my shepherd; I shall not want. He maketh me to lie in green pastures and leadeth me beside still waters. He restoreth my soul: He guideth me in for his name's sake. And whether I have emigrated in the valley of the shadow, I will fear no evil; for thou art with me; Thy rod and thy staff, they comfort me. Thou preparest a table before me in the presence of my enemies. You anoint my head with oil; My cup runneth over."

Anya wiped the tears from her eyes with her fingers as the words brought back the visions of the afternoon of Rosina's burial; the intrusion of the Russian guards, her mother insisting that the guards allow her privacy to bury her child in peace, and finally the placing of Anya's doll, the special doll carved by her father, into Rosina's hands before the dirt was thrown upon the tiny body wrapped in the unfinished white apron.

Yerik watched the sky as he listened to Anya. "Yes, green pastures in the summer for the herds, still waters for the best fishing, oil for the lamps, a good spear and walking stick while trekking through the hills around our village," he mused. "The ancestors are more far reaching than I ever thought. They have obviously had a hand in the teachings of your people, and it seems they are pleased with your words. See that flash of purple streak through the green light? That means they are most happy with us tonight."

Anya offered a melancholy smile, "Yes, Sonia and I have often discussed the similarities between the beliefs of our peoples. There are some definite differences, too, but much is the same if you take the time to think about it."

Snores, emanating from a nearby tent, stopped abruptly with a snort, followed by a sigh and movement of the tent wall as someone rolled over.

"The others will wake soon; you had better try to get some sleep before we leave. We have a long day ahead." Yerik continued to warm his hands over the fire as he nodded his head in the direction of Anya's tent, sending her on her way.

"When will you sleep?" she asked as she turned to leave.

"Suka knows the way; I will sleep while we travel," he smiled and winked.

Anya stopped for one last look at the wind-blown curtains of light, and then quietly reentered the tent. Chilled from the night air, she sat upon her mat and pulled another blanket around her shoulders. She felt something was not quite right. She reached over and placed her hand on Sonia's chest, as she had done earlier. Instead of the soft up and down motion of Sonia's shallow breaths, there was only stillness. Trepidation streaked through Anya as she gave Sonia a quick shake, but there was no response. A particularly bright flash of light illuminated the interior of the tent for a brief second, just enough time for Anya to clearly see Sonia's face. A contented smile graced the lips of the old woman.

Anya tucked the blankets closer around the tranquil body, "The purple streak in the sky was for you. The ancestors are happy you have joined them, and I see you are happy, too. Tell Malvina I said 'thank you' for allowing me to be a part of your life. I will let Rodin sleep for now. We have a long day ahead." She laid her head on Sonia's chest, closed her eyes and dreamt of the cottage and her happy days with Oma.

CHAPTER TWENTY-NINE

Have No Fear, For I Am Near...

"**A**nya, are you up yet? It will be time to leave soon, and your tent needs to be packed."

She opened her eyes at the sound of Rodin's voice and felt as though she had just fallen asleep. She lifted her head from Sonia's body and rubbed her eyes, recalling the events of the night. Pulling the blanket off Sonia and again feeling for any sign of life, Anya was disheartened to find her Oma's body was cold. She quickly stood and threw a blanket around her shoulders like a cloak. When she was ready to face Rodin with the news of Sonia's passing, she opened the door-flap and stuck her head out to see where he might be.

Rodin was standing a few feet away, waiting to take his mother to his sled and dismantle the tent. "Rodin," Anya said quietly and signaled for him to come closer, "please come here."

Rodin sensed something was not right and quickly made his way to Anya. When he was near enough, she pulled him inside and pointed at Sonia's lifeless form. He knelt beside his mother as Anya took his hand in hers. "She is gone, Rodin, the ancestors took her last night. But, as you can see, she is happy. Oma is with Malvina now," she whispered.

Rodin reached out and laid his hand on his mother's lifeless body. He bowed his head and closed his eyes, then, without a word, quickly wrapped the blankets tightly around her. He rose to his feet, lifted Sonia, cradled her in his arms and turned to leave. He stopped, turning again to face Anya.

"We have about a day and a half of travel left, maybe only a day if everything goes well and we make good time. Anya, I have to ask you not to say anything to the others. Can you do that? Can you pretend that all is well until we get to the village?"

"Yes, Rodin, I think so, but why? They know she was old and ill. Why must I keep quiet?"

"If they know she is dead, they will not let her travel with us. They will leave her to the wolves. I promised her that I would give her a Selkup funeral, and I intend to do just that. I must be able to get her to a coffin-boat and give her Malvina's dress."

Anya placed her hand on Rodin's arm, the memories of her own mother insisting on a proper burial for baby Rosina fresh in her mind. "Yes, I will try my best to follow your wishes. I will pretend nothing has changed."

"I am sorry, Anya, I know how much she meant to you. I realize I am asking more than I should, as you will have to share your tent with her again tonight. I will do my best to make it as easy as possible on you." Rodin shifted Sonia's frail weight in his arms and carried her out into the half-light of the pre-dawn.

"Please do not worry about me, Rodin. I will be fine." Anya bit her lip to steel her nerve, began folding the remaining blankets and picked her bear hide mat up off the tent's floor.

As Rodin placed his mother into his sled and tucked her into the basket, the dogs whined uneasily. Rodin knew they could smell death. He commanded them to be quiet and returned to dismantle the tent.

Yerik approached and handed Anya a chunk of dried fish and a tin cup filled with hot tea as she prepared to step into his sled. "Did you sleep well?" he asked, irony in his voice, a hint of a smile twitching at the corners of his mouth.

"As well as I could, considering...," she wanted to say more, but knew Rodin had his reasons in asking for her silence.

"The ancestors were very busy last night; I am surprised any of us slept in the wake of their dancing lights." Yerik chuckled as he helped Anya get settled. "And Sonia, did she sleep well?"

"She did not move all night."

"Good, the old woman needs her rest."

Anya managed a wistful smile, finished her tea and tied the cup to the side of the sled basket. She picked at the fish and ate a few morsels.

"You will wish you had eaten that as the day gets longer, we may not stop until evening," Yerik commented.

"I am just not very hungry," Anya replied as she put the fish onto her lap and laid her head back and closed her eyes. "I think I am more tired than I thought. Maybe I will eat it as we travel."

"I might allow that," Yerik chortled quietly, "just remember that I intend to sleep as we go, so you will have to keep an eye on the dogs for me."

"Just give me some warning, please, so we are not both asleep at the same time."

Soon everything was ready and commands were given to the dogs to move out. Rodin's dogs hung back, refusing to obey his orders. Rodin understood his dogs' reluctance to pull the sled with the body in it, but he had to get them moving before any of the other men suspected a problem. He walked to his lead dog and grabbed her by the nape of the neck. She let out a yelp as he lifted the startled dog off the ground and flung her forward. "Get going!" he yelled at her, then gave a quick jerk on the gangline rousing the other dogs to follow. *I dislike doing that. If I could only make you understand,* Rodin apologized under his breath. As the dogs trotted past him, he grabbed the rear of the sled and jumped onto the runners in a smooth and practiced manner.

The other men saw Rodin's uncharacteristically harsh action and looked at each other, questioning his motives. "He must feel an urgency to get home, to get his mother to the shaman," Yerik commented quietly, and the others nodded in agreement.

As if in response to Yerik's words, Rodin pushed his dogs ahead and set a quick pace for the others to follow. Not wanting to tire the dogs too soon, the remainder of the clan kept their dogs at an easy pace. Rodin was soon a fair distance ahead, nearly alone as he flew across the frozen steppe. Shouts from the men went unheard or unheeded. By mid-morning, the others felt a need to keep Rodin in sight and began pushing their own dogs to catch up....

Anya spotted him first; a gray figure in the distance, keeping pace in a parallel track with Rodin. She waved her arm at Yerik and pointed to the east. She felt Yerik's hand on her shoulder in response. Without slowing his dogs, Yerik reached alongside the sled and pulled his rifle out of the scabbard that hung there.

"Suka! *Apasnast!*" he hollered to warn the dogs of the impending shot.

The other men, hearing Yerik's alert, looked toward him, all except Rodin, still too far ahead to hear. Pointing toward the running figure, Yerik yelled, "*VOLK!*" and fired a shot into the air as a warning to Rodin and at the same time hoping to scare off the lone wolf. Suka and her team dodged to the left a bit, but did not shorten their stride.

Rodin, hearing the report of the rifle, slowed his dogs to a walk and looked over his shoulder. Yerik was gesturing frantically to the east, and the others were all aiming their rifles in that general direction. Scanning the horizon, Rodin picked out the form running along a short ridge. As Rodin reached for his rifle, the lone wolf was joined by the rest of its pack, coming up from the far side of the crest. Soon the one became six, and finally ten.

Knowing his dogs could not outrun a wolf pack, and seeing that the wolves were still too far off to shoot, Rodin debated whether to let the others catch up, or turn around and try to meet the group halfway. Choosing the latter, he swung the dogs in a wide arc, keeping the tiring animals at an easy gait. Rodin was sure of two things at this point; the wolves could smell death, and they were after his sled and his mother's body. His best chance was to join the rest of the men; there was safety in numbers.

As Rodin closed the gap, the wolves turned toward him and accelerated into an easy gallop across the firmness of the frozen snow. The men urged their teams forward. A volley from the rifles shattered the stillness. Two wolves fell, but this did not deter the rest of the pack.

Rodin rejoined the clan and the men pulled their sleds into a tight circle; then rolled them onto their sides. The dogs were hauled into the middle and swiftly unhooked from their ganglines and tied individually to the overturned sleds. As one, the team could easily pull the heavily laden sleds, but without working together the sleds would not be moved.

Anya was ordered out of Yerik's sled, which was quickly overturned. Yerik indicated that she was to crawl under it, and she speedily obeyed. Rodin tried to remove his mother from his sled, but the unforgiving processes of death made her too stiff to move from the basket. Yerik saw Rodin was having difficulty lifting Sonia, so he approached to offer his help, but quickly ascertained the problem.

"She is dead, Rodin!" Yerik declared and launched into a tirade as he grabbed at Rodin's sleeve. "How long has she been this way? Is this why we are being hunted? You have put us all in danger! You, of all our clansmen, know better!"

More shots rang out as Rodin pulled himself out of Yerik's grip. "Yes, she is dead! And I am taking her home!" Rodin screamed back, his anger ambushing his senses. "Yes, the wolves know it, too, and that is exactly why we are being attacked! You and the others would have left her behind. You would have left her to the wolves, anyway."

"And well we should have, then we would not be in this mess now." Yerik countered. He waved his arm in the direction of the other men, poised with their rifles aimed at the wolves, "You would see all of us dead, just to ease your feelings toward your mother!"

Rodin began to respond, when Miko broke loose from his lead and leapt over one of the sleds. A wolf, unseen by the dogsledders, had crept up behind the circle and was getting too near Anya. Miko grabbed the wolf by the throat and the two of them became one twisting, turning blur of gray and silver fur.

As the fight ensued, and the combatants moved away from the men, the other wolves moved into position, ready to join the fray, making themselves easy targets for the rifles' bullets. The tethered dogs jumped against their restraints, barking and yipping excitedly as they tried to slip free of their ties. Unable to get a clean shot at the fighting wolf, Rodin tried to climb over the sleds to Miko, but was pulled back by Yerik.

The snarling and gnashing of teeth continued, until the wolf finally conquered the tired Miko. The dog was on his back, and the wolf stood over him. For reasons known only to the wolf, he hesitated for one brief moment, yellow eyes flashing in triumph at Rodin, before grabbing Miko's throat one last time. A shot reverberated from the distance... and the wolf fell in a heap onto Miko. The big dog squirmed and whimpered under the wolf's weight.

Rodin scrambled over a sled and reached for the wolf. Grabbing the beast with both hands, he jerked the body out of his way. He knelt in the snow and removed his gloves, tenderly feeling Miko from nose to tail, assessing the damage the dog had suffered. He spoke softly comforting the animal, as he lifted him. Only then did Rodin give notice to the origination of the shot that killed the wolf.

Four Selkup sledders, a hunting party, pulled up next to the downtrodden man and his bloodied dog. "How badly is he injured?" one of them inquired.

"With proper care, I think he should heal." Rodin responded, and then asked, "Where did you come from?"

"We were hunting north of here when we heard the shots. We knew someone was in trouble and thought we should check it out. You are not due back to the village for another week, and why are there so few of you?"

"My mother was ill, and I promised that I would get her to the shaman," Rodin began, "but the ancestors claimed her last night."

"I see...and she is still with you? Is that why the wolves attacked?"

"Yes," Rodin said sadly as he shifted Miko's weight in his arms.

"We will accompany you back to the village, in case there are more wolves to deal with."

Rodin and his comrade carried the dog back to the chaos of the overturned sleds. The other men were busy working with the overly excited, and very tangled, dogs.

The newly arrived group included one unlike the others. He worked separately as he proceeded to upright and repack the sleds. As he grabbed the runners of Yerik's transport, something moved underneath it. Pulling the vehicle off the blanketed bundle, he joyfully exclaimed, "What have we here, frightened puppies?"

Anya was doubled over on her knees, her hands covering her head, beneath as many blankets as she could muster under the sled's basket. As the man yanked the blankets away, revealing the back of a sobbing young girl, he stepped backward in unexpected surprise.

"Yerik," he hollered, "did you bring a forest nymph as a surprise for your wife?"

"I am not that foolish," Yerik smiled sympathetically at Anya, "She is, or was, the ward of Rodin's mother. Now, I guess she will be Rodin's responsibility."

"Well, we cannot leave her here in the snow," the man said as he reached a hand out to help Anya to her feet. "The excitement is all over, you can come out now."

As Anya stood, the blankets fell away from her. She blinked and tried to see through her tear-blurred eyes. She looked at this strange man, but could only make out how different he was from the rest of the Selkups. He stood before her dressed in deer skins, just like the others, but he was noticeably taller. Instead of sparse black stubble on his face, he had a thick, light-colored, full beard, now coated with ice. His eyes were not dark ovals, like those of Rodin and Yerik, but round and pale, maybe even blue. She tried to dry her tears with the backs of her gloved hands, and in so doing, the hood of her parka dropped to her shoulders revealing her blonde locks.

The man caught his breath. Finally "Magdalena?" rolled from his lips in near silence, his voice catching in his throat.

"No," the child responded, "my name is Anya."

"Anya, mein kleines Anya! Mein kleines Mädchen, Anya?"

Not having heard German spoken in a very long time, Anya had to think hard making the connection between what had just been said and the feeling that she knew this voice. *But if this is the Norwegian everybody has talked about, how could he know me? Why would he speak German? Why does his voice take me back to the farm?*

The connection jolted her like an electric current. Her heart began racing and the tears started to flow again, "Papi?" she whispered.

"*Sie kennen mich nicht?* You do not know me?" Johannes smiled broadly as he opened his arms to Anya.

"Papi, oh, Papi! Can it really be you?" Anya screamed as she disappeared into his arms.

Johannes embraced his daughter, lifting her off the ground and spinning in his elation. He kissed her forehead and cheeks over and over as she laughed and cried at the same time.

The Selkups gathered in a tight group and watched the two in stunned amazement. Yerik elbowed his neighbor and smiled, "I think they might know each other."

A painful yelp from Miko cut through the revelry and brought everyone back to the moment. Anya pulled away from Johannes and turned to see Rodin examining Miko's wounds more closely. She looked back at her father, torn between reuniting with him and helping her long-time friend. Johannes could see the worry on his daughter's face. He pushed her toward the dog, "Go on, and see to him."

"How badly is he hurt? Is he going to be alright, Rodin?" she asked as she dropped into the snow next to Miko.

"He has some nasty bites, and his skin is torn over his shoulder. He is in pain, but I think he will heal."

"I can help," Anya said as she rose and dashed off to Sonia's bags of herbs and medicinal mixtures. She selected several items, then reached into another sack and removed a small bowl and her sewing kit. She stopped for a handful of clean snow and placed it in the bowl.

Returning to Rodin, she began mixing the plant material into the snow and smoothed the resulting paste onto the wounds. Miko jerked when she first touched him, but the poultice soon began to deaden the pain and he relaxed. She took an additional bit of substance from another tiny bag and pushed it into the dog's mouth. "That should take the pain away," her words were spoken in a soft and calming voice.

As soon as Miko closed his eyes in a relaxed sleep, Anya quickly took her needle and some fine thread and stitched the tear on his shoulder. She turned to Rodin and handed the small bag to him. "Miko will need to be kept quiet and still for a few days. Give him a pinch of this when he stirs. Is it possible for him to ride in a sled back to your village?"

Rodin accepted the bag and the instructions. "I am impressed with your skills, my mother taught you well. We will have to see if there is room for Miko in any of the sleds. If not, then I must leave Mother here, and he can take her place in my sled."

"Rodin, you cannot do that!" Anya pleaded. "You know how much I love Miko; I would do anything for him...and you, but I will not let you leave Oma to any more wolves. If it will help, I will walk to the village."

Johannes had not taken his eyes off his daughter and now listened to this exchange. He stepped forward. "I can make room in my sled for Anya, and your dog can ride with Yerik."

"But, how Papi? Do you not have a full load of meat for Rodin's clan?"

"Nothing that I can not replace, child. The deer are plentiful this year; I will hunt again next week for what is lost today."

"Thank you, Yanochan," Rodin offered his hand in friendship. "I will help you make up for your loss."

Anya came up to her father and wrapped her arms around his waist, burying her head into his coat. Johannes dropped his free hand, and it came to rest on her back as he gripped Rodin's hand, "You have enough loss to deal with, my friend, while I have regained more than I ever hoped."

CHAPTER THIRTY

Reunion

Not wanting to waste good daylight, and needing to put distance between them and the blood of the wolves left to solidify on the icy ground, the group travelled on. The days were becoming noticeably longer as late spring wandered into summer and the sun hung stubbornly in the sky.

When a suitable location to camp for the night was found, the dogs were allowed to rest. Tents were set up and fires were built. The dogs were unhooked and taken to relieve themselves, then tied to stakes placed at strategic intervals around the site, and provided with dried fish and reindeer meat. The men worked swiftly, joking and jostling among themselves, as they did what came naturally to them. For generations their people had done these same tasks, in this same way, on this same desolate Siberian plain.

Rodin removed Miko from Yerik's sled and carried the dog into his tent. Once assured that the dog was comfortable, Rodin set up Anya's sleeping tent near Johannes'. Preparing Sonia's body for the night, Rodin wrapped her in an extra blanket trying to conceal the odor of death. He placed her along an edge of Anya's quarters, allowing the girl a bit of additional space to sleep. When he had completed this task he built an extra fire, outside and to the rear of the tent, as a precaution against any unseen night marauders.

Anya removed her bedroll from the sled, and upon entering her tent found Rodin kneeling beside Sonia. Out of respect, Anya began to back out, but Rodin indicated that she should come in. He took a deep breath and let out a long sad sigh.

"I am sorry you have to spend the night with her," Rodin apologized once more.

"Dear brother, this is not anything you have to be sorry for," Anya empathized as she held his hand. "Oma prepared me for this… for her death…many months ago. I am just pleased the clan is allowing her to return to the village for the rites she is worthy of. I know it is what she wanted, and it is as it should be." Anya pulled on Rodin's hand and led him out of the tent, "Come; we should get some supper before it is all gone."

Johannes, having completed his evening responsibilities, approached Rodin and Anya with an offering of tea and dried fish. "This could have been fresh stew," he smiled through his beard, "but I think one more supper of dried fish will get us home. Rodin, why did you not tell me you were hiding my daughter?" Johannes teased, unable to conceal the pure joy radiating from his steel blue eyes.

"Because the brightness of your affection would have melted my little Snowflake, just as it is doing now, and I would have nothing left of her. Besides Yanochan, how was I to know that such a delicate and pure bit of crystal could have been spawned from a crusty old iceberg like you?"

"She calls you brother, as do I, so I will accept your lapse of good sense this time. In the future, just let me know if you wish to conceal any of my other children, and I will take the responsibility of them off your hands." Johannes gave a quick wink to his good friend.

Hearing the reference to "my other children" caused a spark of hope to race through Anya's heart. "Papi, do you know where they are, have you seen them?"

"Have I seen who?" her father asked, then realizing what he had said, replied, "No, dear Anchen, no. You are the only one of our family I have found. It seems we have much to talk about."

Anya had not heard her nickname in so long, and the sound of it now moved her. Only her father and brothers called her Anchen; hearing it threw her into memories of the past. The vision of Heinreich and Konrad watching and calling to her from the edge of the train tracks, as Sonia led her away five years ago, was as clear now as it had been on that day. Often she had seen this image in her dreams, distorted and hazy, an apparition in the night, but now it was all so clear it could have happened yesterday.

Johannes invited Anya into his tent, unrolled a soft, white doeskin and placed it on the floor for her to sit on. He lowered himself onto another skin and sat cross-legged, facing her. The strange sight of her father, sitting like a school girl during a gossip session at recess, caused her to let out a startled, embarrassed laugh, which she immediately tried to hide by putting her hand over her mouth.

"You have never seen an old man sit in a Selkup chair?" he asked innocently, pretending to be hurt by her giggle. Then he smiled, "Me either, until I joined this group. I never would have believed I could ever have twisted myself into such a knot. But, one learns the ways of those one lives with, in order to become one with them."

Anya sat in silence, staring at the man who sat before her, trying to make her brain believe her heart. *I know he is my Papi, but it has been so long. He has changed. He speaks Russian, as I do, not the language of my childhood. I am unable to remember what he really looked like, and I have never seen him unshaven. But, only my Papi would call me Anchen, so it must be him! This has to be him!*

Johannes reached out to her, "I know you must have many questions for me, as I have many for you. I think you may even doubt my existence. You have changed so much. You have grown into a young woman, and I have missed experiencing that. If you did not look so much like your mother, like my dear Katerina, I might not believe you were my daughter, my Anchen."

"How did you get here, Papi? How did you come to be with these people?"

"Ahhh, good questions to begin our reunion with, as there is a long story attached," Johannes began. Sadness came into his eyes as he related his experiences in the shipyard, and what he remembered of his escape and his rescue by Elena and her family. He told her of meeting Yerik in the village when Pavel picked a promised puppy. His hands were animated as he talked about taking up carving again and how his carvings played a roll in purchasing the puppy and ultimately, his own tenuous freedom.

Anya sat silently, her head cocked to one side as she listened to his tale. Then she reached into her pocket and removed the wooden doll. "Then you did make this?" she asked as she held the doll toward him.

"You know I did, I made that for you when you were very small."

"No, Papi, that doll was buried with Rosina," Anya explained. "This doll was a gift from Rodin shortly after I began to live with Oma. I have always pretended you made it and that you were close by. It has been my reassurance that you were still alive."

Johannes took the doll from her hands and examined the smoothly-worn features closely. "Yes, this is one of the dolls that was given to Yerik for the puppy." A broad smile crossed his face, "Do you have any idea what it means to me that *you* have had this? That it has been a comfort to you?"

Anya shook her head.

"God has indeed had His hand in this. He has guided me in ways I will never understand, but now I am sure He is the reason we are together again." Johannes joyfully handed the doll back to Anya and she returned it to her pocket for safe keeping.

She sat quietly for a brief moment, not taking her eyes off her father, and then asked "Why do they call you Yanochan?"

"Have you heard the word *kulak*?" he asked.

Anya nodded her head slowly, "Once, while Sonia and I were in Onega."

"Do you know what it means?"

"No."

"You do know that we are German?"

"And Russian, too," she quickly responded.

"Yes, we are German because my grandparents came to Russia from Germany over 100 years ago, Russian because we are born in this country. But, the Russian government has decided that our people no longer belong, and they are trying to get rid of us. Originally kulak referred to the wealthy land owners, people with much more than we ever had, but now all people with German heritage are labeled as such, and the kulaks are considered enemies of the government. That is why we were taken from our home and brought to this part of the world. When I escaped from the shipyard guards, I had to become someone other than a German, to keep from being arrested. Elena thought I might be Norwegian, because of my blond hair and light eyes, so I went along with that idea. I needed a name that did not sound German, and Yanochan is Russian for Johannes; I did not know the Norwegian word." Johannes shrugged and smiled with this last statement.

Anya sat thinking and absorbing this information, trying to put it all together in her mind. She decided there was still more she wanted to know, but her thoughts were interrupted.

"Now it is your turn, tell me how you came to be with Rodin's mother."

Anya took a deep breath. "When you and Mama and Karolina and Magdalena were taken away from Heiner and Konrad and me, the soldiers left us standing in the snow by the train. The big guard, the one that spoke German like us, brought an old lame woman to the train to look at the children. She needed someone to help her with her house and other things. She picked me and took me back to her cottage in the forest..." Anya's tone rose and her words quickened as she remembered the experience. "I had to leave the boys behind, but the guard assured me that he would look after them, that they would be safe. That is the last time I saw them!" Her body shook as she began to sob, as the guilt that had plagued her these past years burst out of her soul and consumed her.

Johannes put his arm around her and pulled her toward him. She buried her head in his chest, weeping uncontrollably for several minutes. When she finally quieted, he placed his hand under her chin, making her look up at him. "My little Anchen, you cry for us both. How I wish I had known what was happening to us. When Jakob and I first saw the soldiers, I thought only that they were coming to take your brother for the army. So Jakob was sent away for his safety. Then we were told that we had to leave our farm for our own safety. I should have understood the journey we were forced to take and where it was leading, but I was naïve, as were all of the others. Now, I do not know where your mother or sisters or brothers might be, or even if they are still alive. And, I do not know how to find them. I have cried for them and you. I have prayed that Jakob made the journey safely to Odessa, and that he escaped and found freedom in America. I have also prayed that we would all find our way back home, that we would all be together again. You are not to feel guilt for leaving the boys behind. God had His reasons for sending you to Sonia. She was good to you and taught you many things. And now He has brought us together, and if it is in His plan, we will find the rest of the family. But if reunion is not in the plan, and we never know what happened to the others, we have each other, and we must be happy."

Anya pulled herself onto her father's lap and wrapped her arms about his neck, as she had done so many times in the safety of their farmhouse. She felt she had not aged; she was ten again. She closed her eyes and breathed deeply as she tried to distinguish his essence from the stench of fish and game that clung to his shirt. How foreign these smells were to her, how unlike the pungent odor of soil and sweat that had clung to his being at home; and yet, there was something reassuring about his scent, something that stated that this was, indeed, her father.

Allowing the events of the day to fall from her shoulders, feeling happy and safe and comforted by her father's presence, Anya descended into a deep and peaceful sleep.

Hellos ...

Anya woke in the night to the resonating waves of her father's snoring. She found herself covered with his blanket; fending off the cold, he had put on his coat and slept tightly hunched on the far side of the tent. She rose from the doeskin mat and quietly covered him with the blanket, then returned to her own tent and the silence of Sonia. The thought that this was only a cold body did not occur to her. Sonia was Sonia. And Anya was accustomed to sleeping in her presence.

Intense rays of morning sun streaked pink and orange across the snow as the day dawned bright and clear. The camp bustled with activity and energy as the men geared up to head for home. The dogs, as well, knew they were close to home, and yipped and barked, pulling against their tethers, anxious to get on the trail. Anya crawled sleepily from her tent, stood and stretched her back, then joined her father, Yerik, and Rodin near the fire. Johannes handed her a tin cup filled with hot tea.

"Did you sleep well?" he inquired.

"Not really," she answered, "too many strange noises."

Rodin raised an eyebrow, a puzzled look on his face. "What kind of noises? Did you hear animals prowling close by?"

Shaking her head in response, Anya smiled meekly, "Not animals, at least not wild ones. In fact, I do not think any wild animal makes the kinds of noises that came from these tents last night."

Yerik threw his head back in a hearty laugh, "It is obvious this one has not been around men much, she has a good deal to learn before she becomes a woman."

Johannes smiled and put his arm around Anya, "I do not want her becoming a woman too soon, as I have missed much of her childhood.

She can learn to be a woman in her own good time."

The men nodded in agreement and returned to breaking up camp and preparing for the trail.

The dogs kept up a steady pace across the open ground and soon a line of trees could be seen in the distance. Around mid-day, Anya spotted a scattering of tapered sampas amongst the trees, and she became excited at the thought that one of them might be her new home. Upon reaching the outer edge of the dwellings, the men halted their dogs on a slight knoll. Anya saw Rodin's sled veer off and continue on with Sonia's body.

"Where is he going, Papi? I need to be with Oma!" A wave of panic gripped Anya. She wanted to jump out and follow, and attempted to stand in her father's sled. She felt a firm tug on the back of her coat as her father grabbed for her.

"No, Anya. You must let Rodin's family have their own time with Sonia. She is Rodin's mother, after all. When they have said their good-byes, they will then prepare her for the funeral rites. If your presence is needed, Rodin will come for you."

In silence Anya sat back down reluctantly, and obeyed. Watching Rodin's sled disappear into the trees gave her the first real sense of loss she had experienced since Sonia's passing, and she wanted to cry; oh, how she wanted to cry. Instead, she fought her tears; she wanted to be strong in her father's presence. She wanted to prove she was not a little girl anymore.

Women and children emerged from the trees and hurried toward the group. Excited chatter permeated the air as family members greeted each other in a warm and welcoming manner.

Johannes stopped his sled a bit behind the others, signifying that he was still an outsider to the tribe and did not want to intrude. Anya watched in quiet sorrow as she observed the happy excitement of the crowd. It had been a very long time since she had witnessed such open elation in any group of people, and it frightened her. She shrank down into the sled and hid under her bear hide covering. Before long, how-ever, four young boys crowded around the sled.

"Welcome home, Uncle Yanochan! What did you bring us? Is there some fresh deer for us? Or, maybe, goose or partridge?"

"Not this time," Johannes shook his head, "the hunting trip turned into a rescue of sorts, but I did bring a surprise."

A boy of about twelve was studying the pelt that covered the sled. "Uncle Yanochan, this is bear fur," he marveled as he cautiously touched the black-brown hair. Suddenly he jerked his hand back, "… and it is moving!"

"Nothing to be afraid of, for any of you," Johannes smiled warmly as he reached for the edge of the hide. "Come on out, Anya, and meet some of Yerik's brood. Boys, this is Anya, she is my daughter."

Anya slowly pulled the hide away and smiled bashfully at the group gathered around her.

"Ahhh, Uncle Yanochan, she is a *girl*! We have enough girls around here!" the oldest whined.

"Look, Stepan, she is even whiter than Uncle Yanochan," a younger boy sniggered. "How come she is so white?"

The boys' mother arrived, unnoticed, behind them. She reached out and cuffed the side of the younger boy's head, "This is not how you have been taught to behave!"

The boys' turned toward her in unison, caught her glare of disap-proval, and scattered in all directions.

"That was not really necessary, Polina, they were only curious." Johannes insisted.

"They have to learn to behave sometime, and their father is no help in that matter. Now, who is this fragile child you have brought me?"

"Polina, this is my daughter, Anya. Anya this is Yerik's wife, Polina."

Anya began to rise from the sled in polite greeting, but was pushed gently back down by this round, genial woman.

"Daughter? You have found one of your children? Oh, Yanochan, how wonderful! You must tell me all about it! But, first, we have to get this young lady into the village and get her settled in *my* house."

Polina was waving her hands in the air, pointing first at Anya, then in the direction of the homes in the village.

"Thank you, Polina, but she will stay with me. She is my daughter, after all. I really do appreciate your hospitality, but Yerik might have a different opinion about adding another mouth to feed in his dwelling," Johannes emphasized to the perpetual mother-hen before him.

"We can discuss this later, Yanochan." Polina agreed, but the glint in her eye revealed she had other ideas. "Now, Anya, when you are settled, please come to see me."

"Thank you, I will." Anya knew this woman could not replace Sonia, but she liked her friendliness and looked forward to spending time with her.

The village sat on the high bank of the Taz River, overlooking the swift, fish-laden waters. About a dozen large tents, made of deer-skins stretched over log and reed frames and reinforced with caked, dried sand, were scattered randomly among the tall pines that thrived along the shore. Fishing nets hung over wooden racks to dry, and sturgeon and pike lay in the sun to cure on platforms made of laced rope. Standing apart from the main settlement were a number of smaller wooden buildings, with attached pens and large fire rings. They appeared to be for some kind of livestock, sporting facades indicative of constant use and harsh weather.

Anticipating his daughter's questions, Johannes said, "Those are for the reindeer. The herds are brought into the sheds in the summer when the mosquitoes swarm. The fires are lit with damp green wood, and the smoke keeps the bugs from biting the deer." Anya nodded that she understood.

Johannes guided his dogs toward a smaller sampa on the outer edge of the hamlet. "Here we are," he said to Anya as he came to a halt. "It is not as big as the others, but a single man does not require the extra space."

Anya stood and stepped out of the sled's basket. Taking note that the entry of this abode, as well as all of the others, faced south, she pulled back the skin that served as a door, and looked into the tent-like structure. The single round room was about the same size as Sonia's cottage. An assortment of hides and woven wool rugs hung from the ceiling and down the walls, providing additional insulation from the cold of winter and the heat of the late summer. A fire ring blackened the floor in the center, directly under an opening in the roof. A tri-pod made of iron rods held a blackened caldron over the now-cold coals and ash. A variety of charred wooden utensils lay scattered about the rug-covered floor.

On the west side of the room Anya noted her father's bed. A frame of pine logs with entwined ropes formed the sleeping surface; it sat a few inches off the floor over a pile of folded rugs. A hunting bow and quiver hung on the wall over the bed.

Pots and pans hung along the opposite wall, and a wooden chair, obviously crafted by her father, sat at the back, a Bible on its seat.

"Go on in and make yourself comfortable while I get the dogs settled," Johannes told her. "Just remember to always move clockwise as you make your way around. A Selkup rule I try to observe."

Anya backed out, the idea of moving into this place made her a little uncomfortable. It was nothing like she was used to, and if there were special rules to abide by, she wanted to follow her father's lead. Instead she turned toward her father and asked, "Papi, may I help you with the dogs? I used to help Rodin when he came to the cottage. I would like to get to know them, if I could."

"Of course you can help. Just as on the farm, I always welcome assistance with the chores." He smiled as he handed her the line for a small, but energetic chestnut-brown and silver dog. "This is Adicus; he may be small, but he is strong and fast. He is kept over there," Johannes pointed to a cable tied between two trees on the far side of the tent.

The dog jerked and pulled and danced on his back feet as Anya struggled to get him to his place. She located the line that ran freely along the cable just over her head and clipped it to the dog's collar. She stood over the dog, one leg on each side of him to hold him still, and removed his harness, being careful not to tangle it. When she finally released Adicus, he immediately ran to the end of his six-foot leash and lifted his leg on the nearest tree. Anya giggled as she saw the dog's ears droop and his face relax as relief came to his body.

"I guess I should have allowed you to do that sooner," she said as she hung his harness on a peg drilled into the tree's trunk, just out of the reach of the dog.

When the team was settled and fed, Anya and Johannes emptied the sled of her few belongings. She stood holding her things and watched as her father deftly over-turned the sled to allow the runners to dry. He then secured the vehicle to a stake, to prevent it from blowing over and being damaged in the strong breezes that often came up from the riverbed.

Johannes was aware that Anya remained hesitant about entering his home, so he held the door-flap open and formally invited her in with a gentlemanly wave of his arm.

She stepped into her father's house for the first time, unsure where she should put her belongings, unsure where she would sleep, unsure what was now expected of her.

Luckily, some fathers have a way of perceiving their daughters' insecurities. "I will hang some of these rugs along the crossbeams and make a room for you. I know you will want your privacy. I remember Karolina's wailing about wanting her own room. It will be a few days before I can make a bed for you; I hope you will not mind sleeping on the floor until then. Now, though, I must go to Yerik's and get a start for the fire, once it is burning brightly, things will warm up in here."

Anya placed her possessions on the floor opposite her father's bed, near the pots and pans; somehow, the presence of 'women's things' made her feel reassured, but she still did not want to be left alone in this strange place. "May I come with you?" she asked. "I would like to meet the rest of Yerik's family, and get to know Polina better."

Johannes answered, "Of course." He stopped to think for a moment and then asked, "How much do you understand of the religious beliefs of these people? Are you familiar with the ceremony of the Fire-god?"

"Oma...Sonia...taught me many things about her religion. She said that the people believe that fire is a living being, an old woman. The licking flames of the fire are her movements, and She is the guardian of the sampa. She immediately becomes angry if someone throws trash or trodden wood shavings into her fire, or spits into it, or hits it. Sonia said that one must not use sharp metal to poke or prod the fire, as the fire-spirit could be injured. The spirit of the fire is a good spirit and drives off evil, but if angered, She can cause great harm and destruction."

Johannes listened in awe of his daughter's knowledge. "You know much about these people; Sonia has indeed taught you well. Come on then, we will go see Yerik."

As Johannes and Anya approached Yerik's home, she took note of the heavy wooden door that formed the entry. A multitude of forest animals were intricately carved into its main panel. She looked at her father questioningly.

"Wooden doors show the status of a family within the clan. The heavier the door and the greater number of animals carved on it, the longer the family has been a part of this village."

A quiet knock by Johannes was answered with delight and open arms by Polina. The pair was immediately invited into Yerik's large dwelling. Anya was surprised by the expansiveness of the interior of this seemingly simple tent. A fire danced in the center of the single room, casting light in all directions. Woven mats covered the floor; additional mats were rolled tightly and stacked neatly against the back wall. A multitude of children, all younger than Anya, noisily bounced and tumbled about the room until Polina raised her voice above the din.

"Settle down! We have company for supper!"

The room became hushed, and only the sound of scattering feet was heard while the children scurried to their places and sat cross-legged around a long red rug of felted wool. Anya finally caught sight of Yerik sitting proudly in a chair at the far end of the circle of children, and puffing happily on a carved ivory pipe. He smiled at her as he spread his arms in welcome.

"Anya, Yanochan, do come in! Anya, meet my family! We have a full house, but you are always welcome," Yerik announced jovially.

Anya smiled shyly as her eyes encountered the many staring back at her. She recognized the four boys who met her father's sled earlier in the day and then mentally counted the other faces, all girls it seemed, waiting intently to know who she was. *TEN! Yerik has ten children! No wonder Papi told Polina that I needed to go with him and not stay here.* Anya might have laughed out loud at the notion of her being a part of this large assembly, but she was too overwhelmed.

Polina came up behind her and placed a hand on her shoulder. "Children, this is Anya, Yanochan's daughter!" Several of the younger girls giggled. "You will make Anya welcome in this house," Polina continued, "Anya, I know there are many names to learn; I will not tell them to you all at once, you will get to know them in time. Now children, make room for them to join us for supper."

Johannes stepped forward, "Polina, we did not come to eat. I wanted to ask for a bit of flame to rekindle the fire in my tent."

"Yes, yes, you can have the fire in due time, but first you must eat. I will not allow this child to spend the night cooking for you. We have plenty in the pot, and you *will* join us!"

Johannes shot a glance at Yerik. Yerik shrugged his shoulders in acquiescence to his wife's wishes. Steaming bowls of a salty stew of reindeer meat and blood dumplings were handed around.

Anya was hesitant to try the great red-brown lump of flour and reindeer blood that occupied the major portion of her bowl, and she poked at it with her spoon. As a spongy chunk broke off and fell into the meaty stew, the room grew silent and she felt everyone watching her. She took a deep breath and tried imperceptibly to hold it while she put the bit of dumpling in her mouth. The doughy mass felt worse than it tasted. She swallowed it with a spoonful of broth, and the room erupted into boisterous laughter and noisy cheers by Yerik's children.

Following the meal and an evening of hospitality and acceptance, Johannes and Anya were ready to return to their tent. Remembering the original reason for Johannes' and Anya's visit, Yerik selected a bough from the fire that was burning at one end. Everyone gathered around the flaming object and held their hands out toward it. Yerik intoned a prayer of blessing on the flame and an apology to the fire-spirit of the household for removing its progeny. Johannes accepted the flame with words of gratitude and promise that the flame would be kept alive and burning in his dwelling for all eternity.

Anya followed her father back to his sampa as he carefully carried the burning branch. She held the door flap open, allowing Johannes to enter and place the torch into the prepared fire ring. The fire came to life, casting an ebullient glow into the small room.

Anya rolled out her sleeping mat and removed her coat and boots, placing them at the end of her makeshift bed. Then she quickly settled her belongings. Johannes pulled several blankets from under his bed and handed the bundle to Anya. She layered the blankets over the bear hide and crawled between them. It had been a long day and she was very tired. Her emotions were such a jumbled mess that she was not sure if she would ever sleep. She was thrilled to be back with her father, but she missed Sonia terribly. She lay on her side and drew her knees up close to her body, closed her eyes and succumbed to a deep and dreamless sleep.

Johannes sat in his chair and watched his nearly-grown daughter. "How like your mother you are," he whispered, "she, too, retreated into a tight coil when her heart was troubled. I pray the time will come that you will never have to twist yourself up so tightly again."

CHAPTER THIRTY-TWO
...And Good-Byes

The morning opened on a village alive with activity as preparations for Sonia's funeral developed.

Anya rose early and made her way to the river to fill the cooking pot and get it hung over the fire to boil for tea. Her father was already up and out of the tent, and she wondered where he had gone. While the water warmed over the fire, she changed her sarafan and donned her newly completed knotted belt. She was combing her long locks when Johannes appeared at the door.

"It is time," he told her quietly.

She quickly pulled her hair back and braided it, washed her face with the tepid water from the caldron, and accompanied her father through the trees and past the other homes to Rodin's.

A boat-like structure, carved out of an old hollow log, sat on the ground outside of Rodin's sampa. The boat's interior was lined with fish skins, and small figures of fish and deer had been carefully painted on the outer surface.

As Anya and Johannes arrived, Rodin carried his mother's deer-hide-wrapped body out of his home, and gently placed her into the coffin-boat. Yerik emerged from the trees with two of the other men from the hunting party; joining Rodin, they lifted Sonia's boat to their shoulders. Not being invited to partake of the ritual, Johannes stepped back out of the way as Rodin began a soft and heartfelt chant.

Though she did not know what the words meant, Anya was aware that the chant served several purposes. The passionate words honored the dead and summoned the ancestral spirits to accompany Sonia to the after-life; it also provided a cadence that enabled the men to step in unison, making the boat easier to carry to the burial grounds.

As the group made their way through the village, Johannes and the remaining men fell into line behind the coffin-bearers, adding their voices to the mantra. Rodin's wife and children followed in silence and were joined by Yerik's family and the remainder of the villagers. Anya was not sure where she should be. She wanted so much to be near Sonia and her father, but she knew that as a female she was not allowed to march with the men. Neither did she think it was her place to accompany Rodin's family, as she did not know them. As a result she hung back away from the group and sadly walked alone behind them.

The path took them in a northerly direction, following the Taz for a good kilometer before coming to a secluded cove where the river turned slightly on its way to the sea. The sandy ground was flat and green with moss. Trees growing on the bank leaned toward the river, their branches seemingly reaching out to protect the coffin-boats that were scattered, in various states of decay, about the cove. Bits of clothing hung from some of the branches.

The men lowered Sonia's boat onto an area that had been cleared of moss and rocks. The chanting ceased and the crowd grew quiet. Anya peered between the people in front of her trying desperately to see what was happening. She knew that the entire village turned out for a funeral; all seemed to be here, except for the men who had stayed behind in Onega to complete their business with the Soviet authorities. Feeling alone and heartbroken that she was unable to be a part of Sonia's services, Anya began to back away from the gathering. She intended to run back to her father's yurt, but a tug on her belt stopped her. She turned around to see one of Yerik's young daughters beckoning her to follow.

"Mama says you must come with us," the child whispered.

Anya willingly followed and found herself being pushed to the front of Yerik's family group and particularly near Sonia's casket. She stood very still, but uncontrolled tears streamed from her face as she gazed at Sonia's shroud. The villagers stood in silent observation. Anya felt her face flush hot with embarrassment, sure that the gathering was staring at her, assessing her deep personal grief.

A distant voice drifted through the trees, the tonic sol-fa increasing in volume as its source neared the cove. Small bell-like tones and clacking noises kept time with the solitary male voice. Anya lifted her eyes to the sounds and observed a cloaked figure emerge from the undergrowth of the forest and stand on the bank opposite the group of people waiting for his arrival. He descended the verge and approached the burial ground. As the man grew nearer, he lifted a small drum that hung from his belt and began a slow and methodical beat upon it. His baritone voice picked up the pulse of the drum in a chant more fervent than that of the earlier entourage. As he neared the gathering, Anya discerned the source of the other sounds that had preceded him through the forest. Iron pedants, images of snakes, forest animals, fish and birds, dangled from his belt and swayed and clanked together as he walked, heralding his approach to all who were near.

"That is the teetypy," Polina leaned over and whispered in Anya's ear. "He is the spirit-master of the forest. He is here to guide Sonia's soul to 'the sea of the dead.' She will rest easy now."

He has come for Sonia after all! Anya thought excitedly. *She would be so pleased. She will join Malvina for certain, now.* This realization lifted the heaviness from Anya's heart. She dried her tears with the palms of her hands and looked over at Polina with a silent 'thank-you'. Polina smiled and nodded in response.

As the shaman completed his chant, a woman stepped forward from the group. She raised her hand and moved it in the sign of the cross, then held her rosary over Sonia's casket. The woman spoke with solemnity and reverence.

"Give rest to the soul of your servant fallen asleep," she prayed, "Most assuredly, I say to you, he who hears My word and believes in Him who sent Me has everlasting life, and shall not come into judgment, but has passed from death into life. Most assuredly, I say to you, the hour is coming, and now is when the dead will hear the voice of the Son of God; and those who hear will live."

Upon completion of her words, she repeated the sign of the cross over her chest and stepped back into the waiting group.

Polina spoke quietly into Anya's ear again. "Some of our clan are

Russian Orthodox, so we include some of the prayers in our servic-es. There is no priest near, so we have to make do with those whose knowledge is greatest."

Anya nodded, indicating she understood. *It is nice to hear prayers I am familiar with, even though they are not in German,* she reflected.

The shaman returned to his place of prominence next to Sonia's coffin. Beating his drum once more, he faced the crowd and seemed to beckon people forward. Rodin stepped away from his family and approached the teetypy. Malvina's dress was draped over Rodin's out-stretched arms. The shaman selected a deer-shaped pendant from his belt, held it above the dress and spoke in a hushed tone over it. With the completion of his words, he took the dress from Rodin and hung it from a low overhanging branch of a nearby tree.

Anya jumped in surprise as the shaman hit his drum with a single hard strike. It not only startled her, but a flock of birds feeding nearby took flight in a confused and noisy departure.

After the shaman recited a few more prayers, he disappeared into the forest amid a chorus of chants and vocalizations from the villag-ers. Following his departure, the group slowly proceeded past Sonia, paying their final respects. Some placed food and small offerings of tea or herbs into the coffin; others left dishes, teapots and blankets on the ground next to it, offerings for a happy and prosperous trip to the higher world.

Johannes came from the group of men and stood silently next to Anya and watched with her. When just about everybody had dispersed, he gave his daughter a gentle push forward, and then he, too, left the cove, allowing his daughter the privacy he knew she needed.

Anya approached Sonia's coffin, knelt in the sand and laid her body across Sonia's. She closed her eyes and let her tears flow as freely as the river running next to her. She felt her love for Sonia envelope the two of them, warming her like a blanket on a cold night. But it was more than a blanket. The warmth she felt was tangible and alive. She opened her eyes and tried to focus, but all she could make out was fuzzy gray...and silver... and black. A whimper emanated from the grayness and a cool wetness brushed against her cheek.

"Miko? MIKO!" she exclaimed as she placed her arm around the big dog's shoulders. He licked a tear from Anya's cheek and placed his head on Sonia's body with a quiet moan. "I know," Anya sighed, "I miss her, too. Did you bring anything to give her, like the others?"

Miko's dark eyes gazed at Anya, but he did not move.

"Me either," she responded with disappointment. "I did not think about it, but I wish I had. It would have been nice to give her something to remember me by."

Stiffly, Miko raised himself from Sonia, and sat facing Anya. She reached out and touched his injured shoulder. The dog flinched only slightly. He licked Anya's face again, then ran his nose down her dress and pushed against her pocket.

"Sorry, Miko, I do not have anything in there for you to eat," Anya smiled softly as she reached into the pocket with the intention of turning it out so Miko could see there was nothing inside. Instead her fingers wrapped around her doll, her precious wooden doll that had been her anchor, her connection to her family and her solace when she needed comfort from the trials and tribulations of her world. The melancholy melted from her face as she realized what Miko had been trying to tell her.

Anya caressed the doll one last time. "Oma, you know that I have loved this doll, almost as much as I loved you. Take it with you now as a part of me, to help you remember the little girl you saved. It is our connection, our link across the spheres of life." Anya tucked the doll between Sonia and the side of the coffin-boat, and then she reached into Miko's shedding winter coat and pulled a large tuft of silver hair from his back and placed it under the doll. "Oma, Miko sends his fur so you will remember him, too." Anya placed her hand on the big dog's head, "You see, Miko, we both had something to give after all."

CHAPTER THIRTY-THREE

Decisions

Anya sat in the sand silently contemplating Sonia's coffin; her arm gently resting on Miko's back, her memories floating gently through her mind. Though sounds of chatter and activity filtered through the trees, they interfered little with her thoughts. She knew a celebration of Sonia's life was taking place at Rodin's residence, but she was not sure if she wanted to join in. She preferred to sit and quietly consider, on her own terms, her current circumstances.

A crackling in the underbrush behind Anya caused Miko to turn his head quickly to look over his shoulder. Upon recognition of his master, the normally obedient canine dropped his head with a quiet whine and remained by Anya's side. Rodin emerged from the woodland scrub, and came down the bank toward the young woman and his prized sled dog.

"I have been looking for you, Miko," Rodin spoke quietly as he leaned down and placed his hand on the dog's large head. Miko stared up at his master; his tail slowly wagged in greeting. "Will you come and eat with us, Snowflake? Your father is waiting, as am I."

"Must I? I prefer being here with Miko and Oma."

"You know we feast in honor of the deceased, and to show the ancestors that we have not forgotten them and their teachings. We have a deep regard for our history, and it is important for us to keep the traditions alive. You are now a part of that; we would like to you join us."

"I know, I am just not ready to leave Oma here, alone."

"She is not alone," Rodin smiled tenderly at the woman-child at his feet, "she is in the company of the ancestors, people she has always known; people she contacted for guidance many times throughout her life. She has never been alone, even during the years she lived in the forest before you joined her. Our ancestors walk with us always, and soon you will realize that my mother, your Oma, will be by your side, too, and you will never be alone. But now, we must honor all of our companions, whether we are aware of their presence or not." Rodin offered his hand to Anya, and she took it for balance as she rose from the sand.

"Rodin, I am not one of your people. Even though Oma instructed me on the Selkup ways, and I value them, I was born into a different set of traditions, different beliefs. These past few days have made me remember my Christian prayers, even though I was only ten when I last heard them daily. Oma knew the teachings of the Russian Church, which are similar to the way I was taught, but we did not worship. We did not observe any rites, not even yours. I do not think the ancestors will accept me. After all…"

Rodin interrupted her, "We may never know about *all* the ancestors, but the only one that matters is your Oma, and your connection to her is very strong, maybe even stronger than the one I have with her."

"How will I know she is with me?" Anya's words were as much an inner thought as they were voiced.

"You will know, Snowflake, at times when you least expect her, and other times when you need her most, she will be there. You will see, maybe not today or tomorrow, but sometime. Now, let us go get something to eat. I am starved. My wife would not allow me to eat this morning, as she was preparing the meal we are missing. Come Miko. I am sure we can find something for you as well."

As the trio reached the top of the bank and turned for one last look across the cove and Sonia's burial site, Johannes stepped out from behind the tree where he had been waiting and listening to the guidance being given to his daughter. He offered his hand in friendship to Rodin. He silently mouthed the Selkup words for "Thank you" to his friend as he took Anya's hand.

"There is more to celebrate," Johannes announced, "the rest of the men are back from Onega."

As the little group neared Rodin's home, they were met with a vibrant stream of voices, a blended mix of Selkup and Russian, spilling through the village. The revelry of the celebration for Sonia's afterlife, intertwined with the welcoming of the last of the supply transports arriving from Onega, was punctuated with the clamor of metal and the chinking of wood as pots and pans and dishes filled with food were passed around, and flagons of vodka were distributed. Everyone and everything seemed to be in a constant state of motion. Still not accustomed to large gatherings, Anya bashfully tried to conceal herself behind her father as they entered the hive of activity. However, Yerik's girls quickly surrounded her and in a flurry of laughter and eagerness led Anya into the midst of the action.

With a forward sweep of his arm, Rodin sent Miko back to his sett with a gentle admonition to remain until he was summoned. The dog dropped his head in obedience and limped to his bed, where, upon arrival, he licked his wounds then curled up on his blankets and slept.

Johannes and Rodin were about to join the gathering when Yerik approached them, an uncharacteristic solemnity pulling at his face. "We must assemble the council," he said glumly as he handed Rodin a sheet of paper. "This came back with the men from Onega."

Rodin took the paper and quickly scanned its words. "Yes, the council must be called; decisions have to be made — quickly."

"This must be serious; can I help?" Johannes asked.

"Yerik will gather the men of the council, and we will meet at his dwelling. But I think you should remain nearby; this may concern you and your daughter."

Eight men joined Yerik in his sampa. Johannes stood outside and listened to the raised voices and agitated reactions coming from within. At length, Rodin emerged through the great carved doors and summoned Johannes to join the group. Johannes greeted the circle of men sitting upon the floor; he noted that even Yerik, normally in his special chair on the far side of the room, sat cross-legged upon the mats.

Johannes was not invited to sit, so he stood opposite Yerik. Rodin returned to his place in the circle. The sheet of paper lay in the center of the floor mat. Rodin reached out and picked up the document and handed it to Johannes.

"We are being mandated to send our children to boarding school in Onega," Rodin began. "All children between the ages of five and eighteen must go. The Soviets are sending soldiers to collect the children within the month." Rodin stopped briefly to allow Johannes to read the decree in his hands, and then continued, "We will resist the taking of our children; they are needed here, and we do not want to lose them to the communist teachings. But the council does not feel you or your daughter will be safe here, and we are also worried that your presence may give the soldiers cause for further scrutiny of our people. It is not wise to draw too much attention to the clan. It has been decided that you will leave as soon as possible."

"But, this has become my home; you have become my family, where will we go? I cannot go back to Onega; I will not take Anya there!"

Yerik shook his head and spoke. "No, we agree that you will not go to Onega. We are sending you south. The council must discuss this further, we will advise you of our decisions by tomorrow. Until then, return to the celebration and enjoy it with your daughter."

The next morning the nine men of the council disappeared into the forest. There was much speculation among the women and remaining men about the reasons for their absence. Johannes realized that he was the only one outside of the council who knew the contents of the decree, and he respected the council's wisdom in staying quiet.

Three days passed before the men returned. Johannes was again summoned to Yerik's home. An oppressing silence filled the room as Johannes entered, and he wondered if any of the men was even breathing.

Finally Yerik spoke, his voice rigid and clear. "We have consulted with the teetypy, and he communed with the ancestors. It has been decided that you and your daughter will go south. You will travel by boat up the River Taz and through the great estuary. Once you have reached the junction with the Ob River you will find an outpost. The man who runs that outpost, Oyvind, is a Forest Nenets, but he is a friend. Tell him I have sent you, and he will know what to do. You leave tomorrow."

The finality expressed in Yerik's face, and the obvious avoidance of the eyes of the others, told Johannes that he was not expected to respond. He simply nodded his head, indicating that he understood his instructions, and backed out of the room and the presence of the council. Once clear of the building, Johannes placed his hand against the nearest tree to support himself, as he stopped to absorb what he had just heard.

Have I been judged for some dreadful sin? Is this a death sentence for Anya and me? What is it we have done? What is in store for us? Where will we end up? The thoughts rolled around in Johannes' head, weighing him down with doubt and foreboding. He hesitated returning to his yurt, he was not sure he wanted to face his daughter, to tell her of this new upheaval in her life. *She has been through so much in the last few days, and now this. How much more can she take? She needs so much that I cannot give her. She needs stability. Where and when will it all end? Will we ever have permanence in our lives again?*

Anya was busy preparing to make bread when Johannes returned home. He stood in the doorway for a minute watching his industrious daughter at work.

"Is there ample flour to make enough bread for a couple of weeks?" he asked casually, not wanting to alarm her with his news just yet.

"Yes, I think so. Are you going off hunting again, so soon?" she responded.

"Not exactly, Anchen. But we may need supplies to last us for awhile."

The hair on the back of Anya's neck crawled. She sensed something was wrong. She did not know how she knew, but she had a premonition. "There has been a lot of talk about why the council left for several days. Did it have something to do with us?"

"Yes," Johannes answered as he moved closer to his daughter and took her flour-encrusted hand in his, "there is much to tell you. I was hoping it might wait, but you seem to be able to see through me. Your mother was always good at that, too."

Anya smiled at this remark, and then sadness crossed her face. "I miss Mama so much. Do you think she is still alive? Do you think we will ever see her again?"

"Yes, Anchen, I do. I have to believe that we will be together again, all of us, or I could not go on one more day."

"Then whatever your news is, however bad it may be, we will be fine. We both have Mama to think about and try to find someday. And I have Oma Sonia to guide me, too."

CHAPTER THIRTY-FOUR

Departure

Johannes and Anya spent the morning preparing the narrow flat-bottomed fishing boat for their escape. Anya's past experience, packing for the sled ride to the Selkup village, gave her enough insight to understand the basics needed for this journey—even though it was to an unknown destination. Meanwhile, Johannes loaded his hunting and fishing gear along with bedrolls for sleeping and skins for shelter.

The men with whom Johannes hunted arrived to say their good-byes, and Johannes thanked each with the gift of one of his dogs. Anya was pleased to know where the dogs were going, but she noted that her father had not presented Adicus or a beautiful black female to any-one. By the time the sun reached its zenith, they were ready to leave, and the two young dogs were still tied to their tethers.

"Papi, what are you going to do with them?" she asked her father when all the preparations were completed.

"I am saving them for Rodin and Yerik," Johannes responded.

"Oh Papi, we must say goodbye to Rodin and Yerik and Polina and the children," Anya insisted. She was feeling the pull of family, even though she had not known some of these people very long.

"I see we are of the same mind," Johannes smiled at his daughter, "these people have been good to me these past five years, and I cannot leave without a proper *auf weidersehen*."

Johannes untied the dogs and led them through the trees toward Yerik's sampa. As they set out on their trek, the forest around them resonated with small voices. Yerik's children burst from between the trees and encircled their clan's beloved foreigners. "How soon are you leaving? Where are you going? Are you going to tell us goodbye? Mama says you had better come to see her before you leave." Their unending flight of questions filled the air like a flock of geese on the rise.

"Hold on. Slow down a minute," Johannes laughed, "we were on our way to visit you and your parents. We would not leave without a proper farewell."

"Well, hurry up then! Mama has something for you. She is waiting, *now*! Come on…come on." Small hands grabbed Anya's and pulled her down the path. Johannes smiled through his beard, his face lighting up as he followed the boisterous bunch.

Polina, waiting at the threshold of her door, stood with her hands on her hips. She tried to look stern, as if the group was late for an important appointment, but upon seeing her children with Anya in tow, her face softened into a poignant smile. "It is about time!" she hollered at them. Waving the ensemble toward her, she ushered them into her home. Johannes tied the dogs to a nearby tree and followed the children into the crowded but comfortable lodge.

Yerik sat in his chair puffing on his pipe, a contented, yet worried look on his face. Plates of food covered the eating mat in the center of the room. The children quickly took their positions, sitting in their own spaces around the food. With an invitational movement of his arm, Yerik indicated that Johannes and Anya should sit.

"Polina insists that you have a good meal before you set sail. I suggest you honor her wishes lest you suffer the wrath of *Kyzy*." Picturing the antics of the mischievous, and sometimes evil, gnome-like creature in his mind, Yerik threw his head back in a hearty laugh and winked over his pipe at Anya.

"Watch yourself, Yerik, or Kyzy may show up in your bed tonight," Polina admonished, wagging an index finger at her husband, a sly smile tugging at her plump cheeks.

Over the habitually incessant chatter of the children, the group devoured the repast Polina set before them. When they were done, Johannes rose and took Polina's hand in his. She blushed as he told her how much he appreciated her generosity and the attention she had given Anya. Then he turned to Yerik.

"Without your help and Rodin's, I might not be alive today, and I am sure I would not have been reunited my daughter."

Yerik stood and gripped Johannes' hand and forearm in an expression of profound comradeship. "It has been a joy to watch you learn our ways and interesting to learn some of yours. I will miss you, my good friend. You are a good hunter."

Johannes knew that among the Selkups, being referred to as a "good hunter" is the highest of compliments, and he was beyond being pleased. "I have a small gift for you," Johannes almost whispered, still reeling from the accolade. He led Yerik outside, untied the female, and handed the leash to his companion. "You know she will produce good strong pups; I hope she will be fruitful for you."

Yerik's smile would have illuminated the village on a dark night. "You are most generous, my friend," Yerik thanked Johannes. "She is a fine gift."

Anya hugged each child. She brushed a tear from Polina's cheek, then wrapped her arms around the ample woman. Finally turning to Yerik, Anya stepped forward and kissed him on the cheek. "Please do not worry about us, we will be safe," Anya whispered as she pulled away. The normally affable man's face reddened as nervous embarrassment tangled with heartache. He could only nod his head in response.

Johannes and Anya took their leave from Yerik, Polina and their brood, and headed to Rodin's quarters with Adicus in tow. Anya followed her father in pensive silence.

Upon arrival at Rodin's, Anya went straight to Miko's shelter. The sled dog was curled up on a deer hide that lay at the entrance to his lean-to. She knelt on the ground next to him and embraced the creature in her arms. The dog gave her a questioning look, then fixed his tawny eyes on Adicus, the interloper sitting at Johannes' feet.

"How are your wounds healing?" she asked as she checked the laceration on the canine's shoulder. Finding that the stitches were healing and no infection was present, she took his head in her hands and exclaimed, "Oh, Miko, I am going to miss you so much!"

Rodin appeared at her side. "You have done a wonderful job with his injuries, Snowflake. Your healing skills will be missed."

"I cannot bear saying goodbye like this," Anya murmured plaintively as she rose to face Rodin.

"I do not like this situation either, and wish you could stay, but it is just not safe."

"I know, but I have not yet met your wife and children. I want to be sure Miko will be alright. I wanted one of his puppies," she blubbered.

"Miko will be fine, thanks to you. I wish I had a pup to send with you, but none are due for a few more weeks. There is much I wanted to tell you, as well; stories of my mother; stories of my ancestors. As to my wife, I am afraid it would be a long time before she would grant your wish to meet her." Rodin sighed deeply and continued, "Yeva did not approve of my mother, my *ëmi*. She did not like the way my *ëmi* left me as a child, or that she isolated herself in the forest far from our village. Here, the elders stay with their children and help raise the next generation. Yeva resents the fact that there were no elders in our lives, when my mother could have been with us. Because her parents went to be with the ancestors early in our marriage, Yeva had no one to help care for our children. When I first told her of your presence in Mother's life, she was very angry. She thought you would prevent my *ëmi* from ever returning to our village, that you would keep her from our children forever. I did try to take my boys to see their grandmother, many times, but Yeva would not allow them to be around you. You were a foreigner, and therefore likely a bad influence on our sons. I am sorry, Anya, I very much wanted her to get to know you, and to realize what a mistake she was making." Rodin kissed Anya on the cheek, then held her at arms length and looked at her. "You have grown so much since I first saw you. And, now you must go. Be safe, my sister. Remember that your Oma will always be near."

A rivulet of tears snaked silently down Anya's cheeks. She had nothing else to say, no words could express her confusion about Yeva's resentment toward her, and no words would be enough to express her sadness at having to say goodbye to Rodin.

A deeply uncomfortable silence enshrouded them. Even as Johannes did not want to leave the village and these people, he was anxious to get started on the journey that faced him and Anya. His voice seemed to boom as he pushed the dog's leash toward Rodin. "I would like you to take Adicus. He is small, but quite strong and fast. He will not replace Miko on your team, but he can help until Miko is ready to work again."

"Johannes, this is your best dog..." Rodin began.

"That is exactly why I want you to have him," Johannes interrupted as he quickly placed the leash in Rodin's hand. "You and your mother have done so much for Anya, and this is the only way I can thank you. I know you will treat him well, and he will work willingly for you in return."

As Rodin drew Adicus toward him, a deep growl emanated from Miko's throat. "Hush Miko," Rodin commanded, "he is not here to replace you, just to help, so you had better learn to accept him." Miko looked from Rodin to Anya to Adicus, then lowered his head onto his paws in silence, but kept his gaze on this new addition to his pack.

Silently, reluctantly, Johannes and Anya turned and headed back to where the dory was waiting on the river's shore. Johannes stopped long enough to recheck that everything they would need had been removed from his tent. Once satisfied, he motioned for Anya to settle herself in the little craft and he shoved it into the water.

As he climbed into the boat and prepared his oar, a movement in the tree line above the shore caught his eye. With a sweep of his hand, he directed Anya's gaze to the top of the bank. Yerik, Polina and their children stood waving. Others soon joined the small group of well-wishers, and the verge was soon crowded with smiling faces and swaying hands. Anya and Johannes waved back. Anya scanned the group, hoping for one last glance of Rodin. Not seeing him, her body drooped sadly as she resettled herself into the boat. Johannes rowed upstream, relieved that the current was not yet bolstered by the melting of the mountain snows. As they inched around the first curve on this new quest for freedom, this voyage into the unknown, a shout drew their attention to the shore. Rodin stood waving from the water's edge, Miko by his side.

CHAPTER THIRTY-FIVE

The Outpost

Johannes rowed against the current for five days. He shared much with his daughter during this time, reliving their lives on the farm, telling her about his days serving in the White Army, into which he was drafted following the October Revolution. He wanted her to understand the political influences that forced them off their land and into the place they now struggled to leave.

Captivated by her father's stories, Anya listened intently, learning much about the world she should have experienced as she grew into womanhood. She was especially pleased when he recounted happy adventures he enjoyed with her mother, but it made her sad to see the tears in his eyes when he spoke of the love he and Katerina shared.

"Papi, we will find her," Anya said earnestly. "We will find Jakob and Karolina and Magdalena and Heinreich and Konrad, too. It may take a long time, but someday…someday."

"Someday, Anchen," Johannes responded. He took the oars from the water and rested them upon his knees, allowing the little boat to drift backwards in the current. "Someday…even if we only meet again in Heaven."

Locating small secluded coves along the shore each evening, they would set up a small rudimentary camp on solid ground, when they could find it, as the estuary was rife with marshland and soggy mires that would bog down even the largest of creatures. A fire was built to warm a pot of river water for tea or soup, and to ward off mosquitoes and any wolves that might be roaming in the area. They ate only small amounts of the fish and meat they carried, not knowing how much farther they still had to travel, or what the days ahead would bring. When she could, Anya gathered plants and wild vegetables to supplement their meals. Following their meager meal, Johannes, exhausted from his day's rowing, settled near the fire and was soon asleep.

Sleep did not come so easily to Anya. She quietly sat and watched as the sun set; its rays turning the clouds into an orange and red inferno that streaked across the indigo sky. *If the ocean could burn like a forest, is this what it would look like?* she wondered. She noted that the days were getting longer, and that even after the sun set, there was light enough to see all that was around her for several hours. Dusk eventually sank into darkness, only to surrender the stars to the dancing lights of the northern skies. She no longer experienced the euphoria of the phenomenon, but watched instead for the flash of purple that would signify the presence of the ancestors...of Sonia. Ultimately, her eyes tired of the search and closed against the strain; Anya, too, would yield to the restful slumber her body required.

Early on the sixth morning of their voyage, Johannes noted an increase in the strength of the current. Excitement energized his voice as he said to Anya, "We must be nearing the junction with the Ob River; I feel a difference in the water. Keep watch on the shore for people and buildings; we are looking for the Nenets' outpost."

Johannes put his back into the oars as he struggled against the stronger current. Anya sat forward, scouring the banks for signs of people. A small herd of reindeer, grazing in the short grasses near the water's edge, lifted their heads and casually watched the boat move past.

"We must be getting near," Johannes noted. "If they were wild, they would have scampered away as soon as they saw us. Maybe the outpost is around this next bend," he pointed ahead to where the river snaked past an outcropping of granite boulders.

Without warning, the air was shattered by a long low blast of a steam whistle, followed by two shorter, higher-pitched bursts. Anya bristled at the noise, a vision of the Siberian-bound death-train flashed in her brain. She gripped the edges of their boat, sinking her fingernails into the soft wood of its sides. Instinctively, she made no noise. Johannes pulled the oars from the water and listened more intently to the sounds being carried on the light breeze that blew their way. Quietly, he replaced the oars and guided the fishing boat to the shore.

As soon as he felt solid ground under its bow, he hopped out of the boat and pulled it onto the beach. He motioned for Anya to jump out, as well, and then dragged the vessel further onto the strand below a thick growth of trees. Signaling for Anya to follow, Johannes clambered up the steep bank. Cautiously they crept through the forest, following the river's course around the bend, where a large ship came into view. Another blast of its whistle produced a puff of white steam that billowed into the sky, curled upon itself and, like a miniature cloud, dissipated on a light current of air. Johannes and Anya watched from their secluded location as the ship pulled close to a somewhat dilapidated dock.

Johannes recognized the boat as a freight steamer similar to the one upon which he had been transported during his military service. This one appeared to be about 80 meters in length and sported a double-deck; a small raised forecastle, the crews sleeping quarters, was visible near the bow. Black smoke poured from its single stack, located about mid-deck. No sails were visible, but masts were located at each end of the vessel. Most importantly, Johannes could not see any indication of armament.

"The ship appears to be for transporting cargo and possibly a few passengers," Johannes told Anya. "I can see a building near the dock; it must be the outpost Yerik told me to go to, but we must be careful. If the ship is carrying certain supplies there could be soldiers guarding the freight."

"Papi, we are not going down there, are we? We should wait until it leaves."

"No Anchen, I must locate Oyvind as soon as possible. Yerik said Oyvind can help us get farther away; maybe that ship is how we will leave."

"But Papi, where will it take us? What about your boat? What will happen to our things?"

"I should have those answers once I have spoken to Oyvind."

Anya followed her father through the trees until they emerged on an embankment behind the building. Johannes stopped briefly to gain a perspective of the site, then turned and faced his daughter.

"Stay here," he whispered. "Until I know it is safe, I need you to stay out of the vision of anyone from the ship."

"Paaaapiiii!" Anya started to plead as she pulled on his coat.

"Anya! Shhhhh! Please obey me. Just stay here until I come back for you. I should not be gone long." Johannes turned and started down the bank.

Once he reached the bottom, he glanced back up at the trees. Anya was gone from view. Satisfied that she might be safe for the time being, he made his way around the plank-sided building and stood near the corner. There was no place for him to hide, so he stopped only long enough to ascertain his situation and get a better look at the ship. He tried to appear as if he were a part of the everyday events at the trading post.

Three sailors, busy unloading crates from the ship, were toward the end of the dock. Two more stood, smoking cigarettes, near the entrance to the store. Johannes nodded a greeting at them as he passed and went inside. The men said nothing in return, but their eyes followed his movements until he was out of their sight.

Once inside, Johannes made his way around a large table piled haphazardly with animal pelts, woolen blankets, and bundles of fabric of all colors. He noted that the shelf-lined walls were filled with cans and jars of all sizes and shapes. Picking up one of the cans that sported a hand-written label indicating that it held tomatoes, Johannes noted the rusty bulged top that warned of its longevity on the shelf. He carefully returned the can to its place, and glanced around the rest of the store. The man he assumed was Oyvind was standing behind a counter at the rear of the shop, deep in conversation with a tall Russian dressed in a captain's uniform. The exchange ended with a smile and a handshake, and the Captain left without seeming to notice Johannes' presence.

"You want something?" the proprietor asked in Russian.

"I am looking for Oyvind, Yerik and Rodin sent me," Johannes answered in Selkup, his voice quiet.

The man's eyebrows raised in surprise. Johannes noted that Oyvind's eyes were directed past him as he answered loudly in Russian, "If you are here to trade furs, I need to see them before you paw through all my merchandise." Under his breath in Selkup he added, "Meet me in two hours behind the store. Trust no one."

Somewhat perplexed, Johannes turned to leave and saw that the two men he had encountered outside now stood on the far side of the room pretending, as he had, to examine the goods while observing the situation. He again nodded an acknowledgment to them and left without another word.

Just to be sure he was not being followed; Johannes took a circuitous path on his return to Anya. He found her where he left her. She was sitting at the base of a large cedar with her knees drawn up to her chest and her arms wrapped around them. She had been crying.

Johannes dropped onto the ground beside her and brushed a wisp of hair from her cheek. "What is wrong, Anchen, why do you cry?"

"You left me here alone. I do not like being alone! I have no one here. I am lost!"

"Anchen, you have me. We are together, and we will stay together."

"But what if you had not come back? What if there were soldiers and you were arrested and taken away?" she whimpered.

"I was, and will be, very careful around strangers. You should understand that. I have no intention of being taken from you." Johannes tried to soothe her.

"But…you were angry with me before you left! You called me Anya!" she sobbed. Once the true reason for her anguish was released from her lips, the tears flowed freely.

Johannes wrapped his arms about his daughter and pulled her close. He placed his hand against her cheek and pulled her head to his chest. Resting his chin on the top of her head, he allowed his little girl to cry.

"You have been so strong that I have been treating you like a grown woman. I forget at times that you are still just a child," he whispered. "So much has happened to you in such a short span of time, and so much more is yet to come. I do not know where we are being led, but I am sure God has His reasons. If you detect anger in my voice, it is not because I am upset with you. I am scared, too, and sometimes I am frustrated with the way our lives have been turned inside out. But, I suspect we have a long way to go, and wherever our travels take us will require that we both stay together. We will need each other for the strength and determination this journey will require of us."

As Johannes spoke, Anya absorbed the vibrations of the words through his chest. When he stopped, she could hear the rhythmic beating of his heart. She listened in silence for a moment; she held her breath and closed her eyes. The tears had stopped. She felt reassured and somehow reenergized. She finally pulled away from her father's grasp and sat up looking him straight in the eye.

"What is the plan, Papi? Where are we going next?"

CHAPTER THIRTY-SIX

Negotiations

Johannes and Anya waited in the forest. They watched as the sailors completed their task of unloading boxes from the ship's deck and stacking them near the entrance to the outpost's door. Soon the ship's whistle gave another steam-laden outburst; the sailors returned to the deck, and the riverboat pulled away from the dock and headed back up the river.

"Must not be our ship," Anya whispered to her father.

"Oyvind may well have other plans for us," Johannes answered as he stood and prepared to leave. "We will know soon."

Anya positioned herself in some bushes near a tree at the top of the riverbank where she could see the men's rendezvous, but not be seen.

Oyvind was waiting for Johannes behind the store, as promised. The two greeted each other with mutual wariness. Oyvind was the first to speak.

"You say Yerik and Rodin sent you? How do you know them?"

"I have lived with the clan for the past five years," Johannes responded.

Johannes took note of the Forest Nenets' odd appearance. He was expecting Oyvind to look like Rodin and Yerik, and while his facial features were similar, he was considerably shorter. Oyvind wore dark blue trousers that appeared to be made of wool, and had surely seen better days as they now sagged at the seams, and shiny areas appeared over the knees and on the pockets. The coat was made of fur, but worn with the fur to the outside. Johannes learned from the Selkups to wear his coat with the fur turned to the inside for better insulation. On his head, Oyvind wore a mink Russian *ushanka* with the ear flaps tied up over the crown. He also wore manufactured leather boots; their formerly polished surface was now scuffed and scratched, with the uppers pulling away from the soles along the bottom stitching. Most notably, however, were the leggings this man wore over his trousers. He was covered from just below his knees down to his ankles in long smoky-white fur, featuring open rosettes delineated in black with pale gray interiors. The leggings were topped with a band of the same fur only the rosettes were larger and more pronounced in shape.

"You like my leggings, I see," Oyvind commented with pride in his voice. "They are Snow Leopard. Very rare. A real prize. See the tops? Made from the tails of the big cats…a real treasure to be sure."

Johannes looked more closely at the fur. "Snow Leopard? I have not heard of such an animal."

"Likely you would not know of it. The cats are rare and live in the highest parts of the Altai Mountains, many kilometers south of here, at the origins of this great river you now travel on. I hunted there as a young man; lost a brother there, too. That is when I chose to return here and set up this outpost. It is safer to hunt bargains with the Russians than to hunt wild cats." Oyvind stopped briefly as a thought emerged in his memory. "You must be the Norwegian I have heard about. But why are you here? What is it you need from me?"

"You have heard of me?" Johannes was surprised.

"Word travels along this river," Oyvind smiled knowingly as his narrow eyes squinted into dark slits and nearly disappeared into the deep folds of his face. "Now what brings you here?" Oyvind's smile faded and his expression turned to guarded caution.

"The Soviets sent word that the children in the village were to be collected for boarding school. The elders feared that my presence would bring suspicion that the tribe was hiding something, and that would result in danger for the people. They said you would be able to arrange for papers and passage for my daughter and myself to someplace safe."

Oyvind's eyes opened wide and his mouth dropped open, revealing empty spaces where teeth should have been, "*Daughter?* But, you are alone, where is this daughter?" he exclaimed.

"She is hiding in the forest. I will not expose her presence until I know you will help us and that you will keep our existence secret."

"But, why a secret? Why would the Soviets be concerned about a Norwegian living with the Selkups?"

"Because I have no papers, my daughter has no papers…" Johannes paused briefly wondering if he should reveal any more information; then assuring himself that the council of elders felt this man to be trustworthy, he blurted out, "because we are not Norwegian."

The wrinkles in Oyvind's face slumped into a deep frown. "Who are you, or what are you, then? I have heard impressive things about the Norwegian in Yerik's village— skillful hunter, useful fisher, and talented carver."

"I am that same man, I am just not Norwegian. A long time ago I was mistaken for a Norwegian because of my fair skin and light hair. I accepted that identity to protect my family, to protect those who accepted me into their lives. I was born in South Russia, as was my father before me. We were farmers there. But, my grandfather came from Germany, so we are considered by Stalin to be Germans, and therefore, enemies of the state."

Oyvind took a step back, his eyes seeming to reevaluate the man standing before him. "I must think on this," he said as he turned to leave. "Meet me back here at sunset, and I will have answers for you."

There was no time for Johannes to respond before the owner of the outpost disappeared around the corner of the building. He wondered what help, if any, Oyvind would provide, and at what cost. *Have I said too much? Have I ruined our chance at escape? Will he turn us in to the authorities? What contacts does this man have, anyway?* The questions ran rampant through his mind as he made his way back up the riverbank to Anya.

"What did he say, Papi?" Anya asked anxiously. "Will we leave on the next ship? When will it come? How much longer do we have to wait here in the forest?"

"Oyvind has much to think about, Anchen, I will meet him in a few hours to get the answers to your questions. Meanwhile, we will wait here."

Anya fidgeted through the afternoon, waiting for the sun to set; waiting for the answers she hoped would come. With agonizing indifference to her concerns, the slothful sun eventually faded into the western horizon, and her father prepared to again meet Oyvind behind the outpost's store.

"Be careful, Papi," she whispered as she kissed him lightly on the cheek.

He placed his hand on her arm and leaned over to kiss her forehead, "Do not worry, my daughter, I will be safe, and we will soon be on our way."

Oyvind was not at the meeting place when Johannes arrived. Finding an old wooden crate to sit upon, Johannes' mind again raced with uncertainty and doubt. He took a deep breath to steady his uneasiness and said aloud, "God, I am putting my faith in You that You will lead us in the right direction."

A deep laugh came from around the corner of the building as Oyvind appeared. "I have not thought of myself as a god, but if that is what you want, so be it! In spite of what you may believe, I think I have some answers for you. But, first, I must meet this 'daughter' of yours."

"I am not sure I am ready to reveal her to you. I still do not know your plans for us. I will not put her in any more danger than she has already been through."

"Any *more* danger?" Oyvind scoffed, "The danger for you and your daughter is just beginning! Life is full of danger, do you not see it? In the forest, in the city, in your own home, you can die tomorrow from a hazard you do not perceive today. So do not worry about danger, my friend, worry only about how I will get you on your way. Now, in order to obtain the necessary papers, I need to see what your daughter looks like so I can word her description accurately."

Johannes understood Oyvind's position and signaled Anya to join them. She quickly slid down the hill and, upon landing, brushed the dirt off and straightened her clothing. She approached her father and looked questioningly at him.

"Oyvind, this is my daughter Anya."

Oyvind looked her over and walked around her, taking in all her presence. When he was standing in front of her again he said in Russian, "How old are you?"

"Fifteen," she declared proudly in Selkup and held her head up aloofly, as if to show she was a woman.

"Ah, I see you speak the tribal tongue. Do you speak Russian, as well?"

"*Da*," she responded, "and German, too."

"Well, you had better keep the German to yourself for now. Stay with Russian whenever possible." Oyvind stroked the thin straggles of whiskers on his chin as he thought, "I have heard many stories about your father, but none of you. There has been no mention of the Norwegian having a daughter. How do you explain your existence?"

"I was separated from my family and lived in the forest with Rodin's mother for the last five years," Anya began, "she raised me and taught me the Selkup ways. Rodin was taking us to the village when his mother died. That is when I discovered my father was living with the clan."

"Convenient, but not very easy to believe," Oyvind said simply. "No, we must have a better story for you."

"But it is true," Johannes interjected.

"It may well be true, but it will open the door to too many questions, too many possibilities of revealing who you really are. She must travel as your wife." Oyvind's words were decisive.

"My wife?" Johannes sputtered. "She is so young, how can she be my wife?"

"She said herself that she is fifteen. That is old enough to be a wife. You can keep the story about her being raised by the Selkup woman, but you took her as your wife when she was found. She will be much safer traveling as your wife. Soldiers and sailors will not bother her if they know she is married."

"Papi?" Anya began.

"It is alright, Anchen, Oyvind is correct; you will be safer traveling as my wife." Johannes patted his daughter on the shoulder. "We must follow his instructions if we are to continue."

"Yes, Papi," she replied as she hung her head in reluctant obedience.

"Now," Oyvind continued, "I will get your travel documents ready."

"Once we have our papers, then what? Where will we go? How will we get there? How much will it cost?" Johannes required explanations before he would continue with this venture.

"There is a logging farm in Blagoveshchensk, along the Amur River. I have heard it is owned by German people. They may have work for you there. It is a long journey, but hopefully, not too dangerous if you keep to yourselves. A tramp steamer should arrive in the next few days. It can carry about 30 passengers and has a crew of fifteen. The captain is an old friend of mine who despises the Soviets, but he will swear allegiance if you ask his opinion. He will take you to Novosibirsk. There you will board the Trans-Siberian to Belogorsk. From Belogorsk to Blagoveshchensk is about 100 kilometers, but I have heard that there might be a good road between them."

Johannes and Anya listened intently. "How much will all of this cost? We do not have much money, only a few rubles I saved from some of the hides I had Rodin sell in Onega." Johannes feared the trip would be beyond his affordability, especially with Anya.

"I am a tradesman. What have you to give me in return for enough rubles to get you both to your destination?"

"The boat that brought us here, and a few supplies, some dried fish and deer meat." Johannes replied.

"THAT IS ALL?" Oyvind burst out. "How do you expect to travel thousands of kilometers with only a few supplies? Bring the boat around; I will take a look at it. If it is in decent condition, I may be able to make you an offer, if not, I have no use for it." Oyvind jumped to his feet and stormed off.

"Papi, what are we going to do if he does not take the boat? What if there is not enough to pay for our passage?" Anya fretted anxiously.

"Hush, child, it is only a ploy. He has to act as if he were to get the worst of the deal, in order to come to an agreement on what is really best for him. He knows that he can sell just about anything we have to offer, it is only a matter of time. If we have something that he can sell quickly, then he will give us a better price for it. The boat is in very good shape, so we should get enough for it. You will see." Johannes hoped his explanation would help alleviate some of Anya's fears, even if it did little for his own.

Johannes ran through the trees to the little cove where the boat was hidden. He pushed it back into the water and rowed around the bend and up to the dock. Anya met him and helped pull it up onto the short strip of sand that anchored the quay's supports. Oyvind exited his store and joined them at the edge of the water.

"Nice, but not very big," he mused. "It might get you to Novosibirsk… if you *row* it."

"This is a fine boat," Johannes retorted. "It is sturdy and solid. It does not leak and skims the surface of the water so quietly that the fish come up to it out of curiosity. Any fisherman with this boat will catch his fill in no time, as I have done on many occasions."

"What else can you offer me?" Oyvind sighed wearily.

"I have deer hides, hair on and hair off. They are good ones; tanned the Selkup way so they will last for years. The hair-offs will make good walls for your chums." Johannes insisted as he lifted the bundle of hides from the boat and spread it open on the rocky ground.

"I have lots of hides in my store waiting for someone to buy them. I do not live in a chum any longer; I prefer a solid wooden building now." Oyvind countered. "What else have you got?"

As Johannes hung his head in defeat, Anya leaned over and whispered in his ear.

"No, Anchen, I will not allow that. It was a gift from Sonia."

"But, Papi, if Oyvind will give us a good price for it…if it is enough to get us to the German farm, I will happily part with it."

"Your daughter has something special to offer me? Tell me what it is, and let me decide if it is worth your trip." Oyvind's curiosity was getting the better of him.

Anya took off and headed up the riverbank to their encampment. She rolled up her sleeping mat and tied it carefully, brushing forest debris away from its surface. She hoisted the bundle onto her shoulder and returned to the waterline and the two men waiting there.

"It is a Kamchatka bear," she said as she unrolled the skin, exposing the long dark fur to the surprised Oyvind.

"Kamchatka? Kamchatka bears are rare. They can also be very dangerous. How did you come by this?" Oyvind tried to look undaunted, but his voice betrayed his excitement.

"It was a gift from Rodin's mother. She lived alone in the forest and was attacked by this bear. He caused her great harm. When she healed, she hunted him down. He is a spirit bear. This mat was the first gift Sonia gave me, and it has been my constant companion since. I have been told it is quite valuable, but I would be willing to part with it to pay for our transportation all the way to the German farm."

Oyvind desired this hide. *A Kamchatka bear would bring me great honor and wealth,* he thought to himself. He paced around the hide and he looked at the boat and the deerskins. His eyes were repeatedly drawn back to the bear.

"All right," he said at last, "I will take the boat, the deer and the bear. That will get you to Belogorsk. Then you are on your own."

"NO!" Anya shouted angrily. "The bear alone is worth more than that, *and you know it!* I want enough money to take us to the German farm *plus* extra rubles to pay for food and lodging along the way."

"What?" Oyvind countered, "That is too much. I will give you enough to get to the German farm, but that is all. You ask too much for your precious bear; you are too attached to its memories."

"Come on, Papi, we will get more for my bear elsewhere. I think there is a village not far from here, and someone there will want it more than he does." Anya's intensity was unexpected and frightened her father a bit. In response, Johannes bent down and started to pick up the bear hide.

"No, wait!" Oyvind exclaimed. "I will give you what you want. Your papers are ready, and I will give you enough money for your tickets and food. You will need little lodging, as there are sleeping quarters included in your transportation."

"Fine!" Anya signaled to her father to leave the hides where they were and headed into the store.

Johannes helped Oyvind pick up the hides and carry them into the outpost.

"I do not normally do business with women," Oyvind shook his head in disgrace, "and that is why. They always get the better of me. Are you sure she is only fifteen?"

Johannes smiled but said nothing. He realized that Anya was playing Oyvind's game. *She is a fast learner! I will have to be careful around her from now on,* he mused.

 Selkup Village

 Johannes' Route

 Forest Nenets' Outpost

 Route of the *Korkino*

CHAPTER THIRTY-SEVEN
The Korkino

A light breeze toyed with the loose strands of hair that hung around Anya's face as she sat on the end of the dock watching for any sign of the expected boat. The sky was threatening rain, and dull gray bulbous clouds floated together and then parted slowly. The dividing clouds allowed crepuscular rays of sunlight to reflect upon the river's surface, resulting in a brilliance that prevented Anya from seeing anything that might be coming down the river.

She reached up to push the strand of hair from her face and came away with dark soot on her fingers. Oyvind had instructed her to rub ash from the campfire into her hair to dull her golden locks, and her father had agreed to this meager attempt at disguising her fair appearance. She glanced at her darkened fingertips, then rubbed the soot onto her skirt with animated disgust, and gazed into the river below her. The water flowed with urgency past the dock, swiftly making its long journey to the sea. *If only time would pass as quickly* . . . she mused. It had been two days since she and Oyvind sealed their deal for her bear hide and now with travel papers, tickets and money in hand, she was anxious to leave.

The day seemed to be endless for Anya, and she grew bored of watching the river flow past her. Rising to her feet, she turned and headed toward the forest.

"Papi," she called as she made her way up the dock, "I am going to gather some herbs and look for some mushrooms for our trip."

Johannes spent his time helping Oyvind unpack and sort the boxes that were left by the previous ship, and now he was lugging a heavy sack of salt toward the door of the store. "Be careful, Anchen, do not wander too far into the trees."

"Yes, Papi, I will stay close. I do not want to miss the ship, should it come today."

Staples like salt, sugar, and tea arrived in forty-five kilogram sacks. These were set aside for the local natives and placed in an easily accessible location near the entrance to the outpost store. Cans of fruit and vegetables, on the other hand, were packed in crates with straw filler and considered by Oyvind to be as valuable as gold, so while Johannes moved the heavy sacks to the stockpile, Oyvind squirreled the cans away under the counter at the rear of the store.

Anya proceeded to clamber up the bank behind the outpost. Just as she reached the tree-lined crest, a long, low blast of a ship's horn called out as it approached a bend in the river. Excitedly, Anya turned to see if she could catch sight of the boat as it drew near, and in so doing lost her footing and slid back down the bank, landing at the bottom in a tangled heap. She sat up and took stock of her situation, then deciding that she was dirty, but unhurt, she rose and ran back around the building and out onto the dock, anxious to see the vessel that would take her father and her on the next leg of their expedition into the unknown.

Anya squinted against the periodic sunlight and waited anxiously as the steamer slowly emerged into sight. Her first thought about this boat was that it was considerably shorter, but wider, than the previous ship. It seemed similarly rigged to the first, but this one also sported a sail fully unfurled at its helm, taking advantage of the increasing winds of the impending storm.

As she stood transfixed by the sight of the nearing vessel, Oyvind's voice rang out to her. "You there! Come closer to the store! If the ship hits the dock, you will end up in the river!"

Anya turned her attention to the voice and saw her father emerge from the store and begin waving at her, motioning for her to come to him. Reluctantly, she walked back down the dock and joined the men to watch the ship arrive.

It took nearly an hour for the steamer to complete its voyage and maneuver alongside the dock. As crewmen prepared to throw the heavy docking ropes overboard to moor to the berth, the ship lightly bumped the dock causing it to shudder and groan in response. The *Korkino* had arrived.

"As usual," Oyvind growled, "that captain always hits my dock."

The boat berthed, the sailors disembarked, and the captain met with Oyvind and dealt with him for various hides and pelts. It seemed forever to Anya, but she and her father were finally advised that they could board and locate their cabin for the trip. Anya had never seen a vessel such as this before, and she was amazed at its size and all that it contained. Wide-eyed with excitement, she carefully walked up the gangplank carrying her possessions neatly rolled up in a blanket and tied with strands of braided leather. At its apex a young sailor dressed in dark blue wool pants with a matching blouse, reached out and offered his hand to assist her as she stepped onto the main deck, then took the bundle from her.

"*Spasiba*," she said politely as she took his free hand to steady herself.

"You have never been on a ship before?" the young sailor asked.

"No," she responded bashfully and reached up to straighten the scarf that covered her head.

"Then, I believe I should show you around our vessel." The sailor bowed as he eagerly offered his services.

"Oh, that would be wonderful but... my husband... would have to approve." The words felt so strange in her mouth, and nearly choked her as she tried to speak them aloud. She turned to look at Johannes as he came up behind her on the walkway.

The young man noticed her difficulty with the words and took note of the great age difference between this young girl and the older, grizzled man she was traveling with, and instantly surmised the union was not of her choosing. He took in her disheveled appearance and the streaks of dirt and mud down the back of her skirt. *Does he beat her?* he asked himself.

"Can you show us to our quarters?" Johannes asked. "We would like to get settled."

"Yes, sir," the young man responded curtly, "right this way."

Following in his footsteps, Anya gazed wide-eyed with wonder, absorbing all the new sights she observed on the deck. She stood in awe at the base of the first mast and looked straight up to its top, nearly falling backward in the process. She drew her fingers along the glass-smooth white surface of the forecastle walls and peered curiously into an oval-shaped opening that led to the interior of the boat. She watched the massive round smoke stack puff clouds of black into the dreary sky, as coal heated the water to make the steam that would propel them to the next port.

They reached another elliptical opening, and the young man swung the heavy metal door wide, revealing a dark hallway illuminated only by the gray afternoon and the flickering of a single lantern. Anya stepped over the threshold and into a passageway lined with narrow wooden doors. She noted that each door sported a Cyrillic number in brass at the top of the head frame. The sailor stopped in front of door number four, opened it wide, and stepped aside to allow Anya to pass. Once she was in the little room, he placed her bundle on one of the two bunks that lined the interior wall and positioned himself between Anya and Johannes, temporarily blocking Johannes' entrance into the cabin.

"I am Vasily," he introduced himself, "if you need *anything* just let me know." He looked past Anya, narrowing his eyes at Johannes. "I would still very much like to show you around when you are ready," he continued, as he stepped past Johannes and re-entered the hallway.

"Thank you, Vasily," Johannes dismissed the young man as he placed his own bundle on the other bunk. "Anya would like that after she gets settled. Is that right, dear?"

"Yes..." she started to say Papi, but quickly stopped, and nodded her concurrence instead.

Vasily's eyes met Anya's with a look of sympathy and offer to help, but not understanding his viewpoint, she thought he was expressing disapproval of her. When he was gone, Johannes closed the door and sat upon the lower bunk.

"You handled that very well, Anchen, I am proud of you."

"I almost called you Papi," she said apologetically, "It is going to be very hard to treat you like a husband. I do not know how I should act."

"As I said, you handled that very well," Johannes smiled at his daughter. "Just remember that it is for your protection."

"But, Papi, did you see how that Vasily looked at me? He must think I am horrid for being married to someone so old!"

"Old? You think I am old?" Johannes laughed heartily, "No, Anchen, that look he gave you had more to do with your current appearance and thinking that I must treat you very badly. I think you should see yourself; here is a mirror." Johannes moved to a small cupboard in the corner of the room and opened the door in the top half of the cabinet.

"OH, PAPI!" Anya was horrified at her appearance, "Why did you not tell me I looked so dreadful?"

"Because then I would have to fight off all the men on this ship, not just Vasily." Johannes smiled a fatherly smile. "Now, I think we should get settled and you can clean up in the basin."

Anya finally stopped to actually take in the little room and what it had to offer. Its walls were formed of smooth white vertical slatwall panels with a chair rail partway up its surface. The beds seemed to be made of long, shallow boxes, painted black and bolted in place. Anya ran her hand over the white sheets and thin wool blanket that covered the soft mattress inside the bunk box and wondered if it was as comfortable as her bear hide. Simple white curtains, hung for privacy along the top of each bed, had been pulled back and secured with ribbon ties. She rubbed the end of one of the ties between her index finger and thumb, letting the silkiness captivate her. The opposite wall was adorned with a curtain-covered porthole above a long bench-seat. The lid of the bench was covered in a pale blue floral-patterned cushion. Opening the lid revealed ample space to store their possessions, meager as they were. Exploring the corner cabinet, Anya discovered that it contained many wonderful things. A drawer in the base of the cabinet pulled out to reveal a chamber pot, well hidden when not in use. A white ceramic bowl was inset into the white enameled flat surface over the drawer, and a matching pitcher filled with fresh water sat beside the basin. The cabinet with the mirrored door was attached just above the basin, and inside Anya found two clear glass tumblers, a bar of lard soap, and four neatly folded white towels. The entire cabin was little more than two meters wide and barely three meters long, but every inch of space was well used.

As Anya completed her survey of the room, she stopped and frowned, and turned to Johannes. "But, Papi, where do I cook?"

Johannes was standing by the closed door and was watching his daughter explore. He expected her to ask such a question and smiled in understanding of her confusion. "You will not need to cook, Anchen. The food will be cooked for us. At mealtime, we will go to a separate room, and there we will eat with everyone else on board."

"Oh," Anya responded with disappointment in her voice. "I thought we could just stay here and avoid all the other people. That would make it so much easier to pretend that I am your wife."

"You will be fine. Just remember to follow my lead, say nothing that will endanger us, and speak only when spoken to."

"Yes, Papi. I will do my best to remember."

Upon leaving Oyvind's dock, the boat turned around and proceeded back up the river from whence it came. They were well underway by the time Anya cleaned herself up, put on her only other sarafan, and combed and re-braided her hair, pulling the long plaits up over her head and securing them with fasteners made of deer bone. When the expected knock came to summon them for supper, she was ready to face a room full of strangers.

Vasily stood in the passageway; he smiled when he saw a trans-formed Anya standing behind Johannes. "Please come with me," was all he said as he made his way to the nearby stairway that led to the upper floor.

At the top of the stairs only two doors were visible in the pas-sageway. A set of double doors on the left had the word "SALOON" stenciled in large Cyrillic letters across them. The single door oppo-site was lettered with "PANTRY." Vasily opened the double doors and entered the saloon. Following him in, Anya observed two long tables that filled the room from end to end. Their surface was made of wide wood planks that had been polished to a high shine. Simple, well-worn benches provided seating on either side of the tables. About a dozen or so men currently occupied various places around the tables; some had already been served, while others waited in anticipation of their impending meals.

Vasily placed Anya and Johannes near the end of the table closest to the door and then quickly left the room. Johannes nodded a greeting to the men sitting across from him. Anya sat quietly with her head down, avoiding the eyes that were obviously staring at her.

Soon Vasily returned. He was wearing a white apron with pockets across the front and carrying two plates laden with noodles and chunks of white fish. He approached Johannes from the right and set a plate in front of him; he moved to Anya's left side and set her plate down, then reached into a pocket and removed a hot biscuit and added it to her plate. From another pocket he retrieved the necessary tableware and cloth napkins, and upon placing them on the table, again disappeared. In a few moments he returned, this time he placed a small cup of tea in front of Johannes and a large glass of milk near Anya.

"Oh, I think I am going to like this ship. Look at this milk! It has been a very long time since I had milk." Anya whispered as she lifted the glass and took a long drink. "And it is so cold!"

"Something tells me you will be getting special treatment, Anchen," Johannes replied as he looked at all the men around the tables. "Enjoy it while you can. But do not let it get the better of you. We still have a long trip ahead."

CHAPTER THIRTY-EIGHT

The Captain's Concerns

"When will we arrive in Novosibirsk?" Anya asked as she prepared herself for bed.

"I think even the captain of this ship cannot answer that question with any certainty," Johannes responded. "This boat is called a tramp steamer, because there is no set schedule for its voyages. The captain sets into a port only if he so desires, whether he thinks he might have business there, or because he needs supplies."

Johannes discreetly turned his back while Anya removed her clothing down to her chemise, climbed up into the bunk and lay upon the down-filled mattress. She was used to sleeping on hard surfaces, but as the thin mattress settled onto the boards that held it in place, she began to miss her bear hide sleeping mat and wondered if she would be able to rest.

Outside, the rain began to fall in earnest, the drops pinging against the porthole glass like pebbles thrown upon a rock. Johannes sat on the edge of his bed with his elbows resting on his knees, his head cradled in his hands. The constant chuff-chuffing and rhythmical "*eins, zwei, drei, vier; eins, zwei, drei, vier*" of the steam engine below them was causing the old injury to his head to throb in pain. Hoping to distract himself from the ache and unvarying noises of the ship, he began to pray aloud softly. He had not taken the time to pray in awhile, and felt that now was a good time to renew his faith and devotion to his God.

As she lay on her bed, Anya listened silently and soon the harmonious timbre of the rain, steam engine and her father's voice lulled her into a dreamless slumber.

Upon completion of his prayers, Johannes stood and removed his trousers, shirt and boots. He pulled Anya's blanket up over her and kissed her on the cheek. Lowering himself into his own bunk, he tried to get comfortable and questioned if he, too, would sleep. *Will I ever get used to that clangorous racket?* he wondered. Forcing himself to close his eyes and disregard the pain in his head and the clamor about him, he tried to rest. In time, the gentle rocking of the boat on the water calmed Johannes enough that he fell into the lap of Morpheus.

A loud knock on their cabin door startled Johannes and Anya to consciousness. "Breakfast in ten minutes" Vasily's voice carried down the passageway.

"Breakfast? So soon?" Anya asked as she rubbed the sleep from her eyes.

Johannes rose, dressed and proceeded to wash his face in the basin. Anya rolled on to her stomach, eased herself off the bunk and dropped onto the polished wood floor. She straightened the wrinkles in her chemise, and then pulled on her blouse and sarafan. She sat on the edge of the bench to pull on her fur boots, but the close quarters allowed little room for such maneuvers, and she accidently kicked her father in the backside. Johannes straightened up from the basin and turned to look at the offending party, his face contorted in an expression of astonished shock.

"Sorry," Anya sputtered as she stifled an embarrassed giggle.

Johannes feigned anger, "Young lady, I will allow you one indiscretion, considering the pocket-sized area of this room," he waggled his finger sternly at Anya. "However, should it happen again, there will be the devil to pay!"

Standing out in the passageway, Vasily overheard Johannes' words through the cabin's thin door. His eyes narrowed in fury as he turned and broke into a run, and scrambled up the stairs to the main deck. Unaware of Vasily's eavesdropping, Anya and Johannes simultaneously erupted into a fit of laughter over her lack of caution in the tiny room.

Anya was pleased to find that the morning meal consisted of foods with which she was familiar—a version of potato pancakes, called *Dranik*. These were accompanied by *Smetana*, a thick sour cream reminiscent of the product her mother made from the milk of the family cow. Spicy sausages sat in pools of grease on great platters and steamy pots of black tea dotted the long tables with random profusion.

Unlike the evening meal that had been served individually, this meal was presented "family style," and the ship's crew used the opportunity to sate their bodies and prepare for a long day ahead. Anya watched in fascination as some of the men devoured large quantities of food as they talked noisily, while others ate in silence, attempting some effort at decorum. *It is easy to tell the difference between the crew and the passengers,* she thought.

Partway through her meal, Anya realized that not only was she the youngest person in the room but she was also the only female present. A pang of extreme loneliness swept though her. She lay her fork down and sat glumly staring at her lap, idly fingering a small stain on her dress.

Johannes quickly realized something was wrong with his daughter and leaned over, whispering in her ear, "Anchen is something the matter?"

"I miss Mama," she sighed.

"Me, too, Anchen… me, too," Johannes murmured.

The words were no sooner spoken than they were interrupted by Vasily tapping Anya on the shoulder.

"I am sorry to disturb you," the young man said to Anya as he glared at Johannes behind her back, "but the captain would like to see you… *alone*… in his quarters after you have finished eating."

"Me? Why would he want to see me?" Anya was astounded at this request.

"I am only delivering the message," Vasily shrugged. "Let me know when you are ready to go, and I will be your escort." Vasily turned and disappeared through the doorway as quickly as he had materialized.

"Why? What would the captain want of me? What should I say to him?" Anya whispered, as fear began to grab at her heart.

"I am sure it is nothing. Just be yourself. He likely has questions about our 'relationship'. You know what is on our papers. Answer his questions with as much truth as you think is reasonable, and fill in the rest as you can. You are smart, and I have confidence in you. Remember the verse from Proverbs that says, '*When words are many, sin is not absent, but he who holds his tongue is wise*.'" Johannes smiled gently at her.

Too disconcerted to finish her meal, Anya excused herself and went to locate Vasily. She found the young man waiting for her just outside the doors to the saloon.

"What do you think the captain wants of *me?*" Anya asked with concern as she approached Vasily.

"I am sure he just wants to know that you are comfortable. We get few women on board these days," he shrugged nonchalantly. "Come on." Vasily reached out and took Anya's hand in his, leading her out onto the main deck.

The rain had stopped, but a strong south wind billowed the foresail, filling the sky with the massive canvas and pushing the ship up the river. Anya stayed close to Vasily as he led her to the rear of the forecastle and the captain's quarters. Arriving at an unmarked door, Vasily knocked politely and stepped back.

"COME!" a man's voice boomed from the other side of the door.

Vasily opened the door and pushed Anya inside and then closed the door behind her, leaving her to stand alone in the captain's room.

The man that occupied this room was sitting in a rattan-backed chair on the far side. He was hunched over a flat desk-like table, studying a large paper that lay across the surface. Anya stood silently gazing about the room. Her first impression was of its overall size. *It must be at least three times as big as 'number four'*, she speculated. She was fascinated by the ornately carved ends of the wooden bunk situated to the left of the desk. The pine-branch pattern stood well away from the panel's smooth background. A tufted edged pillow at the head of the bed repeated the pattern with green embroidery.

Shelves with protective horizontal bars lined the wall over the pillow. Books packed the shelves so tightly Anya wondered how one could be removed without disturbing many. Above the bed, on the long side wall, a single picture in an oval frame presented a smiling young woman holding a baby lovingly in her arms.

Occupying the wall to the right of Anya was a marble-topped dry sink. Sitting in the center of the marble surface, a large porcelain pitcher and matching basin sported a nautical theme in blues and pale greens. An azure-colored mustache cup held a brush and razor on a small railed shelf across the back of the sink behind the basin. Over the sink a simple oblong frame held a beveled-edge mirror, balancing out the appearance of the wall.

Over the captain's desk an assortment of strange-looking instruments hung on either side of a simple wooden gun rack. Though made to hold several rifles, the rack actually held a brass looking-glass, a walking stick, an umbrella, and a plain wooden dowel haphazardly adorned with a semi-clean face towel.

The man finally turned in his chair and looked at Anya. He perceived the adolescent he rested his eyes on to be little more than a street waif.

"I am Captain Pleshakov," he introduced himself. "I believe your name is Anya, is that right?"

Anya now stood with her head down, arms at her sides, staring at the floor in humility, and hiding her pale blue eyes. "Yes," she answered.

The captain picked a paper up off his desk and perused it. "Your travel papers say you are married, is that right?"

"Yes." Anya felt a trickle of sweat roll down her spine.

"How did you come to be with this man?"

Anya rubbed her clammy hands against her skirt. "He rescued me from a wolf attack near the Selkup village."

"I see," Captain Pleshakov responded as he drew his free hand over his mustache-less beard. "Where are you from, child? You are not a native Siberian; anyone could see that. Are you Russian?"

"Oh, yes sir!" Anya exclaimed. "I was born in South Russia," she blurted.

The captain turned back to his desk and opened one of the long flat drawers under its surface. He removed a map and placed it on the desk. "Where in South Russia?"

"The village is called Sofienthal; it is near the Dniester River." Anya was starting to relax, somehow the interest this man was taking in her eased her fears and she looked up at him for the first time.

"Ah, yes, here it is," he said as he put his finger toward the bottom of the paper. "How did you end up with the Selkups, child? This is not a simple journey."

"No, sir, it was not simple at all. Soldiers came to our farm and made us travel by wagon for many days. The entire village…actually many villages from our area…was made to go. Then we were put on a train and taken to Onega. When we were removed from the train, the men were marched west and the women were sent to the east. We children were left behind."

"When was this?" the captain interrupted.

"I think it was about five years ago. I was ten at the time, and now I am nearly sixteen."

"And how did you end up with the Selkups?"

"When my brothers and I were standing in the snow by the train, one of the soldiers brought an old woman to pick someone to help her with her household. She chose me and took me to her forest cottage to live. She was Selkup."

"What about the rest of your family?"

"I have no knowledge of them. I saw none of them after I went to the forest."

"And your 'husband', where is he from?"

"He is Norwegian, according to the Selkups. He was living with them when we met." Anya was starting to get nervous again, she was always taught not to lie, and it agonized her to do so, but she also understood that the truth, the total truth, could put her and her father in great danger.

"Somehow, I do not think he is Norwegian. His way of talking is more like yours than any Norwegian I have ever heard. And Jahnle does not sound like a Norwegian name to me. What was your name, before you married this man?"

Anya hesitated briefly; this was not a question she had anticipated.

"Lutz," she answered, her mother's maiden name was all that came to mind.

"Yes, that fits someone from your area of Russia. You are more German than Russian, I think. But that is not important to me. Now, how does this man treat you?"

"I am not sure I understand what you are asking."

"I have had reports that he might beat you, that he raises his voice to you. Is this true?"

"Oh, no, sir. He loves me very much. He would never beat me. He is a very kind and gentle man."

"He is so much older than you, closer to your father's age I would expect. Do you love him?"

"Yes, very much!" An easy question to answer, Anya thought, though not in the context she suspected this man was suggesting.

"Well, then I will inform my son that all is well with you."

"Son, sir?"

"Yes, Vasily is my son. He works for me as a cabin boy and general all around helper. He is the one who has expressed grave concern about your welfare."

"Oh, yes, Vasily is a very nice boy. He said he would like to show me around the ship, with your permission."

"I will let him do so, but I ask that you do not lead him into a broken heart."

"I do not understand." Anya was perplexed by this statement.

"I fear he may be smitten by your beauty. He meets few young ladies his age on this boat. He is my only son; his mother died when he was quite young." The captain's eyes drifted toward the picture over his bed. "I had little to do with his upbringing and now, as I groom him to captain this ship someday, I must protect him from outside influences and beautiful distractions."

"I am afraid I do not know how to deal with this. I would like to be his friend, but I do not want to break his heart, as you said. Maybe I should just avoid him altogether."

"I think that would only serve to enhance his fascination with you.

No, I will explain to him that you are happy with your situation. That should suffice."

"May I go now?" Anya was again very uncomfortable, though her fears took on a new light.

"Yes, you are free to go. If you see my son, tell him I would like to have a word with him."

"Yes, sir. Thank you, sir." Anya quickly made her way out of the door and into the empty passageway. She leaned against the wall and took a deep breath, relieved that she did not have to give more information than she was prepared to give. But, now she had a new issue to deal with. *How will Vasily take his father's admonition? I like Vasily. Would we be more than friends under different circumstances?*

CHAPTER THIRTY-NINE

New Adventures

Anya leaned on the railing that surrounded the ship's deck and watched as the vessel passed yet another potential port of call. This harbor seemed popular, as a number of boats traversed in and out of the waterfront. *We have not stopped anywhere, I wonder why?* Anya mused. *But, that is all right. The sooner we get to Novosibirsk, the better.*

Anya and her father had been on the *Korkino* for seven days. Most of those days were accompanied by copious amounts of rain. During the worst of it, she had stayed cooped up in her cabin reading and washing and mending clothes; today was different. The clear sapphire sky allowed the sun's rays to dance on the water, causing the surface to glint and sparkle among the ripples that undulated from the passing traffic. She pulled her headscarf tighter about her face as protection against the chilly spring breeze and wondered if she should go back to her cabin.

Turning from the railing, she saw Vasily watching from behind her as she gazed at the river, wrapped up in her thoughts of her mother and Sonia. Anya nodded a polite greeting and smiled a courteous smile at him, but said nothing as she walked past and headed for the opening to the passageway.

"Wait," Vasily said as he approached her. "I promised to show you around the ship, and I have not yet done so."

"That is not necessary," she answered politely.

"Please let me," he pleaded. "I think you will find it very interesting."

"I should inform Johannes first, and maybe you should clear it with your father."

"The captain has already given his permission, and your husband is busy with some of the other passengers."

"Well...if you have the time, I would like to see that noisy engine."

"Good!" Vasily could hardly contain himself. He placed his hand on Anya's elbow and guided her into the stairwell that took them down into the bowels of the ship. They walked past the staterooms and cabins on the second deck, with Vasily pointing out the differences between the first-class rooms, the couples' rooms, the gentlemen's quarters and private ladies' cabin. From there he escorted her down to the next deck and showed her a small room that held trade goods. She recognized the hides from Oyvind's piled in one corner; sacks of wool, and small wooden crates and boxes filled up the remainder of the space. Proceeding along the passage they came upon a room labeled "Wine Cellar."

"The name is not accurate," Vasily chuckled, "as the room is filled with Vodka. Wine is difficult to obtain these days, but Vodka seems simple enough to procure."

The tour continued down into the coal hold, past the mounds of chunky black rock, and through a narrow corridor into the engine room. As they entered the large room, Anya threw her hands over her ears and cast an apprehensive look at Vasily. She had never heard anything like the roar this engine was emitting. Her companion put his arm around her shoulder, in reassurance that everything was as it should be. The throbbing of the engine vibrated within Anya's chest, and she felt as if her breath was being sucked from her lungs by the heat of the coal-fueled firebox.

Anya recognized the four burly men who took turns shoveling the coal steadily into the hot chamber. Though never all at the same time, she had seen their ash-blackened faces at several of the meals, most notably breakfast. A fifth man scampered between several dials and gauges scattered about the engine's many pipes and spigots, opening a valve here and closing another there. He looked up long enough to see the youngsters, waved a quick hello, and resumed his continuous monitoring of the dials.

Anya stopped to try to catch her breath. She looked up at the great smoke stack that emerged from the engine and followed it with her eyes as it disappeared through the ceiling. *I have only seen this from the main deck. Is it taller than the sail masts?* She wondered. *I will have to ask Vasily later.*

He continued to lead Anya around the base of the engine, into another narrow corridor and through an additional coal hold; he showed her the large cargo space in the bow of the ship that was usually filled with grain, but was now nearly empty. He took her back up to the middle deck and opened doors to reveal the mail room and the sail storage area. Anya took in the smell of the damp canvas. On a large wooden bench at the rear of the room, she watched a crewman making repairs to one of the smaller sails.

Anya was so immersed in the fascination of the workings of the ship that she was not aware of Vasily's fascination with her. As he led her up the last staircase that would return them to the main deck, he grabbed her wrist and pulled her to him. He kissed her squarely on the mouth. The heat of the engine room was no match for the heat she felt boil up through her body. She did not know what she was experiencing; was it fear, or embarrassment, or pure joy? Her first response was to pull away. She wrenched her arm from his grip, and stood looking at him in bewilderment. Her cerulean eyes dissolved into pools of tears.

Vasily knew he had overstepped his limits and reached out to her again, but only to apologize. He was too late. Anya ran up the remaining stairs, out of the door and across the main deck, heading for her cabin. She bumped into someone as she made her way to the door that led to her room. Looking up, she recognized the captain through her tear-glazed eyes. Not stopping, she arrived at her room and was relieved to find that her father was not present. She collapsed on the bench, weeping.

On the deck the captain's voice boomed, "VASILEEE!"

The young man answered his father's call, a sheepish look on his face.

"WHAT DID YOU DO?" the captain yelled as the young man stood in front of him.

"Nothing!" was the response as Vasily examined the toes of his father's boots.

"Do not lie to me, boy! If you had done nothing, she would not have run past me in tears!" the captain continued with raised voice pointing towards the passengers' entrance.

Vasily felt his face flush; he was aware that passengers who had been milling around the main deck were watching. "Can we talk in your quarters?" he pleaded.

"No, we will discuss this here. Tell me what you did!"

The words balled up into a mass in his throat and stuck there. His face reddened even deeper as he sputtered, "I kissed her."

"You did *what?*" the captain asked in astonishment.

"I KISSED HER!"

The captain grabbed hold of his son by the shoulder and pulled him into his quarters. Those who saw this action assumed a whipping was soon to commence. Vasily, too, envisioned his father's razor strop plied against his bare back.

Upon reaching their destination, the captain threw Vasily to the floor as he slammed the door behind him. As the boy cowered waiting for his punishment, the captain strode across to his chair and sat heavily upon it.

"Do you realize how disappointed I am in you? We talked about this; you know you were to keep away from her."

"But, Father…" Vasily began.

"No, do not speak. I had a feeling something like this would happen, but I trusted you to behave like a responsible adult. I have been trying to get this boat to Novosibirsk as quickly as possible, in an effort to avoid this very situation. We need supplies, but I have not docked. I am sure you have realized that. I have doubts that Jahnle is who he says he is. He does not seem Norwegian to me. I do believe the girl was telling me the truth as to her origins; if that is the case, she could be trouble for us. We need to get these people off my boat as soon as is feasibly possible. Had I not owed Oyvind a favor, they would not be here now. My feelings are that if the government authorities were to discover their presence, we would be in grave danger. Meanwhile, you need to be taught a lesson. No son of mine will be an interloper in another man's marriage, regardless of how you feel about the arrangement. Therefore, you will apologize to them at the evening meal, in front of anyone who happens to be present."

"I will ask for forgiveness from Anya for my actions, but not in public. I will not apologize to her husband. I have no need for his clemency," Vasily muttered as he cringed under his father's demands.

"YOU WILL NOT SHOW CONTEMPT FOR MY AUTHORITY!" The captain seethed at his son's disrespect. He turned his back on the boy in order to regain his composure. He took a deep breath before speaking again in a calmer voice. "Vasily, you are a member of my ship's crew as much as or more so than any other man under my command. And as such, I expect you to readily obey my orders. You are not allowed to question my motives or disobey my directives. Doing so will bring consequences you do not want. Were you a regular crewman you would likely be flogged, but as I am not just your captain, but your father, as well, I could easily turn you over to the army. You are old enough to be enlisted; all that is keeping you here is me. The choice is yours. If you are not man enough to apologize to the man whose wife you dishonored, then you can learn to be a man at the hands of an army commandant."

Vasily had not experienced this side of his father before, and he was frightened. It was not the heated words that scared him, but the cool demeanor that accompanied the threat to send him away. He quietly rose to his feet and stood at attention before his father. "I am sorry I have disappointed you. I will do as you ask, sir."

"Thank you, son. I know you will handle this situation in the proper manner. You may go now."

Anya had regained her composure by the time her father returned to their room. She washed her face and combed and re-braided her hair. She chose not to tell her father about Vasily's impulsive indiscretion, as she was not sure how she really felt about it herself. She considered not going to supper, as she was uncertain she could face the young man. But, she also knew that refusing food would cause her father to ask questions she did not believe that she wanted to answer.

Anya was relieved to see that Vasily was not in the dining area when she and her father entered and took their places at the table. They were a bit early and only a few other passengers were present. Anya relaxed a bit, hoping that the captain had taken Vasily off of kitchen duty. She was sitting with her back to the main entrance and did not see him enter. She jumped in surprise, and her heart thumped hard against her ribs when she heard his voice.

Vasily stood straight as a board as he spoke his well-rehearsed words to Johannes; "Sir, I wish to apologize to you and your wife for overstepping my boundaries this afternoon. My rashness was unpardonable, and I am ashamed of my actions. If there is anything that I can do to rectify the situation, please advise me."

Johannes was quite astounded and caught off guard. He looked over at Anya. Although she sat in silence with her head down, he could see her ears and cheeks flush red and figured out what may have occurred. Choking back the urge to chuckle, he feigned a very serious look.

"Thank you, Vasily. I was not made aware of any indiscretion on your part. After I have spoken with Anya, I will determine the consequences…for both of you."

The silence of the room hung heavily in the air, as all that were present eavesdropped into the conversation. Beads of sweat emerged on Vasily's forehead as he nearly dissolved into a pool of guilt. He thought of grabbing Anya and running away, but he knew there was no place to hide on the ship, and his father was not planning on putting into a port soon. So he stood in his place, unable to move.

Johannes turned to his daughter and placed his hand on her knee. "Well, my dear, how serious was this indiscretion?"

The room held its collective breath as Anya whispered, "It was only a kiss."

"I see." Johannes patted Anya's knee under the table in a gesture of reassurance, but faced Vasily with an angry look, "And did she return your kiss?"

"Oh, no sir!" the young man exclaimed.

"Do you think that because she is near your age, you have the right to take special privileges with her? Have you no respect for the sanctity of marriage?" Johannes seethed.

"Nnnno, sir; yyyyes, sir. I mean it was *only* a kiss." Vasily stumbled over his words, as fear of what might happen to him gripped his mind.

Johannes stood and took a breath, as if to calm his anger. "Young man, while I am of the opinion that what you have done is a direct intrusion on my manhood, I respect your coming forward and admitting your error. I will forgive you this once. However, I think that you should avoid such contact for the remainder of this voyage."

The occupants of the room exhaled in relief, but none more so than Vasily.

"Yes, sir," he responded. "The captain said the same."

Vasily gazed regretfully at Anya as he turned to leave; she did not return his look. She remembered the captain's admonition; "I ask that you do not lead him into a broken heart." *Is this what I have done? Will Vasily be all right? Will the captain forgive me?*

As the men in the room returned to their normal conversations and diverted their attentions away from the young people, Johannes perceived that his daughter was struggling with hurt and confusion. He took her hand and led her back to their cabin. Anya was very troubled by her father's actions toward Vasily. She did not expect this overt displeasure at such an innocent gesture.

Once they were safely inside their room, Johannes smiled at his daughter and placed his finger to his lips. "The walls have ears, Anchen, be careful of what you say," he whispered. "I am not angry at you, but we must appear as true to our perceived image as possible; remember that.

A first kiss is always awkward, and some circumstances are more difficult to manage than others. But you will both live through this and will be stronger for it. I might not understand the perspective of a young woman, but I think I am aware of what happens in a young man's mind. Avoiding each other is the best approach for this situation,

Anchen. And, with any luck, we will be at our destination soon, and you can put all this behind you."

Anya stood silently, trying to understand her father's words and sort through her feelings. Her mind kept focusing on the instant of the kiss and the sensation she experienced.

CHAPTER FORTY

Novosibirsk

The *Korkino* arrived in Novosibirsk in the late evening. As Captain Pleshakov maneuvered his ship carefully amongst the vessels of all shapes and sizes that filled the harbor, he noted a significant presence of the Soviet military. By the time the ship was docked and moored, the sky had settled into a gray dusk and yellow dots of light began to flicker in the windows of the buildings beyond. Several of the passengers of the *Korkino* quickly disembarked as soon as the gangway was put into place.

Johannes watched from the porthole in the cabin; he too, noted the military's existence within the harbor. *Is this a good place to leave the ship?* he wondered to himself as he watched Anya double checking that all of their belongings were well secured within their bundles. A sharp rapping at the door startled Johannes out of his thoughts.

Cautiously, Johannes opened the door and revealed Vasily standing diplomatically before him. "I brought your papers," the young man began, "and the captain has instructed me to lead you through the city to the depot as part of my penance for my irrational actions." Vasily paused briefly as his eyes singled out Anya; he returned his attention to Johannes. "He says there are too many soldiers roaming the streets, and your passage will be safer by going the back roads and alleyways," Vasily continued.

"You are familiar with these back roads and alleyways?" Johannes asked as he stashed the papers in an inner pocket of his coat.

"Yes, sir. I grew up here until I was old enough to join my father on the water."

"But I thought your mother died when you were very young." Anya interrupted from behind her father.

"Yes, that is true. After my mother died the captain sent me to live with an elderly aunt, here in Novosibirsk, until I was twelve. I ran the streets at will and became accustomed to the ins and outs of the seldom used lanes and paths of the city."

"In that case we are at your mercy," Johannes nodded his acceptance of this offer. "We are ready to go when you are; it will be dark soon."

"All the better," Vasily replied as he politely took Anya's bundle from her. "It will be easier to slip past the Soviet Guard or any NKVD agents that might be roaming about."

Without another word, the trio left the ship. Vasily's confidence grew with each step. He was excited to be out from under his father's grasp. *The 'Almighty Captain' has no control over me here*, he gloated to himself as he led his charges away from the *Korkino*.

They made their way up the pier and through the docks crowded with all sorts of people, cargo, and activity. Anya gaped at the terminal building that loomed over them. She had never seen such a huge building and wondered what fascinating things it might contain. However, Vasily led them past the main entrance through a small gate, into a dark passage, and up a ramp to a single wooden door labeled CREW ONLY BEYOND THIS POINT. Johannes reached out and took Vasily's arm. Vasily stopped and turned; he understood Johannes' questioning look.

"It will be okay; just follow me," Vasily whispered as he opened the door revealing a brightly lit room filled with sailors and soldiers. The entranceway was partially blocked by a waist-high counter, behind which stood a man in a dark brown uniform. Anya observed that the guard stood slightly taller than Vasily, though was much older and more rotund. His uniform coat pulled tightly across his middle, and the bright blue epaulets curled upwards on their ends, indicating it had been some time since the coat was properly cleaned. His black-visored blue cap sat tilted back on his head, as if he had just wiped sweat from his brow. A leather strap stretched tightly across his chest and attached on his left side to a holster belt; this appeared to balance the weight of the holster and its resident pistol on his right. Several brightly ribboned medals hung over his left breast pocket and clinked together when he moved.

"Vasily! It has been a long time!" the guard jovially boomed, his baritone voice carrying throughout the room. "How good to see you! Where have you been off to this time? And, who have you got with you, a new wife maybe?"

"Hello, Alexei!" Vasily returned the greeting with enthusiasm as he shook the guard's hand. "Yes, it has been quite some time since I was here. The captain took us farther north than usual, all the way to the Forest Nenets' territory." Vasily's face took on a resigned expression as he continued, " For some reason, Father felt I needed additional tutoring in history and economics and hired Johannes, here, to teach me. Johannes is Norwegian, and quite a good tutor, I might add. This is his wife, Anya," Vasily swept his arm toward his companions, as Johannes smiled obligingly and offered his hand to the entry's sentinel. Anya stood quietly behind her father, looking at the floor and feeling her heart rapidly pulsing against her ribs at the idea that they were speaking to a member of the NKVD.

Alexei returned Johannes offer of friendship as he eyed the man's fur coat, "That is an odd coat you are wearing; it seems to be inside out. Where did you get it?"

Johannes ran his hands over the coat as he responded, "For the last five years I taught the Sami children in the villages on the Taz River, and this is how they make their garments. The fur is warmer when worn on the inside."

"Really?" Alexei's broad smile dissipated a bit as he asked, "And why have you left the villages of the north? What brings you here?"

"Great Papa Stalin has decided that the Sami children should be sent to boarding schools. They need to learn their lessons in the uniform manner that all of the other children of this great country learn. So I was without employment."

"I see," Alexei seemed a bit dubious of the explanation. "And where are you off to now?"

"Oh, it is wonderful, Alexei! Johannes has been hired to teach at the new university!" Vasily interrupted.

"You mean the Novosibirsk State University of Economics and Management?"

"Yes!" Vasily stated excitedly. "And I have the honor of taking him there, can you believe it? So we are in a hurry, to get him there before the gates close for the night. That is why I brought them this way, to avoid all the waiting and delay of the main terminal."

"Well, I am not so sure that was a good idea. You know I am only supposed to allow crew members through here. I am not authorized to allow anyone else past this check point."

"I can understand your concerns, Alexei, but their papers are all in order, the captain made sure of that. And you know that I know my way around here very well; no one will ever suspect that they are anything but crew members. If you think about it, Johannes was essentially a member of our crew; he was *hired* by my father."

"Since you put it that way…" Alexei hesitated as he thought about the boy's words. "I will allow them through, on one condition," the smile returned to Alexei's face, "when you return to your father's ship, you will bring me a honey *prianik* from the little bakery down on Lenina Street."

"That, my good man, is definitely a plan," Vasily said as he picked Anya's bundle up from the floor where he set it during his conversation with Alexei. "Now we must be on our way, we do not want to be left out on the streets tonight."

The little group was again on their journey. Vasily led them around the gathering area for the various ships' crews and past what appeared to be sleeping rooms for the men. Finally, they entered a long hallway that seemed to Anya to go on forever.

The walls and floors were tiled with highly polished, small white ceramic squares that reflected the light of glass bulbs encased in wire cages, hanging singly, and several meters apart off the ceiling. Anya was curious about these little lanterns. She wanted to stop and examine one closely, as they did not flicker like a candle or seem to need air like an oil lamp. But, she knew there was no time for curiosity or examination, so she kept up with the rapid pace Vasily established. Soon they went through yet another door and found themselves standing outside the terminal at the edge of a very busy street.

Anya stopped in her tracks and looked up and around her. She drew in her breath and held it as she slowly rotated her body full circle. The sky above her was black, but light emanated from every direction. The buildings hovered over her like giants in a fairy tale. She let out her breath and stood with mouth agape staring at all the strange sights she was trying to absorb.

Something that appeared to be a small one-car train stopped in the middle of the street in front of her and expelled a hoard of noisy people covered in fur from head to foot. Suddenly she was lost in a sea of humans that jostled her from one place to another as they rushed past on their way to their own destinations. Unable to regain her breath, she felt as though she was going to faint, when a hand grabbed hers and pulled her to safety; Vasily had come to rescue her.

"Stay with us, or you will get lost," he warned as he pushed her up against a wall and out of the line of pedestrian traffic.

Johannes put his hands on Anya's shoulders and steadied her. "Are you all right Anchen?" he asked.

"I have never seen such a place as this! There are so many people in the streets, and enormous buildings, and the lights…so many lights… and they do not seem to be candles or lanterns!"

Vasily smiled at the realization that Anya had never been to a city before, and she was unaccustomed to the many wonders of the likes of Novosibirsk. "There is much to see in this city. It is the third largest city in Russia and the largest in all of Siberia," he declared. "The buildings rival those of Moscow or St. Petersburg."

"I think it is now called Leningrad," Johannes interjected.

"Oh, yes, Leningrad. It does not matter. Our city is more beautiful than either."

Anya stepped away from the wall and watched the people who passed by. She felt out of place in her simple, and somewhat tattered, clothing. Spotting a small group of soldiers milling about on the opposite side of the street, she pulled her scarf up over her head and drew it tightly around her ears and under her chin. "I do not like it here. The buildings frighten me and there are too many people. I think we should keep moving."

Vasily led them along the sidewalk for another block or so, and then turned down an alley. The hard surface of the walkway turned to gravel and mud puddles, and the bright lights of the main thoroughfare faded into the distance. Enough ambient light flowed from windows above and on either side to allow them to see much of their way among the shadows. At some places on their journey the air was filled with wonderful aromas of food cooking, or bread and pastries baking. In other places the stench of rotting sewers nearly made them gag. The back streets were not without peril. Anya was nearly bowled over when a door was abruptly opened and a drunken soldier was shoved out into her path. He grabbed at her skirt as she maneuvered around him.

"Tell your father I will pay good money for your company tonight!" he bellowed after her as he stumbled and fell into the mud. Amid a myriad of expletives, the soldier rolled onto his back and passed out.

Vasily continued his quick pace as he rounded some corners to the left, and others right, and Anya wondered if they would be lost in this quagmire forever. Then, without warning, they stepped into another busy well-lit street and upon the edge of a vast open square. The wind blew off the river and across the bare space before them, and sent a chill through Anya as they continued their trek.

"That is the main depot building," Vasily pointed ahead toward a structure unlike any either Anya or Johannes could have envisaged.

Johannes admired the stately construction that consisted of pale blue-green walls outlined with white cornices and moldings that emphasized each transition within the architectural entablature. He noted the long rows of columns rising on either side of the center section and the mullioned glass windows that filled the spaces between them. He appreciated the fact that the windows were repeated within the central arch that formed the main entranceway to the station, giving a completed look to the facade. Finally, he was surprised and yet pleased to see that just above the entrance doors a small triangular edifice sported a double cornucopia resting on scrolled sleigh runners and topped with a rendition of the crown of Tsar Nicholas. In the center of the conjoined cornucopias a clock advised all travelers of the time with its black Roman numerals and intricately ornamented hands. *I can not believe the government has not removed or defaced this reminder of the Tsar, but I am glad it remains,* he silently mused as he watched the hands move toward eleven. Vasily's voice jarred Johannes out of his thoughts and admiration of the Tsar's facility.

"The *Korkino* with its masts at full sail would fit in this building with room to spare," Vasily declared authoritatively to his companions as they made their way to the central entry. "During the day the square is filled with vendors selling all kinds of goods to travelers. Or at least they used to, before…"

"Before what?" Anya asked.

"Before the government…" again Vasily stopped in midsentence. "I can not say anymore…there are laws against criticism of the government."

"Yes, I understand," Johannes acknowledged. "Now, I am afraid we must part company. We need to get inside and purchase our tickets, if they still sell tickets this late."

"The ticket window is inside and to the right, and is open at all hours. I think it would be best if I take Anya around the edge of the building and onto the main platform. When you have purchased the tickets you can meet us there." Vasily reached into his pocket and pulled out a handful of Ruble notes and pressed them toward Johannes.

"What is this for?" Johannes asked with surprise.

"A ticket for me, I am going with you."

"Does your father know? Do you have travel papers? When did you decide this?" Johannes demanded as he put his hand out to push the money back to Vasily.

"Please take me," Vasily pleaded. "I do not want to go back to the ship; I want to go with you and Anya."

"I am sorry, but you cannot go with us. Anya and I have a long way to go, and we know not what dangers lay ahead. You have no papers, and I doubt you have your father's blessing. We appreciate that you have assisted us in getting this far, and we can never thank you enough for that, as you have saved us many hours and possible arrest…"

"You can thank me by taking me with you!" Vasily begged.

"Why, Vasily. Why do you want to go with us?" Anya implored of him.

"You know why, Anya," his eyes expressed the love he felt in his heart, but he refrained from speaking the truth in front of Johannes. "On the ship, I am only a slave to the captain's bidding. He does not care what happens to me. He will only miss me if I am not there to serve his needs. I am nothing but a disappointment and a burden to him. That is why I will not go back!"

"No, Vasily, you are very wrong about your father. You may not see how proud he is of you, that he loves you very much; but I saw it the first day we were on the ship. Do you remember when he summoned me to his quarters? He spoke highly of you and told me how much he missed seeing you grow up. He is only protecting you and trying to teach you…" Anya hesitated briefly wondering if she should say the words that would really get through to this young man, the words that should send him away for good. Finally she blurted, "Oh, Vasily, he wants you to take his place as captain of the *Korkino*!"

"That is not true!" Vasily countered. "If he wanted me to be captain why does he only give me boring jobs, things any child could accomplish? He has never mentioned that I am to be captain someday. He only orders me around. Vasily do this, Vasily do that, is all I ever hear from him."

"How did you father become captain in the first place? Did he just buy a boat and put on the uniform?" Anya inquired.

"No, the boat was his father's. All the men in our family have been sailors."

"And how do you think he learned to handle such a ship? Did he not learn from his father?" Anya demanded.

Vasily thought for a moment, then lowered his voice in acquiescence, "He claims that he was a cabin boy, like me."

"Do you realize that you have a clear path ahead of you? You know where you belong and that you will have a job, no, a profession, for life. You like traveling on the river, do you not? Johannes and I must keep going, too, only we are not sure where tomorrow will lead us. We could be arrested at any moment; you know that. Do you want to spend your life in prison, or at some desolate labor camp, just because you think you are in love with me— in love with a *married* woman?" Anya did not know from where her words were coming. She felt they were far more mature than her years should have allowed, but her heart seemed to be dictating her thoughts and she would say anything to turn Vasily away.

"But Anya…"

"No, Vasily, you must leave now. Go back to the ship; go back to your father; go back to your future." Anya saw her father slip off toward the passenger terminal during the conversation, so now she took hold of her belongings and turned to make her way to the platform at the rear of the building.

"Anya, please never forget me," Vasily entreated.

She stopped with her back to him, and slowly turned to face him. He took a tentative step toward her. She reached deep into the pocket of her skirt and pulled out a small cloth packet. She handed it to Vasily.

"What is this?" he asked as he stood riveted by the bouquet of its contents. "It smells like you."

"Yes, dear Vasily, my Oma Sonia told me to always carry a bag of dried flowers and herbs. It is my essence, the aroma of my spirit. Keep it near your heart and remember me well. And when you find the love, the real love, of your life you must throw it away."

"But if I take this, what will you do? Where will your spirit be?"

Anya smiled, "This essence is of my life past. When Johannes and I reach our new life, wherever that may be, I will gather new herbs, the herbs of the new land, and they will become my new spirit." She moved closer to him and kissed him on the cheek. "I can never forget you; you will always be in my heart," she whispered as she quickly pulled away and broke into a run in the direction of the platform.

Vasily stood and watched as she disappeared around the corner; his heart seemed to have fallen to his feet, and he could not move. He was hurt and confused and suddenly consumed with an unexplained loneliness. *Who would I miss most?* He asked himself. *Anya or my father?* He saw the train pulling into the depot and after several more moments of thought, he squeezed the little pouch in his hands, inhaled its sweet perfume, put it in his shirt pocket and began walking back across the great square, back to his father's ship.

Route of the Trans-Siberian Rail Road

Novosibirsk to Chita approx. 2,500km or 1,564 miles
and three time zones

CHAPTER FORTY-ONE

The Train

Anya was breathless by the time she arrived at the platform. She knew she could have stopped running as soon as she was certain Vasily was not following her, but she was somehow afraid to stop. She feared that if she paused long enough to even think about her actions, she would return to the young man she left in the square.

Anya searched the platform, which rose between the rear of the great terminal building and the tracks, looking for her father. Lights shown from all directions, illuminating the fifty or so people who were waiting to board or waiting for loved ones to disembark. She came to a standstill; she felt her heart pounding from her exertion, and from the overwhelming sight of the great locomotive that sat chuffing on the tracks in front of her. She had spent days steeling herself against this moment, telling herself over and over that this was not the death-train of her youth. Now, here she was face to face with the monster of her nightmares, her personal big black beast of dread.

She took a deep breath and stepped forward toward the big engine. She let her eyes examine the machine, taking in the red running-board alongside the engine's rounded body. She noted that the red again appeared behind the silver-colored drive-wheels and in a sleek stripe running the length of the coal-tender that followed. The bright red stripe repeated itself along the side of the passenger cars, which were painted as green as grass. The cars were topped with rounded grey roofs, and their walls were lined with windows, lots of windows. As she looked down the length of the connected cars, she saw none of the brown cattle-cars of the train that took her family to Onega. *Definitely NOT the same train*, she tried to convince her doubting mind.

In only moments, her father found her and beckoned for her to follow him down the tracks to the fifth car in the line of twenty or so identical units. These were trailed by a number of flatbed cars loaded with logs headed toward the mills somewhere farther east.

Anya lifted her bundle up the short stairway leading to the entrance of their unit. She stopped at the top step and looked to her right and down a narrow hallway—lined with doors on one side and windows on the other—then stepped forward to allow her father to pass and proceed to their compartment.

Johannes, tickets in hand, checked the numbers on each walnut-veneered door until he came to 16. The window forming the upper half of the door revealed that no one was present inside, so he turned the knob and entered. The room was small, barely big enough for the two of them to stand. Thickly-stuffed bench seats, each with a railed shelf over it, were situated along the two longest walls. The outer wall consisted of a large window over a small table that folded down flat.

Johannes smiled as he lifted his bundle up onto one of the shelves, and then did the same with Anya's. He picked the seat with its back to the direction of the train, quickly sat to make room for his daughter to come inside, and gestured for her to sit on the seat across from him. Anya cautiously ran her hand over the rust-colored velvet, feeling its unique softness. Slowly she sat down, and looked directly at her father with a smile of her own.

"I have never seen anything like this, Papi," she whispered breathlessly.

"Neither have I, Anchen. I think this is why they called it the Tsar's travelling office. He would only have had the best."

"The window is so large; I can see everything from it." She reached up and placed the palm of her hand against the glass, as if needing to be sure it was real. She was startled out of her gaze, across the city that shone in the dark, by a long blast of the train's whistle. The car gave a quick lurch and began to move. Within minutes they were leaving the station behind and heading off across the steppe-land to the east.

A robust woman in a smartly tailored uniform of dark brown gabardine knocked at the door. "Tickets!" she demanded in a firm voice.

Johannes stood, opened the door and handed her their tickets. The woman examined them closely, checked that the number on the door matched that of the tickets, punched holes in the corners of the salmon-colored papers and handed them back to Johannes. As she did so, she looked over his shoulder at the girl in the seat. "Travel papers," the woman said as she put her hand out.

Johannes reached inside his coat and removed the papers and placed them in the woman's hand. She scrutinized the document, looked again at Anya, and handed the papers back to Johannes with a disgusted "Humph." After a slight pause she said, "There is hot water for washing and tea next to the toilet at the rear of the car; your dining car is the second one back; meals are served between seven and nine—Moscow time— morning and evening." With that, she again cast a repugnant look at the occupants before her, and continued on her way to the next compartment.

"Well," Johannes said as he returned to his seat, "the *Provodnitsa* may not approve of our relationship, but she seemed to approve of our papers. I guess Oyvind knew what he was doing after all."

Once the train was well away from Novosibirsk, it settled into a constant pattern of gently rocking as it rushed along the tracks. The darkness concealed the landscape they were traversing, and Anya soon became tired of seeing only her reflection in the window. She sat back and relaxed into the soft seat.

A little lamp, located on the wall just inside the door, illuminated the compartment and flickered and dimmed on occasion, but cast enough glow that one might read. Anya looked around, but found nothing for her to study, so she began fiddling with the knot on her belt. Johannes sat back in his seat and soon his eyes were closed. She guessed it must be nearly one in the morning, but she could not relax enough to sleep.

It was not long before the Provodnitsa walked through the car ringing a small brass hand bell and announcing "Eight-thirty, dining car will close in one-half hour!"

Anya watched as the woman disappeared past their door. "What kind of food do they serve, Papi?" She had not realized that she was hungry, but now the suggestion seemed to make her stomach growl with anticipation.

"Well, it does not look like I am going to get much of a nap, so I guess we should go see." Johannes replied with a gentle smile.

As they made their way through the car, Anya took note of the rooms as they passed. Some were empty, but items inside indicated that passengers were in residence; others were a void of non-occupancy. She saw a single man in one, and a couple of men in another. A family of four was crowded into the last little space. The mother was rocking a toddler in her lap, while the father tried to entertain a boy who appeared to be around five or six.

At the end of the car, Anya and Johannes stopped to wash their hands and faces in the warm water provided by a spout that emerged from the wall just above a metal basin. A small bar of lye soap sat at the edge of the bowl, and a linen towel hung on a peg nearby. Next to the basin, a large metal samovar, with a glowing firebox under it, exuded steam from its sides and across a stack of nested metal cups on a small shelf. Next to the cups, a jar of black tea leaves and a plate of hard cheese sat ready for a passenger's needs. Anya looked for milk or sugar, and was disappointed that she found none.

Upon entering the dining car, Anya counted six tables down each side of the room, each table directly under a window of equal size to the one in their compartment. Each table was flanked by four simple wooden straight-backed chairs, and was covered with a plain white cloth. A fork and spoon rested in front of each seat, delineating each person's place. About half of the tables were taken, so Johannes chose the first available place and sat down. Anya sat across from him. Neither spoke. A middle-aged man, with the swarthy complexion and almond-shaped eyes of Rodin and his tribe, quickly appeared and placed steaming hot cups of tea before each of them. The man was dressed in white shirt and trousers, and a white apron hung from his waist to his knees.

"Vodka, sir?" he asked Johannes in Mongolian-accented Russian.

Johannes nodded and a small glass was placed next to his tea. The waiter reached into the pocket of his apron and removed a bottle of clear liquid from it. He poured the liquid into the glass, then left and entered a small space at the front of the car. When he returned, he carried two plates. Each plate held a bowl of *schi*, a brothy cabbage soup, and a single link of spicy sausage. Using the fork to cut the sausage into little pieces, Johannes added them to his soup. Anya chose to eat her meat separately. Together they enjoyed the hot and tasty combination in silence.

While she was finishing her meal, Anya noticed a man a few tables away. There was something about him that bothered her, but she did not know why. She observed his handsome face and guessed that he was a bit older than she, maybe closer to her brother Jakob's age. He was nicely dressed in a dark suit with a white shirt and thin black tie. His clothing appeared cared for, but was not new by any means, as the pants revealed a shininess that only time and wear imparts. His flaxen hair was neatly combed back away from his face. He imparted a presence of self-assurance and position, and she wondered if he came from a family with money. She caught him looking at her more than once, and it made her uncomfortable.

The waiter returned to remove their dishes and serve dessert. The small pocket of fried dough contained farmer's cheese and was topped with a dab of Smetana and a bit of dark jellied fruit. Anya closed her eyes as she let each bite melt in her mouth and trickle down her throat. She could not remember when she had eaten anything so wonderfully smooth and tangy with just the right touch of sweetness. Johannes was pleased to see that his daughter was taking so much pleasure in such a simple meal.

When they returned to their compartment, they found two blankets and pillows neatly resting on one of the seats. Anya wrapped herself in the dark wool blanket, shoved the pillow against the outer wall and lay upon her bench.

"I wish there had been more money," Johannes said as he watched his daughter trying to get comfortable, "I would have liked to have given you a first class room with beds and better food."

"Papi, there was certainly nothing wrong with the food, and now I think I am tired enough to sleep anywhere. I think we have done well, and it is only a few days until we reach Blagoveshchensk and our new home."

Morning came early, but was not eventful. Anya watched the passing scenery as the train kept its rapid pace across vast open spaces of flat steppe, up moderate grades through hills and down into valleys of marshland, sporting wildlife of all sorts. She occasionally dozed, as did Johannes, trying to catch up on their short night. Just past midday the train crossed a large river and slowed into a port town. Anya could see the dockyards from her window, and a large factory of some sort spewed gray smoke from its giant stacks. A sign along the tracks declared that they were in Krasnoyarsk.

"Papi, is it all right if I look from the windows across the hall?"

"Yes, Anchen, just do not leave the car, please. I have been told the train only stops for a few minutes at each depot; I do not want you left behind."

"Oh no, Papi, I will not leave; and, besides you will be able to see me from here."

Anya opened the door and stepped across the narrow hall. She stood close to the window and stared at another vast collection of buildings of all shapes and sizes. She could pick out the onion tops of the Orthodox churches and the smoke stacks of more factories against the skyline. The river flowed east and seemed to contain islands of refuge in its center, whether for people or animals she could not know. In the far distance she could make out rising mountains. *I wonder if they are covered in forest like those of the north,* she reflected wistfully.

Her gazing was interrupted by an older couple coming down the passageway struggling with two large satchels. The woman depended on a cane for balance, and she was showing signs of exhaustion. Anya left her place in front of the window and went to the couple.

"May I help you?" she asked politely. "What is your room number?"

The woman looked up without saying a word, appreciation written all over her face. The man grumbled "Nineteen, we are in number nineteen. Who are you? You do not work for the railroad, are you going to steal our things?"

"No, sir, I only want to help. My name is Anya, and I am a passenger like you."

"Why would you want to help us? No one helps anymore, unless you expect to be paid. If that is what is going on here you can go away, I have no money to pay you," he groused as he waved her off.

"My Oma Sonia needed a cane to walk, and I always helped her. Now I will help you." Anya lifted the heavy satchel confidently from the woman's grasp, and led the way to their compartment. "Where is the conductor? Why has she not assisted you?" Anya asked as she opened the door and placed the satchel inside on the floor.

"Because we are Jews, no one helps an old Jew, not these days." The words were spat from the old man's lips as if he had eaten something very bitter. He began to lift his bag up onto the overhead rack, and Anya stepped forward and pushed from her side. They repeated the process for the woman's valise.

Anya smiled at the couple as she prepared to leave. "I am afraid I do not know what a Jew is, so it is acceptable for me to help you." With that she closed the door behind her and smiled to herself as she began her return to her own room. She was startled when a man's voice came from behind her.

"That was a nice thing you did; not just anyone would have done that."

Anya turned to face the person speaking and found herself face-to-face with the attractive stranger from the dining car. She now noticed that he appeared thin, but not emaciated like many men she had seen recently. Unlike the straightly combed-back style from last night, his hair now fell casually in a wisp over his forehead. His green-brown eyes shone happily from his square-jawed handsomeness.

"I do not understand why that is. If someone needs help, you just help them," Anya shrugged.

"You are not from this part of the world, are you?"

"I am not sure what you mean. I am Russian. Is this not Russia?"

"Basically, yes, but this part of Russia has its own customs, its own way of life."

"And helping others in need is not a part of that? If that is the case, I am glad I am not from this part of Russia."

"In this district, one helps only if it will lead to a better circumstance. Did you receive any pay or political gain from your efforts?"

"Of course not!" Anya was appalled at the idea.

"That, my dear lady, is how I knew you were not from this vicinity. I am Piotr, and I am not from this area either," he said with a great flourishing bow. "I am happy to make your acquaintance."

The train gave a lurch as it began its trek out of the station. Anya steadied herself against the wall as she offered her hand in introduction. "My name is Anya."

"Will you join me for the evening meal? I would like company." Piotr asked as he took her hand in his and kissed it.

Anya blushed bright red, but managed to say, "You may sit with my husband and me, if you wish. I think he might like someone to talk with…as well… but I will have to request his approval."

"Husband? I was sure he was your father." Piotr was a bit unnerved by her response, but straightened and continued, "But I would like that. See you at seven then?"

Anya nodded her acknowledgment of this proposal and returned to her room, where she found Johannes dozing in the afternoon sunlight that flowed in from the window. He woke as she brushed past him on her way to her seat.

"Anything of interest to see?" he asked.

"Another big city like the one we left. Big and dirty. I do not think I could breathe in such a place. I met an older couple just getting on the train, and helped them to number 19. Then I met that man from the dining car, you know, the one in the suit. He said his name is Piotr. He has asked to sit with us during the evening meal, with your approval, of course."

"Well, you were quite busy in such a short amount of time. Yes, I might like some company with our meal. But, remember to be careful what you say; we do not yet know this man or what his intentions might be."

"Yes, Papi," Anya responded causally as she watched the Provodnitsa pass their door. "Papi?"

"Yes, Anchen, what is it?"

"What is a Jew?"

"That is an odd question for you to ask. Why ask it now?"

"The man in Number 19 said no one would help them because they were Jews."

"I see. I know it has been a long time since you have studied your Bible, and you have likely forgotten a lot of what you did learn. The Jewish religion is very old, even older than Christianity. Jesus himself was a Jew. And that is where the difference begins, because many of the Jewish faith did not believe that Jesus was the Messiah and refused to follow his teachings, they stayed with their own beliefs and denied Our Lord. The *Hebrew Bible* consists of much of what we call the Old Testament, but they do not recognize the New Testament that we Christians profess to live by. As a result there have been many wars, and constant dissention, ever since. That is the simple version, but I think you get the idea."

"Oh," Anya replied thoughtfully, "but there was no reason for me not to help them, was there?"

"No, dear, we all need help now and then, and our religious beliefs should have no bearing on whether we offer a hand to those in need."

"I must have remembered something of what I was taught, either by you and Mama or at church or school; because I did not think I should just ignore those people. They just seemed like they needed me."

"I am sure they did," Johannes yawned. "Now, may I return to my nap?"

Promptly at seven—Moscow time—the conductor rang her bell and announced the opening of the dining car. Johannes and Anya again stopped to wash at the basin then proceeded to their supper. Piotr was waiting for them at the door.

CHAPTER FORTY-TWO

Piotr

Piotr offered his hand in friendship to Johannes. "I am Piotr Giess. I met your wife, Anya, earlier. She was performing a very caring act toward an older couple."

"Johannes Jahnle." Johannes returned the greeting as he sized up the man standing before him. *Only an average man,* he thought, *he could be just about anybody*. "Yes, she told me about the encounter. She was only doing what comes naturally to her. She was always taught to be considerate of others and to help where she could." He stopped for a moment and then said, "Giess…that does not sound Russian."

Piotr laughed. "No, I am Polish. I am a sales agent for a lumber company. I am accompanying the cargo in the rear cars, as my employer requires only the best prices from the mills, and that only happens when an agent is present at delivery." His bright face took on a temporarily serious look. "Jahnle does not sound Russian either."

"Norwegian," Johannes said softly and quickly added, "Shall we find a table?"

Piotr led the way to the rear of the car, politely offered Anya the chair nearest the window, and sat on the opposite side of the table, facing the couple. The waiter arrived with tea and vodka, followed by their meal, which consisted of a hot bowl of *rassolnik*, accompanied by a plate of *churek*, a simple flat bread. Anya was not familiar with the soup before her and tasted a small spoonful. The salty-sour tang of cucumber pickles mixed with onion and chunks of poultry giblets danced on her tongue, waking her taste buds to new flavors. She liked it.

The men engaged in small talk as they ate. Anya respected her place and said nothing, unless spoken to specifically.

"So what brings you to this part of Russia? A bit out of the way for a Norwegian, is it not?" Piotr inquired.

"I suffered a grave injury to my ear, and can no longer sail on the fishing boats. While berthed near Onega, I began seeking work on land. I have been told of employment in the area of Blagoveshchensk. Anya and I have been heading that way for some time now."

Piotr listened with interest, and as little cake rolls, called *bushe*, were served to complete the meal, he asked, "Do you smoke?"

"A pipe, on occasion."

"Excellent, then please join me in the vestibule of your car. I take pleasure in a fine pipe, and a good companion would enhance my enjoyment immensely."

"I will take Anya back to our cabin and locate my pipe. I am afraid it has been relegated to a coat pocket somewhere."

"I fully understand," Piotr again smiled, "One of the many inconveniences of travel."

Although it was late June, a chill wind blew through the opening over the coupling of the train's cars. Johannes and Piotr lit their pipes and in unison, drew deeply on their mouthpieces. As the smoke quickly degenerated into the atmosphere, Piotr lifted the collar of his coat as he stepped closer to Johannes.

"Do you know what this is?"

Johannes examined the small circular pin that was kept hidden beneath the lapel. The white enamel background was emblazoned with a scarlet cross. Johannes shook his head as he stepped back, "I must presume you are Christian, but I do not recognize the emblem."

Piotr let the lapel return to its natural position, again hiding the little pin, "Yes, I am Christian, but that has nothing to do with the pin. The badge symbolizes that I am an agent of the Red Cross. The society helps people everywhere, and I am here to help you."

"I do not believe I understand."

Piotr looked over his shoulder to the window in the car's door; to be sure they were indeed alone before continuing. "The work you think is in Blagoveshchensk no longer exists. The people with the farm along the Amur River were of German heritage. They hired many more German-Russians to assist them with the farm, only to aid them in traversing the five kilometers of frozen river each winter. They have been instrumental in helping many of their kind to escape across the border into China. But the Soviets were closing in, as they suspected such a clandestine operation. The family escaped this past February with the last of their refugees."

Johannes drew deeply on his pipe but choked on the inhaled fumes; his face flushed red with the effort of his coughing.

"Now, under my protection, I can get you to China as well. I work for the society in Harbin. There are many émigrés there waiting for transport to North and South America. Many more have already completed their journey."

"Why would you think I am interested in leaving Russia?"

"I can clearly see that you are not Norwegian. Your name is nothing like any Norwegian name I have ever heard; it does not ring true to that language. Your accent is heavy with German tones. I would venture a guess that you are from Odessa, or someplace near there." Piotr spoke very matter-of-factly, without emotion in his voice.

Johannes was stunned. "How...how do you know all of this?" he stammered.

"My family is of German extraction, too. They settled in Poland most likely about the time your family settled in Russia. I am very familiar with the little things German people do without thinking. The first night I observed you, you cut up your sausage and put it into your soup. The only times I have seen someone do that is with people of German background. I also believe Anya is your daughter, not your wife. There is too much resemblance in your facial features. I do not know how long you have been able to get by with your ruse, but I feel it will not get you through much longer."

Johannes was recovered from his choking spell and listened carefully to Piotr's words. "How will we get to China? We only have tickets to Belogorsk and just enough money to get to Blagoveshchensk. Our travel papers are not good for China..."

"That is where I come in," Piotr interrupted. "But first, I just want to know if my assessment is correct."

Johannes studied the ash burning in the bowl of his pipe while he carefully weighed his words. "Yes," he spoke softly, "Anya is my daughter, the only one I am certain exists. I will do anything to protect her."

"Good. I know what it took to tell me that, and I respect you. We will arrive in Verkhneudinsk tomorrow. I will be assisting the Schneider couple, the people Anya helped to their room. Bring whatever baggage you have and follow me to the other train that will be waiting in the station. I will take care of all the papers."

"But at what cost? I have told you we have little money."

"There is no cost. I will transfer your tickets to the other train. They will get you to Harbin."

"But why do you do this?"

"This is what the Red Cross does; I am only their agent." Piotr emptied his pipe and tapped it against his boot. "While I work for the lumber company, which pays for my travel, I help as many people as possible to leave this downtrodden country. Call it my mission in life. I have access to what is needed and the knowledge to be useful. Now, I will see you on the platform tomorrow." He opened the door to the car and disappeared through it.

Johannes stood in the little space for a while longer, listening to the clickety-click, clickety-click of the wheels rolling on the tracks. He, too, emptied his pipe and put it in a pocket. *Oh, Lord, where are you leading us now?* he asked. Holding onto the railing across the vestibule's outer opening, he closed his eyes and prayed deeply.

When he returned to the room, Johannes quietly explained the conversation to Anya. She sat for some time contemplating the possibilities that lay before them.

"Are you sure we can trust this man? What if he is actually an agent for the NKVD? What if he has only told you lies about the farm in Blagoveshchensk? If we do follow him, and he really takes us to China, what happens then?" Her questions seemed endless.

"Anchen, in my heart I feel very strongly that this man is who he says he is, and I am willing to place my trust in him. And if I am wrong…if I am wrong… then we must suffer the consequences, whatever they may be. God has led us this far for a reason; do you doubt Him now? Isaiah said there would be a course and a way, which will be called the Holy Way that no impure one may go on it. Once we are across the border, there will be no more NKVD to worry about. I believe it is a chance we must take."

"Oh, Papi, I am frightened, so very frightened..."

"I think we should pray together on this, and see if we get any answers," Johannes took his daughter by the hand. He was about to kneel when he spotted the conductor in the passageway outside their door, so he pulled the shade down over the window, and listened at the door until he heard her footsteps fade into the other noises of the train. He and Anya then knelt together and asked for guidance.

All night and for most of the following morning the train meandered along the shores of the giant Lake Baikal; just past noon the train angled south and pulled into Verkhneudinsk about an hour or so later. Anya was disappointed to see that they were in yet another large and bustling city. She longed for the villages and isolation to which she had become accustomed. As she sat gazing out of the window she spotted Piotr making his way to a train sitting on the opposite side of the platform. She could see him talking to someone she thought might be a conductor, though his uniform was nothing like the Provodnitsa of the train on which she was sitting. Soon, Piotr returned and gave a short rap on their cabin door as he proceeded to Cabin 19.

Silently, Johannes picked up both of their bundles of belongings and indicated for Anya to follow him. They stepped off the train and began their journey across the platform. Without warning a voice rang out, "Where are you going? You cannot leave this train now!"

Johannes and Anya stopped in their tracks. Both recognized the crusty intonation of the Provodnitsa. "Papi?" Anya whispered.

Johannes understood the question without hearing it, "Just pretend you did not hear and keep moving."

They continued on and again the voice called out, "You cannot leave here! You have no tickets for that train!"

Hearing the sound of running boots quickly approaching, Anya stopped and looked behind her. She saw the Schneiders, the older Jewish couple, struggling to haul their baggage across the platform and the conductor hastily coming after them. Piotr appeared at their sides and waved the Provodnitsa off with a handful of papers.

"They are coming with me," he yelled at her. "Can you not see that this lady is ill? I am taking her to the doctor. We will all remain here until the next eastern-bound train arrives, then we will proceed to our destinations."

"What about your shipment of logs? Who will accompany them to the mills?"

"I was just at the telegraph office, notifying my superiors of my delay. They will have someone waiting at the offload point." Piotr picked up one of the Schneider's heavier bags, "Now please let me get these people to a doctor."

"Why are you helping these Jews? What is in it for you?" the conductor demanded.

"I should think you would be happy to be rid of them. I am taking them off your train, and you will no longer be responsible for them."

The Provodnitsa looked at Piotr with narrowed eyes, uttered a very disgusted "Harrumph" and returned to her train.

Piotr caught Anya watching him and with a quick smile, jerked his head in the direction of the new train, signaling that she should catch up to her father. Not understanding why the conductor had not seen her or her father, Anya hurried to Johannes side. As they quickly proceeded to their new transport, Anya observed that this train looked very much like the first, only the cars were brown, not green, and the horizontal stripe along their sides was a dirty yellow, instead of the bright red of the Trans-Siberian.

They found their way to the fifth car, per Piotr's instructions, climbed the stairway and were met by the new conductor, who led them to berth number 8, opened the door and bowed as Johannes and Anya entered.

Chita to Harbin by Trans-Manchurian Rail Road
1,745 km or about 1,084 miles

CHAPTER FORTY-THREE

The Road to China

Safely berthed in their new cabin, Johannes and Anya waited for Piotr to arrive with their tickets. They silently watched as the train they just left pulled out of the station and continued on its way toward Belogorsk. Johannes' palms began to sweat as he worried whether he had made an error in judgment in trusting a man he knew nothing about.

Anya moved about uneasily. The brown cloth seats were not as luxurious as the rust-red velvet ones of the Trans-Siberian, and they carried the odor of rancid cigarette smoke. Additionally, they were not as long, which meant that sleeping would be a bit cramped. Shabby gauze-like curtains hung at each side of the exterior window, their fabric yellowed with age. Idly running her fingers along the edge of the windowsill, she came away with black dust on them, which she wiped on her skirt with a disconcerted sigh. *Has Papi made a mistake?* she wondered. *I think we should leave this train and find another way to get to Blagoveshchensk.* As she tried to make up her mind about leaving, Piotr knocked at the door.

"I have your new tickets," he smiled as he handed the pale blue papers to Johannes, "these will get you to Harbin. The train will be leaving soon and heads east to Chita, where it should arrive by mid-day tomorrow. The stop will be short, as the city is closed to outsiders. You will not be allowed off the train. About nine tomorrow night we will be crossing the border into China. That sojourn will likely be close to an hour or longer. You will need to present your travel papers to the border officers as they go through the car. The Chinese agents are hospitable; they seldom question Russian travel documents, as Harbin is populated primarily by Russian émigrés. Be respectful; stay in your room and do as you are asked; there should be no problems."

From the border-crossing to Harbin will be about another twelve hours. You will officially be out of Russia in less than two days."

"And then what? Where will we go? What will we do once we reach Harbin?" Anya could contain herself no longer. "We have no money; how and where will we live?"

"I have already discussed many of those details with your father, but do not worry. I will get you to someone who will assist you. I realize you must be frightened; you are heading into a strange new country with strange new people. But somehow, I think you have been through experiences like this before. Just have faith and trust that everything will work out for the best." Piotr turned to leave, and then stopped again. "Life does not always work out as we plan, but it always works out the way God knows is best for us. Accept the intrusions and interruptions that block your path, and you will be amazed and astonished at the outcome."

As Piotr disappeared down the passageway, Anya sat and stared out the window at the barren landscape rushing past. Something about Piotr's words touched her heart, and now she dwelled on them. She came to realize that each major event, each major disruption in her life, had indeed led to a change that brought something better for her, maybe not right away, but in time.

The evening meal consisted of a simple soup of clear broth, a few vegetables and wide white noodles. Anya was still hungry as she and her father left the dining car. The always present samovar provided the hot water she expected, but the tea being offered was pale and flavorless compared to the rich black Russian teas she had become used to—nor was there a plate of cheese for between meal refreshment as on the previous train. *Now I understand what Papi meant by calling the Trans-Siberian the Tsar's train*, she pondered.

The night hours passed in a fitful and uncomfortable sleep for Anya and her father. By morning the train began to climb out of the steppe lowlands and into forested mountains. Anya had seen no towns or villages or cities along the way and, except for the occasional goat herd, few indications that people even existed in this remote part of the world.

She was pleased to see the expanse of trees filling her window with life only the forest can provide. As the train began a long slow curve toward the impending noon hour, the forest floor became saturated with a lavender sea of Rhododendrons flooding the open spaces between the dark brown trunks. The splendor of the forest pulled at her, and she longed to run with abandon through it. She felt the train decline into a valley and was startled out of her reverie when the trees abruptly ceased and cleared land gave way to a city nestled between two rivers.

Small wooden cabins sat on rudimentary farms on the outskirts, giving way to the contrast of the grid pattern of streets and neat rows of houses and shops forming the city. The skyline was pierced with the occasional church spire, Orthodox 'onion tops' and golden turban-like towers of mosques. As the train slowed to a stop, Anya noted some buildings with a strange upward curve to the roof eaves and she wondered how the rain drained off them.

The train halted in the station, but other than soldiers scattered along the tracks, there were no people present.

"Papi, where are the people? Why is this big station so deserted?" Anya asked.

"Piotr called this a 'closed city'. My guess is that it is so close to China's border that the government officials fear citizens will try to leave, or foreigners might try to come in and claim it." Johannes shrugged.

"Why does the train even stop here then?"

"I would suppose it would be to off-load supplies and trade goods for the people who live here."

"Oh," Anya replied distractedly as she watched a man who looked a lot like Piotr leave the train and hand a cloth-like bag to one of the soldiers, the soldier handed back a similar bag and the man returned to the train.

Although she wondered about the exchange, Anya said nothing to her father. She dozed off and on throughout the afternoon, bored with watching the passing of large expanses of rolling hills covered in short grasses and scraggly bushes.

When they went to supper, Johannes and Anya found few people in the dining car, so they ate in relative silence. Piotr had not been seen all afternoon. Shortly after their meal was served, the Schneiders appeared and sat a few tables behind Johannes. Though breakfast had consisted of a hearty meal of an egg and meat mixture, it had not stayed with Anya for long, and she was now quite hungry.

After serving the necessary tea and vodka, the waiter set plates before them bedecked with smoked meat resting atop some sort of white grain substance. Anya picked at the grain and cautiously tasted this new matter; rolling the little grains around in her mouth she found them to be a bit sweet and sticky on her tongue. She was about to sample the meat when she caught sight of the Schneiders pushing their plates back toward the waiter.

"What is this meat?" Mr. Schneider asked. "Is it pork?"

The waiter shrugged his ignorance of the contents of the plate.

"We can not eat this, whatever it is, unless we know it is kosher."

Anya took a bite of the meat on her plate and chewed it thoughtfully, then rose and approached the elder couple's table.

"I believe the meat to be goat," she offered helpfully.

"Oh, thank you dear," Mrs. Schneider smiled, "but if it is not kosher, we still cannot eat it."

Anya wrinkled her brow, not understanding the problem.

"It is a Jewish matter," Mr. Schneider grumbled, then turned to the waiter, "just bring us each a plate of plain rice."

"It was good of you to try to help us, dear," Mrs. Schneider said apologetically to Anya, "maybe you will understand someday."

Anya returned to her seat and proceeded to eat her meal in silence. Johannes reached across the table and gently touched her hand. "I will explain it to you later," he whispered.

They returned to their cabin and were settling in for the night, when the train slowed and stopped near a small building seemingly in the middle of nowhere. Anya looked out of the window, but could see nothing in the darkness.

"We must be at the border-crossing," Johannes offered as he retrieved their tickets and travel papers from the inner pocket of the coat he had laid across the back of his seat.

Anya sat quietly, but she was nervous not knowing what to expect. She watched as two Chinese men, in brown tunic-like uniforms, made their way through the narrow hall followed closely by two Russian NKVD agents looking in at each door. She cast a surprised look at her father, as Piotr had not mentioned the possibility of the NKVD being present. Johannes moved closer to his daughter.

"Act like it does not matter who they are," he whispered.

The sound of loud knocking, followed by angry voices, filled the passageway and continued for some time. During the mêlée, the Chinese men came to the door and requested papers from Johannes. Johannes politely offered his and Anya's papers and tickets to the men; after a quick perusal, the papers were handed back, and the men moved on. With great commotion, the NKVD envoy stomped back through the car and into the next.

Once things got quiet and the train was on its way again, Anya settled down to sleep, but she thought she could hear a woman sobbing somewhere in the distance and wondered if it had anything to do with the presence of the Russian agents.

Following breakfast the next morning, Anya began packing their bundles in anticipation of reaching Harbin. She was chatting idly with her father about what they might expect upon their arrival, when Piotr appeared outside their door and knocked lightly.

"I am here on behalf of Mrs. Schneider," he stated when Johannes opened the door. "She was wondering if Anya can sew."

"Of course I can," Anya asserted, "why?"

"I know you heard the tumult last night. The NKVD agents searched the Schneiders' belongings. In the process, Mrs. Schneider's best dress was ripped and she had hoped to wear it to synagogue this evening in Harbin. But her eyesight is poor, and she needs help repairing the dress."

"That poor woman!" Anya declared with anger in her voice. "Why were those men even here? I thought you said it would only be border guards coming on the train."

"They were a surprise to me; I have not encountered agents at that border station before. They seemed to suspect that the Schneiders were carrying valuables of some sort. They went straight for the poor old couple. Someone, somewhere, evidently told the NKVD the Schneiders were on this train."

Anya pushed past Piotr and ran to the Schneider's compartment. She was greeted by a tearful Mrs. Schneider holding a black dress in her hands. Mr. Schneider sat solemnly on the bench seat, holding a long white cloth to his forehead. For the first time, Anya noticed the yarmulke on his head. In the past few evenings, her father had taught her quite a bit about the Jews, and she was now quite curious about these people.

Anya gently took the dress and held it up to see how much damage had been done to it. "It only seems to be ripped along the seams," she smiled, "easily repaired if you have a needle and thread for me, Mrs. Schneider."

"Please call me Fredrika, dear. And he is Otto," the woman said as she rummaged through a small pouch she pulled from her large bag.

"I am Anya…"

"Yes, yes, we remember from the first day in Novosibirsk," Otto growled.

"Oh, pay him no mind, dear, he is always like that," Fredrika asserted.

Anya sat on the seat across from Otto and began to piece the garment together. Fredrika sat next to her and chatted animatedly, happy to finally have someone to talk with. Fredrika told Anya all about how they had come to Eastern Siberia following the uranium strikes nearly thirty years earlier.

"It was good work until the Japanese invaded and occupied the city," Otto interjected.

"Yes," Fredrika continued, "the Jewish quarter was a wonderful place to raise a family in the years before the Japanese arrived. Then we moved to Novosibirsk with the later intention of returning to Stuttgart, where we were both born. But it seems we never had enough money to do that. Now, we have been told that Jews are not welcome in Germany and are being sent to Poland. So we have decided that Harbin is where we will be protected best. There are many Jews in Harbin."

"We are German, too," Anya stated excitedly, "well, sort of. My father's grandfather came to Russia from Germany, but we still speak and worship in German. Papi and I hope to go to America!"

"Ah, America, the ultimate dream," Otto interrupted. "I should have guessed."

"Why are you not going there?"

"We are just too old. Harbin will suit us just fine. We are out of Russia, we are safe from the German government, and we do not need to go any farther."

Anya finished the repairs on the dress and handed it to Fredrika.

"Oh, look, Otto! What a beautiful job she has done on my dress!" Fredrika exclaimed. "My dear Anya, you deserve something special for this fine work."

"Thank you, but no, it was a pleasure visiting with the both of you; that is my reward."

"I will not hear of it!" Fredrika reached deep into her bag and pulled out a pale blue scarf, and handed it to Anya. "Here, child, wear it with the satisfaction in knowing that you helped a couple of poor old people in their time of need."

Anya let the fine cloth slip through her fingers. She had never felt cloth as smooth and soft as this. "It is too beautiful; I can not take it."

"Yes, dear, you must. Refusing a gift is not allowed," Fredrika smiled and wrapped the scarf around Anya's neck. "It is made of silk, you know."

"Silk?" Anya asked as she prepared to leave.

"Caterpillar waste," Otto grumbled.

CHAPTER FORTY-FOUR

Edna

As the train rolled into the city of Harbin and neared its stop, Anya was dismayed that this was yet another large city, but was somehow captivated by the many buildings that seemed to fill the streets with an endless tangle of East bumping into West. She watched as all sorts of conveyances, many she had never before seen the likes of, traversed the boulevard that ran alongside the tracks.

The train slowed, and prepared to stop, as vendors and merchants crowded the depot platform, noisily pushing their way toward potential buyers arriving in their midst.

"Papi, there are so many people here!" Anya whispered aloud in wonderment.

"Yes, Anchen, there are too many. You must stay close to me while we look for Piotr; if we were separated, we would both be lost."

Anya picked up her bundle of personal belongings and took her father's free hand in her's. She smiled a worried smile and took a deep breath to quell the anxiety she felt building within her. "This reminds me of market days when I was small and we would all go to the village. You were always afraid I would wander off somewhere."

Johannes squeezed his daughter's hand tightly. "It was always an adventure with you, as it will be now," he smiled gently at her as they left their little room and made their way through the passage to the train's exit door. Johannes descended the steps first, then turned to assist Anya with her belongings. Handing her rolled up clothes to her father, she spotted Piotr a short distance up the tracks, hovering over the Schneiders and fending off overzealous tradesmen. Making their way through the crowd as quickly as they were able, Johannes and Anya caught up to Piotr and the old couple, just as two more men and a woman carrying a little girl on one arm and dragging a large suitcase with the other, arrived from farther sections of the train.

Piotr stood his full height and counted the familiar faces around him. "Good," he said, "everyone is here. Now, stay together and follow me out of this din!" He picked up Mrs. Schneider's bag, adjusted it in his hands and was off at a brisk walk. The vendors seemed to sense his urgency and fell away from the little group, causing a clear path to open before them.

Anya was concerned that the young mother with her extra load would not be able to keep up, so she handed her bundle off to her father and took the heavy suitcase from the woman. A thankful smile melted the woman's face as she shifted her daughter's weight and scurried to catch up with the rest of the group.

They kept up the hurried pace until they cleared the train depot, then Piotr slowed to a more accommodating stride, allowing everyone to breathe a little easier while managing their individual loads. After about three city blocks, Piotr stopped near an entryway that led to what appeared to be a small shop. A circular wooden sign, its white background emblazoned with a red cross, hung over the doorway. Piotr opened the door and invited the group into the building.

Anya followed her father and the others into a simply furnished room. She looked around at the walls of dark paneling. A single bench ran the length of the wall to her right; a wall at the end of the room contained a barred window above a simple countertop.

Alerted by the noise of the entering ensemble, a woman's face appeared at the window and examined the intruders. She instantly recognized one of the members and greeted him with a smile and a hearty, "Piotr! How good to see you! Who have you brought this time?"

Piotr smiled broadly, "Edna, how are you? Where have you been? It has been a few months since I saw you last."

"Regina had her baby, a fine boy. Named him Horst. I spent some time with her, wanted to be sure the boy got off to a good beginning," Edna grinned proudly.

"Well, then give my congratulations to Karl and Regina! Tell them I wish them the best."

"I will do that, Piotr. Now, what business do we need to do today?" The plump-faced grey-haired lady pushed her dark-rimmed glasses back up her nose, as an indication that business was paramount to her presence.

Piotr turned to the waiting group and indicated that they should sit on the bench. He then turned his attention to Edna, and lowered his voice to guard the information he was about to reveal.

"I brought you two men who wish to work in the bakeries; they are brothers and come from St. Petersburg. It seems they irritated the local constabulary and found it necessary to flee Mother Russia," Piotr grinned at his sardonic description. "Someday maybe we will find out the real reason for their leaving," he whispered conspiratorially, "but it does not matter now. They are both skilled in the bakery trade. They just need entry permits and job placement.

"The young woman...the one with the child...was widowed at the hands of the NKVD. She claims to have family in Canada and would like to find them. She will need proper travel papers and preferably a sponsor from Alberta or Saskatchewan.

The other young woman and her father are exiles from Onega..."

"Do you mean escapees?" Edna interrupted. "How does anyone escape from Onega? And there are two of them!"

"The girl was not taken to the camps, but lived with a villager. The father did escape the shipyards; however I have not really obtained the entire story. At any rate, they wish to go to America."

"North or South?"

"I do not think it matters. If you can get a sponsor for them, they will go where they are sent. Their current documents have them traveling as husband and wife, but I think you can fix that, can you not?" Piotr's smile expanded into a blatant flirt.

Edna outwardly disregarded the faux advances as nonsense and proceeded with her inquiries. "And the old couple...where do they wish to go?"

"I am taking them to the elder hostel, Moshav Zkenim, in the Jewish quarter. They have good papers, so you have nothing to prepare for them. I have plans to get them settled before evening worship, so if you can relieve me of the rest of my wards, I will arrange transportation for the Schneiders."

"Will you come back to dine with us this evening?" Edna inquired. "It has been so long, I would like to know where you have been and what you have been up to of late."

"I am sorry, dear Edna, but I need to catch up to the east-bound train and complete my deliveries to Vladivostok. My lumber company job takes precedence over my love life, I am afraid," Piotr concluded, as he reached through the window and took Edna's hand, brought it to his lips and kissed it gently.

"You are a horrible man!" Edna's face beamed as her cheeks blushed pink, "Alfred will be upset that he missed you."

"Tell your husband that he had better keep his eyes on you lest I sweep you away." Piotr turned with a wave of his arm and bent into an extravagant bow. When he rose, he turned to the now-seated group he had brought with him. "Edna will take good care of you at this time. I must be on my way. I am pleased to have made your acquaintances and wish you all a safe journey and a good life." He assisted Mrs. Schneider to her feet and picked her satchel up off the floor, then gestured for Mr. Schneider to follow. He glanced back at Anya and offered a reassuring smile as he departed through the door.

A door opened to the left of the barred window and Edna filled the opening. She wore a blue and white checked print dress under a full length white apron. A bright red cross was centered over her amble bosom and was repeated on a band she wore on her upper right arm. She pointed at the brothers.

"You two, first."

The brothers stood and walked through the door, which was shut behind them. After a short wait the door opened again, and Edna gestured toward the young woman with the baby. The woman stood, repositioned her child in her arms, and proceeded to the door, leaving her suitcase behind on the floor near Anya.

"No bags?" Edna asked.

"Yes, that big one there. I thought I would leave it with them until we were done with my paperwork." The woman said as she pointed toward the suitcase near Anya.

"Bring it with you now, dear. You will not be coming back this way." Edna's voice was sweet and yet her words frightened Anya a bit.

Anya rose to assist with the luggage, but Edna waved her away.

"No dear, she can bring it herself. She will need to travel alone for now and must be able to handle both her child and the bag." Turning to the young mother, Edna asked, "Can the child walk? It might be easier for you if you let her."

The mother put her daughter on the floor and lugged the bag through the door. The little girl took hold of her mother's skirt with one hand, while she sucked the thumb on the other, and followed in silence.

When the door was closed, Anya quietly spoke to her father. "That Edna frightens me; I do not think we should trust her, Papi."

"Hush, Anchen. I am sure it will be alright. Just remember we are no longer in Russia; we are in a safe place now."

Anya toyed with a seam in her dress while she waited for Edna to call her into the room. *Will I go alone, or will Papi come with me?* She worried silently. After what seemed like an eternity to Anya, the door opened one last time, and the amply-filled apron appeared in the entry.

"Now I think I am ready to see what I can do for you." Edna smiled at Anya and put her arm around the girl as she passed through the door. Johannes followed closely and stayed near.

This room was quite the opposite of the ante-room they just left. Anya was a bit dazzled by unadorned white walls reflecting the bright light of several large fixtures hanging from the ceiling. The room was divided into two main areas simply by the arrangement of furniture. One half was dominated by a heavy wooden desk and four straight-backed chairs. The other half featured a wall full of white metal cabinets, each sporting the bright crimson cross of Edna's apron. A starkly unadorned metal table occupied the space in front of the cabinets. Anya expected to see their travel companions waiting in the room, but except for Edna, she and her father were alone.

"Please sit," Edna said as she pulled a sheaf of papers from the top drawer of her desk. "I need your travel documents, and I will have to ask you some questions. I would appreciate honest answers. In return, I will do my best to make your lives easier and possibly get you to where you want to go. But, be prepared to remain here in Harbin for awhile; the wheels of progress do not always move swiftly."

Johannes pulled the documents from his jacket pocket and settled into a chair. Anya chose a chair that was situated a little farther from the desk, indicating her apprehension.

Edna looked up from her paperwork and smiled at Anya. "You do not trust me, do you? I understand your misgivings; I was in your place myself once. Let me tell you about this office and our organization." Edna sat back in her chair and folded her hands in her lap. "The Red Cross is a strictly humanitarian society. It was founded about seventy years ago by a man from Switzerland who was unhappy with the treatment he witnessed of wounded soldiers during armed conflicts in several battles. He was primarily concerned with the lack of nursing and medical care. The order was founded to protect human life and health, to ensure respect for all human beings, and to prevent and alleviate human suffering, without any discrimination. We are mandated to protect the life and dignity of the victims of international and internal armed conflicts, but we also have been charged with additional humanitarian tasks to aid and assist civilians in need due to political unrest in their home countries. This includes arranging for emigration to another country; finding living situations during the wait while sponsors in the new countries are located; providing medical treatment if needed; and managing an exchange of messages regarding prisoners and missing persons. In other words, we do everything we can to assist those who need us, regardless of who they are. I am sorry if I sound like a brochure, but I have had to repeat this to so many people over the years, it has become second nature."

"Why is your symbol a red cross? Does it represent blood?' Anya inquired.

"Nothing as exact as that; as I said, the founder was from Switzerland and the Swiss flag is red with a white cross. Our founder just reversed the colors to remind people where the organization was started, and yet have a distinctive difference," Edna answered.

"See Anchen, I told you there was nothing to worry about," Johannes responded.

Anya sat forward in her chair, "Did you say you could get messages to prisoners?"

"I did not say that exactly, but we do have a system in place for some camps."

"Is the lumber camp at Onega one of them?" Anya was starting to become more than interested.

"Yes, I think so," Edna began, "here let me check." Pulling a thick pamphlet from her desk drawer, Edna began skimming through the pages. "Yes, here it is, OA74693, Onega forced labor camp, lumber division."

"Papi, we can send a letter to Mama! She can tell us how Karolina and Magdalena are doing, and how she is managing!"

"Now, wait a minute," Edna jumped in, "I said we could send a message, I did not say a message could be sent back."

Johannes shook his head, "Anchen, I do not think that is a good idea. Your mother has probably been told that I am dead. We can do nothing to get her or your sisters out of that place, and God only knows how much I wish that could happen. Why get their hopes up? It has been so long; we are not even sure they are still at that camp."

"But, Papi, we have to let them know we are alive and where we are going. They have to know where to find us when they are freed from the camp," Anya pleaded.

"Anya, dear, can you write?" Edna asked.

"Of course I can."

"Good, then why not take this paper and go over to that examination table and write your mother a letter while your father and I complete our business? But I suggest that you do not say where you are now or exactly where you plan to go. That information could put you and your father, as well as your mother, in great danger. You are not completely safe yet," Edna advised as she handed Anya a pencil and tablet.

By the time the woman asked all her questions of Johannes and completed several documents and issued instructions regarding housing and work prospects, Anya had finalized her letter to her mother. Edna took the letter, read the Russian print and looked up at Anya.

"Would you mind if your father read this?"

Anya shook her head, "I would like very much if Papi read it. He might have something to add to it."

Edna handed the letter to Johannes. He accepted the missive and began reading.

> *Dearest Mama,*
>
> *I do hope this finds you and Karolina and Magdalena well. I miss you so very much. When we were separated at the train, I was taken by a Selkup woman to live in the forest. She gave me a good life for the five years before she joined her ancestors. As we were traveling to live with her family, we met a hunting party from the same village. Among the men in the party I found Papi. I know you must believe him to be dead, but he is alive and well and doing what he can to get us all back together. While we are not yet there, our goal is to find Jakob. I do not know what happened to Heiner and Konrad, but I am sure they are doing well, too. Tell my sisters I love them. Papi and I pray for you every night. He loves you more than you can ever know.*
>
> *Your loving daughter, Anya*

As Johannes completed the letter, he reached up and wiped a tear from his eye. He looked at Anya with a sad smile, as he handed the letter back to Edna. "You may send this," was all he could manage to utter.

Edna folded the letter into quarters and placed a small sticker over each end to hold it together. "To whom should I address this?"

"Katerina Jahnle," Johannes and Anya spoke in unison.

When Edna completed the camp designation on the letter and a return code in one corner, she pulled a small metal ring containing two keys out of her apron pocket, unlocked the bottom drawer of her desk with the largest key and removed a leather pouch. She used the second key in a small hasp on the pouch, releasing the strap that secured the small bag. She opened the pouch and placed the letter inside, relocking the hasp. As she put the pouch back into the desk drawer, she patted it with an affectionate tap.

"It will leave here on Thursday, but I can not guarantee that it will arrive at its destination or, if it does, that there will ever be an answer." Her voice was resigned and meek.

"We understand," Johannes said as he rose from his chair and prepared to leave.

Edna handed Johannes two of the documents she had just completed, along with several bills of paper currency. "You will need these," she said. "Come back here in three days, and I will have the rest of your travel papers ready. Everyone leaves by the back door; it is safer and easier for you to find your next stop. You will be staying with the Zeigler family until you can arrange for more permanent accommodations. Just tell them I sent you. Phillip...Herr Zeigler...will advise you on locating employment. Now from here you turn left and follow the alley to the next street. Turn right at the corner and look for a shop with a sign that says "Ziegler's Watch and Clock Repair." Do not go into the shop. There is a passageway just past the shop that will take you to the apartments. I wish you luck."

Edna offered her hand to Johannes. He shook it politely and thanked the lady for her assistance. Anya, however, having finally been won over by this lady's kindness, threw her arms around the woman with a grateful hug.

CHAPTER FORTY-FIVE

The Letter

The contents of the leather pouch from Edna's desk were placed into a dirty canvas sack and carried by a messenger to the train depot on Thursday morning as promised. The sack was tossed into the mail car at the back of the train and lay in a pile of similar bags as it traveled north to the Russian border. Once the sacks arrived at the first check station, they were unloaded and emptied onto a large table for sorting and inspection.

"Not many this week," one of the guards commented as he rummaged through the dozen or so missives on the table before him.

"Good, I find that I tire of this task quickly, and I have more important things to do," a second sentry replied as he picked up a letter and removed its seal. Sitting down in a chair at the edge of the table, the man checked each name mentioned in the letter against his long list of those wanted by the NKVD for one reason or another. When he was satisfied that the letter was not coming from, or going to, someone the government considered derisive, he passed it to his colleague. This man would then read each letter, and with a bit of sponge and a large well of ink, daub through any divisive comments about the government, routes of possible escape, locations of safe houses or anything else he chose to censor, before sending the item on.

Picking up the folded bit of paper addressed to "Katerina Jahnle," the sentry checked her name against his lists. Finding no matches, he continued to read the childish scrawl. "What kind of name is Papi?" he asked aloud.

"Might be a soubriquet, or alias," his partner commented. "Is there a last name and are there any like it on the lists?"

"It appears to be written by a daughter to her mother. The mother's name is Jahnle, and I am not finding any names like that on the list."

"Where is it going?"

"Umm, according to the code, it is headed for the lumber camp in Onega."

"Send it on, then. It is unlikely that it will ever reach its destination, and if it does, the recipient has probably 'departed,'" the guard chuckled.

The letter was refolded, stuffed into a bag with other items being sent to Northern Siberia, and tossed into the corner of the room to wait until the bag was sufficiently filled to warrant being sent on its way.

Eight weeks passed before the Onega-bound satchel was dispatched.

"What is this?" the commandant asked as his aide handed him a canvas sack.

"It seems the government is allowing mail to be sent through the Red Cross to our inmates."

"Amazing! Do they actually think these creatures can read and write?" The commandant opened the sack and dumped the contents onto the aide's small desk. "How many letters are there and how are we supposed to distribute them?"

"There are eight total. I will have to check them against the resident list to determine which barracks they should be sent to."

"No, that will take up too much of your schedule! Just staple them to the wall outside of the latrines. If the addressees are still here, they will find them in due time."

The aide gathered the letters into a small stack. "Yes, Commandant, I will do as you wish."

The women of the camp had little expectation of receiving anything, much less a letter, so few took notice of the bits of paper tacked up on the wall. Those who did take notice suspected them to be government fabrications and feared the implications of making a claim to one of them. But, gradually, one by one, the letters disappeared.

Sofia Becker had not been to the latrines in quite some time. Following the typhus outbreak nearly six years before, she was ordered to serve as a nurse at the make-shift hospital. The doctor who came from the shipyards arrived only when summoned by the camp staff, and he required someone to care for those who were too ill to work or needed minor emergency attention when he was not present. For sanitary reasons, the infirmary building had been given its own set of toilets, so Sofia had no need of the camp latrines. But, there had been a number of illnesses of late that might have been connected to the conditions of the latrines, so she was here to inspect them and report back to the doctor on his next visit.

A bit of fluttering paper connected to the outside wall caught her eye as she entered the laystall, so she stopped to examine the item. The paper had yellowed from exposure to the constantly changing weather, but Sofia could still read the hand-penciled name on its surface. She carefully removed the paper from the wall and tucked it in her pocket.

Upon returning to the infirmary, Sofia sat down and carefully removed the letter and spread it open on a small table before her. She gasped as she read the words carefully printed on the page and wiped the tears from her eyes when she finished. She rose from her chair and made her way past the mostly-unoccupied bunks that lined the walls of her improvised hospital.

The bed located farthest from the office contained an individual who appeared to be sound asleep. Sofia sat on the edge and gently tried to arouse its occupant.

"Katerina, wake up, please. Katerina, I have a letter for you," Sofia called softly. When she received no response, she tried again, a little louder, "Katerina, please wake up. I have a message from your daughter…I have a message from Anya!"

The woman in the bed gave a quiet moan, but did not move.

"I will read the letter to you, then. I think if you know its contents, you might come out of your despair." Sofia proceeded to read the letter, being careful not to mention Karolina and Magdalena. When she finished she again tried to arouse Katerina, "Katerina, wake up! Did you hear the words? Your Johannes is still alive! He and Anya are well and safe!" Still not receiving a response, Sofia rose from the bed and looked back upon the wasting body that lay before her. "I will answer the letter for you, my beloved friend. I will tell them not to worry about you," Sofia sadly sighed.

Upon returning to her station, Sofia rummaged through the doctor's desk looking for an unadorned sheet of paper on which to write. She gave much thought to the words she would use to tell Anya what she could about her mother's situation and the fate of her sisters. Finally, she began:

04 September 1934
My Dear Anya,

I am answering your letter on behalf of your mother, as she is too ill at this time to do so herself. I do hope you remember me, Sofia Becker, the Byrgermeister's wife from our home village. Your mother and I have become cherished friends during our time here in this camp. We have lived and worked together, and supported each other through all manner of grief and hardship. She is the one I have turned to when I could not find strength in prayer, and she is the one who always brought me back to God and the reality of my life. Now, I wish I could say the same of my abilities, but painfully, I have not been able to provide that same sustenance for her. I regret to tell you that both of your sisters have been lost to serious accidents, and combined with the reports of the death of your father, your mother has descended into a deep melancholy from which she may never recover. She wastes away a little more each day, and I fear she may not make it through the month. I am praying your letter will bring her hope and she will return to her vibrant self. I must say that I selfishly need her, and miss her spirit intensely.

We have had no news of your brothers, or my boys, either. I was informed that my husband Josef was killed in an accident at the new canal project, a few years ago, and for that reason, if for no other, I attached myself to your mother for strength and spiritual nourishment.

I am so pleased to hear that you have found your Papi and that you are together for whatever Our Lord has in store for you. I will pray that you are kept safe and that you will find Jakob. I once told your mother that we will never know what has happened to our children or husbands or any of our people. Future generations will never know we even existed; that we will all just vanish...like footprints in the wind. But your letter gives me hope. When you arrive at your future destination, tell all you meet about us. Tell them who we were and what happened to us. Our generation is lost; do not let us be forgotten.

Please do not bother to answer this note, I only ask for your prayers in return. Do not worry overly much about your mother; she is where she wishes to be, and I will do my best to serve her needs.
God bless you and keep you,

Kindest Regards, Sofia Becker

Sofia returned to Katerina's bed and read the letter to her. When she had completed it, she folded the epistle and returned it to her pocket.

"I wish you would tell me if I said the right things, or if there is more you would like to say. I only want your approval, your agreement to what I have written. Please, Katerina, please tell me." Again there was no response, so Sofia tucked the blanket tighter around Katerina's shoulders, kissed her on the cheek and whispered, "I will take this to the commandant's office now, and send it on its way. Just know that their prayers for you will be heard, and that they will grieve intensely for you."

As the door clicked into place following Sofia's exit, a single tear trickled onto the pillow from Katerina's closed eyes. She allowed her body to relax into the bedding, took a deep breath and relinquished her soul to God.

CHAPTER FORTY-SIX

Finite Duration

EARLY 1935

Months passed as Anya awaited an answer to her letter. She busied herself through the fall and winter helping to care for the young children of Phillip Zeigler, the watch and clock maker, while his wife recovered from her most recent childbirth.

With Herr Zeigler's help, Johannes found employment at a fabric mill. He spent his days refilling the great spools of thread on the machines that wove continuous bolts of fine material, for the many clothing makers in the city. In order to earn a little bit extra, Johannes spent evenings fine-tuning his carving skills making clock cases for Herr Zeigler to fill with the intricate workings of his timepieces. When Johannes had saved enough of his wages, he and Anya moved from the tiny apartment behind the clock shop into a larger flat a few blocks closer to the mill.

When her assistance was no longer needed by the Ziegler's, Anya found herself alone in the apartment while her father worked. Although she said nothing to her father, Anya found that the usual chores of housekeeping soon bored her, and as she was anxious to hear any news of her mother or sisters, she often found her way back to the Red Cross office to briefly inquire "any news for me?" And always the answer was "Not yet, dear, not yet."

One morning, as she prepared her father's breakfast, Anya asked. "Papi, do you think Edna would mind if I offered to help her around the office?"

"Only she can tell you that, Anchen. But I have no issue with you going to volunteer your services."

"Thank you, Papi. I will go as soon as I have finished clearing up the dishes."

"Do you think you will have any trouble finding your way?"

Anya smiled, "No, Papi, I have been there many times already, checking on an answer to my letter."

Johannes frowned, "Anchen, I have told you before, do not get your hopes up. There is a very likely possibility that the letter never reached your mother, or if it did, that it will ever be answered."

"I know, Papi. But, I just have to be there if it does come."

As soon as her father left for the mill, Anya wiped her hands on her apron, pulled it off and hung it on a peg next to the sink before straightening her hair and donning her coat. It was late April; even though signs of spring were in abundance, there was still a chill to the air as the wind blew briskly between the buildings that lined the streets and alleyways of her path. Arriving at the Red Cross office she pushed the door open, but found no one inside. She crossed the empty room and went to the shuttered window in the back wall and knocked lightly.

The shutter opened slightly. "Who is there?" Edna inquired.

"Hello Edna, it is me, Anya."

"Why did you not say so, dear?" The window closed and the adjoining door opened wide; Edna in her white apron filling its space. "I have not received a letter for you yet, if that is why you are here. Or are you ill? You are not ill are you? What about your father, is he well?"

Anya stood with a slight smile on her face, waiting for Edna to give her a chance to say something. Finally, when the woman paused for a breath, Anya found her opportunity.

"I am well, and so is Papi. While I was hoping that a letter had come, I was actually wondering if maybe there was something I could do for you. Would you have some job I could do to help me pass the time? I get so lonely in the apartment all day and there are only so many corners to clean…"

"Well, let me think on this a bit. Things have been relatively quiet around here of late, but I expect an abundance of arrivals soon, what with the improving weather and the increase of Nazi activity in the west, so I believe we may have something to keep you occupied. I cannot pay you, though."

"I do not expect pay, Edna, I just want something to keep me busy, and maybe then I will be here if an answer comes from Mama." She hesitated for a moment then asked, "Edna, what is a Nazi?"

"In Germany there is a new political group called the National Socialist Party, which many refer to as the Nazis. The man leading this party claims that the defeat of the Imperial German war effort during the Great War was because the government was internally sabotaged by Jews. He has been sending Jews to prison, just because they are Jews, and his army is working their way across Europe conquering everything in their path for his benefit."

"He is doing to the Jews what the NKVD did to us? But why? Are the Jews not German too?" Anya asked.

"Many are indeed German citizens, but the Jews have always been singled out for one reason or another. It seems this man has a relentless hatred for them. I do not understand it; it makes no sense to me, but the word coming from those who seek refuge here in Harbin is that another war may soon be upon us. God only knows how much more this city can take. Japan bombed Harbin heavily only four years ago, and it is just now recovering many of its major losses. I do not know if China will ever be able to reclaim their rule of this area, and now it could be lost to the German fascists or Russian Red Army.

But my lot is not to worry about what is happening in the rest of the world, only to get those who wish to find a safe haven a place to stay and maybe a chance to find freedom on another continent."

"Do you think Papi and I will ever get to go to America?"

"I have been trying to find a sponsor; but because there are others that have been waiting far longer than you, I must make their arrangements first."

"I understand, and besides, I cannot leave until I know that my mother has read my letter."

"Then I think we should find something for you to do."

Anya soon found herself assisting Edna with many things, but she relished the chance to work on the healing skills she had learned from

Sonia. Piotr, as well as two other Red Cross "agents," arrived periodically with new émigrés. Many of the new immigrants came with minor wounds or uncomplicated illnesses, and Edna was charged with their treatments. She was surprised at how much Anya knew about curing simple ailments and injuries with herbs and homemade potions, and was open to understanding more about the medications that could be obtained just by gleaning the woods and forests. In return, Edna taught Anya about the need for sanitation, and some of the modern medical practices performed by Red Cross staff.

Spring breezed into summer; summer turned to fall and the frozen ground of winter finally gave way to another promise of new life and hopes for a new future.

The sun was hidden behind pallid clouds that loomed on the horizon above the inner-city buildings. The sky turned grey, threatening to transform what had been a beautiful June day into a depressing afternoon. Anya was alone in the Red Cross office as Edna accompanied her husband, Alfred, to the train depot to retrieve needed supplies for the agency. Heavy droplets of rain began splashing against the streetside windows causing Anya to become restless as she waited for Edna's return. She swept the floors and dusted the tables and chairs. She desperately wanted to return to her apartment, but she had promised Edna she would stay in the office. She plopped down into Edna's chair and began fiddling with the papers on the desk. She picked up the wooden box that held the numbered pages of the calendar and looked at the date.

"A year," Anya said aloud to the walls around her as she slammed the box back onto the desk top. "We have been here for a year, and where has it gotten us?" She folded her arms on the table in front of her, cradled her head in the crook of her elbow and closed her eyes as she listened to the rain intensify. Her thoughts drifted to the farm and her memory of running barefooted along the dirt track that led to the fields where her father and Jakob would be hard at work. She envisioned the dust rolling up from the ground behind the plow as Hans and Georg, the big farm horses, leaned into their harnesses walking their straight lines, forming rows for planting. She saw her mother holding baby Rosina in one arm, while she stirred the stewpot with the other. She was so engrossed in her memories she did not hear the door open.

"Anya, are you ill?" Edna's voice startled Anya and she jerked her head up at the unexpected utterance.

"No, I am fine," Anya began, but the words lodged in her throat and tears began to well up in her eyes.

Edna's hands were gripping a number of items, which she quickly placed on the examination table. She removed her coat, shook the rain off of it and hung it on a rack and then lowered herself onto a chair next to Anya.

"Please tell me what is wrong, dear. Why are you so sad?"

"Oh, Edna, I was just remembering my family and life on the farm." Anya took a deep breath and sighed loudly. "I just miss home."

"I wish I could tell you that you could go back, but I think you know that part of your life is gone forever. On the other hand, you have so much to look forward to."

Anya detected a slight smile begin to appear across Edna's face. "You have a sponsor for us?" Anya's eyes widened with anticipation as the thought formed her words.

Edna nodded fervently.

"Where are we going? When do we leave? Are we going alone or are others going with us?"

"One question at a time, please," Edna laughed as she rose and walked over to the bundles she left on the table. She pulled a leather portfolio out from under a bunch of carrots and beets, opened it and removed a folded packet of papers. Returning to the desk she opened the papers, spread them out across its top and began to peruse the contents.

"It says here that a church in California is offering to sponsor up to seven people of German heritage. The United States of America is allowing only fifteen people per month at each port of entry, so your arrangements will have to be coordinated through the Consulate to give you priority at the port. We have much to do, but I think your father should be involved in this, too. I suggest you go home and talk to him, then the two of you come back tomorrow and we will get things started."

"Cal…if…orn…ia," Anya pronounced the word slowly, thoughtfully. "I am not familiar with that place. Papi has always just said we were going to America. Is Cal… ifor…nia a big place? As big as Harbin?"

"California is more like a country, dear. It is a place with many cities. The United States is a land of many small countries, called states, that all have names, but are banded together into one giant nation, just as Russia has oblasts."

"Oh," Anya responded. "I did not get to study the countries in school, I was too young. I have always understood that America was a place full of great wonders. When we were still on the farm Papi would receive letters from his uncle who lived America. Papi has always desired to take us…all of my family…to America, but I do not remember ever hearing that it was separated by states. It has always just been 'America.' Now, I guess I will have much to learn about that great land and the part of it called Calif…fornia." Anya stood and began to put on her coat. The relentless downpour had eased into a light trickle, and she was impatient to inform her father of their news.

"Before you leave, I have something else for you, Anya." Edna pulled another folded bit of paper from the portfolio and handed it to the young woman. "Maybe you should read *this* with your father, too."

Anya took the document and looked at the writing on the outer surface. Her name was clearly written in a curved scroll that she did not recognize. She looked questioningly at Edna.

"It is from Onega, dear. I think you have an answer to your letter."

CHAPTER FORTY-SEVEN

Mixed Emotions

As she hurried from the Red Cross office, Anya fingered the letter that lay nestled in her coat pocket. She felt the need to touch it; to be sure it did not disappear before it could be read. While Edna had helped her re-learn her spoken German, she now regretted her inability to read it. Though anxious to get back to the apartment, she felt torn between telling her father the news that they would soon be able to depart this city and having him interpret the correspondence from Onega.

She had secretly planned and saved since their arrival in Harbin for a special supper to honor the event of their leaving, so now she turned down a narrow alley and headed to the lane that contained many street vendors and shops in the Russian-German quarter.

Anya hurried past the fabric and flower stalls, the book shop, and newsstands. Locating the butcher's stall, she went inside. She made her way through the de-feathered ducks and chickens dangling by their feet from a low rafter, and found the proprietor standing behind a low glass-fronted counter filled with cuts of red meat.

"Would you like a nice fat stewing hen today?" the man behind the counter inquired.

"No thank you," Anya answered, "I would like a fine slice of pork. I am making *schnitzel* tonight."

"Must be a very special occasion," the butcher winked as he selected a couple of nice pork cutlets and carefully wrapped them in newspaper. Anya cautiously counted out her money and paid for her purchase.

Upon reaching the street, she stopped briefly and again counted her coins. She had just enough to purchase a jar of sauerkraut to accompany the schnitzel. Sauerkraut was a staple at the farm, but cabbage was hard to locate here in this city, and purchasing a jar-full was truly a delicacy.

Anya visited the lady at the vegetable stand on a nearly daily basis and knew she carried the jars of pickled cabbage. The lady was pleased to see Anya arrive toting a package from the butcher.

"Ah, I see you are having meat tonight," the woman enthused as she eyed the red juices seeping through the paper wrapping.

"Yes," Anya smiled. "This is a very special occasion and I am fixing my father a very special meal. We are having schnitzel and kraut tonight!"

"It must indeed be an extraordinary occasion," the woman agreed. "And are you here for the kraut?"

"Yes, Frau, I am. You do have some, do you not?"

"Of course! I keep jars on hand just for these unique events." She laughed heartily as she went to the rear of her stand and pulled out a clear jar that displayed the finely shredded and fermented contents.

Anya handed the woman the remaining coins from her pocket. "Is this enough?"

The woman counted the money and smiled, "Yes, this is quite sufficient. In fact, there is also enough to purchase some fresh dill for the schnitzel. Would you like some dear?"

"Oh, yes, I would like that very much!"

Supper was nearly ready when Johannes arrived from the mill. As he removed his wool beret and jacket, he stopped as he inhaled the aroma that filled the little flat.

"Anchen, what is that you are cooking? It smells so wonderful! It smells like… schnitzel? It must not be, though; we do not have the money for such a meal."

"Papi, I have very good news for us tonight, and I have been saving a bit here and there, so we could have this special meal."

Johannes' face clouded a bit as he thought about what news his daughter might have for them. Suddenly his face brightened, "We have a sponsor? We are going to America?"

Anya could no longer conceal her excitement and grinned broadly as she nodded her head. Johannes rushed over to her and lifted her off of her feet and swung her around in a circle. "WE ARE GOING TO AMERICA!" he shouted.

"Papi, put me down!" Anya laughed. "Supper will burn!"

Johannes replaced his daughter in front of the cook stove and took his seat at the table. Anya fretted over the knowledge that she had the letter from Onega in her pocket. She wanted to wait for the right time to show it to her father, without destroying the excitement of news of their sponsorship. Anya prepared plates with the fried cutlets, then topped each with sour cream mixed with chopped fresh dill. She added a large serving of warmed sauerkraut alongside the meat. As she placed a plate before her father, he beamed with delight.

After saying a prayer of thanks for the meal, Johannes added, "My darling daughter, you will make a fine wife for some lucky man someday. But, I am afraid he will have to be German, as I do not think an American man would appreciate such a fine dish as this."

Anya blushed as she prepared to take a bite, "Papi, if the man I choose to marry is American and not German, then I will have to teach him how to enjoy my cooking."

Johannes chuckled at his daughter's remark, and then entreated, "Now, tell me what you know about our trip."

"Edna said we are being sponsored by a church in Calif...fornia." The word still felt foreign to Anya as she stumbled through it. "There is a limit as to the number of people being allowed into The United States of America each month, so we will have to go to the Consulate to make arrangements. Edna says this will give us priority at the port. She wants both of us to come to her office tomorrow to begin the paperwork."

Johannes chewed his mouthful of schnitzel as he contemplated his daughter's words, then responded, "California...I somehow never thought of going there. I just imagined that we would go to the Dakotas or someplace in the center of the country. All of the people I have known who had relatives go to America talked about them going to the Dakotas. My own uncle went to South Dakota in the eighteen-nineties. I do not think I have heard of anybody going to California."

"Papi, you sound disappointed…"

"Oh, no, Anchen. I am very excited that we are finally going, just a bit surprised by our destination, is all. Just being in that country will be such a blessing, it really does not matter where we are going." Johannes' face brightened again as he reassured himself and Anya that all was satisfactory, indeed much more than satisfactory. "I will meet you in Edna's office tomorrow, after I have completed my shift at the mill."

"Papi… I have something else." Anya reached into the pocket of her dress and removed the letter. Her hand trembled as she offered the folded paper to her father. "It is from Onega."

Johannes took the letter from Anya's hand and looked closely at it. He turned it over and studied both sides. The folded paper was covered with black markings delineating each time it had been opened and read by a censor or other agent of the Russian government. He ran a finger over the penciled words 'Anya Jahnle' on the surface. The letters were in the script of an educated person, not the stilted print his wife always used. Apprehensively, and with careful motions so as not to tear the delicate paper, he removed the censor's seal, unfolded the note, and laid it out on the table. Anya pulled her chair closer to her father and sat on the edge of the seat, straining to see the words written in German script.

Johannes quickly realized Anya's difficulty in understanding what was inscribed, so he began reading aloud:

"'04 *September 1934*

My Dear Anya,

I am answering your letter on behalf of your mother, as she is too ill at this time to do so herself. I do hope you remember me, Sofia Becker, the Byrgermeister's wife from our home village.'" Johannes stopped reading, "Do you remember her?"

"Yes, very much so, she treated you after you were beaten by the

NKVD men early in our journey. She was a nurse in the army and taught me how to stitch up your wounds. I liked her and wondered why our families were not better friends at home."

"The Byrgermeister and I did not agree on many subjects, so it was best we avoided each other," Johannes explained and then continued reading, "*Your mother and I have become cherished friends during our time here in this camp. We have lived and worked together, and supported each other through all manner of grief and hardship. She is the one I have turned to when I could not find strength in prayer, and she is the one who always brought me back to God and the reality of my life. Now, I wish I could say the same of my abilities, but painfully, I have not been able to provide that same sustenance for her. I regret to tell you that both of your sisters have been lost to serious accidents, and combined with the reports of the death of your father, your mother has descended into a deep melancholy from which she may never recover. She wastes away a little more each day, and I fear she may not make it through the month. I am praying your letter will bring her hope and she will return to her vibrant self. I must say that I selfishly need her, and miss her spirit intensely.*'"

Again, Johannes stopped reading and stared at the paper, "I thank God that your mother found someone from our village that she could be close to. Sofia also says that Karolina and Magdalena… have both met with fatal accidents," Johannes had difficulty repeating these words and his vision began to blur from the tears that coated his eyes. He cleared his throat, and wiped his shirtsleeve across his face. "*We have had no news of your brothers, or my boys, either.*' They could be anywhere, or nowhere," Johannes sighed. "Either way I fear they are lost to us forever. '*I was informed that my husband Josef was killed in an accident at the new canal project, a few years ago, and for that reason, if for no other, I attached myself to your mother for strength and spiritual nourishment.*'

'*I am so pleased to hear that you have found your Papi and that you are together for whatever Our Lord has in store for you. I will pray that you are kept safe and that you will find Jakob. I once told your mother that we will never know what has happened to our children or husbands or any of our people. Future generations will never know we even existed; that we will all just vanish...like footprints in the wind. But your letter gives me hope. When you arrive at your future destination, tell all you meet about us. Tell them who we were and what happened to us. Our generation is lost; do not let us be forgotten.'* We must remember these words, Anchen. Your mother and sisters and brothers must never be forgotten." Johannes reached out and took his daughter's hand. "They must *never* be forgotten," he repeated firmly.

"*'Please do not bother to answer this note, I only ask for your prayers in return. Do not worry overly much about your mother; she is where she wishes to be, and I will do my best to serve her needs.*

God bless you and keep you,

Kindest Regards, Sofia Becker.'" With these last words, Johannes re-folded the letter and laid it on the table between him and Anya.

"Papi, how ill is Mama? This letter has taken so long to get to us; do you think she is still alive?"

"I wish I knew, Anchen, I wish I knew. But, Sofia said that your mother might not live out the month in which this letter was written, so unless your letter had such an impact on her that it gave her the strength to fight back, then no, I do not feel she is still with us."

Anya sat motionless, absorbing all that she had just heard. Tears streamed silently down her cheeks and dripped onto the tabletop as Johannes picked the letter up and held it in his hand. He tightened his fingers around it, gripping his one last connection to Katerina— his wife, the mother of his children, and a very large portion of his heart.

Anya reached out and gently placed her hands over his clutched fist. Johannes, lost in his own thoughts and grief, looked up at his daughter and stared blankly at her. He focused on her normally sapphire eyes, now reddened and swollen in sorrow.

"I think we should pray," she said quietly.

Without a word, Johannes rose from his chair, went over to the small table by his bed, and picked up his Bible. He turned and stood with his back against the wall, and opened the tome. His eyes became hollow and sunken with the emptiness that overcame him. As he began reading, he slowly slid to the floor and sat with the book in his lap. Slowly he raised his hand and reached out for Anya to join him. Sitting close to her father, she laid her head on his shoulder as he thumbed through the pages and found verses that he read aloud; words to bring strength, words to express their sorrow, words to ask for forgiveness and safe passage for Katerina, Karolina, Magdalena, Heinreich and Konrad.

Together, father and daughter asked that Jakob would be kept safe, and that someday they would find him. They prayed that their own journey to the new land would be a good one. They prayed that God would bless all who had helped them get to where they were now and for blessings on all who would help them in the future.

Between verses and prayers, they reminisced about their lives on the farm, and some of the happier times. Anya recalled romping in the barnyard with Konrad and Heiner, and cradling baby Rosina in her arms. She explained how the sewing skills she learned from her mother had become so important in many instances in her short life.

Johannes offered stories about his good workhorses, especially his favorites, Hans and Georg. Then, at length, he described meeting Katerina for the first time, and how hard he worked to gain her attention—and the difficulties he encountered getting her father's approval. He did not need to speak of his love for her; that was obvious from the look in his eyes and the manner in which he spoke.

Anya talked about Sonia, and her deep attachment to the woman who raised her. She prayed for Rodin, and Yerik, and their families, and wondered if the children were still with them, or if they had been sent off to school by the government. She offered a prayer for Miko, and the other dogs; that they remain strong and fast and live good long lives.

Johannes and Anya continued their worship late into the night, bolstering each other with solace and encouragement; reconnecting with what had been, and contemplating what was to be. Finally, after an exhausted last "Amen," they both closed their eyes, drained from the emotions and memories that seized their minds and bodies. The Bible lay open across Johannes' lap, and they slept until a ray of early morning sunlight crept across the floor and warmed their faces.

END

But I focus on this one thing; Forgetting the past and looking forward to what lies ahead, I press on to reach the end of the race and receive the heavenly prize for which God, through Christ Jesus, is calling us.- Philippians 3:13-14

History of the German-Russian People

Few people know of the German-Russians, and fewer still comprehend why Germans were even in Russia. It is important to understand the history of these people in order to appreciate what they endured at the hands of the Soviet Government.

Germany did not become a cohesive country until 1815 when the Confederation of German States was formed. Prior to that time it consisted of a large group of fiefdoms, small principalities and political alliances unified by the factor that they all spoke the German language, though in a variety of different dialects. These entities were often at war with one another. Additionally, religious coalitions frequently did not see eye to eye, again resulting in upheaval and turmoil amongst the populations. In other words, war was a constant feature in daily life, and conscription of young men into the military was the normal state of affairs. This resulted in an offer that many Germanic people could not refuse.

Empress Elizabeth, ruler of Russia from 1741-1762, seeking to create a buffer zone with Turkey, and hopefully eliminating the frequent raids of the Turks and Mongols into the sparsely populated southern areas of her country, designed an extensive scheme to colonize the border with immigrants. Serfdom made relocation of her own people into the area impossible. Her plan was completely orchestrated as early as 1752, but havoc in war-torn Europe, caused by the Napoleonic hostilities and the Seven Years War, delayed any attempt at implementation until after the Empress's death. Elizabeth's daughter-in-law, Catherine I, by default, became the executor of Elizabeth's will in this matter. Catherine, later known as Catherine the Great and being German herself, began her campaign in the Germanic provinces by publishing her Manifesto of 1763.

In order to better understand why so many people were drawn to Russia by this Manifesto, I will list some of the provisions she stipulated for the immigrants:

1. Those wishing to settle in Russia, but did not have the means would be provided with travel money.
2. For farming and manufacturing purposes, free and suitable land would be provided.
3. Free and unrestricted practice of religion, according to the precepts and usage of their Church.
4. Thirty years tax exemption for all who have settled as colonists and their families.
5. For the building of dwellings, the purchase of livestock needed for the farmstead, the necessary equipment, materials, and tools for agriculture and industry, each settler will receive the necessary money from the treasury in the form of an advance loan without any interest. The capital sum to be repaid only after ten years, in equal annual installments in the following three years.
6. Complete duty-free import of all property.
7. They shall not be drafted against their will into the military or the civil service during their entire stay. Only after the lapse of the years of tax-exemption can they be required to provide labor service for the country.
8. They will forthwith receive food rations and free transportation to their destination.
9. They will be permitted to sell and export freely for ten years, without paying export duty or excise tax.

Although exclusion from military service was repealed by Alexander II, one-hundred years later in 1874, this Manifesto remained in place until its replacement by the Toleration Act of 1905. Additional manifestos by Catherine's grandson, Alexander I, in 1804 and 1813, colonized the annexed territory from the Azov to the Dniester, including Crimea, during the first and second Turkish wars (1768-1774 and 1787-1792) and Bessarabia by the Treaty of Budapest in 1812, opening up those areas for additional expansion and settlement.

The German settlers soon established their own villages, maintaining their language, culture and religious beliefs. They were productive and hard-working, and their efforts fed much of Russia for many years.

By the beginning of the twentieth century, political upheaval began turning the German-Russians' lives into turmoil. The Russian Revolution of 1905 called for a constitutional monarchy, and Tsar Nicholas II signed a resolution establishing the Duma as the central legislative body; however, lives had already been lost and political divisions had been established. The German-Russians, though primarily pacifists, were supportive of their Tsar and aligned themselves with the White Army.

Nonetheless, with the onset of World War I, and the major losses Russia suffered under the leadership of Tsar Nicholas II, the majority of the Russian population was turning to the Bolsheviks and their Red Army for direction. The resulting Revolution of 1917, and the establishment of Vladimir Lenin as the leader of the Bolshevik Party, eventually led to Soviet rule and prompted collectivization of the farms. The German-Russians objected to the confiscation of their farms and, in many areas, fighting ensued. Following the death of Lenin in 1924 and the rise to power of Joseph Stalin, the "Purge of the Kulaks" began.

A *kulak* was described as the higher-income farmer who was presumably more successful and more efficient, and had a larger farm than most Russian peasants. By 1929, The Council of People's Commissars labeled a kulak as any farmer who used hired labor, owned a "complex" machine, rented agricultural equipment or facilities, or sold his surplus goods on the open market. Grigory Zinoviev, a well-known Soviet politician, said in 1924, "We are fond of describing any peasant who has enough to eat as a kulak."

The German-Russian farmers of the southern Russian regions

were particularly targeted as kulaks, resulting in systematic removal of the people from their lands.

In 1930, Stalin declared: "In order to oust the kulaks as a class, the resistance of this class must be smashed in open battle and it must be deprived of the productive sources of its existence and development... That is a turn towards the policy of eliminating the kulaks as a class."

The Communist party agreed to the use of force in the collectivization and dekulakization efforts. The kulaks were to be liquidated as a kind and were subject to one of three fates: death sentence, labor settlements (not to be confused with labor camps, although the former were also managed by the GULAG), or deportation "out of regions of total collectivization of the agriculture." Tens of thousands of German-Russians were executed, property was expropriated to form collective farms, and many families were deported to unpopulated areas of Siberia and Soviet Central Asia.

Often local officials were assigned minimum quotas of kulaks to identify, and were forced to use their discretionary powers to "find" kulaks wherever they could. This led to many cases where a farmer who only employed his sons, or any family with a metal roof on their house, being labeled as kulaks and deported.

The overwhelming majority of German-Russians executed and imprisoned were male, but precise numbers are somewhat difficult to obtain. Many historians consider the great famine a result of the "liquidation of the kulaks as a class," which complicates the estimation of death tolls. A wide range of death tolls has been suggested, from as many as 60 million, suggested by Aleksandr Solzhenitsyn, to as few as 700,000 according to Soviet news sources. A collection of estimates is maintained by historian Matthew White.

According to data from Soviet archives, which were published in 1990, 1,803,392 people were sent to labor colonies and camps in 1930 and 1931. Various books state that 1,317,022 reached the destination. The remaining 486,370 may have died or escaped. Deportations to Siberia, and other remote locations, continued on a smaller scale after 1931. The reported number of kulaks and their relatives who died in labor colonies from 1932 to 1940 was 389,521. Former "kulaks" and their families made up the majority of victims of the Great Purge of the late 1930's, with 669,929 arrested and 376,202 executed.

In the words of Walter Kiesz, in a paper which was presented to the San Joaquin Historical Society, "These people were hardy, resilient, and industrious. Above all they had a deep faith, not only in their own abilities, but in their God. They were a devout and religious people and their faith was tried, but it triumphed."

Many were not released from the labor camps until the late 1960's and early 1970's. Those who survived the labor camps and deportation have never been allowed to return to the land from which they were removed. Even today, they are banned from living in the villages from which they originally came.

Thank you for reading my book, I hope you enjoyed it. I would appreciate your review on Amazon.com, B&N.com or Goodreads.com. With deepest gratitude.

CPSIA information can be obtained at www.ICGtesting.com
Printed in the USA
BVOW04s0411160614

356398BV00003B/5/P